Also by ROBERT CONROY

1901

1862

1945

1945

ROBERT CONROY

BALLANTINE BOOKS

NEW YORK

A Ballantine Books Trade Paperback Original

Copyright © 2007 by Robert Conroy

All rights reserved.

Published in the United States by Ballantine Books,
an imprint of The Random House Publishing Group,
a division of Random House, Inc., New York.

BALLANTINE and colophon are registered
trademarks of Random House, Inc.

ISBN 978-0-345-49479-5

Printed in the United States of America

www.ballantinebooks.com

8 9 7

Book design by Barbara M. Bachman

ACKNOWLEDGMENTS

As always, I am thankful to my wife, Diane, my daughter, Maura, and friends for their support of my lifelong dream of having a career in writing, however belated. And thanks to Tim Mak for his insights into editing, and Ron Doering for buying the book in the first place.

By the summer of 1945, the Japanese were thoroughly and utterly defeated. Their cities were rubble, their navy nonexistent, their economy destroyed, and their people near starvation. By all rights, they should have surrendered.

But surrender wasn't in the vocabulary of the militarists who ran the nation. They lived by the code of Bushido, which condemned surrender. Instead, they wished to fight until an honorable peace was achieved and felt they had good reasons for doing so.

First, they considered the recent agreement among the Allies, the Potsdam Declaration, to be a plan to destroy both Japan and her culture. This was intolerable to them.

Second, they considered any possible occupation of Japan and any subsequent war crimes trials to be mortal insults. So too were any thoughts of making the powers of the emperor subject to the will of the people. After all, didn't the emperor own the people?

Third, a few were pragmatic and felt that defeat would mean their personal doom.

Many in the military felt otherwise, and a great number of the civilian government and population wanted peace, but these people were powerless to do anything about it. In the naïve and racist hatreds of the day, many Japanese thought that the Americans would rape, murder, and then cannibalize Japanese dead.

It took the shocks of the nuclear assaults on Hiroshima and Nagasaki, along with the Soviet attack into Manchuria and elsewhere, to give the Japanese peace movement the motivation and the rationale to seek peace. Even then, the governing Japanese hierarchy was sharply divided. The military, led by the army, wished to continue fighting. The army was largely intact and had several million armed and trained men ready to defend the home islands against invasion.

When Emperor Hirohito required that they sue for peace, the army bent to his will.

Yet peace was still far from certain. That night, a handful of rebellious officers led several hundred enlisted men on a rampage throughout the Imperial palace in search of Hirohito and the recordings of a peace message he'd made to be broadcast to the world the next day.

The rebels begged the war minister, army general Korechika Anami, for support. Anami was torn between his desire to continue the war and his loyalty to his emperor and, as a result, did nothing. If the coup succeeded, he would support it. If not, he would not oppose the surrender.

The rebels then confronted the commander of the Imperial Guards at the palace. When he refused to support them, the rebels shot him. This infuriated the guards, who then began to fight the rebels, thus dooming the coup. By morning the coup was over and most of the rebel leaders had committed suicide.

But what if Anami, who had all the armies of Japan at his disposal, had decided to support the coup? The Imperial Guards would have aided the rebels, Hirohito would have been captured or killed, and the war would not have ended on August 14, 1945. Instead, it would have required an invasion of the Japanese home islands by the armed forces of the United States of America. Instead of peace, the United States would have been forced into Operation Downfall, the bloodiest campaign in its history.

The first phase, Olympic, would have been the invasion of Kyushu on or about November 1, 1945, while the second phase, Coronet, would have been the invasion of Honshu about six months later. Most American planners agreed that a bloody American victory would have been won by the end of 1946. The soldiers, sailors, and marines who would have constituted the invading force were nowhere near as optimistic.

Additional atomic weapons would have been used against Japan. Cities such as Kokura and Niigata were already on the short list of targets, and more would have been added.

This novel tells what could have occurred if the coup had succeeded, and the United States been required to invade Japan.

TO SIMPLIFY MATTERS, I have given all Japanese names and relevant terms in the American manner and have ignored any references to dates that might be different because of the international date line.

My major sources for the planned invasion were *The Invasion of Japan* by John Ray Skates, *Downfall* by Richard Frank, and *Code-Name Downfall* by Norman Polmar and Thomas B. Allen, all of which give great detail and were invaluable resources: Also, *Mr. Truman's War* by J. Robert Moskin provided marvelous insights into the issues, personalities, and motives of the people involved, while *The Fall of Japan* by William Craig detailed the attempted coup.

—*Robert Conroy*

1945

*T*he Son of Heaven sat cross-legged and stoic on the simple bamboo mat that covered the stark concrete floor of the shelter. His head and shoulders were covered by a fine layer of dust, and his nostrils recoiled at the smell of smoke that carried the sickly sweet stench of burning flesh. He felt as if he were suffocating, but he willed himself to remain calm. This squalid room was almost all that remained of an empire that, only a few short years earlier, had encompassed half the world.

The bomb shelter had been constructed to provide him and a select handful of others in the government and the Imperial family with a degree of safety from the incessant rain of American bombs. Although the B-29s and other bombers appeared to have been ordered not to aim for the Imperial palace grounds, mistakes occurred and the sacred buildings in central Tokyo had sustained damage, enough to set up protection of the mortal body of the frail and nearsighted emperor from the death that fell from the skies.

Someone explained to the incredulous emperor that a demonic gust of wind could send a bomb far off its intended course. He thought it amazing that mere air could alter the course of a falling bomb and change the fate of those beneath it. Some would live and some would die, all because of an errant zephyr.

But now, Hirohito thought bitterly, the concrete and steel shelter that had cost such great manpower and material was likely to be his tomb, not his refuge. Above him, Japanese soldiers fought and died to change Japan's future. Tragically, these were not Japanese fighting the Americans, but Japanese fighting other Japanese over the right to die for him and for Japan. Like the wind on the bomb's descent, uncertainty of his and his nation's fates pervaded his thoughts.

Hirohito had fully understood the determination of the military, particularly the army, to prolong the uneven struggle against the hated Americans beyond all reason. Their fanatic devotion to the code of the warrior, Bushido, screamed their defiance of an implacable enemy who had the power to destroy all life on the home islands of Japan. Hirohito decided on a course of action that would preserve life, not destroy it.

The first atomic bomb used in warfare had destroyed Hiroshima in a ball of fire that consumed many tens of thousands of men, women, and children and left many thousands more to live their lives in unspeakable horror. Three days later, a second bomb had incinerated Nagasaki with the same results, although Hirohito's experts had informed him that the death toll was somewhat lower than Hiroshima's. Why, they did not know.

This, coupled with the continuing nonnuclear fire bombings and bombardments of cities and towns throughout Japan, convinced Hirohito that there was no sense in further struggles against the inevitable. Most of Japan's cities were scorched rubble, and there was no way of stopping the Americans from inflicting more pain on his beloved nation.

At a meeting with his war cabinet, he shocked them by doing something never before done in such a meeeting. He had spoken directly to them. The emperor, always present, maintained a regal silence regarding the issues under discussion. It was, in fact, against the Japanese constitution for him to voice an opinion.

There were eight on the council: Hirohito and the seven others who debated and voted. Five of the seven were militarists, and even he had been shocked when they'd acquiesced with his demand that they surrender.

This time, however, he told his cabinet that it was time to think the unthinkable and endure the unendurable: to surrender the nation unconditionally to the Americans. If they did not, no Japanese child would grow to adulthood and thus preserve the exquisite and priceless culture that was uniquely Japanese. Of that Hirohito was convinced. He was also convinced that the only alternative to unconditional surrender was death. Several in the group had broken down in tears, but they had agreed to comply with his wishes. For his part, he now bitterly regretted his earlier enthusiasm for the war, which had cost the people of Japan so much and which even threatened the continuation of his throne. How could he have been so foolish? Now he had to salvage what he could of his honor, his country, and his throne.

The meeting took place in this same shelter, where now, alone but for his hopes, Hirohito awaited his fate. The emperor knew that the radicals in the military would rebel with a maniacal fury to prevent Japan's surrender. All of Japan should die and become a scorched cinder rather than a degraded vassal of the hated and despised Americans.

Hirohito had recorded a message to the Japanese people, then gone into hiding. The message was to be broadcast by radio to the steadily shrinking empire, and the war would come to a swift end.

Hirohito cocked his head. Again he heard the chatter of machine gun fire as it echoed down the corridors of the upper levels. A grenade exploded nearby, causing another rain of fine dust to fall upon his head and onto the lenses of his thick glasses. He took a handkerchief and tried to wipe them off and wondered, had War Minister General Anami found the will and support within the army to defy him, or was this uprising spontaneous, the actions of a few score of misguided young zealots?

General Anami believed in fate and would likely let the efforts of others decide his destiny. There was much precedent in current Japanese history for such an uprising by angry young officers. In recent years, other such young warriors had developed the unpleasant habit of murdering their political enemies and often did so without fear of retribution. They had learned it in the 1930s when they had set the nation on a course of conquest through the simple expedient of assassinating their more peaceful and reasonable opposition. That course of conquest, initially so glorious and successful, had now nearly brought an end to Japan.

Hirohito winced in surprise at another sharp burst of gunfire, this one close by. Whatever his and Japan's future would be was going to be determined in a short time.

The shelter's door flung open and an army colonel stood silhouetted by the smoke and light behind him. He wore the uniform of the Imperial Guards, but with a white sash about his waist. He looked young for his rank, probably in his early thirties, but he carried himself like a grim-faced veteran. He was covered with dust, and blood from a cut on his forehead had carved a path down his face. Hirohito did not know him and did not speak.

The officer entered and bowed deeply. "Your Excellency, I am here to take you to a place of safety."

"Do you have a name, Colonel?"

The colonel flushed. In his haste he had forgotten the courtesy and respect due his emperor. "Forgive me, Your Excellency. I am Col. Tadashi Sakei and I am on the staff of the Twelfth Area Army, which is responsible for the safety of the city of Tokyo."

Hirohito declined to look directly on Sakei. "And this place of safety, where is it and why should I accompany you? Am I your prisoner or your emperor, and what is the significance of the white sash you wear?"

"Your refuge will be away from Tokyo, Excellency. Here we fear that your life is in danger from more than just American bombs. More I am not at liberty to say. As to your other questions, you are my emperor. The sash signifies that I am one of those who are your protectors. Your enemies wear no sash." Sakei again bowed deeply, reverently.

"And what does General Anami know of your actions?" The man still had not said which side he was on. The term *protector* meant nothing. Protection from whom? Would there be blessed peace or the continuation of death?

The colonel raised himself proudly to full height. He was quite tall for a Japanese, and the blood drying on his face made him look barbarically fierce. "General Anami," he said with a glint of satisfaction in his eyes, "has finally condoned the actions of men of honor who wish to preserve Japan and keep her safe from her enemies. He now supports us and honors us with his leadership."

Hirohito began to grieve inside for his beloved nation, but did not let his disappointment show. General Anami, once his friend, had betrayed him.

"It does not matter that you have me. My message will go forth without me," Hirohito said proudly.

Colonel Sakei smiled tightly. He left the room for a moment and returned with two small packages wrapped with string and brown paper. "Do you mean these? The treasonous message your traitorous advisers forced you to make and record for broadcast to the world?"

Now it was all Hirohito could do to keep from sobbing in his dismay and frustration. His enemies had both himself and the recordings of the royal rescript. His voice calling for peace would not go forth to the people of Japan. There would be no end to the war. The killing would go on. And on. And on.

"Do you have any idea what you are doing?" Hirohito gasped.

"Saving Japan," Sakei snapped.

"By destroying her? Why don't you kill me?" Hirohito asked sadly. "The shame of your foolishness is too much to endure. Get it over with and then depart and return to your misguided comrades." Hirohito shook his head in dismissal. Colonel Sakei was now beneath his contempt.

Sakei reacted as if slapped. A couple of white-sashed soldiers who had peered into the room gasped and darted away. If the angry colonel had seen them in his shame, he would have had them beaten to a pulp, perhaps killed. That was the way discipline was maintained in the Japanese army.

"Excellency," Sakei said in a strained voice, "you are a living symbol of Japan, her living god. Your presence and your pronouncements will add credence to our efforts to defend the home islands from invasion by the Americans."

Proclamations would be issued in his name, but by the hand of Anami and officers like Sakei. On the other hand it seemed obvious that he was the only member of the royal family who had been taken, and that the twelve-year-old Crown Prince Akihito was elsewhere and safe, as were the emperor's two younger brothers. If he, Hirohito, was assassinated, then Akihito would become emperor. With Hirohito alive, any comments that might be made on behalf of or by Prince Akihito would have no weight. It was a small ray of hope, but he grasped it. Most important, his only and well-loved son was alive and apparently safe, if only for the moment.

"Why would you extend this battle?" Hirohito asked. "The Americans will drop more atomic bombs on our cities and then invade our few islands. Our lands are already surrounded by their warships, and their planes fly overhead without opposition. If you persist, all Japan will be destroyed because of your misguided stubbornness."

Sakei gestured for the emperor to rise and follow him. Reluctantly, Hirohito did as he was told and emerged into the hallways that connected the palace to the shelter. He was dismayed to see several bodies lying in bloody disarray. Some wore sashes and some did not. It grieved him to realize that loyal soldiers had died on his behalf. Sakei, however, did not share his feelings. Instead, he pointed to a dead soldier who also wore a sash.

"Then we die with honor, not as prisoners!" Sakei said proudly. "Let the Americans bomb our cities. We will live in the countryside. Let them destroy our homes and we will live in caves in the hills. Let them invade our shores and we will fall upon them with every weapon we have. If we must, we will tear at them and destroy them with our hands and teeth. We have millions of soldiers and tens of millions of civilians willing to die to preserve our sacred culture. We will gnaw at their throats, and eyes, and testicles, and bleed the Americans until they come to their senses and negotiate an honorable end to this war."

It was all Hirohito could do to keep from laughing at Sakei's pompous and irrational speech. How could the deaths of all those people preserve anything Japanese? He had been told that the Americans thought of December 7, 1941, as the Day of Infamy. Now he had his own Day of Shame—August 14, 1945. God help the people of Japan.

Part One

THE WAR UNENDING

CHAPTER 1

•

GERMANY

*T*he muffled sounds of the nearby explosions cut through his sleep-fog and Lt. Paul Morrell leaped from his cot. A surge of fear ruined his warm and pleasant dream about his girlfriend, Debbie Winston. He grabbed his carbine and ran outside the tent and looked for the source, all the while trying to ignore the nausea and splitting headache that assailed him.

Another explosion came from behind the low hill just to the rear of the camp.

Morrell looked about for help as he ran up the hill. No one was around. They were probably still out celebrating the end of the war, although it sounded as if someone didn't believe it. Could they be under attack from some Nazi fanatics? It sure as hell sounded like it.

Another blast jarred him. He breasted the hill on the run and looked down below him. Then he started swearing softly. Two of his soldiers, Sgt. Cecil Wiles and Cpl. Tommy Nevins, were standing by the stream that ran through the gentle valley. Wiles, staggering ever so slightly, pulled the pin on a grenade and lofted it into the center of a wider section of the stream that formed a nice little pond.

Water geysered up from the pond and so did a number of dead fish. Wiles and Nevins whooped loudly at the sight.

"What the hell are you men doing?" Morrell snapped as he approached. He was furious at their stupidity and enormously relieved that he was not again at war. The two NCOs looked at him dumbly, then Wiles made a waving motion with his arm that might have been a drunken attempt at a salute.

"Fishing," Wiles said, then after a long pause, "sir. We are fucking fishing." Nevins giggled at the witticism and almost fell into the water.

Morrell looked about. The banks of the stream were littered with dead fish. Some had been blown to pieces by the grenades, while others had had their lives snuffed out by the concussion.

"All right," Morrell snarled, "this is enough." His anger was growing. Not only had they scared the crap out of him, but they were endangering themselves along with anyone else in the vicinity. They were destroying government equipment as well as blowing up someone's private property. Worse, his headache was throbbing and he felt as if he would heave.

It wasn't the first time the duo of Nevins and Wiles had gotten into trouble, usually alcohol-related. Even when sober they were only marginally efficient. He wondered just how they had gotten their stripes.

"Why is it enough, Lieutenant?" Wiles asked with mock innocence.

Morrell iterated the reasons and added a last one. "Because I'm ordering you to, that's why."

Nevins hiccuped. "Lieutenant, why don't you fuck off."

Morrell was stunned and took a deep breath to calm himself. "Tell you what. You're both drunk, and so's probably half the army. Now I'm gonna be a real nice guy and pretend I didn't hear that. You two get back to camp right now."

Nevins's face flushed in anger and he looked as if he might take a swing at Morrell. However, he quickly thought better of it. Along with being an officer and someone you just didn't hit, Morrell was sober and fit-looking. At five-eleven, he weighed a compact 180, and despite his curly blond hair and innocent-looking blue eyes, Morrell looked as if he could take care of himself, especially in a fight with two staggering drunks.

"No," said Sergeant Wiles. "Let's not forget about it. What the hell's the matter with you, Lieutenant? You know you got a reputation around here as being the choirboy officer. You're a pain in the ass, Lieutenant. Look, the war's over and we got a right to celebrate, and if you don't like it, why don't you get the fuck back to your tent and stay there."

Morrell was livid with anger. He'd been with the outfit only a short time in comparison with many others, and he knew he wasn't getting respect from many of the men. Second lieutenants were the lowest of the officer ranks and all too often the butt of jokes by others with more experience. A joke, or even a veiled insult, he could deal with, but this was outright insubordination.

He turned to Wiles. "I think you and your little pal have gone too far. I regret this, but I am going to see Captain Maxwell."

Wiles and Nevins looked at each other, then burst out laughing. "Sure," said Wiles, "you go see the captain. You just do that."

Morrell turned and, in a rage, his headache and hangover forgotten, almost ran the half mile to where Captain Maxwell had set up shop.

Captain Maxwell had commandeered an old two-story farmhouse that had escaped the ravages of both the German retreat and the American advance. Like so many places in Germany outside the major cities, the area in which they were camped looked as if nothing had changed in it for a hundred years. Whenever he saw Maxwell's ornate headquarters, Morrell was reminded of the story of Hansel and Gretel.

Maxwell's clerk looked uncomfortable at Morrell's request, but told him the captain would be downstairs in a minute. Morrell nodded and went into the living room, which served as the captain's office. Maxwell, a stocky National Guard officer about thirty years old, arrived and waved him to a chair. Morrell briefly explained the situation regarding the grenade-tossing and the two NCOs' drunken insubordination. The captain lit a cigarette and stared at the ceiling.

"Dammit," Maxwell finally said.

"Captain?"

"Lieutenant, how long you been with us?"

"About three months. Just before the Nazis finally surrendered."

Maxwell leaned forward. "That's right, just before the war ended. That means you came in on the ass end of a lot of fighting those boys had been going through for more than a year. You even replaced an officer who, while not particularly smart, was fairly well liked. So, how much combat did you see?"

Morrell flushed. "Not much at all, Captain." Only a few minutes, and he'd been scared to death and scarcely able to function. It was nothing in comparison with what the others had gone through, even the two assholes, Nevins and Wiles.

"That's right, and what were you doing a year ago?"

"I had just finished college and been called up."

"That's right, Lieutenant, you finished college. Then you did your basic training in the good ol' US of A, became an officer, and then got your butt shipped over here to us just in time to see the curtain go down. Do you know what we were doing a year ago? We had just arrived in France and had begun shooting our way across Europe. Know what I was doing four years ago?"

"No, Captain."

"I was managing a grocery store with my father. Then I got called up, and while I was gone, my dad died and they had to sell the store. All that while you were starting college and maybe reading *War and Peace*. When you go back, you'll have a degree and a future, but for people like me and a lot of others out there, there'll be nothing but shit for a future."

"Captain, are you saying I should have let them keep doing what they were doing?"

"Why not? They were just a couple of hillbilly assholes blowing up some grenades we don't need anymore and killing some kraut fish. Think, Lieutenant, what should you have really done?"

Morrell took a chair and sat down. His anger ebbed. "You're right. I should have taken any remaining grenades off them and left them there to do whatever they wished. If they had protested, I should have gone back for you or someone else to help me."

Maxwell relaxed after his tirade. "Paul, it gets worse. You want me to discipline those guys and I'll do it, only it'll just be an ass-chewing and nothing more. They know they deserve to lose their stripes, but it'll be their word against yours as to what they said, and you know they'll both lie like rugs. When I'm through chewing on them, they'll go back to their ugly friends and laugh at you because they got away with fucking with you."

Maxwell stood and paced the little room. "Look, I dislike those two clowns as much as the next guy, but they're veterans, NCOs, and heroes with Bronze Stars, even though they'll steal anything that ain't nailed down."

Maxwell told him that the two men had been ambushed by some Germans and had to shoot their way out, thus getting their medals. In his opinion, they had been looting a farmhouse when the Germans caught them, which made their fighting their way out something less than heroic.

Damn, thought Paul. He had really screwed up.

"It gets worse, Paul. They've got more than enough points to be discharged. So, in a couple of months, maybe sooner, they'll be home screwing their women and their sheep, and newcomers like you'll be here trying to run an occupation army. Who knows, maybe I'll be away from here too."

Morrell seized on the comment. "And that's the point, Captain, we are still an army, not a mob. Those guys are destroying what we came here to liberate."

Maxwell laughed harshly. "Liberate? Let me tell you something, Lieutenant; we liberated Belgium and France, but not Germany. This fucking country we conquered with a lot of our friends getting killed or wounded in the process, and there's a helluva lot of difference."

"To the victor belong the spoils?"

"Exactly."

"But what about our orders to maintain discipline and protect the people?"

The question amused Maxwell. "Things don't always work out like they were intended, now do they? Take Ike's nonfraternization order, for instance. Did anyone really think they could keep a couple of million horny GIs away from German pussy when the kraut chicks will give you anything you want for some cigarettes, or chocolate, or even a meal? Hell, the Russians are raping them wholesale and we're willing to pay for it. That makes us the good guys."

Grudgingly Paul agreed. That particular order truly was nonsense.

"And, Lieutenant, I am also supposed to employ Germans to run this area and get their local economy going again. Only orders say I can't use anyone who was a Nazi. Now tell me, just who the hell does that leave in a country where even the little krauts became Nazis before they could walk and wore swastikas on their diapers? Communists, that's who, and the brass'd kill me if I used commies to run the joint. At any rate, there aren't too many commies left after Herr Hitler got through with them, so I work with what I got, and that's what you're going to do as well."

"I see the problem," said Paul softly.

"Yeah, and we might as well settle down and enjoy it while it lasts. And might I ask just where the hell were you last night?" Maxwell said with a sneer.

Paul flushed. "At the gasthaus celebrating the Japanese surrender," he said sheepishly. There was no way he could lie about it. The captain had been there as well. It was where he had gotten this morning's headache, which was starting to come back. Shit.

"Yeah, and Herr Gasthaus-meister, or whatever the fuck his name is, probably was a good little Nazi just a few weeks ago. Now he's doing his smiling best to get rich and get the U.S. army drunk and laid, and that makes him one of the good guys too."

"Okay, you've made your point, Captain. Now what do you think I should do?"

"Take some aspirin for your hangover and let me think. Now get out of here."

After Morrell had left, Maxwell's clerk told him that Major Lewis had come in the rear door and gone upstairs. Maxwell nodded, went upstairs, and found the major sitting on the edge of the bed in the largest of the bedrooms. One of the two dark-haired fräuleins they'd brought back from the gasthaus the night before was still sleeping, while the other sat in front of the dresser and combed her hair. Both were naked. The sleeping one snored slightly. He couldn't recall just which one he'd fucked and seemed to recall they were sisters. He was slightly concerned that they looked so much younger than they had last night.

The major looked extremely somber, and that worried Maxwell. "What's the problem, Bob?" Maxwell asked.

Lewis pulled a bottle of schnapps from a drawer and took a long swallow. "Tell me first about young Lieutenant Morrell. What's his problem?" Maxwell quickly filled him in on the situation.

"The problem is," Maxwell went on, "that those two idiots are gonna tell everyone they made a fool out of him, and it'll be difficult for him to regain control of the troops. He barely had it in the first place."

Major Lewis took another swallow. It was apparent to Maxwell that the major wanted to get drunk and do it right now. Why? Maxwell wondered.

Lewis belched. "Then ship him out. Put him on the levy to Japan."

Maxwell blinked in surprise. As a prelude to invading Japan, the army had begun sending individuals off to the Pacific. It was rumored that full units would follow. People with a lot of combat experience in the European theater would be returned home to civilian life, while others with less experience would either be retained in Germany or used in the invasion of the home islands of Japan. Orders had come down asking units to "volunteer" individuals, which meant that everyone was taking the opportunity to get rid of oddballs, troublemakers, and incompetents.

Maxwell shook his head in confusion. "Bob, the Japanese just surrendered, didn't they? I thought the levy was going to be canceled?"

Major Lewis looked at the naked woman at the dresser. She had completed combing her hair and was now picking at the remains of some C rations, ignoring them both. "I have bad news for you, my friend. The Japanese may have just unsurrendered."

"Bullshit!" Maxwell sagged into a chair in disbelief.

"It's the truth. Seems there's been some kind of a coup or revolution over there, and the crazy people are back in charge. The invasion is on, at least until the next revolution, and the levy is not likely to be canceled anytime soon. So get Morrell out of here while you still have the chance. Send him off to fight the Japs with our blessing."

Maxwell nodded assent. It was an easy decision to make and would solve a lot of problems. If only he could get rid of Nevins and Wiles just as easily. At least, he consoled himself, they'd be shipped out somewhere soon enough.

Too bad for Lieutenant Morrell, though. He genuinely hoped nothing happened to the young man. Despite being naïve about some things, Morrell was a pretty good kid. On the other hand, Maxwell had a life to live in Germany for the foreseeable future.

God, Maxwell thought, let it be in Germany and not invading Japan. He reached for the schnapps and patted the sleeping woman on her bottom. She moaned slightly but didn't move. Maybe people would get their heads out of their asses and end this thing for good. Maybe the war would end a second time before Lieutenant Morrell even got there. But, what the hell, he had his own life to lead.

CHAPTER 2

•

Nothing in the first six decades of his life had indicated that Harry Truman of Independence, Missouri, would ever become president of the United States and one of the most powerful men in the world. Born in 1884, he'd seen combat as an artillery captain in World War I, served as a county judge, and, to the astonishment of many, was elected to the U.S. Senate in 1934. He'd stayed there, accruing seniority and serving his nation honestly, anonymously, and well. In 1944, President Franklin Delano Roosevelt had surprised everyone and tapped him to be his vice-presidential running mate.

Although a high honor, the office under FDR was a thankless one. Roosevelt ignored his vice president once the election was done. Roosevelt considered it his constitutional obligation to have a vice president, but nothing said he was required to actually use one. One of Roosevelt's earlier vice presidents, John Nance Garner, had referred to the job as not being worth a pitcher of "warm piss." The word *piss* had later been changed to *spit* in an attempt to sanitize history. Roosevelt could accept this comment, but not Garner's temerity in trying to unseat Roosevelt as president. Garner had been dumped from the ticket, and it had brought about the 1940 pairing of Roosevelt with Henry Wallace. When Wallace's infatuation with Joseph Stalin and all things politically far left, if not Communist, became known, he too became unacceptable.

Enter Harry Truman, who was loyal, hardworking, honest, American, and not likely to lust after FDR's job. For the eighty-odd days he had served as vice president, Truman had been content to accept the honor of the office as a reward for long years of faithful service to his country and the Democratic Party. He considered it a pleasant prelude to a comfortable retirement.

On April 12, 1945, Roosevelt unexpectedly died of a massive stroke in Warm Springs, Georgia, and Harry Truman, the dapper little man with the often snappish temper, had become president of the United States.

Now, as he paced the Oval Office and waited for the others to arrive, he could only ponder how wholly unprepared he had been for the job he now held. He had known absolutely nothing about the development of the atomic bomb or the agreements made by FDR at the Yalta conference in February 1945, where the United States and the Soviet Union had set the pattern for the world's future. FDR had operated in a world all his own, and Truman was only beginning to plumb its depths. He felt he had not disgraced himself at the recently concluded Potsdam conferences and was learning more each day about the office of president. But he sometimes came near to despair at how little he knew and how much he had yet to learn.

Truman had made few changes in FDR's cabinet or command structure. Jim Byrnes had succeeded Stettinius as secretary of state, although Ambassador Grew had been a decent interim choice. Stettinius was now the first ambassador to the United Nations in San Francisco, while the sixty-six-year-old Byrnes had a wealth of government experience to draw on. Roosevelt had referred to Byrnes as his "assistant president," both insulting and ignoring Truman with the term. To the surprise of some, Byrnes and Truman functioned together efficiently.

James Forrestal was the secretary of the navy, and Henry Stimson remained the secretary of war. Adm. William Leahy was chief of staff to the Commander in Chief of the Army and Navy. Leahy, a quiet man, sometimes seemed to be dominated by Adm. Ernest King, the navy-chief of staff, and George C. Marshall, the army chief of staff. Truman could easily imagine anyone being intimidated by King and Marshall. Forrestal and Stimson would not attend this day. Byrnes, Leahy, King, and Marshall were expected, along with anyone else they chose to bring.

Truman thought it ironic that he, a man who'd never graduated from college, could be in charge of such highly educated and well-qualified men of great renown, and that he now hobnobbed with kings and premiers. It could easily be an ego-swelling experience, and at times Harry Truman thought he could learn to like his new job.

Truman entered the conference room, took his place at the head of the table, and gestured for the standing men to be seated. The only additional member of the group was Maj. Gen. Leslie Groves, the man who had administered and ramrodded the Manhattan Project and the development of the atomic bombs that had recently been dropped on Hiroshima and Nagasaki.

Truman gestured them to their seats and began with characteristic abruptness. "Gentlemen, have we learned anything new in the last few hours?"

Byrnes responded, his brow wrinkled with concern. "As of yesterday, we thought we had a deal with the Japs. The Swedish government, acting as an intermediary, informed us that Hirohito and Premier Suzuki's government had accepted the terms of the Potsdam Declaration, which required them to agree to unconditional surrender. Their radio even warned the Japanese people that a major announcement would be broadcast at noon their time. It now appears that a bunch of fanatic young officers have seized the palace and kidnapped Hirohito. When the noon radio announcement was made, it said nothing about surrender. War Minister Anami, who alleged to be acting on Hirohito's behalf, called for continued resistance and made reference to using the entire population of Japan as human weapons against the United States should we be so foolish as to invade. Anami also said that the rumors of surrender were false and made by officials in the government who had treasonably conspired to act on behalf of an unknowing emperor."

Byrnes shook his head in dismay. "Sir, this was not wholly unexpected. There were many factions in the Japanese government and military who were opposed to any surrender, and they have taken control of both the government and the emperor."

"We were so close," Truman muttered. "So damned close. We were even willing to let them keep their emperor, even though most of the United States would like to see the little bastard hanged. Didn't they understand they could keep Hirohito?"

Byrnes nodded grimly. "I've spoken with the Japanese experts at State and they've informed me that the Jap hierarchy knows full well that Hirohito gets to stay. The problem, as they see it, runs much deeper. It really goes to the fact that their culture and values are so different from ours that we, in their eyes, might as well be from another planet."

Adm. Ernest King's voice was a snarl. "If they don't surrender and do it soon, they may well be blasted to another planet."

Truman hushed him with a wave. "The problem is, do we recommence hostilities or try to wait this out?"

Marshall spoke for the first time. "I don't think we have a choice. What Anami said was a complete rejection of any surrender at this time. We must continue the war."

"I agree," said King firmly. Leahy looked away in dismay. He had taken the failure of the Japanese to surrender very hard. After a moment, Byrnes too agreed.

Truman groaned. "The country has been anticipating an end to the Jap war for several days now. There have been premature and false announcements of peace, and people have been celebrating and dancing in the streets. Now, they have to be told that all their hopes have been dashed and we're still at war with a bitter and fanatical enemy." He turned to Byrnes. "I must go on the air and make an announcement very quickly before the rumors get out of hand."

General Groves coughed lightly to get attention. Although a belligerent and highly confident man, he was outranked and somewhat awed by the people in the room. "Mr. President, gentlemen, I presume you will want a continuation of our atomic bombings?"

Truman nodded. Destroying Hiroshima and Nagasaki had almost brought the Japs to their knees; perhaps more bombs would succeed where the first two had not. It had been Truman's decision and his alone to use the little-understood weapon against the Japanese. He had made the decision hoping to save lives, American lives, and now that decision again confronted him.

As before, Truman did not hesitate. "Do that. When can we atomize another city?"

Groves paused. "Not immediately, sir. It will be at least two weeks before we will have the materials in place at Tinian to assemble another bomb. We are beginning production of the bombs at our facility in Hanford, Washington, but the pace will be slow. We estimate that we can make at least one a month, with a strong possibility of accelerating that pace once we learn more about the process."

Truman mused out loud, "Two weeks. Well, I daresay we can't roll them off an assembly line like Ford does cars." It brought a small, bitter chuckle from the others, even from the dour Leahy, who was vehemently opposed to using the bomb.

Just two days prior, Ford had begun the production of civilian vehicles at a plant in New Jersey, and the other carmakers were lusting to follow. Even without the surrender of Japan, the United States was starting to ease back into a less restrictive economy.

"We might have had a bomb ready a couple of days sooner," Groves continued, "but, with peace so likely, we canceled the planned shipment of fissionable material to Tinian. No need, we thought."

Truman rose and the others did as well. It was a gesture of respect for his new rank that still surprised him. "All right, we have a war to win and I have an announcement to make to the world. I'm afraid our people are going to take this as yet another example of Jap duplicity, and I can't say as I blame them. This is going to make the real ending of the war just that much more brutal and bloody to achieve."

Truman returned quickly to his office. Even without taking into consideration what the fanatics were causing to be inflicted on the civilians of Japan, the thought of sending still more young men to die in battle had almost caused him to weep. He had been so hopeful that the shocks of Hiroshima and Nagasaki, along with the Russians' declaration of war and subsequent invasion of Manchuria, would have caused even the most radical Jap to see the light. It was a horrible responsibility, and he silently cursed Roosevelt for dying and thrusting it upon him.

Japan was not the only problem of immense magnitude that he and the United States had to deal with. The war had ended in Europe, but not the killing, as the oppressed took savage revenge on their oppressors or, sometimes, just the weak. Poles had massacred several hundreds of Jews who had survived the concentration camps and who had tried to reclaim their possessions from Polish squatters. What to do with the Jews, along with the millions of other refugees, was an enormously complex problem.

General Eisenhower had just informed him that the "breadbaskets" of Europe had not produced much in the way of crops this year, and since those lands were now in Russian zones, what grain that would be harvested would be heading for the Soviet Union. Along with feeding England and France, the United States was going to have to find enough foodstuffs for Germany and other countries.

Russia was also on the march in Asia. Stalin was openly supporting the Chinese Communists under Mao Tse-tung in their war against the Nationalists, who, however corrupt and incompetent, were allies of the United States. Russian armies were driving the Japanese armies from Manchuria and Korea, and it looked as if those lands would come under Soviet control. Any hopes that the American possession of nuclear weapons would deter Stalin's ambitions had been dashed.

Last, but hardly least, was the question of the U.S. economy. The country had been on a total war footing for years, and there was a real need to begin boosting the production of civilian goods and integrating millions of returning servicemen into the fragile economy. This had to be done carefully to prevent a return to the Great Depression. After twelve years of economic pain and ruin, there were those who felt that a depressed economy and great numbers of unemployed might be the normal state of capitalism for the twentieth century. Truman fervently wanted to prove them wrong.

At least, Truman thought with some satisfaction, the Widow Roosevelt had finally moved out of the White House and returned to her Hyde Park residence in New York. His wife, Bess, and his daughter, Margaret, were only a few steps away, and their presence was a great comfort to him. He was surprised to find that the Roosevelts, who'd lived in the White House since 1933, had never truly considered it their home and had allowed it to fall into neglect and disrepair. Bess had been appalled at the filth.

Harry Truman grinned. Bess would take care of that little problem. All he had to do was end this damned war.

.

CHAPTER 3

P-47 fighter pilot Dennis Chambers had been shot down over northern Kyushu in May 1945. The twenty-six-year-old Army Air Corps captain had endured harsh interrogations from his captors, during which, in accordance with new air force policy, he told them everything he knew rather than resist until the information was pulled from him, piece by bloody piece. Like many downed airmen, he fabricated wild stories that seemed to satisfy the Japs rather than the bland truth that he didn't really know much at all about grand strategy.

Routine beatings left him bloody but not badly hurt, and then he was taken to the prison camp just outside the port city of Nagasaki.

Dennis was left counting his advantages. First, he understood a smattering of Japanese, courtesy of an immigrant houseboy his parents had employed. He gradually picked up enough from his captors to be reasonably fluent, which he kept secret.

A couple of his friends were beaten to death for minor infractions, and he'd watched in horror as one man was beheaded for some unintended insult to a guard. At least that kind of death would have been swift. All too often, punishment consisted of having rations reduced, and since the rations were already below subsistence level, that meant lingering death by painful starvation.

Although bruised and cut, he still had his health, and being a small man a little under average height and build, he didn't require much in the way of food to keep him going. Early in his captivity, Chambers realized that he could stomach eating anything if it meant surviving, and he made a point of digging up worms and eating insects to supplement the small balls of rice the Japanese provided.

This only delayed the inevitable. He was a lean man, and when he did lose weight, it came from muscle and not from any fat. He soon felt himself wasting away and knew that he would soon look just like the others. Men who'd been POWs longer than him looked like corpses, skeletal and covered with ulcerating sores. Several suffered from infections of the scrotum that caused the sac to balloon up several times larger than it should be. Dennis could only guess at their agony.

Chambers tried not to torture himself by thinking about his wife and his home the way so many of the other POWs did. Whenever an unbidden thought did break through his defenses, he blocked it out.

Despite his privations and bleak future, he didn't contemplate escape. After all, where the hell would he go? A white man in the middle of Japan would stick out like a sore thumb. If he tried and was caught, the punishment would be savage and fatal. He and his buddies talked it over. They would wait.

Like every able-bodied American, British, or Australian POW in the camp, Chambers had to work for his meager rations. He and a handful of others had been put to work in one of the small factories on the outskirts of Nagasaki, where he performed menial work under the scrutiny of his masters. He welcomed the work. It broke up the monotony of the days and frequently kept him away from his guards.

Better, many of the civilian workers in the factory were not sadists like the guards and treated him reasonably well. A couple of them even slipped him bits of food from their own meager supplies out of pity for him. He knew he was fortunate to be working where he was. Many POWs were forced to work in the area's coal mines, under extremely harsh and primitive conditions that caused deaths and numerous injuries.

He had been alone in the basement of the factory moving storage boxes when the entire world had lit up about him with an unearthly, incandescent glow. Stunned, thinking only that one of the many American planes often seen overhead had bombed the factory or crashed nearby, he'd simply frozen.

Seconds later, the fist of a shock wave hurled him against a wall and covered him with debris. He later thought he might have lost consciousness. When he did revive to the point where thought was possible, he began to dig himself out, knowing only that the proper direction was up.

It might have taken him hours, but he finally broke through to fresh air and to sights that stunned him. All about him, Nagasaki was destroyed, buildings flattened and burning. Then he looked up and saw a black storm cloud of immense fury churning and roaring above him as it fought the winds that sought to push it away.

Then he knew. Rumors had been rife in the camp of a superbomb that had been dropped on Hiroshima. Most people dismissed it as the hallucinations of starving men, just like the ones that had thousands of Negro cavalrymen on white horses riding to free them. Now he knew the stories of the bomb were true and that it had now decimated Nagasaki.

The bomb had freed him. There was no sign of his guards or his fellow prisoners. If they were dead, it was a shame, but he was alive and he intended to stay that way. If he stuck around, he might get lynched by an angry Japanese mob. There would no longer be any small kindnesses from the Japanese civilians. They would want revenge and he wasn't certain he blamed them. His plans for waiting out the end of the war had suddenly changed. He had to run for his life and hide.

He'd gathered his thoughts. It was reasonable to conclude that no one would ever look for him, and the Japanese people he saw milling about were distracted and would ignore him for the time being.

He was covered with dirt and most of his clothes had been shredded by the blast and the effort of digging himself out. Dennis looked no different from any of the scores of others who milled about him aimlessly and in shock.

Alone in a sea of Japanese people, he'd seen that many had been horribly burned. Some were nothing more than walking corpses who stumbled along on charred limbs before they pitched over and died. Many of the normally modest Japanese people were naked and seemingly unaware of it as the blast had seared clothing right off their backs or burned the fabric into their flesh. Many of them had folds of flesh dangling from them as if someone had tried to skin them and then, for some demented reason, stopped.

In front of him, a specter reached its clawed hand for Chambers.

It might have been a man once. Its teeth were visible as stumps in a lipless mouth, and it tried to speak but only a gurgling growl came forth. The thing had no face, and white liquid was where the eyes once were. Dennis realized that the creature couldn't see or hear him, but reached with blistered hands for anything in its mindless path. Dennis stepped aside and let the horror pass. He had to get the hell out of Nagasaki right away.

He selected the corpse of a man who still had most of his clothing and pulled the body out of the roadway. No one noticed him. Then he stripped the body and put on the dead man's Japanese clothing. They were a little small, but he could make them do. For once he was thankful that he had lost so much weight in the camp. No one paid him the slightest bit of attention as people trudged past, their eyes glazed over with their own shock and horror.

He covered his face and hands with dirt and some grease he found by a ruined car, hoping it made him look less Caucasian. Then he'd joined the torrent of humanity, most of it frighteningly silent, as it flowed out of the ruined city of Nagasaki and into the bleak hills that rose out of the northern part of the island of Kyushu. On his way he saw the shattered hulk of the Catholic cathedral of Nagasaki. However small the numbers of worshipers might have been, the only center of Christianity in Japan had been destroyed by an allegedly Christian United States.

As he walked, it further struck him that no one was doing anything for the people of Nagasaki. There was no plan; there was no government left in the area to start helping its people. All had been destroyed and no one knew where to begin. He looked behind him and saw that the pillar of the cloud had finally begun to stream away, and that it had lost much of its peculiar mushroom shape. It had begun to rain large, warm drops, and he wondered if the explosion had caused rain as well. Could the bomb have been so powerful that it changed the weather?

At a point, he broke away from the main throng and struck out into the more rugged area around Mount Tara, which was to the north of Nagasaki.

Hours later and high on a grass-covered ridge, he found the remains of a farmer's hut that must have been abandoned a few years before. He propped up stones and pieces of wood to keep the rain off him. The weather was warm so he didn't fear exposure, but the efforts of the day had exhausted him. He had to rest and he had to find food and water.

Near his shelter, he located a puddle and lapped it like a dog when his cupped hands wouldn't retain enough to quench his suddenly enormous thirst. Then he took a stick and began to dig in the soft ground. It was as he had hoped. The damp earth was full of insects.

As he ate, he decided that, whatever happened from here on in, he was not going back to a prison camp. Even if he died in the hills of Kyushu, he would do so as a free man.

Later, as the days stretched on, he began to wonder. How long could he endure and survive on his meager diet in the mountains of Kyushu? The weather was mild, but winter was inevitable. He had no idea how cold it would get, but it would certainly be much cooler than the present. What if he had to spend a long time in the hills? What if it took years for the war to end? Then he thought of something even more awful, and it made him shudder, nearly cry. What if it never ended? If that was the case, then he was condemned to spend whatever remained of his life running, hiding, and slowly starving to death.

Despite his circumstances, he saw black humor in the alternative possibility that the war would end and he would never find out. That would be just his luck.

CHAPTER 4

"**I**'m not too sure which appalls me the most, the rioting by our servicemen in San Francisco, or the civilian riots in other cities," said Marshall.

"They all sicken me," Truman said. "Look at the numbers for San Francisco. An estimated twenty thousand soldiers and sailors ran amok for two days before other military and state police could take control. They rampaged through Chinatown and killed anyone who looked even remotely Asian, hoping, I presume, that they were somehow killing Japs. God, more than a hundred dead and a thousand injured."

"Are you counting the rapes?" Marshall asked.

The riots in San Francisco had begun as a drunken celebration of victory over the Japanese by tens of thousands of servicemen overjoyed that they were not going to be fighting the Japs. When they found out the truth, the celebrations turned ugly. Most of the rapes had occurred during the celebration phase, the murders later on.

"No," Truman said sadly. The document on his desk indicated three thousand reported rapes in San Francisco alone, and God only knew how many unreported. "And will somebody tell me why the people of Detroit felt it necessary to kill another score of Negroes? Hadn't they had enough of race rioting in 1943?"

Where there had not been an Asian population to attack, the colored people of many large cities had become the target of the mobs' wrath.

Secretary of State Jim Byrnes lit a cigarette. "What is happening to these people, these criminals? May I presume there will be a lot of arrests and court-martials?"

Marshall shook his head. "Presume nothing. Most of the rioters in San Francisco are unidentified, except for a few score picked up by the police as drunk and disorderly. As to the rapes, most women won't testify, even if they could identify their assailants. The San Francisco hospitals reported giving out several thousand douches and sending the women home. There were so many raped women they had no other way to treat them. In order to defuse the situation, we are shipping as many of the soldiers and sailors out of California as quickly as possible and have confined the rest to their barracks.

"The police in Detroit and other cities finally seem to have everything under control, and there have been some arrests, although there does seem to be a lack of enthusiasm regarding actually prosecuting people."

"Not if I can help it," Truman snapped.

"Will we get convictions?" Byrnes asked.

Truman rose and paced. "Realistically, in today's climate we don't stand a snowball's chance of convicting someone for killing a Jap, Chinese, or colored man, but women and children were killed and that's something else entirely."

Truman took a deep breath to calm himself. "Which brings me to the point of this discussion, gentlemen. We must show ourselves as striking back at the Japanese in Japan and doing so extremely harshly. The actions of the mobs simply show how much the people's hatred of everything Japanese has increased. General Marshall, what is the status of the next bomb?"

Marshall answered quickly, "The bomb components have been flown to Tinian, and it is being assembled now. We will be ready anytime after the twenty-second of August."

"Good. Now, General, what about a target?"

Marshall paused, knowing that his answer could condemn thousands to death. The sixty-five-year-old five-star general had built the army from a scratch force to a massive entity in only a few short years. He had been the confidant of Roosevelt and was now Truman's trusted adviser.

"Sir, the original list included four Japanese cities that were largely spared conventional bombing in order to get maximum effect from the atomic bomb. Along with Hiroshima and Nagasaki, the list included Kokura and Niigata. If we stick with the original list, then only the last two remain. Air force generals Spaatz and LeMay would like to expand that very short list by also adding Tokyo and Kyoto, and they are backed by General Arnold."

LeMay and Spaatz commanded the air forces in the Pacific, while Gen. "Hap" Arnold was the air force representative on the Joint Chiefs of Staff. Since he was technically subordinate to Marshall, he was not present.

Byrnes answered quickly, "We've gone over that ground before and there is no reason to change the list. If anything, the decision to not atom bomb Tokyo and Kyoto is even more compelling. Simply put, we need both those cities relatively intact if we are ever to end this war. Tokyo is the administrative hub of Japan, and if we destroy it and the government, possibly killing the emperor, we could wind up with no one remaining in charge to call an end to the war. Quite frankly, gentlemen, I believe that the emperor is the only person who can surrender Japan.

"Kyoto's the religious center of Japan, virtually a city of temples. It would be tantamount to bombing the Vatican and then informing Italy's Catholics that we respected them and their culture. Using atom bombs on Kyoto could easily result in millions more fanatics ready to die for their country than there are now.

"General, we have too much to lose, and, yes, I do recognize the fact that we have been firebombing both cities with tremendous loss of life. But atomic bombs are so devastating that there is no comparison between the two events."

Marshall had expected the response, even supported it, but he felt obliged to forward the thoughts of his generals. "After we bomb Kokura and Niigata, we really don't have any more targets. Kokura's prewar population is less than a hundred thousand, and Niigata's only a little more than that. Further, the Japanese are finally getting the message and have commenced evacuating their cities. I rather doubt we will be dropping any kind of bombs on civilian refugee camps."

Truman laughed harshly. "Are you telling me we sit here with the greatest and most awesome weapon ever made, and we have bombed Japan so thoroughly that we might not have anything to use it on?"

Marshall nodded. "Precisely."

Truman sighed. "Jesus."

"Mr. President," Marshall continued, "it may be worse than that. According to General Groves, Dr. Oppenheimer and others are reporting that the lingering effects of radiation from the bombs may be far worse than what they expected. They've examined the ground at Alamogordo and the items recovered from there, and the radiation count is still very high, even lethally so. Further, there is a significant body of anecdotal evidence coming from Japan which confirms that hypothesis. It now seems that radiation does not dissipate in a matter of hours or days, but may linger on for months, perhaps years. There are many reports coming from Japan of otherwise healthy-looking people sickening and dying days after exposure to radioactive items. This means that our own soldiers could be at risk if we send them into a bombed-out area without proper precautions."

Truman was exasperated and his voice rose. "General, Jim, we must use a bomb. We must show both the people of the United States, and the fools in Tokyo, that they cannot refuse to surrender without suffering the consequences. If we do not punish the Japanese for this new act of treachery, there might be calls for my impeachment, if not my head. Now, if we cannot expand the list of targets, which of the two cities do you prefer?"

Marshall responded without hesitation, knowingly condemning thousands to incineration and worse. "Kokura. If we have to invade the home islands, the first assault will be on the island of Kyushu. Kokura is a city near the narrow straits between Kyushu and the almost adjacent island of Honshu. Destroying Kokura will have the effect of making it more difficult for the Japanese to move soldiers into Kyushu to reinforce the armies already there. By stretching the definition, Kokura could be considered a military target."

Truman turned to Byrnes. "Any cultural or political problem with Kokura?"

"None whatsoever."

Truman took a deep breath. "Then we will bomb Kokura."

"Yes, sir."

"Very good," Truman said softly. "After Kokura is destroyed, I wish to be fully updated on the plans to invade Kyushu, along with any other options that might be available to us. God help the people of Japan." And God help me, he cried to himself as he considered the additional deaths his decision would cause. But what choice do I have?

■

CHAPTER 5

"I'll get it," the pretty blonde yelled as the doorbell rang for the second time, this time insistently. Who could be in such a hurry? Nobody was expected this August evening. She pulled it open and stood there in disbelief.

"Hi," the young man said shyly. He was in uniform, and his gold lieutenant's bars shone in the light from the house.

Debbie Winston screamed and hugged the man at her door, then covered his face with kisses, which he urgently returned.

"Wow," 2nd Lt. Paul Morrell said when they finally broke for air. "Just think, I was worried that you might not be glad to see me." Debbie stopped any further attempt at conversation by again covering his face with kisses while she dragged him into the living room.

The clamor had brought the rest of Debbie's family, and they greeted Paul warmly with hugs and handshakes. Debbie's mother asked him if he had seen his own family, and he assured her that he had, and that he had just come from there. Then they sat him on the couch with Debbie beside him with her arm entwined with his.

"How much time do you have?" Debbie asked, dreading the answer.

"Only a couple of hours. A friend of mine is picking me up and driving me downtown to the train station." He laughed. "I'm not supposed to be here at all. The army flew me from Germany to England, and then from England to New York. My orders say I'm to take the most direct route to San Francisco, and then overseas. I guess they want me in a hurry. I saw a lot of other officers getting the same treatment. However, I just figured that the war would wait a little bit or, better yet, go on without me."

Debbie's mother stood. A whimsical smile was on her face. "Two hours? Somehow I think you two want to spend it alone and not talking to us." She grabbed her husband and Debbie's younger brother and steered them out of the room.

Debbie took Paul's hands in hers and kneaded them in quiet desperation, as if willing them to stay. "Paul, it isn't fair. You shouldn't be going to fight the Japanese. Didn't you do enough in Germany?"

He put his arm around her and pulled her to him. It was a hot evening and she was wearing only a blouse and skirt cut short because of the wartime shortage of materials. He could feel the warmth and tantalizing smoothness of her skin underneath her clothing, and her slender legs were gorgeous.

"Apparently not," he managed to say. "A whole lot of people are being sent from Europe to the Pacific." He decided not to tell her about the incident in Germany that had caused him to be put on the levy to fight the Japs. No need disturbing her with accounts of his own stupidity. "I'm just hoping it's over by the time I get there. Even if everything moves according to somebody's schedule, I don't see how we can do anything about Japan for several months. Of course, maybe if we drop a few more atom bombs on them, there won't be anything left to invade."

She nodded into his chest, conscious that she was staining his khaki uniform with her tears. She was trying not to cry but it was futile. News of the continued war had hit home with a bulletin that said yet another atomic bomb had been dropped on Japan, this one on a place called Kokura. *Kokura* sounded like a bird calling, not a city that had just been wiped off the face of the earth.

"Paul, it was so terrible here after the peace collapsed. Everybody had been celebrating victory, and then the rug was pulled out from under our feet and the crash was sickening. Instead of your coming home to me, we all realized that soldiers were still going to be shipped overseas to fight and maybe die. There was a lot of rioting here, and a lot of people were killed in downtown. Would you believe someone even smashed the window at Ginsberg's store and stole a couch? Mr. Ginsberg tried to make a joke of it by saying it was an ugly piece of furniture and that the thief had no taste, but I could tell he was shaken by it. Did you know that the governor declared martial law because of all the killings around the riverfront? There was even a curfew for a few days and everyone stayed home or got arrested. I just never believed it could happen here in the United States."

"I know," he said sadly. "I saw a lot of it in the barracks with men getting murderously drunk and then going into town simply to break things and hurt people. It was like the whole world had gone crazy with anger and everyone felt they'd been cheated out of the rest of their lives. Since I was an officer, they had me trying to settle things down and take charge. Funny, but what I really wanted to do was join them and break some stuff myself."

Debbie lifted her head and they kissed again. She was sobbing and realized he was crying softly as well. "Paul, I'm so scared for you. Somehow I thought that your going in the army was a lark, and I was playing at being the brave but lonely woman waiting at home for her man while you marched off with your uniform never getting dirty. After all, the Germans surrendered just after you got there, and then the Japs were going to give up. Now I'm scared that I might actually lose you."

Her voice broke and her chest heaved. "I just want you to come back to me."

Debbie did not add that she wanted him there so she could resolve her own doubts about their future. When he was with her, she was confident that she was in love with him. When he was gone from her, she wondered whether she was doing the right thing by continuing their long-distance romance. She gave no thought, however, to telling him of her doubts this evening.

Paul took a deep breath. "I love you," he said, and they kissed again. "And I am coming back." Then he grinned through his anguish. "Damn, I am glad I took this little detour even though it means I'm going to be late reporting."

"Can you get in trouble?"

He chuckled wryly. "Yeah, maybe they'll fire me. Wouldn't that be a shame?"

She laughed. "Come outside." She took his hand and led him out to the backyard. He smiled as he saw Debbie's family's car, tireless and propped up on cement blocks, testimony to the shortage of rubber and the rationing of gas. Debbie's father took the bus or trolley to work and had been selling his gas-ration coupons in return for other items. It wasn't legal, but everyone was doing it.

Some patio furniture was underneath a tree, and they sat on a porch swing, rocking gently.

.It was amazing, he thought, but her entire family seemed to have disappeared. He wondered if they were peering through windows at them and didn't give a damn. His own parents had wished for him to stay and spend what little time he had left with them, but they understood his need to see Debbie before he headed on to the West Coast. Both his parents had been weeping when he left them, but this was the worst departure of all.

"Do you want to get married?" Debbie asked softly, surprised at her own boldness and wondering if she really meant it. "We could run off to Kentucky and get married right away. I know some people who've done it."

He held her even more tightly. "I want to marry you more than anything in the world, but not until I return." And in one piece, he thought. "You're much too young to be a war widow and I won't wish that on you."

"Don't even think like that," she gasped. "Even my brother, Ronnie, is starting to talk like death is just around the corner. He'll be eighteen in a few months and now they're talking like he won't even get to finish high school before he gets drafted. My God, Paul, now they're taking babies in the draft! Isn't anybody left? Ronnie's scared and I don't blame him. I'm terrified for both of you."

Paul wondered what it was like in Japan. Were they drafting children the way the Germans did? He'd seen so many little boys in German uniforms, pretending they were soldiers, but using real bullets. Some were only ten or eleven years old, and a number of them had been killed or wounded by Americans who didn't stop to ask their age. An enemy soldier with a gun was a threat, no matter how old he was. It occurred to Paul that the winner of this awful war might just be the last country with anyone left standing.

They held each other in silence. They kissed and sometimes sobbed. This was not a night for giggling and petting. It was a night for remembering every sound, every word, every scent of each other.

They didn't even look up and comment on the sea of stars that was visible. They wanted nothing to distract them from what might be their last memories of each other.

After what seemed like only a few minutes, they heard the sound of a car horn. The interlude was over. She walked with him to the front of the house and they kissed one more time before he got in the car and drove away into the darkness.

Debbie kept a stony façade until the car turned the corner and was out of sight. Then she dropped to her knees and let out a wail. Her parents came running.

.

CHAPTER 6

*T*he dust-covered jeep stopped in front of a long row of identical brown army tents. The two MPs in the front watched as the disheveled young lieutenant eased himself stiffly out of the back and removed his duffel bag. They made no effort to help him, nor did any of the soldiers in the area manage to notice the situation either. The sight of MPs delivering a soldier to the area wasn't the slightest bit unique.

One of the MPs, a sergeant, glared before speaking. "Lieutenant, if I was you, I would trot my ass down to tent 721 directly. Do not try to clean up, do not get a bite to eat, do not pass go, do not collect no two hundred dollars. Just get down there and pronto before you get in any more trouble."

"Thanks for the lift, Sergeant, and the warm night of hospitality," he added, and dropped the heavy bag by his left side. He waited and stared until the sergeant reluctantly saluted him. Morrell returned it and turned away.

Tent number 721 was but one of thousands like it in the massive tent city that had been thrown up on the outskirts of Oakland, California, as a means of processing the transient troops en route to the war in the Pacific. The whole camp had an air of temporariness, as if it belonged to a migratory horde that had suddenly appeared and could disappear at will. The roads were dirt and rutted, and the tents were small and shapeless. However, the camp was laid out in a sensible grid that made it possible for the MPs to drop Paul off only a little way from his destination, tent 721. They could have dropped him off right in front, but they wanted to show a little more of their superiority by letting him take a walk.

Paul tapped on a piece of plywood attached to the front of the tent as a crude knocker. "Come in," a voice called, and Paul had that feeling that he'd been here before. It was uncannily like that last time in Germany.

He ducked his head and entered. Then he started to stand upright and come to attention. "Sit down, Lieutenant," said the voice, interrupting that effort. Paul found a camp chair and did as directed.

As his eyes became adjusted to the dimmer light, he saw that the man facing him across a card table that served as a desk was a captain in his late twenties or early thirties. He had dark, brush-cut hair and looked to be fairly tall and rangy.

"Lieutenant Morrell, I presume?"

"Yes, sir."

"Wonderful. Lieutenant, I am Captain Tom Ruger. Now just where the hell have you been? You were supposed to be here three days ago. Almost all the rest of the regimental officers have gone on ahead with the enlisted men, with me left behind to round up strays like you."

Tradition dictated that he was to say "no excuse," or something like that. Right now, Paul was too tired and dirty to care. "Sir, if I hadn't been thrown in jail for no good reason yesterday, I would only have been two days late. As to the rest of it, my orders weren't realistic. I may have had travel priority, but that couldn't get me on planes that weren't flying or trains that weren't moving."

To Paul's surprise, Ruger laughed. "The orders may not have been realistic, but most army orders aren't. If we had told you to arrive as soon as you could, how long would you have taken? A year? Two? As to the other part, you were arrested for the crime of wearing a uniform in San Francisco, which, after the peace riots of a few weeks ago, is now off-limits to all military personnel and will remain that way for the foreseeable future.

"When the cops stopped you, your orders caused the police to worry about your intentions because they showed you were already two days AWOL. If you'd been on time, they'd just have put you on a bus or truck and shipped your sorry ass out here. Since your paperwork condemned you as a probable felon, they decided not to take chances, and that's why they held you in jail. To tell you the truth I don't blame them. There are a lot of people showing up late in hopes the war will be over by the time they arrive."

"I admit the thought crossed my mind."

"As to transportation problems, Lieutenant, the military in the Northwest states are going crazy, which is completely screwing up everything that moves on wheels. The Japs have started sending over firebombs attached to balloons that drift along over the prevailing air currents by the hundreds, maybe the thousands, and into the U.S. They've only caused a little damage: a couple of small forest fires, and a handful of people were killed while trying to examine them. But rumor has it that one of the bombs apparently started a fire at some supersecret installation near Hanford, Washington, and cut the place's electricity. It may have been chance, but it's the sort of thing that drives the brass crazy and disrupts train schedules."

Ruger's voice dropped its tone of banter and turned stern. "Be that as it may, you were still supposed to be here on time. Do you understand that?"

"Yes, sir."

"You planning to make the army a career, Lieutenant Morrell?"

"Hell, no. I mean, no, sir."

Ruger took a piece of paper off his makeshift desk and wadded it up. "Then there's no point in disciplining you, is there? I could maybe have you court-martialed and stripped of rank, but that would be a waste of the time and money the government's got invested in you, and a written reprimand that would ruin your career wouldn't mean squat if you don't have a career to ruin in the first place." He threw the paper away. It landed on the ground, a few feet from an overflowing wastebasket. "You got a family in Detroit? A girl?"

"Yes to both, Captain."

Ruger leaned forward and glared. "I'll bet you deviated from a true straight-line course and spent some time with them, didn't you?"

Why lie? Paul thought. "Yes, Captain, I did. I was off course for about seven hours."

Ruger shook his head in disbelief. "That all? Jesus Christ, Lieutenant, I would have spent a lot more than that with them. After all, you're not likely to see them for a helluva long time."

Paul blinked and Ruger started laughing. "Like I said, Lieutenant Morrell, how can I punish you? Can't fire you, now can I?"

Paul worked up a reciprocal smile. "It wouldn't hurt my feelings if you did."

"Morrell, I'm a reservist myself, so I can't wait for this pile of shit war to end so I can get home to my loving wife and two kids and start working on kids three and four. In the meantime, I've got an infantry company to staff, along with filling a couple of other openings in the battalion for Major Redwald and General Monck. The enlisted men and the rest of the officers left via troopship shortly after the riots, and we are trying to fill the last officer vacancies. It's an unusual procedure, but this whole damned war is highly unusual. You, Mr. Morrell, look like you can do the job. Let's see, you're twenty-three. How the hell did you stay out of the draft for so long?"

"Captain, I was in ROTC in college, had a mild knee injury from high school football, and my dad knew someone on the draft board. Of the three, I think the last was the most significant."

"Not exactly dying to get in, were you?"

"I don't think anybody is. I guess that's why we have the draft in the first place since any rush to enlist ended shortly after Pearl Harbor. But now that I'm here, I'll serve and do my best."

Ruger grunted acknowledgment. "I see you've been in combat."

"Very little. Twice my unit in Germany was under indirect artillery fire, and once we might have been shot at by a sniper. In all cases, I just kept my head down and tried to keep my people from being killed."

"But you actually did something. You didn't lie there frozen in your own crap, now did you?"

"I guess I did manage to move about and function usefully."

"So why'd they get rid of you in Germany? How badly did you fuck up?"

Paul explained the situation with the grenades and the discipline. "Funny," Paul concluded, "but all I was trying to do was the right thing."

Ruger nodded. "The road to hell is paved with people trying to do the right thing or something like that. I presume you've learned a little discretion."

Paul grinned. "A lot."

"Fine. Let's get back to you in those combat situations. Were you scared?"

"Shitless."

Captain Ruger nodded. "My first time was in the Philippines last year. I was so scared I maybe did shit, although the place already stank so bad I don't think anybody could tell, and I suppose I'll be scared again when we invade Japan."

Paul's heart sank. "Then it's official?"

"Yep, and you're gonna be part of it. Since you look reasonably human and have almost satisfactorily explained yourself, I'm taking you for my company. We are part of a now-forming infantry regiment, the 528th, Brigadier General John Monck commanding. We are going to be assigned as a reserve force for one of the divisions that's going to invade. We'll be shipping out from here faster than you can say jack shit, so don't even think about unpacking or even leaving this tent without me as a chaperone."

Paul sagged. That soon? Not even a few days' respite? "Do I have time for a phone call? How 'bout a shave and a shower?"

Ruger looked at his watch. "If we move fast, we can both make a phone call. Unless somebody changes their minds, we'll be on a C-54 in about two and a half hours. You can forget the shower. The plumbing around here is terrible at best."

Ruger stood up and Paul realized the captain was not as tall as he'd first thought, only an inch or so taller than he was. Ruger held out his hand and Paul took it. Ruger's grip was firm. "Morrell, welcome to whatever the hell we're getting into. Now, let's go find us some phones, some food, and maybe even something to drink. You mind eating and drinking in an ugly old tent?"

Despite his apprehensions, Paul smiled. "Not in the slightest, Captain. Uh, do you have any idea where we're going from here?"

"Paul, after a few stops for food and fuel, we will be catching up with our enlisted personnel on that resort spot of the Pacific, Okinawa, and God help us."

Paul's first steps in the Pacific theater would come soon.

.

CHAPTER 7

The third atomic bomb followed its precursors at Hiroshima and Nagasaki and fell on Kokura, with the same devastation. Gen. Korechika Anami, minister of war, stared at the small group of grim-faced men who sat with him in that same bunker where Emperor Hirohito had been taken prisoner. The austere walls were now covered with maps and reports that charted the flow of the war that was raging over their heads as American bombers pounded targets in Tokyo and its suburbs. The new leader of Japan wondered what was left for them to destroy in Tokyo.

Beginning with the March fire raids, the city had systematically been destroyed. More than a hundred thousand of her people had burned to death as the fragile wooden dwellings that housed her population of 3 million had gone up like matches.

It was the same in the other cities of Japan. Fire and death.

As news from the bombed city of Kokura filtered in through the shattered lines of communication, and as the death toll from Hiroshima and Nagasaki continued to mount, the sixty-three-year-old General Anami wondered if he had done the right thing by supporting the rebellious young officers whose palace coup had caused the killing to continue. He dismissed the brief spark of doubt. What had been done was right and Japan's fate. Japan would fight on and so would he. He had to. He was samurai and bound by the oath of Bushido to never surrender. But what would Japan fight with? They had to stop the rain of nuclear terror from the skies.

Grudgingly, he acknowledged that the traditional definition of war had been changed. Japanese bravery would count for naught unless he could find some way of halting the bombings. Not for the first time he wondered if he had been born too late. Better that he was already dead and his ashes scattered than to see what was happening to his beloved Japan.

Because of his role in the coup that had captured Hirohito and prevented the planned surrender, General Anami had taken the duties of prime minister as well as war minister. The previous prime minister, Suzuki, had not resigned. He had died of a sudden and massive stroke while being taken into custody, and it offended Anami that the American and British press insisted that the seventy-seven-year-old Suzuki had been murdered. The doddering old man who had survived other coup attempts and outlived assassins' bullets had simply died.

Foreign Minister Shigenori Togo had been imprisoned, although in the comfort of his own home. The fool had insisted on trying to negotiate a peace settlement with the Allies on terms that were unfavorable to the Empire. Later they would decide whether he had committed treason. Probably not, as he was not a soldier and had been following the wishes of his misguided emperor, Hirohito. Togo's replacement, ex–prime minister Hideki Tojo, had been chosen by the military, and the news had sent shock waves through the Allies. Tojo had been one of the architects of the Pearl Harbor attack, but had borne the brunt of blame for the later failures of the military and been forced to resign.

Anami hoped that Tojo's appointment and apparent return to power would send a clear message that the Japanese Empire was deadly serious in its intent to continue the war. Tojo, however, was a figurehead appointment. The real power to lead and control Japan lay with the handful of men in the room.

Of the other important pacifists, only Marquis Kido, a friend and relative of the emperor's, remained at large. General Umezu, who had openly agreed with the decision to surrender, was also under house arrest. In Anami's opinion, Umezu was definitely a traitor and would be dealt with accordingly.

Anami began the meeting. "The emperor sends his greetings and wishes us well."

Admiral Toyoda's mouth flickered slightly in what might have been a smile. "Then he has not decided to choose an honorable death?" Toyoda was delighted that the war was continuing and, like the others in the room, knew that Hirohito was a prisoner. "And where is our beloved emperor?"

Anami nodded slightly at Toyoda. "Colonel Sakei said that Hirohito intends no such thing as an immediate honorable death. He believes that he can best serve the Empire by living."

The implications were clear. Hirohito would remain alive to forestall his replacement by someone more extreme. Should he die, then the crown would pass to his son, Akihito. But the crown prince was far too young to reign, and a regent would be appointed, presuming, of course, that the crown prince could be found. A second choice would doubtless be Hirohito's younger brother, Prince Takamatsu. Takamatsu stood solidly behind the militarists in their continuing fight.

"As to the emperor's physical presence," Anami continued, "Colonel Sakei has moved him to a place of greater safety. He is in a secure location near the city of Nagasaki. That was chosen because the Americans would not again bomb the ruined place. It also places him away from Tokyo and the possibility of a countercoup." Anami quickly looked upward and the others followed. They could hear the distant thudding of bombs. "It is ironic, but dead Nagasaki is now far safer than Tokyo."

The group nodded agreement. Anami was still taken aback by the way they looked to him for guidance and leadership.

Anami again directed his glance at Admiral Toyoda. "Are there any improvements regarding the navy?"

Toyoda flushed. There was no navy. With the exception of sixteen destroyers and a number of regular submarines, the conventional navy no longer existed. Fewer than 10 percent of navy ships were still afloat, and all other ships of consequence had been sunk or so severely damaged that they could not move.

"We have no carriers, no battleships, no cruisers, and almost no frontline planes. Unless they have been found and destroyed by the Americans, only about a hundred fighters remain, and they are dispersed all over Japan."

Once, the Japanese navy and the swift Zero fighter had ruled both the waves and the skies. Now it was all ashes, and the surviving planes were hidden rather than rising to fight. Even the guns from the remaining ships had been removed and placed in tunnels and bunkers where they would have a better opportunity to repel the Americans.

Just before Pearl Harbor, the late and revered Admiral Yamamoto had said that the Japanese navy would run amok for six months or a year, but that the weight of American arms would be too much. Events had occurred precisely as Yamamoto had forecast.

Anami wondered what role Yamamoto would have taken in these proceedings had he not been killed by American fighter planes.

"General Sugiyama?" Anami asked.

Field Marshal Hajime Sugiyama had been appointed to coordinate the land defenses of the home islands. Anami considered him pompous, but he was a loyal supporter of continuing the war.

"The army is ready," Sugiyama said proudly. "We are two million strong and undefeated, although I have to admit that many of our troops are inexperienced, and not up to our previous standards. Additional formations are crossing over from Manchukuo and Chosen and will assist in the defense of the home islands. Further, we are beginning to enroll millions of Japanese civilians into either militia units or civilian shock troops."

With the exception of the battle for the Philippines, only fairly small units of the Imperial Japanese Army had encountered the Americans. In China, the Japanese army had been victorious and all-conquering up until the Russians had advanced into Manchukuo and threatened the Kwantung army's rear. Now that army was withdrawing its best troops back to the home islands while leaving second-rate soldiers to fight off the Soviets in the lands known by the Americans as Manchuria and Korea.

"General, when will the Russians be halted?" Anami queried.

Sugiyama's confidence was unshaken as he stated unpleasant truths. "The remainder of our armies in China and Manchukuo will be split by the Russian advance. Those in China have been directed to build strong fortifications and defend themselves bravely until relieved, while those in Chosen are withdrawing south and will form defensive lines where the peninsula narrows. By that time, the Russians should be out of fuel and, with their supply lines extended, will be vulnerable to our counterattacks."

Anami prodded, "The Soviets have crossed and landed on what they refer to as Sakhalin Island. Have we overlooked their amphibious potential?"

"No," the field marshal answered tersely. "What was overlooked was the defense of those islands. Our predecessors thought that the treaty with the Soviet Union would render moot any need to protect those lands from those we thought were our allies. Thus, the Russian landings were virtually unopposed. I guarantee you that will not be the case if they wish to proceed farther or attempt to land on Honshu."

Sugiyama's report did not mention the hundreds of thousands of Japanese soldiers either still fighting battles in the islands of the Pacific, or who were withering and starving after being bypassed by the American navy, which could sail anyplace it wished. He was told almost four hundred thousand of Japan's best soldiers were isolated from the home islands by distance and the American navy. They might as well be dead.

"Army fighter planes?" Anami asked. "What numbers are there?"

Sugiyama shrugged. "A few hundred, and they too are dispersed and well hidden until the time is right. But that is not important. We will win this war with courage and adherence to the code of Bushido, not with machines. Victory will go to the brave, and there is no one more courageous than the Japanese soldier!"

Anami said nothing, but again wondered just what good courage was against an enemy who was tens of thousands of feet in the sky and capable of dropping bombs of all kinds on the heads of those brave Japanese soldiers. What good was bravery if the brave warrior could not even reach the craven enemy?

Thousands of American planes flew daily over Japanese lands, and the Japanese military was helpless to stop them. Those few fighters that did fly up to attack them were inevitably shot down. As a result, the draconian order had gone forth that the cities would not be defended from the American bombers. The few remaining planes, along with the precious few warships, would be husbanded until the time of the American invasion. As this occurred, the Japanese military and civilian population would dig into the hillsides and await their opportunity for revenge.

Anami clenched his fists. "Victory is a qualified statement. What we want is to end this round of fighting on terms that will not destroy or humiliate Japan or cause us to violate our oath to the code of Bushido, and which will enable us to prepare for the next round. The question then is, how do we accomplish this most reasonable goal? We understand quite well that the Americans have a different definition of the worth of a soldier's life. In Japan, a soldier's goal is to die for his emperor, while the American wishes nothing more than to survive and go home. Thus, while our soldiers fight to the death, the cowardly Americans surrender at the earliest opportunity."

Sugiyama sniffed. "They are women."

"Be that as it may, the fact of their unmanly behavior has given us a weapon. General Sugiyama, you spoke of arming millions of civilians, but with what? We have very few guns to give them."

"Spears and knives," Sugiyama said proudly. "They will rush the Americans. Then they will stab them and disembowel them."

Anami appreciated the thought, but questioned its effectiveness. However, while uncountable tens of thousands would be killed and stacked in bloody piles before the American guns, many Americans would indeed die as well.

"Good," Anami said, "but the key to our success is the kamikaze." They recalled the sacred story of the kamikaze, the divine wind, that had sprung up those hundreds of years ago to destroy the ships of the Mongol horde and kept Japan safe from invasion.

"The purpose of the kamikaze," he continued, "is not to die uselessly for Japan, but to kill for her, and we must not forget that. If death comes as that which is inevitable and right, then such a death is an honor to one's self and family. But it is far, far better to kill first than to just die, and that is what we must ensure. General, how many kamikaze planes and pilots are ready for the final battle?"

Sugiyama's chest swelled. "At least five thousand, and there are an additional ten thousand planes of all kinds that can be converted into flying bombs. Getting pilots is no problem, and we are hoarding fuel enough for them to make their one-way flights to glory. They will kill for Japan."

"Good. Now, what about the navy, Admiral Toyoda?"

The admiral responded proudly. "While we lack larger craft, we have over three hundred midget submarines, along with many manned torpedoes and many hundreds of smaller craft that are intended to attack and ram American ships. Again, the fuel, while scarce, will be sufficient for a onetime thrust. The navy too will kill and die for Japan."

Anami permitted himself a smile. "Then all we have to do is make this rain of nuclear death stop. I must confess that, when the first bomb was dropped on Hiroshima, I thought that the Americans would have no others. Sadly, I was wrong and I apologize for my ignorance. Yet, we are not without recourse."

He paused and saw that he had their attention. "To my surprise and dismay, the Hiroshima bomb was followed by the Nagasaki attack only three days later. This was obviously intended to make us think they had many bombs in their arsenals." Anami paused again and smiled grimly. "Yet, it took almost two weeks for a third to be dropped on Kokura. That tells me that their number of bombs and their ability to produce them is extremely limited. They likely had two to begin with and used them at Hiroshima and Nagasaki, thinking we would surrender as a result. When we did not, they had to manufacture a third. I am certain they are right now building a fourth and fifth of the infernal devices. But, I am just as certain that we have a couple of weeks before any will be ready for use."

Anami looked about, waiting to see if they agreed with his logic. When no comments were forthcoming, he continued, "During these few weeks given us, we will prey upon the American weakness regarding the deaths of their soldiers to force them to stop using atomic bombs on us."

"How?" interrupted Toyoda.

Anami ignored the breach of protocol. "We hold many thousands of American and British prisoners of war, along with numerous Australians and Dutch. I propose that those prisoners now held in the home islands be brought to our cities and held as hostages against nuclear attack. I further propose that Allied prisoners in Manchukuo and elsewhere, particularly those senior officers like Wainwright and Devereaux, be transported to the home islands to swell the numbers who will die if we are attacked. I also propose that we immediately inform the Americans and British of our intentions."

There was a stunned silence, then the men in the underground bunker rose and applauded General Anami.

CHAPTER 8

Sgt. Joe Nomura knew he was in trouble when he saw the two men walking briskly down the row of beds in the hospital ward. He was the only person in the ward in Saipan, so he couldn't hope that they would pass him by.

Joe lay back on his bed in his underwear and relaxed as they stopped in front of him. "Gentlemen, what can I do for you?"

The two men appeared to be in their thirties. They were dressed as naval officers, commanders, and carried briefcases. While one was dark-haired and the other light, the two looked disarmingly like tall and well-muscled twins. The lighter-haired one spoke. "Sergeant Nomura, I am Commander Johnson and this is Commander Peters. We would like to speak with you for a few moments."

Nomura sat up. It was awkward because his left arm had been amputated at the elbow. "Has my discharge come through?"

Peters and Johnson looked at each other; slight confusion registered on their faces. "No," said Johnson, "we don't know anything about that."

Nomura waved his half an arm. "Do you mean that the army intends to keep me on as a one-armed soldier? That's ridiculous. There's nothing more I can do. I've given enough, don't you think?"

"I understand," said Peters.

"Do you?" Nomura sneered.

Johnson opened his briefcase and pulled out a sheet of paper. "Let's see. Sergeant Jochi Nomura, aged twenty-eight. You were born on the island of Oahu in Hawaii, in some town I can't pronounce. At age eight, your parents, who were employed by a shipping company, took you to Japan, where you lived until you were seventeen. At that point, you returned with them and lived in Honolulu, where you remained until the start of the war."

Johnson halted for a moment to see if Nomura would comment. He didn't. "Almost immediately after Pearl Harbor, you volunteered for the army and, after basic training, were assigned to the 442nd Regimental Combat Team and were later shipped over to Italy. You were wounded slightly and returned to combat. Then, while rescuing comrades who were pinned down by a Nazi machine gun, you were shot and suffered the loss of your left arm just below the elbow. You were awarded the Silver Star for that action. That, however, did not stop you, and you were voluntarily assigned as a translator to help the army convince Japanese civilians here on Saipan that they would not be harmed by us, and that they should surrender."

Joe Nomura laughed harshly. "Helluva great job I did. I stood there and yelled for them to come in, while all the time they were throwing themselves off the cliffs only a hundred feet away from me. I'm through. I want my discharge. One-armed soldiers with Silver Stars get to go home, and you goddamn well know it."

"Joe," Peters said, "we'd like to make you an offer."

Now it comes, Nomura thought. "Who are you guys? I know you're not navy."

"We're not?" asked Peters, looking a little hurt. "I'm disappointed. I rather thought we looked the part."

"Hell no. First of all, your insignias aren't correctly put on, and more important, I haven't said *sir,* haven't stood up, and haven't been very nice to you at all. Real officers would have eaten me alive for that, one-armed hero or not."

Johnson laughed. "Good call. We're from the Office of Strategic Services, the OSS, and we'd like you to help us."

Joe was momentarily puzzled, but then the light dawned as the bottom dropped out of his stomach. "Oh, shit, you want me to go into Japan, don't you?"

Both men nodded. "You're perfect," said Johnson. "You've lived there, you're of Japanese descent, and you're wounded, which means their secret police won't bother you."

"Fuck off."

"Joe," said Peters, "we have to know what's going on in there, and we desperately need the damn few people in the world like you. We don't have any spies in Japan and we can't land regular agents. To belabor the obvious, a white man in Japan would stand out."

Nomura had to laugh. "Well, ain't that the truth. Having a white skin ain't always an advantage, now is it?"

"Will you at least consider helping us?" Johnson asked.

"What's in it for me?"

Peters saw the small opening and responded quickly, "You'll be discharged, but kept on as a government employee with the equivalent pay and privileges of an army captain."

Joe stood slowly, his calm Japanese face suddenly an alien mask of scarcely controlled rage. The change in his bearing and demeanor startled the two OSS recruiters, and they stepped back quickly and in shock.

"God damn it!" Joe screamed. "You think you can buy me? Look, assholes, in the past couple of years a lot more has happened than my losing my arm for a country that doesn't give a shit for me! I'm alone in this fucking ward because, after spraining my ankle out on those cliffs, no one wanted to be around a Jap, not even one with a Silver Star. Y'know, in Italy I saw white Americans shoot Japanese Americans and ignore the fact that we were supposed to be fighting the Germans together. Whenever we went to a town in Italy, we were spit on and called yellow Japs and a helluva lot worse."

Jochi Nomura glared at them. "And that ain't all. My dad lost his job because of his skin and nobody cares that he's a naturalized citizen. And now my parents are living in squalor in some fucking concentration camp like convicts whose only crime is having a yellow skin. And do you know what's the worst?" A stunned Peters and Johnson shook their heads numbly. "A couple of weeks ago some white guys who'd busted into the camp grabbed my mom and raped her because she was a Jap. They fucked my mom! Anybody besides your daddy fuck your mom lately?" Nomura sat down heavily. "Now, try to tell me again why should I help you?"

Johnson lowered his head in embarrassment while Peters looked away. "I'm sorry. We had no idea," Johnson said softly. "Sergeant, we're both truly sorry. It was just our fervent hope that you and others like you would be able to go into Japan and provide us with the information we need to help stop the killing. Look, nothing can ever make the past good again, but we have to start somewhere building the future, and we can't do that until the war ends. I guess I don't blame you for telling us to kiss off. We'll go now. Good-bye, Sergeant." The two men turned to leave.

Joe sighed, "I'll go."

Both men blinked. "What?" Johnson managed.

Nomura smiled bleakly. "My parents are fine. They're living in Honolulu and not in some camp, and if somebody touched my mom, she'd cut their balls off. The rest of the shit I told you about the white soldiers picking on us is true, and it's also true that no one is in this ward with me so they don't get confused and think I'm one of Hirohito's boys who are still hiding out in the hills. In a way it's okay, though. I kind of like it being alone. Besides, despite the fact that me and people like me are getting fucked over royally, it sounds like I might actually be able to help end this fucking war, right? I want to prove once and for all to the government that Japanese Americans are not the enemy."

Johnson smiled, while Peters looked a little angry at being misled. "Mr. Nomura, you're a real bastard," Johnson said, "but we like that in an agent. When can you leave?"

Nomura looked around at the empty room, hostile in its silence. "Is right now soon enough?"

■

CHAPTER 9

President Truman could barely contain his anger and frustration. First, the destruction of the city of Kokura had elicited no response from the Japanese. It was inconceivable to him that the deaths of tens of thousands of Japanese civilians could be ignored by the Japanese government. What would it take for them to surrender? Hiroshima, Nagasaki, and now Kokura had ceased to exist, and so many Japanese civilians had been reduced to ashes. And all for nothing. Were the Japs even human? he wondered. At least their leaders weren't, he concluded. But this was not the only problem.

President Truman's voice tended to rise an octave when he was upset. "I thought I now understood at least a little of what I needed to know in order to be president, but now you're telling me there are still more deep, dark secrets that have been kept from me." He sagged in his seat. "This is beyond incredible."

Secretary of State Jim Byrnes leaned over and touched the president's sleeve. "Mr. President, I just found out now myself, although I have to admit I suspected and am not surprised." They were seated on facing couches in the Oval Office. An uncomfortable-looking Gen. George C. Marshall sat on a colonial-style chair at Truman's left.

"So," Truman said resignedly to Marshall, "what you are telling me is that we're reading the Japs' mail and that we've been doing it for some time, unbeknownst to both them and me."

Marshall nodded. "Yes, sir, and the secret is so closely held that I'm not at all surprised you weren't told. Much of our success in this war has been dependent upon our ability to decode Japanese transmissions and to keep that fact secret."

Truman almost sneered in his frustration, but held himself in check. "Really?"

"Yes, sir. With the exception of those actually working on the project, very few are aware of our successes in this area. Sir, at one point we thought that President Roosevelt was careless in his handling of secret Japanese documents that we'd decoded, so we took him off the list of recipients for almost a year."

Truman's jaw dropped and Byrnes gulped in astonishment. Byrnes stammered, "You arbitrarily deprived the president of important information?"

"Mr. Secretary, we gave him all the summary information he needed. We did deprive him of source documents and other items that would indicate we had broken the Japanese codes. Our term for the effort is 'Magic,' and through it we've been able to read virtually all Japanese diplomatic radio transmissions and most military ones. The British have done the same thing with the Germans, and they call it their Ultra program. They are, by the way, as secretive about it as we are. The important thing is to keep in mind that neither the Japanese nor the Germans yet have any inkling that this is going on. As a result, the Japanese continue to use the codes they have been using. Even though the war with Germany is over, we still think that retaining secrecy will prove useful.

"Sir, if the Japanese were to find out, they'd change their codes and we'd be blind for a long, long time. It took almost two years to break the Japanese diplomatic code, and we don't have that kind of time to go through all that effort again."

Byrnes took a sip of his coffee. "What you're telling me, General, is that President Truman, should he be elected on his own in 1948 and have his own vice president, would be well advised to keep this secret from that poor soul just as FDR kept it from him."

"Exactly," said Marshall with just a trace of a smile.

Truman waved his hands. "The next election will keep. Unless this war is brought to a speedy and successful conclusion, I won't be able to run for dogcatcher in 1948. Now, what does all this message reading tell us."

"It tells us that there is turmoil in Japan's hierarchy," said Marshall. "The military is in fairly firm control over the armed forces and is moving to consolidate, but their grasp is not as solid as it could be in other areas."

Byrnes agreed. "From what I've gleaned, Japanese diplomats both in Japan and in their embassies in neutral nations are virtually unanimous that the war must end on almost any terms. Tojo may have been appointed foreign minister, but he does not have the support of his staff. We also feel that the other nonmilitary sectors feel that way as well, but are powerless as long as the military remain in control. We are getting further indications that the majority of the civilian population wishes for an end to the war, but they too are helpless."

Marshall continued, "Even so, our military intercepts also indicate that the Japs are moving to reinforce their existing forces in Kyushu. They have anticipated correctly that Kyushu will be the first target of our assault on the home islands."

"Damn," said Truman.

Marshall paused. He knew this would be the most difficult to tell the volatile Truman. "Mr. President, we are also hearing that the Japs may be moving Allied POWs into strategic positions to deter us from using any more nuclear bombs on their cities."

Truman sat bolt upright. "No!"

"I'm afraid it's almost undoubtedly true, sir, although their effort is incomplete as yet. The Japs hold about a hundred and forty thousand Allied prisoners, maybe ten thousand of which are Americans, and we think about half of those numbers may be on the Jap home islands. The rest are scattered all over the place with large portions in Malaya and Burma. Many of our captured senior people are in camps in Manchuria. According to the intercepts, they are among those being sent to Tokyo and other important places in the home islands."

"That's against the Geneva Convention," Truman said sadly.

"Yes, it is," Marshall responded, "but we never signed the Geneva Convention, although we have been adhering to its terms on a voluntary basis. The Japanese have never shown any interest in obeying it."

Truman's face turned red in frustration. "I will presume that the Japs plan on making this a public pronouncement fairly soon, don't they?" Marshall nodded, and Truman threw up his hands. "First you tell me that we're running out of targets, and I agree with you.

Kokura was a wretched little place to destroy. Then I'm informed that the Japs are evacuating their cities, which further reduces our nuclear opportunities, and now you tell me that American and British POWs are going to be used as human shields to prevent our using atom bombs against whatever happens to be left in Japan. Is that right?"

Marshall sat unmoving. "That's right, sir. Other than causing the movement of our prisoners to target areas, you're right, the bombing of Kokura has had virtually no impact on the Japanese. I would suggest that we suspend nuclear operations against Japanese cities and create an inventory for tactical use in support of the landings on Kyushu. Conventional, nonnuclear bombing of Japanese targets will, of course, continue."

"Of course," Truman said in a dejected whisper. "Agreed."

"I'm sorry, Harry," Byrnes said solicitously, "we all had such high hopes that the bombs would end the war."

Marshall paused. There was another point to make. "We are starting to see the volume of decodeable traffic dry up, and that will hinder us. The Japanese now have few outposts and even fewer ships with which to communicate, and their home island radio transmitters have been destroyed to a very large extent by our bombers. They are now relying on telegraph and telephone, which we cannot intercept, as well as using human messengers and couriers."

"Another ironic price of success," Truman mused. "May I presume we are reading Stalin's mail as well?"

Marshall nodded solemnly. "Not as well as we'd like. You may also presume that we are reading British messages, and that they are reading ours."

Byrnes found it amusing. "Lord, what a wicked, wicked world we live in."

Truman stood and the two others left. Now he could walk the corridor to the real White House and try to relax with Bess and his Margaret. Maybe he could have a drink and play the piano. Maybe, he laughed aloud, he would play the piano so loud the whole wretched building would collapse on his head.

He chuckled. At least that would solve one of his problems.

•

CHAPTER 10

In the six months since she'd been commissioned, the officers and crew of the U.S. submarine *Moray* had seen only limited action in the Pacific. With the Japanese military and merchant fleet shrinking through combat attrition, there were fewer and fewer targets for a prowling sub to find and sink. Locating even those handful that remained involved hazardous trips through Japan's Inland Sea, that myriad of channels that separated and flowed through the multitude of large and small islands in the Japanese archipelago.

To the *Moray*'s captain, Comdr. Frank Hobart, the last patrol had been a frustrating disgrace. Nothing sighted and nothing shot at. They had returned to base with all torpedoes snug in their racks and were silently ridiculed by their more successful and experienced peers. Thus, he was delighted to be sent to Okinawa for what was described as a special mission to Japan. How special he didn't care. One more chance, Hobart thought, for a few kills, and a better chance at staying on in a postwar navy that was sure to shrink and want to keep only the best and the brightest. And the most aggressive, he kept adding. He had to make a name for himself before it was too late.

Neither he nor his crew were unduly surprised when the five men and their equipment came on board at Okinawa. The men were all dressed in black and all had their faces covered like bandits. Even more curiously, one of the men, the smallest of the five, had only one arm.

The *Moray* was a Gato-class submarine stationed off northern Kyushu, one of more than sixty in that efficient and effective category. She was 307 feet long and displaced 1,525 tons. Along with ten torpedo tubes, she had a three-inch deck gun and a 20mm Oerlikon antiaircraft gun. The *Moray* was a formidable weapon and had been built at Mare Island, California, in late 1944.

The sixty-five men in her crew normally lived in cramped and abominable conditions, which were exacerbated by the presence of the five additional men and their equipment. To make matters worse, the five secreted themselves in the captain's cabin and wardroom and stayed there for the duration of the short voyage, thus pushing out the officers who would normally have lived there.

From Okinawa to Kyushu was less than five hundred miles, and Captain Hobart was confident he and his crew could gut out the overcrowding for another chance at the Japs. His crew was not as confident. While skilled and professional, many had this nagging feeling that Hobart was aggressive to the point of recklessness, and most did not share his confidence in wanting to tweak the enemy one last time. They also wanted the five interlopers gone from their boat and their little breathing room back in their cramped world of tubes, pipes, and bad air.

When the *Moray* surfaced at night just a mile off the northern coast of Kyushu, everyone was relieved that at least part of their journey was over. With precision and dispatch, the five men, still black-clad and masked, emerged on deck with their gear and a rubber raft. Silently, they pushed off, and four men paddled while the fifth, the one-armed man, sat unmoving in the center of the small craft. Within minutes they had disappeared into the darkness. The sky was only partly cloudy, and starlight and moonlight made the *Moray* fairly visible if anyone knew where to look. Prudently, her skipper submerged her farther, until only her conning tower was above the surface of the gently rolling sea.

"Skipper?"

"Yes, Randy?" Hobart tried not to show his impatience. His second-in-command, in his opinion, did not show proper aggressive spirit. Randy Bullard was a reservist who'd made it known that he wanted to go home more than anything else. Well, he would go home when his captain decided, and not before.

"Captain, I strongly suggest we submerge to periscope depth. There's just too much of us showing and we are very close to enemy territory."

Hobart sniffed the air and looked about. It was humid and he thought it might soon rain. There was no sign of anything on the sea or in the air, and the brooding hills of Japan, so tantalizingly close, were dark and still as well. It was the middle of the night and the Japanese were asleep, even those who had survived the nuclear assaults on Nagasaki and Kokura. He wondered if he should risk a look at Nagasaki's harbor after finishing this assignment.

"Negative, Randy. Let's air the place out. It stinks like a stable down there. Besides, those banditos in the raft have to be able to see us in order to find their way back to us." Besides, Hobart thought silently, he didn't want to give in to his weakling of an exec.

Only just before the raft had shoved off had Hobart been given the final portion of his orders, which informed him that only one of the five men—he presumed they were Marine Raiders—would actually be leaving the sub. He was dismayed and knew his crew would be unhappy as well, because it meant that the intolerable living conditions would be improved only slightly. Screw it, he thought. Get them back here so I can look for some Jap shipping.

After what seemed forever, a lookout spotted the raft on its way back. Despite his annoyance at having to keep them, Hobart felt relief and admiration for the boys who had paddled their human cargo to Japan and come back without incident. Hobart thought it would be wonderfully exhilarating to be able to say he'd actually set foot on Japanese soil. He ordered the sub to surface higher so that the men and their raft could be taken aboard via the deck hatch.

A little less than half a mile away, Comdr. Mochitsura Hashimoto looked transfixed through the periscope of his submarine, the I-58. The I-58 had just returned from its last patrol confident it had sunk an American battleship, only to find that Japanese naval intelligence now believed it was the heavy cruiser *Indianapolis* that he'd sent to the bottom of the Pacific. No matter, he had been successful. For quite some time, Japanese sub victories had been few and far between; thus, it was with a kind of delight that he saw the silhouette of the conning tower piercing the surface. The shape was American and he was insultingly close to Japan.

The I-58 was a fairly new addition to the Imperial Japanese Navy and, at 355 feet long, was believed to be larger than any American sub. She could simultaneously fire six thirty-foot-long, oxygen-driven torpedoes that had a range of several miles and a speed of over forty knots. She also had a 5.5-inch deck gun and several machine guns as antiaircraft protection.

Attached to the I-58's deck were four *kaiten* human torpedoes. Because of the need to make room for a rider and a rude steering mechanism, the *kaiten* were slower and had a smaller warhead.

But they would never miss. The *kaiten* would be launched at a suitable target and the pilot would steer into it. The human torpedoes were a German device so there was a release mechanism that, theoretically, would save the pilot. The release would not be needed. Not one of the *kaiten* pilots would think of not dying.

During the cruise, the *kaiten* pilots had been a problem for Commander Hashimoto. They had begged for the opportunity to hit the American battleship that had turned out to be a cruiser, but Hashimoto had denied them because he thought their efforts would be wasted. The shot was so easy that human guidance was unnecessary. Wait, he'd counseled.

Now they were at him again, begging and whining like children for the right to obliterate themselves against an American ship. In a way, he felt sorry for them. They had pledged to die, and to return safely to port was a disgrace, even though it wasn't their fault. They had set out to die, so die they must or suffer shame. A kamikaze pilot generally went out with only enough fuel in his plane for a one-way trip, so a return was unlikely. Even if a kamikaze didn't find an American warship, he would find a reasonably honorable death by crashing into the sea.

Not so the *kaiten*. Commander Hashimoto was adamant that in their use they would not jeopardize the I-58 or waste themselves in any attempt. The I-58, and a few like her, were all the Imperial Japanese Navy had to fight off the Americans, and while suicide might be a future option, Hashimoto did not think that now was the right time. Hashimoto was also acutely aware that many of the large Japanese subs were now being used solely to ferry troops and supplies to isolated garrisons, and he was gratified that he was still able to carry out combat operations and not have to operate as an undersea transport.

The American sub looked just about right for the *kaiten* to make their final efforts. The target was small and a miss would be too likely with a conventional torpedo.

"Two," he said to the eager faces, and two men ran forward to climb through the connecting hatches and take their places in the *kaiten* while the others moaned their dismay.

The American sub insolently rose farther out of the sea. It appeared that there was activity on her deck as well. Hashimoto's senior torpedo officer signaled that the *kaiten* were ready, and the commander gave the order to fire. The I-58 rose slightly by the bow when the human torpedoes were launched, and the helmsman kept tight control on the ship to ensure that she wouldn't breach and reveal her position.

On board the *Moray*, the deckhands had just about finished stowing the raft when a lookout screamed. "Torpedoes!"

Without looking, Hobart yelled for an emergency dive. Men tumbled down the hatches, breaking bones in their haste to be off the deck and into the perceived safety of the *Moray*. In seconds, her bow had started to move and dip beneath the gentle waves. Hobart, who had been overseeing the reloading operation, saw that the sub was going to dive with him still on the deck. He turned and watched in horror as twin lines of bubbles shifted and directed themselves toward the *Moray*. As the sub struggled to find the safety of the depths, Hobart knew it was useless. The devil-guided torpedoes would find her. He bowed his head and waited. In his last second of life, he thought he saw a face looking at him from the torpedo as it crashed into the sub.

JOE NOMURA, ALONE on a hill overlooking the sea and with his gear safely hidden, sat in silence. The first explosion was immediately followed by another, and the *Moray*'s dark shape lifted out of the water before plunging, broken, to her death.

From the suddenness and totality of the explosions it seemed highly unlikely that anyone on the *Moray* had survived. Even if they had, he could not jeopardize his mission by going after them. God help them, he prayed silently, and God help me. He felt the despair of being completely alone.

The explosions would bring attention from the Japanese military. A chill breeze blew by him and he clutched the tattered remains of his Japanese army uniform tighter to his chest. It was time to begin his mission.

CHAPTER 11

.

Brigadier General Monck saluted. General Eichelberger returned it and held out his hand. "Welcome to Manila, General, and congratulations on your promotion."

Monck flushed with pleasure. "Thanks, General, but it was really quite unexpected."

"Nonsense. I understand you did a fine job with that armored unit in the Ruhr. I just wonder how you'll adapt to being an infantry commander fighting Japs after riding around with a hundred tanks at your disposal and taking on the Nazis?"

Monck chuckled. "I'll make do. General, I was an infantryman well before I knew anything about armor, and I didn't expect to find much armor here in the Pacific theater. Island-hopping and amphibious warfare don't call for massed tank formations. It'll be like a homecoming for me to be working with infantry again."

An orderly brought coffee, which Monck took gratefully. He'd spent a lot of time on an airplane and felt the caffeine stirring in him. Eichelberger took a sip and put his cup aside.

"General Monck, as soon as I've briefed you and you've finished your coffee, you'll meet MacArthur. Then you'll be heading off to Okinawa to take command of your new regiment. Current planning has that regiment in reserve for one of the divisions that will take part in the initial phase of the invasion of Japan, the assault on Kyushu. It'll likely be the 41st, which is still being reorganized. The 41st has a long and proud history of action in the Pacific, but, like so many others, has taken a lot of casualties and has lost a lot of men because of the damned policy of rotating long-service soldiers back to the States."

Monck said nothing. While he privately agreed that men who

had endured years of hell should be sent home, it meant that the best and most experienced soldiers were being replaced by men with little or no combat experience.

"So," Eichelberger added, "your regiment will be overstrength at just under four thousand men and filled with recruits who don't even know each other. You'll have about a month, maybe two at the most, to whip them into shape, so work them wisely and hard. Their lives will depend on it. General Krueger, who is unavailable to meet you right now, will command the attack on Kyushu. I am functioning as MacArthur's planning and operations chief for the second phase of the fighting, which will be the final attack on the island of Honshu and the city of Tokyo."

Monck hoped they would not pay dearly for that rush. And he knew the reason for his new command to be overstrength. It was expected to go in early and would be taking heavy casualties. The regiment would need the extra men to function after getting mauled. It further answered the question why he, a brigadier general, was getting a command that would ordinarily fall to a bird colonel. Thanks for nothing, he thought.

"General Eichelberger, just how firm are the plans for the invasion?"

"As firm as anything that is being thrown together in haste. I've got to admit we didn't think it would really come to this, and we didn't start planning in earnest until recently. Only two things are certain: first, that the invasion will be in the very early part of November, and second, that it will be on the island of Kyushu rather than anyplace else. Don't worry, Monck, we'll get this all sorted out and muddle through. Now, have you ever met MacArthur?"

"No, I have not."

"Well, it should be an experience. MacArthur is a very complex person, though I presume you've heard horror stories about his monumental ego?"

Monck grinned slightly. "I don't think I should answer that, General."

"That's right, you shouldn't. First rule is never speak ill of a living legend. Seriously, General Douglas MacArthur is both a genius and his own worst enemy. You know that he graduated at the top of his class at West Point and achieved academic standards that no one's ever come close to?"

Monck did, of course. MacArthur had graduated in 1903 and gone on to be decorated for valor in the Vera Cruz incursion in 1914 and then again in France in 1917. Whatever his faults, MacArthur did not lack personal bravery. MacArthur had then gone on to be army chief of staff, had worked organizing the Philippine army, had retired, and had then been brought back to both command the Philippines and help defend them against the pending Japanese threat. His work had been far from complete when the Japanese attacked in December 1941.

MacArthur now commanded the American armies in the Pacific, had controlled the Southwest Pacific and the Philippines, and, if the rumors were true, would be in overall command of all the ground forces that would take part in the invasion of the Japanese home islands.

"General Eichelberger, I went to the Point with the class of '14. MacArthur the student was a legend, even then. I was one year ahead of Eisenhower."

"Why'd you leave the military, General?"

Monck shrugged. "A perceived lack of a future and cruel economic conditions. I didn't get to France in World War I, so I thought my career was shot. That and I was married to a wonderful woman who insisted that the children I kept impregnating her with be able to eat."

Eichelberger sympathized. Military pay in the days before the current war had been horrendous at best. "How many kids?"

"Four. Two boys and two girls. One of the boys is in England, while the other is, thank God, still in school."

"You know, if you'd stayed in, you'd likely have three stars like I do."

"Or I might be an over-the-hill and overweight major at a desk in the Pentagon. Can't change the past, General, I'm just glad I've gotten this far. Thank God I stayed active in the reserves."

"Are you planning on staying on after the war?"

"If the army'll have me, yes. It took me a while to realize it, but this is my calling." Monck grinned. "Of course, my kids are almost all old enough to find food on their own now."

Eichelberger rose. The interview was drawing to a close. "Good, then you will not want to screw up your meeting with MacArthur. He is a very proud and complex man, and some people find it comical. He also doesn't trust everyone, and some people think him paranoid for that. He strongly feels that Washington betrayed him and left his Pacific command to wither on the vine in the early days of the war when they declined to rescue his men from Bataan and Corregidor. History will decide whether he is right or wrong when everything about those tragic events comes out.

"But make no doubts about it, MacArthur is a very strong and forceful commander who has conquered about a quarter of the globe and done so with very little resources. He will not suffer incompetents or anyone else who stands in his way."

Monck had also stood. "General, there are those who say he wants to be president."

"They may well be right. He may just run for president on the Republican ticket when this war is over, and, yes, that would be very interesting. It also may well be the reason he makes certain that all battle announcements come from his office. You came from Europe, where people like Patton and Bradley got a lot of publicity, but that's not MacArthur's style. For right or wrong, damn few people back home have ever heard of anybody named Eichelberger or Krueger, and you would be well advised to make sure that no one hears of John Monck either."

"Understood."

"Good, and stay on the good side of Generals Willoughby and Sutherland as well. They work directly for MacArthur and think the sun rises and sets on him. They will cheerfully ruin anyone who they think is either working against their leader or who has a private agenda. If you run afoul of them, you will be through in the military, and there won't be anything either Krueger or I could do to change things."

"Understood."

General Sutherland was MacArthur's chief of staff, while Willoughby was in charge of intelligence. Willoughby was rumored to be haughty and arrogant, while Sutherland had recently returned from a brief banishment because of what may have been an affair with another officer's wife. The banishment was supposed to have been permanent, but MacArthur would hear nothing of it and Willoughby had returned.

"Good," Eichelberger said. "Let's go."

They walked down a short corridor and entered a large waiting room. They were immediately admitted to MacArthur's large and well-appointed office. It looked more like something in the Pentagon than a place where a major battle had been fought only a few months earlier. Monck wondered if this was what a papal audience was like. Like a young plebe, Monck snapped to attention and reported. This pleased MacArthur, who rose from behind his ornate wooden desk and smiled. MacArthur was surprisingly tall, slim, and had a stern and hawklike face. His eyes seemed to flash with excitement.

"Welcome to the Pacific, General Monck," MacArthur's stentorian voice boomed.

"Thank you, sir, it's a pleasure to be here and working for you." Monck noticed that both Willoughby and Sutherland had taken up positions flanking MacArthur. The set of their stance said that they were ready to protect their liege lord. MacArthur, erect and dark-haired, looked to need little protection from anyone. It was hard to realize that MacArthur was sixty-five and had already retired once.

"I see you served under Eisenhower. Fine man Ike. He was my chief of staff in Washington for a while, and I thought he was an excellent clerk. I'm a little surprised he's gotten as far as he has, though. Did you know him well?"

"Very little, sir. While I recalled him from the Point, our paths never crossed in Europe. He sent me a letter of congratulations on my promotion, but that's about it."

The answer seemed to satisfy MacArthur that Monck was not a part of the Eisenhower club. "General Monck, I am supremely confident that your tenure as a combat commander here will be a brief but successful one. The Japanese are finished and it's only a question of time before they realize it. We have done our studies"—MacArthur turned to Willoughby, who almost smirked—"and we firmly believe that the Japanese military will break when we invade Kyushu and that there will be minimal casualties."

MacArthur then laughed sharply. "There are those in Washington and elsewhere who think the Japanese will resist strongly, but they are wrong. The Japanese will be defeated in open battle by our overwhelming strength, and they will break and retreat, just as it happened here in the Philippines. When that occurs, the war will be over. Do you know what happens then, General?"

Monck felt that he was sweating and almost prayed it didn't show. "No, sir, I don't."

MacArthur had an almost dreamy look on his face. When he answered, it was almost as if he were giving a speech or were a missionary preaching to the heathen. "When the Japanese surrender, I will become the military governor of Japan. When that occurs, every man, woman, and child in Japan will be under my thrall, and that includes the emperor. Yes, General Monck, the emperor of Japan, the God-Emperor Hirohito, will acknowledge me as his superior. Think of it. After all these years of fighting, they will kowtow to an American."

Sutherland whispered something to MacArthur, who nodded impatiently. There was doubtless another appointment, and Monck's brief time before the throne was up. He departed with Eichelberger, who patted him on the back and said he'd done just fine, and don't forget to avoid correspondents and publicity like the plague.

Brig. Gen. John L. Monck assured him he wouldn't. He found his driver and rode back to the airstrip wrapped in thought. He needed a drink and a conversation with Major Parker, whom he'd sent on a snooping expedition of his own.

He found Parker in the shade of a tent, sipping a can of cold beer. Parker took one from a cooler and offered it. Monck swallowed half the can in one gulp.

"Did you meet God?" Parker asked irreverently.

Monck finished the beer and grabbed another one. "No, I met his boss, MacArthur. Jesus, you wouldn't believe it. I wonder just what the hell we've gotten into."

"General, did you get the crap about taking only light casualties if we invade?"

"Yeah, and I believe it about as much as I do the tooth fairy. What did you find out?"

Parker took another can for himself. "MacArthur has this disturbing habit of proclaiming victories before the fighting's over. Yes, the Japanese were defeated here in the Philippines and have retreated, but they haven't surrendered. After causing more than fifty thousand American casualties, they've just gone to ground in the hills and are awaiting word from Tokyo of what to do next."

"How many are still left?"

"Maybe fifty thousand under General Yamashita here in Luzon, plus smaller groups elsewhere. They don't have any tanks, damned little artillery, and less ammunition, and they may be starving to death, but unless they are ordered to surrender, someday someone's gonna have to go in and root them out, and that's gonna be bloody painful."

Parker rubbed his forehead with the cold can and continued, "Mac thinks the campaign is over and he can move on, but it's far from complete, and I don't like his casualty estimates any more than you do. I don't know what the exact numbers are, but he based his estimate on what happened here in the Philippines and not the fanatical resistance we met on Okinawa. A little bird told me he's now saying we can have all of Kyushu for only fifteen thousand casualties because the Japs are in such bad shape and we are so unbeatable."

Monck crumpled the can and threw it against the side of the tent. How could MacArthur say it would cost only fifteen thousand to take one of the home islands of Japan when the battle for the Philippines had already consumed four times that? How could he ignore the horrific casualty percentages that had been suffered on Iwo Jima and Saipan, as well as most recently on Okinawa. It didn't make sense. "Then why is he doing it, Don? Why the low numbers?"

Parker checked his watch. "Two reasons, and then we'd better catch our plane. You may be a general now, but that plane has a schedule to keep and other brass to ferry around the Pacific.

"First, he actually believes the battle for the Philippines is over and that he's won, and in a lot of ways he's right. The fact that it's incomplete is irrelevant to him. That's just the way his mind operates. He's finished with the Philippines and he wants to move on to the next challenge. He's right that he's won the campaign, but the fighting is still subject to flare-up at any time.

"The second reason is a little more insidious. It is widely believed among some members of his staff who used to be my friends that he avoided giving a higher estimate of casualties because he feared Washington would have called off the invasion. No invasion, no glory, and no victory. No victory and he can't become Hirohito's boss. Thus, Willoughby and Sutherland baked up some wild-ass low numbers on his behalf, and MacArthur grabbed them like the Holy Grail. Now he can invade with a clear conscience because his staff said it's okay."

"Oh, Lord," Monck said with a groan. An enlisted man told them their plane was ready. They grabbed their carry-on bags and headed across the hot runway for the transport plane. "What do your friends say about the real estimated numbers?"

"General, there is the slight possibility that Willoughby and Sutherland are right. But as to my friends, they're all scared to death that it could be a bloodbath."

CHAPTER 12

.

Reluctant OSS agent Joe Nomura knew that the *Moray* would sail away and leave him, but its sinking left him wondering if anyone in the United States even knew he was alive.

He'd hidden his supplies quickly, so not to attract enemy attention. A patrol had indeed confronted him in the rugged terrain after the explosions that signaled the end of the *Moray*.

After a few questions from their sergeant, Joe realized that his disguise worked. A one-armed veteran in a tattered uniform was of no concern or threat to the patrol. The soldiers were solely interested in whether he had seen or heard anything unusual regarding the explosions. They didn't even ask to see his carefully forged army papers. He was just too innocuous. He told them he had heard the explosions, but had seen nothing, and they brusquely sent him on his way.

The next day, Joe joined the milling throngs of refugees that clustered around hospitals and stood in long lines at food distribution centers near Nagasaki. He'd seen refugees before, but never so many, and never with so many of them injured. The hospitals were obviously overwhelmed by the catastrophe and could only handle the more serious injuries. Simple burns and broken bones didn't qualify one for medical care. These victims either found help elsewhere or endured. There was no choice for them.

Joe had also never seen so many people who both looked like him and who were in such obvious physical and emotional agony. The sight of the children, mute with horror, moved him more deeply than he ever thought possible.

However, without an arm and dressed in tatters, he blended in perfectly. This made him confident and he wandered about, listening to conversations, and occasionally asking questions of medical personnel who were helping to treat the most horribly injured. To his surprise, many were more than willing to talk about their experiences, although he got depressed when people inquired of him about their loved ones. He was a soldier, wasn't he? They thought he should know these things. It almost made him weep when they asked him about missing children.

That gave him the idea of volunteering to work in a hospital, and in the ensuing days, his services were accepted at several places where he helped with some of the more odious tasks, such as carrying out bodies. When one doctor asked him why he was doing it, Joe had drawn himself to attention and announced proudly, "Even a one-armed man can serve his emperor." The doctor had sucked in his breath and bowed to Joe in deference and respect to his sense of honor.

From several nurses, he heard the complaint that they had no bandages, no medicine, and, even if they had, these wouldn't work against the new sickness caused by the bomb.

From doctors he heard puzzling comments over the weakening effects of radiation. They wondered why some were spared while others were dying, and they compared notes while in his hearing.

The doctors were perplexed by people who appeared healthy, then collapsed, sickened, and died from radiation poisoning. How, they wondered, did one treat wounds that would not heal and burns that could not be quenched? Almost to a man they cursed the United States for the agony it had brought to Nagasaki. There were no curses for the Japanese government. Whatever thoughts the medics might have had in that regard were kept prudently in check. Anyone might turn someone with dissident thoughts in to the national military police, the *kempei*.

Usually the *kempei* wore ordinary military uniforms with distinguishing red and khaki armbands, and Joe saw several of them. Just as often, though, they wore civilian clothes and kept their identity a secret. From his briefings, Joe knew they were ruthless and, as the situation in Japan deteriorated, were becoming brutal. In many cases, they had the right to inflict summary judgment and punishment upon individuals.

Joe never stayed long at one place, often just a few hours, as he drew himself closer and closer to the center of Nagasaki. As he passed through the devastated and flattened city, he wondered just how the damage at Hiroshima could have been worse, yet he had been told that it was. Kokura, he'd heard, had suffered about as much as Nagasaki.

But it was Nagasaki that interested his superiors in the OSS. Nagasaki was on Kyushu, and that was considered relevant because of the open rumors that gave Kyushu as a probable, but still secret, target for the invasion. Hell, he thought, some secret. Even the Japanese he overheard speculated that Kyushu was a likely place for the Americans to land.

Nagasaki's destruction had occurred more than a month earlier, and the United States was concerned about the effects of lingering radiation on both places and people. Joe'd been given little packets of film to utilize in areas or on things where he suspected radiation. He was told that the extent to which the film was exposed would indicate the strength of radiation. He unobtrusively tagged these and checked them in private.

As he performed these experiments, a disturbing picture emerged. First, while radiation had dissipated somewhat, it had done so inconsistently. Areas in Nagasaki were still so hot that the Japanese had cordoned them off and permitted no one to enter. He wondered what effect the radiation would have on an American army moving through the area.

He found that people who had been under the mushroom cloud when it slowly fell back to the earth were seriously ill, with many of them dead or dying. The bomb had generated dirty outbursts of rain, which contaminated drinking water.

Most disturbing were the continuing incidents of seemingly healthy people who suddenly came down with serious cases of radiation sickness. Joe could only speculate on the causes. Either they had come in contact with something that was radioactively hot and had cooked them, or they had been contaminated earlier and it had taken days, even weeks, for the sickness to reach a point where they were incapacitated.

Joe found both options equally disturbing when he again contemplated the idea of GIs moving about and fighting in the poisoned land.

As to the other wounds he saw, the burns and fractures were nothing he hadn't seen before, only multiplied a thousandfold until the sheer numbers became numbing. That so many civilians had died came as no surprise to his sensitivities either. He had seen what modern warfare could do to Italian villages and knew that death in war was indiscriminate. However, he was concerned by the many cases of blindness. Most people who had seen the atomic explosion had suffered at least some vision damage. It was worth noting and he filed it mentally.

He was also intrigued that not all people near the center of the blast were killed or injured. The many hills in the area seemed to have shielded some from the effects of the blast, although others had been hit by the radiation that fell from the bomb cloud if they were unlucky enough to have it blown in their direction.

It was time to unearth his radio and report. Not only did he have enough information to give his masters, but he felt a strong urge to let them know he was still alive, and that he had not gone down with the *Moray*, which he presumed was listed as missing. He hoped he wouldn't have too much trouble with the code they had given him. Joe would have to keep his messages short and to the point, changing frequencies and radio locations with each message. Trouble was, he now had a lot to say and doing it would entail a lot of risk.

Nomura trudged the weary miles out of Nagasaki and onto the hill where he had squirreled his precious cache of supplies and equipment. With his stomach aching with hunger, he was even looking forward to army rations, although he would have to be careful and not eat them all up. At best, he had enough to last him only a few weeks. After that he was adrift along with the civilian population of Japan.

He looked across the valley and saw motion on a hill about a mile away. Joe squinted and watched. It was definitely a human, although he—or she for that matter—seemed to be moving erratically. Probably someone else who was injured or deranged, he decided, or even one of the numerous blind people. Well, well, he had neighbors.

Nothing surprising and certainly nothing to be alarmed about, although he made a mental note to check out the surrounding area once more. With so many refugees about, things could literally change overnight, and there was always the possibility of the *kempei* doing some random snooping.

As long as the threat was not too great, he was not worried about taking care of himself. Along with the radio and the food, the OSS had thoughtfully provided him with a number of weapons, including a couple of Japanese ones. If necessary, he had no qualms about using them on some of those people who looked like him.

Joe glanced across the valley again and realized that the person he'd seen had disappeared from view. Now he definitely thought he should check things out a good deal more thoroughly. And he would take a Japanese pistol with him when he did it.

•

CHAPTER 13

*T*heir first look at the tortured island of Okinawa came when the C-47 transport plane banked slightly while still several miles away from the long, thin island. From that distance, the island looked to Paul Morrell and Capt. Tom Ruger like a pale strip on the horizon, an item in the vast ocean that was barely worthy of notice.

Okinawa was innocuous and deceptively like a score of other islands they had either flown over or stopped at briefly. Even as they flew closer, they had a hard time thinking of the apparently tranquil patch of land as a cause of so much bloodshed.

"They fought like hell for this place," Ruger muttered. "I wonder what they'll do when we actually land on Japan proper?"

Paul Morrell craned his neck to see out one of the plane's few tiny windows. Okinawa, roughly sixty miles long, narrow, and only 340 miles from the Japanese mainland, had been invaded by Lt. Gen. Simon Bolivar Buckner's Tenth Army on April 1, 1945. For a while it seemed as if the Japanese weren't going to fight as the Americans overran the northern two-thirds of the narrow island in only a few days, with little in the way of resistance. The army's big problem had been the care and feeding of the thousands of terrified Okinawan civilians who had clogged the island's few roads. The gentle Okinawans had been told that Americans were monsters and they had been delighted to find out otherwise.

But as the Americans moved toward the southern tip, the island became a study in hell. It took until June 22 for them to secure Okinawa, although individual Japanese soldiers and a few small units were rumored to be still hiding in Okinawa's more rugged areas.

Both sides paid an enormous price. Of the almost one hundred thousand Japanese soldiers on the island, only seventy-four hundred had been taken prisoner. Most of those taken were Okinawan militia who had been poorly trained and equipped, and not as fanatic about fighting to the last man as their Japanese neighbors. The nearly eighty thousand Japanese regulars had chosen to die along with their commanding general, Mitsuru Ushijimi, who had committed suicide on the last day of the battle.

General Buckner had been killed in an artillery barrage at about the same time. Nearly eight thousand soldiers and marines had died in the campaign, and another thirty-two thousand had been wounded.

The campaign for Okinawa had brought additional terror as Japanese kamikazes were used in large numbers for the first time in the war. A large number of ships had been sunk or damaged by these kamikazes, and many, many sailors had been killed or wounded. If Okinawa was a forecast of the future, both men felt the future was to be dreaded.

Yet, as Morrell and Ruger drew closer and overflew the anchorage, their spirits were buoyed. The waters around Okinawa were filled with what looked like limitless numbers of warships of all sizes and types, all massing for the assault ahead. Battleships and carriers, along with attendant cruisers and destroyers, were arrayed farther offshore in the deep waters, while transports, landing craft, and other and more plebeian and utilitarian craft huddled nearer the shore.

The island itself appeared to have been transformed into a floating military base. The central and northern portions in particular were an ocean of tents and temporary buildings that made the transit camp back in California look minuscule in comparison. The flatter central portion contained several airfields, and their C-47 landed without incident and taxied quickly off the crowded runway to make room for the next plane. They were just another flight ferrying in from somewhere as part of the huge buildup of forces.

As they climbed, stiff-jointed, out of the transport and onto the hot field, Ruger remarked, "One more plane and the goddamn island's gonna sink, Lieutenant." Several other planes circled and waited their turn to land, while hundreds of others were parked wingtip to wingtip on the fields adjacent to the air bases.

"I almost wonder if there's any room for us. My God, why doesn't someone take a picture of this and send it to the Japs. It'd scare them into surrendering," Paul said in awe.

Ruger and Morrell had arrived at the shattered island several days ahead of the troopship carrying the other officers and the enlisted men of the company. This gave the two men time to reconnoiter the area and make plans for the training the men would have to have. Paul took it as a compliment that Ruger seemed to both like him and respect his opinions. Why the hell hadn't he had a captain like Ruger back in Germany?

Thus, when the rest of their men came ashore from their cramped transport, the situation was fairly well organized. What Paul and Ruger were not prepared for were the sullen looks on the men's faces, along with the hatred and disgust in their eyes. They bitterly resented that they had been sent out to fight while so many of their buddies were heading home.

"Shit," Ruger whispered, "we got a helluva morale problem on our hands. I thought the troops would be unhappy, but this is a lot worse than I ever thought it would be."

With that, Ruger distributed the almost 250 men in his command to their respective platoon officers. Before they got settled in their barracks tents, Paul gathered the sixty men in his platoon around him in a large and informal cluster. Only his platoon sergeant, S. Sgt. Frank Collins, a rawboned and red-haired Kentuckian, looked even remotely friendly. Collins looked exhausted; it had been a rough and tedious transit from California as he and the other officers and NCOs had gotten little sleep. Much of their time was taken up with breaking up fights.

"Gentlemen," Paul began after Collins introduced him, "how many of you have eighty-five points?"

Eighty-five points was the magic number a man needed to be rotated back to the States and discharged. The number was based on a formula that included a man's total years in service, time in combat, number of dependents at home, and a handful of other things. But the bottom line was simple. Eighty-four or less and he stayed put.

There were exceptions, of course, and they almost always worked in the army's favor. First, the program only included combat soldiers, so support and administrative types were in for the duration. Also, if a person had a unique skill, such as the ability to speak Japanese, then he was screwed no matter how many points he had.

Paul looked at his men. "Since I don't see any hands raised, I guess nobody's going home. Well, I'm not either, and I'm not any happier than you are. In fact, I'm kind of pissed off about it. I don't have eighty-five points or anywhere near that, so we're stuck with each other."

Paul had spent a little time going over their service records and knew that a few of them were achingly close to that magic number. Most, however, weren't anywhere near it.

"Let me be blunt. Like you, I'd much rather be home with my family and friends too, but it's not gonna happen. I'm not going to give you a bullshit rah-rah speech or insult your intelligence about how much we're going to do to win this war. But we're not going home until this thing is over, so we're all gonna have to make the best of it. Captain Ruger's goal, and mine too, is to have everyone make it through this safely. By the way, that includes my ass getting back in one piece too.

"In order to do that, we're going to start first thing tomorrow morning doing some of the hardest training you've ever seen. It's gonna make basic training look like a high school dance. The purpose will be to get you back in shape—some of you look like you haven't exercised since the Japs hit Pearl Harbor—and improve your weapons training along with small-unit tactics. We figure we've got about a month before we ship out, and we're going to make the most of it."

With that, Paul dismissed the men to get a meal and a good night's sleep. He saw Collins looking at him carefully.

"How badly did I do, Sergeant?"

"You gonna be marching with us tomorrow, Lieutenant?"

The question surprised Paul. "Of course. Where the hell else would I be?"

Collins relaxed and smiled. "Well, not every officer does what he asks his men to do. I was on Luzon with an officer who rode in a jeep every chance he got, regardless of what his men were doing. Nobody was too upset when his jeep ran over a mine. You march with them and share their problems with them, then they'll come around. They won't love you, but they'll respect you." Collins saluted casually. "See you in the morning, Lieutenant."

Paul looked around at the small and undistinguished portion of Okinawa his platoon called home. He heard a throbbing noise and looked skyward to see a pair of American fighters streak overhead. In the darkness, he couldn't see what they were exactly, although he thought they might have been F4U Corsairs from one of the outlying carriers.

It struck him that they were on patrol, and that he was a few hundred miles from Japan, on an island jammed full of targets. He wondered if the next planes he saw or heard would be Japs and shuddered.

·

CHAPTER 14

*I*t occurred to Joseph Grew, the former ambassador to Japan, that an assassin with a bomb could force the United States to end the war simply by killing the people who were now staring at him in some expectation.

In the Oval Office along with President Truman and Secretary of State Byrnes were Secretary of the Navy James Forrestal and Secretary of War Henry Stimson. Directly representing the military were General Marshall and Admirals Leahy and King.

"I have asked Ambassador Grew to talk to us today to help us put the Japanese situation in perspective," Truman began. "You will recall that Mr. Grew served as ambassador to Japan from 1932 until that fateful month of December 1941. Along with his staff and their families, they were exchanged for the Japanese ambassador and their staff and returned to the United States in early 1942."

Grew nodded. "First, let me say that my own opinions are not particularly in total favor at State." He glanced at Byrnes, who smiled slightly and nodded for him to go on.

"I learned to love the Japanese people and their culture during my almost nine years as ambassador. I found the ordinary people to be gentle and friendly. However, a few, primarily some of those in the military, have proven capable of the most bestial cruelties to their fellow man, and that includes their own fellow Japanese. In my opinion, this war should be ended by negotiations and we should forswear the idea of forcing the Japanese to accept unconditional surrender. To do anything else will only extend the bloodshed needlessly."

It was a paradox in Truman's administration that the State Department, led by Byrnes and Dean Acheson, was pressing for unconditional surrender and the bloodshed that would ensue as a result of that policy, while the military wanted a negotiated peace that abandoned the position of unconditional surrender and, thus, eliminated the need for an invasion. Truman thought it surprising that, in this regard, his generals and admirals were far less warlike than the diplomats.

"We appreciate your candor," Truman said. "Now please proceed."

Grew reminded them that the Japanese archipelago, referred to as the home islands, consisted of four larger islands and hundreds of smaller ones. The island chain ran from the southwest near Korea and northeast toward Siberia and extended for more than twelve hundred miles. Honshu was by far the largest of the islands, and all were hilly and rugged, which forced much of the population into a number of crowded cities. A great deal of the land was not suitable for farming, although the Japanese had incredible ingenuity regarding agriculture. They grew a large quantity of their food, primarily rice, and they also fished extensively in the surrounding waters.

"The islands are warmed by four currents coming from the south. This results in a climate that is astonishingly mild and temperate."

"And that could mean several growing seasons, couldn't it?" Truman inquired. As a Missourian, he knew a bit about farming.

"In some instances, yes. Which is why, despite our bombings and blockades, there has been no starvation. Severe food rationing, yes, but no starvation. At least not yet.

"Over time, the remoteness of the Japanese islands insulated the people from the activities on the mainland so that they developed a concept of uniqueness. That uniqueness resulted in the Japanese thinking of themselves as a master race. That idea on their part predates the Nazis by centuries."

King interrupted, "Then how the hell did the Japs get in bed with Hitler? What would have happened if the Axis had won the war? After all, you can't have two master races on one planet, can you?"

Grew smiled at the thought. "God only knows. For the short run, they probably would have divided up the world between them; but, in the long haul, I'm certain they would have fought for each other's portion.

"One other thing," Grew added. "They hate being called Japs.

They vastly prefer the word *Japanese. Jap* is a term they consider an insult. It's almost like referring to them as niggers."

King laughed hugely. "Well, ain't that too goddamn bad. They should've thought of that before they started this war."

Grew continued, "Gentlemen, in Japan we have a military-ruled society that considers itself superior to other races and nations and is destined to rule the world. Japan considers any other peoples to be inferior to them, and that includes other Asian and yellow-skinned people as well as whites and blacks. They define the Chinese as barbarians, and the Koreans they control are virtually enslaved. The Okinawans are considered second-class citizens, as are several peoples of the islands north of Japan.

"When Japan took Formosa in 1895 and Korea in 1910, they were profoundly shocked when the inhabitants of those lands wouldn't see things their way. This caused the Japanese to react harshly to this inconceivable situation. It is consistent with how they later behaved in Manchuria, the Philippines, China, and elsewhere. They are baffled and infuriated when someone disputes what they religiously feel is their right of primacy in a world destined by God to be Japanese."

"Jesus," muttered Byrnes.

"Indeed. Those in charge will not—can not—surrender even though they have been defeated in every definition of the term, and even though they know it. The code of Bushido is sworn to by every officer in the army and navy. In it he promises to never retreat or surrender. If he does surrender, he is considered dead by his family and government. If a surrendered Japanese soldier should ever be repatriated, he expects to be executed; thus, many of them are quite willing to fight to the death once death is an inevitability.

"They are a little more pragmatic about retreating. It is recognized as a part of maneuvering and it is an accepted virtue for a commander to save his men for another day. We've all noted that the Japanese fight to the last man only when there is nowhere else for them to retreat to. But a defeated general will often commit suicide in his shame at having failed his code and his emperor.

"In our recent announcements, we offered to let the Japanese keep their emperor subject to the wishes of the Japanese people, required that Japan be occupied by us, and further required that alleged war criminals be tried by us and, if found guilty, punished. Those officers, those modern samurai who consider themselves descended from medieval warriors and who follow Bushido, simply cannot do this. In fact, they cannot even comprehend what we are talking about. We tell them they must surrender unconditionally when they are not allowed to surrender at all. As to surrendering unconditionally, I'm not certain the concept even translates into their language.

"They also feel our terms desecrate the emperor. After all, how can the emperor be subject to the will of the Japanese people when he owns them? Although very much a figurehead, Hirohito is titular owner of every person and every piece of property in Japan.

"Additionally, the occupation of Japan by us is unthinkable according to Bushido. As to them being tried by us for war crimes, that too is inconceivable because they do not feel they have committed any crimes. How can living according to the code of Bushido, and aiding in the destiny of the master race, be any sort of a crime? Unthinkable. All of this goes to the essence of their fears: that Japan and her culture will disappear in the wake of an American victory."

Truman was aghast. "We plan no such thing."

"Unfortunately," Grew said grimly, "our words and actions conspire against us. For proof, all they have to do is look and see how we've dismembered Germany and replaced the Nazis with our own administrators. They see that happening to Japan and are terrified. Their propagandists have also done a marvelous job of scaring their own population half to death. There are millions of civilians who adamantly believe that Americans are monsters with blood slavering from their teeth, who will rape their women and eat their children alive.

"Laugh if you will at the absurdity of it all, but think of what we thought the Japanese would do if they landed in California in 1942. Bear in mind too that the overwhelming majority of the civilian population has never seen a European, much less an American. We might as well be from another planet as far as most of them are concerned."

"Do they all feel this way?" Truman asked, thinking of an earlier conversation in which that same "other planet" analogy was used.

"No. The diplomatic and administrative officials did not take any oath to adhere to Bushido, and the civilians, like the enlisted men in the army and navy, are stuck in the middle and just do what they're told. Some of the military give only lip service to Bushido."

Marshall was unconvinced. "Isn't it possible that they're not wanting us to try them as war criminals is nothing more than an attempt to save their own evil skins?"

Grew shrugged. "Absolutely. As to those who have pledged to die for Nippon, I really don't know how many will actually do that when the time comes. Almost surely a large number will fight, although many of them will be under orders and not necessarily enthusiastic about the idea. The enlisted military are trained very brutally and will obey without thought, while many of the civilian volunteers will be sent to battle under guard and be shot if they falter."

"Absurd," said Leahy. "The idea of a whole nation committing suicide is not rational. Nor is sending people out to certain death."

"Why not?" Grew admonished him gently. "We revere Nathan Hale and others who give their lives to save others when they had the chance to do otherwise. And"—Grew turned directly to Marshall and King—"haven't you or your field commanders ever sent someone out to do something that would likely result in their death?"

"But that's the exception," said Marshall, "while what you're describing is the rule. When we order men to fight a battle, we know that people will die, but we're elated when they don't. We don't have a national policy that requires suicide."

"Yes," said Grew. "And that is part of the cost of Japan's developing in such an isolated manner. As I said, their sense of values is, in many ways, so alien to us. I'm certain," he added wryly, "they feel the same about us."

"If their emperor is a god and god wants peace," Truman asked, "why are we still fighting? Why don't they obey their god and stop?"

Grew answered, "Because we should never think of Hirohito as god in the same Judeo-Christian way we were brought up to use the word. At best Hirohito is a demigod, or godlike. He became godlike when he became emperor and not before. When he dies, the new emperor, now a mere mortal, will become godlike. Which brings up a point. Hirohito must avoid being assassinated. If the military doesn't like the god-emperor they have, they are perfectly capable of killing him and putting a new one on the throne. Japanese god-emperors grow old, sick, and subsequently die—or can even be overthrown and murdered—and that's much the way it is with Hirohito.

"This is a paradox: only the emperor can order the Japanese to surrender. No one else will be obeyed by the fanatics in the Japanese military. We can defeat them and conquer them, but without the word of their emperor, many will not surrender. They have their own intelligence sources and must be aware that we are reducing the size of our military, which they will take as a sign of weakness and be encouraged by it. It will not alter the fact they are defeated and know it full well, but they will not, can not, surrender. Again, only Hirohito can release them from the code of Bushido."

Truman stood and looked out the window. "And the fanatics have Hirohito."

■

CHAPTER 15

As he vomited bile onto the ground, former POW Dennis Chambers was happy that at least the diarrhea had let up. He had thought he was doing so well. His diet, one he would once have considered repulsive, had actually been helping him gain strength. The bugs, worms, and occasional mouse, coupled with leaves and grasses, were filling and apparently nutritious.

He thought he knew what had disagreed with him so violently and vowed never again to eat the leaves of that particular broad-leafed plant.

"Jesus," he moaned, and lay back on the earth and belched hugely. Right now he didn't care if fucking Hirohito himself came by and took him prisoner. After a while he noticed that he had stopped vomiting. Of course, he had nothing in his stomach to puke, but that hadn't kept him from trying before.

After a few more minutes, he even began to feel a little hungry, but he didn't think his stomach could handle a nice, juicy worm. And he had been doing so well, he thought again.

But doing better had come with a price. With hunger pangs satisfied, he was no longer able to avoid thinking of life back home in California. When he slept, he saw his wife's face. In his dreams Barb was always smiling at him with that half-wicked, half-insolent look that he loved, and her golden hair was loose and hanging down on her tanned shoulders and to her firm breasts. Then, when he awoke, he felt empty and alone.

Then he heard the voices. At first he thought he was delirious and imagining things. But then he realized that the voices were in Japanese, that they came from the other side of the ridge, and that the voices were all males. This was bad. He had checked out the area before and found it empty, but obviously something had changed and it couldn't be for the better.

He stayed where he was until night fell. Then he moved carefully up the few yards from where he lay to where the hill crested. Crawling on his hands and knees, he slithered over the top and found a place where he could look down the slope to the valley below. A handful of men were hard at work heaping leaves and branches on sections of canvas that covered a pair of Japanese fighters. He blinked in disbelief. The planes were Zeros or, more precisely, Mitsubishi A6M2 carrier fighters. Once they'd been the finest plane in the air, but they'd been eclipsed by the newer American planes, and Dennis had shot down two of them himself. But what were they doing here? Of course, he answered himself, without carriers to launch from, the Japanese had to stash them on land.

The Japanese were dispersing their aircraft in small groups to avoid the overwhelming superiority America had in the air. During his strength-building and worm-eating days in the hills, he had seen a number of U.S. planes flying overhead. B-29 bombers, like schools of silver fish, flew high up in the sky, and hordes of fighters searched and stalked their prey from much lower altitudes.

Once, he had stood on the top of a hill and watched a P-51 Mustang streak through the air below him. Below him! He was lost in a strange land and standing above an American plane! He had screamed at the sight of the Mustang so near, yet so far away. The fighter had swept the valley again and had flown so close that he could see the pilot's face as he insolently surveyed his domain and looked for targets. The P-51 pilot gave no thought to the ragged-looking man on the hill, if he saw Dennis in the first place.

Dennis jerked his thoughts back to the present. What was he to do about the Jap planes and the men who were so close to him? He counted four people at the little camp. That made sense. Two pilots and two mechanics. There were no other guards—after all, they were safe in Japan, weren't they?—but all four probably had weapons. All Dennis had was a piece of metal he had sharpened against a rock and used as either a knife or a shovel, depending on the need of the moment.

It was, he decided sadly, time to move from this place to a safer one. Then he saw something that changed his mind. One of the mechanics opened the flap of a tent and, stacked neatly in the back, were several bags of rice. Even better, they were filled with wild rice, which was much more nutritious than the white version. If he could somehow get his hands on that rice, then he would be able to really improve his health and his chances of surviving. But was it worth the risk? He closed his eyes and wondered what Barb would have him do. The answer came quickly. Her last words to him had been "Come back to me."

ON A DENSELY WOODED hillside in Kyushu near Nagasaki, Joe Nomura struggled with the radio supplied him by the OSS. It wasn't that the thing was bulky. It was surprisingly small and compact. The problem was operating it with only one hand with a beginner Boy Scout's skills with Morse code. There simply hadn't been time to make Joe Nomura an expert, and he struggled with what he had to say. This too was difficult. Never a great scholar, he now had to be the soul of brevity and conciseness, which were language skills he'd never considered important.

Of the two, brevity was the most in his best interest. It had been hammered into him that the Japs had listening devices and would, sooner or later, likely pick up his transmissions. Then they would try to locate him using triangulating devices that he only barely understood. He could only hope that they would discover him later, much later. Like 1950.

To help maintain his security, he'd been given a number of radio frequencies to use and the order in which to use them. All of this, coupled with the need to frame a concise yet accurate message about what he'd learned about conditions at Nagasaki and the other parts of Kyushu he'd seen, made him sweat with frustration. Then, of course, he had to put it into the very basic code they'd given him to use, which was basic to Johnson and Peters, but was difficult for him. Joe wondered how long it would take the Japs to decode it if they picked up his transmissions.

Finally he tapped out his message. It told his superiors of the lingering horrors of Nagasaki, of the people still dropping over and dying from the radiation sickness, and of the Japanese government's total inability to do anything about it. He closed his message by telling his unseen compatriots that he would have more information for them soon.

As he shut down the radio, he automatically looked skyward. He had been told that he would be transmitting to specially equipped planes that would be waiting for him to call. He fervently hoped they were indeed up there, circling. Then, using his teeth and his one hand, he repacked his gear. It was difficult, but he half-dragged and half-carried the equipment to a new site about a mile away. He didn't think the Japs had picked up this first signal, but he wasn't going to take unnecessary risks by transmitting from the same place twice.

When he'd finally hidden the radio in the ground and covered the site with leaves and branches, he walked away. In a few minutes, he was just another displaced and crippled Japanese soldier. Only he knew just how lonely and afraid he really was.

•

CHAPTER 16

President Truman slowly read through the handful of summary sheets while the others waited for him to finish. He was reading the updated overall plan for the invasion of Japan. It bore the code name Downfall and was divided into two different and sequential operations.

The first phase of Downfall, Olympic, was scheduled for November 1, 1945, which was only a little more than six weeks away. The second phase, Coronet, had a tentative date of March 1, 1946. Truman noted that the invasion dates were called X-Day, in silent testimony to the fact that *D-Day* would forever be associated with the Allied landings in Normandy in June of 1944. Prior to Normandy, every invasion date was referred to as D-Day.

Olympic was the invasion of the island of Kyushu, while Coronet was the invasion of the Kanto Plain on the island of Honshu. The Kanto Plain contained the cities of Tokyo and Yokohama and was the ultimate goal of the operation that would end the war. With Coronet clearly dependent on the success of the imminent Operation Olympic, the president found himself staring at the numbers and trying to assign them some identity.

Olympic would be the largest amphibious invasion ever attempted in military history. Nine divisions in three corps would assault three separate landing areas simultaneously. They would be backed up by five other divisions and at least one independently operating regimental combat team. Three of the divisions in the initial assault were marines, while the rest were army.

The numbers for the navy were even more staggering. Halsey's Third Fleet contained fourteen large carriers and six light carriers, along with nine new battleships, twenty-six cruisers, and seventy-five destroyers. Halsey was to attack targets inland.

Spruance's Fifth Fleet was even larger, with scores of escort carriers and more than four hundred cruisers and destroyers. Spruance was charged with protecting the amphibious force, which counted the almost fourteen hundred ships that would carry more than half a million men to battle.

The island of Kyushu had been chosen because it contained reasonably satisfactory landing areas, two magnificent deepwater anchorages, airfields, and, most important, was within range of land-based air cover from Okinawa and Saipan. This latter point was critical. Without land-based cover, the invasion would be dependent on carrier planes, whose operations were limited and could be shut down by the weather and were vulnerable to Japanese kamikaze attacks.

Despite its gigantic size, the Olympic part of Downfall had specific goals and only called for the conquest of the lower third of the island. Kyushu was about twice the size of Massachusetts and roughly divided in two by mountains that separated the north from the south. The army believed that the Japanese could be driven from the southern part and contained in the north while the south was developed as a base for staging and supporting Coronet.

November first had been chosen because it represented both the amount of lead time necessary to develop and launch the attack as well as being after the end of the annual typhoon season. Typhoons had savaged the American fleets off Okinawa and elsewhere, and a recurrence could be disastrous for the expedition. One typhoon had ripped through Okinawa in early August and caused a great deal of damage to equipment being gathered for the landings on Kyushu.

All of the units involved in the operation were among those already in the Pacific theater. No divisions would be drawn from Europe for Olympic, although two armored divisions were scheduled for deployment from Europe for Coronet in 1946. There were no appropriate areas for massed tank assaults on Kyushu, although there were such places on the Kanto Plain. The infantry and marine divisions would still have their regular quota of tanks, many of which would have flamethrowers instead of cannon.

On X-Day, the marines would attack the southwestern tip of the island and begin to drive overland across the Satsuma Peninsula toward Kagoshima Bay, which ran north-south and roughly split the southern end of Kyushu in half. The two army corps would land on the east side of Kyushu, and one corps would also drive on toward Kagoshima while the second took Ariake Bay. Ariake was on the southeastern end of the island and, even though it was the smaller of the two anchorages, was itself large enough to hold a large fleet.

Truman was bemused because someone responsible for planning must have been a car buff and had named all the sites and areas accordingly. Thus, the marines' main landing areas were Taxicab and Roadster, while the army would be in Town Car and Station Wagon. Specific beaches were named after particular brands, and it was a little unnerving to see future battlefields named Ford, DeSoto, Buick, and Chrysler, along with many others. Attacks just prior to November first would take place on several smaller islands off Kyushu.

Truman put down the folder. "Casualties and options, gentlemen."

As usual, Marshall answered. "Casualties are impossible to predict, as they are based on several unknowns. First, we don't know how many Japs will be facing us on Kyushu, and second, we don't know how hard or how well they'll fight." He took a deep breath, obviously reluctant to give such an estimate. "We have run several analytical models based on the invasions and campaigns of Leyte, Luzon, Iwo Jima, Okinawa, as well as the latter stages of the European war from Normandy to its conclusion. Right now our best estimate for Olympic alone is two hundred thousand casualties from all causes, combat and noncombat.

Truman shook his head. "And if we have to go forward and attack Tokyo, how many for Operation Coronet?"

Leahy took his turn. "Perhaps another ninety thousand battle casualties, which, if the noncombat casualties are added in, would bring the total for the campaign up to nearly a half a million. And these are only for the ground forces. We estimate at least another ten thousand naval personnel will be casualties, primarily as a result of kamikaze attacks for Olympic alone. The Japs are hoarding their planes for just such an attack, and they will come at us in the thousands. Some are bound to get through, just as they did off Okinawa."

Truman wondered, "How many kamikaze planes did the Japs throw at us at Okinawa?"

"About two thousand," King said, "and they sank almost forty ships, although all were smaller ones. While several hundred ships were damaged, nothing larger than a destroyer was sunk. A couple of our carriers suffered grievous wounds. The *Benjamin Franklin* was struck by a kamikaze and eight hundred of her crew were killed with hundreds more wounded. We think that many more than two thousand kamikazes were launched, but that a goodly number of them simply got lost or just fell out of the sky for mechanical reasons. That won't happen at Kyushu since we'll be hundreds of miles closer to the kamikaze bases. When the *Franklin* was hit, she was just off Kyushu.

"The kamikazes, Mr. President, scare the hell out of the navy, and I don't mean just their planes when I use the term *kamikaze*. They have kamikaze boats and subs, even human-piloted torpedoes."

"Scares the hell out of me as well," Truman muttered.

"Of course," Marshall injected, "we are of the opinion that a decisive American victory on Kyushu stands a good chance of making the Japanese surrender. If that's the case, we won't have to launch Operation Coronet and invade near Tokyo."

Sure, Truman thought bitterly, just as the atomic bomb was going to make them surrender. "After all that's occurred recently, do you really believe that?"

Marshall was not intimidated by the response. "Sir, our intelligence intercepts indicate that the Japs are massing virtually everything they have on Kyushu. If—I mean *when*—we beat them there, they won't have anything left to fight with. The battle for Japan will be won or lost on Kyushu."

"Then why," Truman asked, "don't we do an end run and drive straight for Tokyo if they have all their forces on Kyushu?"

King responded, "Because of the threat of their kamikazes and the fact that we absolutely need land-based air cover to protect our men and ships from those assaults, as well as to bomb Japanese strongpoints."

Truman sighed. The cold statistics were making him angry. These were people, flesh-and-blood people, and not abstract numbers. "I talked to Secretary of War Stimson, and he feels your figures are far too low. Churchill felt the same way, and that was before he was booted out of office by the ungrateful British people. What do you say about that?"

Again Marshall met his stare. "These are all estimates. God only knows what the reality will be. I will say that both of the gentlemen you mentioned are highly emotional and tend to overstate issues."

"All right," Truman said resignedly. "Run my other options by me."

"Yes, sir. Even before the atomic bomb, we felt we had only three alternatives, and that only one, invasion, was viable. The first of the other options was to carry on limited offenses against other Japanese-held lands, such as Formosa and Korea. This first idea was discarded almost immediately as we believed it would not cause the Japanese to give up and would only create needless American casualties."

"Agreed," said Truman.

"The second option was to continue the blockade and the bombing offensive. While we believe this would minimize our casualties, we are convinced that it would take an unacceptable length of time, perhaps years, to bring down the Japanese."

Truman tapped his fingers nervously. "Too long. The American public demands a quick victory and an end to the war's privation. We cannot have millions of our boys sitting on their duffs while we blockade the Japs and wait for them to give up. Good Lord, the public is after us to bring the boys home now. If we tell them there might be years of relative inaction while we wait for the Japs to quit, there'll be hell to pay."

Marshall nodded. "There are other reasons why a blockade wouldn't work. It would cause millions of civilian deaths among the Japanese from bombing and starvation, and it still wouldn't necessarily cause them to quit. After all, they are capable of providing for their own food needs, however meagerly. It is possible that, after enough deaths, they would arrive at a food-to-population equilibrium that would enable them to sustain themselves forever."

Truman shook his head in disbelief, but the basic idea seemed chillingly correct. There was no certainty that blockade would bring victory. Not ever. "We cannot wait an eternity to find out. Gentlemen, we cannot wait more than a year and there must be action. The American people demand it."

"Agreed," said Marshall, and the others murmured assent. "It goes without saying that our prisoners of war would continue to suffer terribly during this period of time, and that other casualties would still occur. There is ongoing scientific work on defoliants that would destroy the Japanese rice crop, but we will not have the herbicide in any quantities until next year at the earliest. If we do use defoliants, then the result will be tens of millions of Japanese men, women, and children dying of starvation along with our own prisoners, who would, of course, be the last to be fed."

"Which leads us back to an invasion," sighed Truman.

"Yes, sir, it does," Marshall almost whispered, and it struck Truman that the man was upset at the prospect.

"Thank you, General," Truman said. With undisguised distate, he picked up Operation Downfall's thick folder of information as well as the summary sheets. He hated reading long reports. He recalled that he'd had to be talked into reading an earlier report on the Manhattan Project shortly after taking office. "This, I presume, is current?"

"Yes," said Marshall. "At least as it has been developed to date. Changes are being made almost constantly."

"Do these changes include using atomic bombs?" Truman asked.

"Yes, but it is doubtful that we will have enough bombs or targets to make a difference," Marshall said. "The Japanese are scattering, hiding, and digging in their units to minimize the effect of both conventional and nuclear weapons."

"So we have to do it the old-fashioned way?" Truman asked bitterly.

"Yes, sir."

Truman glanced over the figures. It was an awesome 'enterprise. In scope it would dwarf the landings in Normandy on D-Day. No other Allied forces would land with MacArthur's army, although some Royal Navy ships were operating in the Pacific in conjunction with Nimitz. Discussions that might lead to the later inclusion of

British, Australian, and Canadian troops were ongoing, but there were no plans to use them at this time.

"Well thought out. Should we attempt to deceive the Japanese into thinking we won't attack Kyushu?"

"Yes, sir," Marshall again responded. "And those efforts are called Operation Pastel. They involve feints at Korea and Formosa, as was discussed as our first option, along with a sham thrust toward the island of Shikoku, which is actually closer to Tokyo than Kyushu, but, again, out of land-based air coverage."

Truman understood what he was hearing. The inescapable conclusion was that Kyushu was the only logical target. If the American military minds could realize that, so could the Japanese. "Gentlemen, will any of our deceptions work?"

Marshall's expression changed to one of sadness. "Probably not, sir, or at least not to any great extent, but they must be attempted."

"Then, General Marshall, what will the Japanese be doing on November first, 1945?"

Marshall found it difficult to look Truman square in the eyes. "Mr. President, they'll be waiting for us on Kyushu with everything they have."

CHAPTER 17

Religion amused Col. Tadashi Sakei. Once it had been important to him, but that was when he had been very young and before so many of those he loved had been incinerated by the Americans. Since then he had seen the uselessness in believing in any god or gods who cared nothing for him. Thus, he became a convert to the cause of Japan and believed in it with zeal and fervor. Japan did care for him. Japan had nurtured and strengthened him. Japan was his god. Now he would repay her faith in him by protecting her with his life.

On the other hand, he did nothing to discourage religious beliefs in others. It mattered nothing to him whether a person believed in the gentle Buddha, the ancient rites of Shinto, or even the confusing and ridiculed logic of Christianity. All that was important was that the believer dedicate his or her life to Japan.

Thus, placing Emperor Hirohito in protective custody in a Shinto shrine near Nagasaki was an act of opportunity and expedience, not sacrilege. The Americans rarely attacked anything that looked religious, and he had gone to great lengths to keep his five-hundred-man Imperial Guards battalion dug in and out of sight during the day. Lookouts scanned the skies in all directions to watch for the enemy, who could drop like hawks on unsuspecting prey.

Shinto stood for the "way of the gods" and was the oldest religion in Japan. Devotees worshipped many gods, called kami, which were the basic force present in trees, rocks, rivers, and other parts of nature. Japan was liberally sprinkled with shrines, and this was a fairly large one with several buildings, including a charming garden that had been well tended by the priests who had run the shrine.

Sakei had chased off the religious occupants and installed Hirohito in the quarters of their senior priest. It was hardly palatial, but it was safe and secure. The buildings also kept most of his men out of sight while the others camped in a nearby grove and, to the extent possible, limited their movements to nighttime, when even the American predators slept.

As he started to walk the dirt path to the nearby village, Sakei was confident that American planes would not notice one man walking along one of the miserable excuses for roads that were so typical of Kyushu. He looked to his right and was dismayed by the sight of a score or so of his soldiers running in a single line across a field. It was probably a work group, and he made a mental note to find out who was in charge of them. He would give that unfortunate soul a harsh lesson in the virtues of staying out of sight during the day. Their officer probably thought it was safe to cut across the field since none of their hand-cranked sirens had gone off in a while, as they did several times each day to warn of American planes prowling the sky.

Sakei ignored the virtually omnipresent and high-flying bombers as they were off to bomb the cities and other major targets, but the swooping and darting fighters and dive-bombers were another matter. They were the ones that sniffed out the smaller targets and went after them like birds of prey after rodents in a field.

Sakei looked down the road and saw the man he wished to meet, Captain Onichi, the senior *kempei* officer in the area. In deference to the fuel shortage, the overweight captain rode a bicycle, with some difficulty, and a rare smile crossed Sakei's face. He had no love for the *kempei*, but the secret police, or "thought police," had their purpose. He could only wonder, however, just why the fat *kempei* captain wished to meet him under these private and discreet circumstances.

Before he could go farther, a dark shadow crossed over Sakei, and he heard the shriek of engines as the gust of air swirled dust around him. It was an American plane and it had passed just a few feet over his head.

He watched in horror as the work party scattered in blind panic with many of them heading for the presumed safety of the shrine buildings. Perhaps the plane hadn't seen them as it swept by, but then he remembered—the Americans never flew alone.

The second plane roared overhead with its guns spitting at the prey the first one had flushed. Rows of dirt exploded in the field, sending soldiers tumbling and flying, landing in bloody heaps. Within seconds, the first plane returned and it strafed the shrine, while the second sliced bloody ribbons in the grove where so many of his men were bivouacked. Sakei could only hope that his men had made it to the protection of the numerous slit trenches dug in the area.

In the grove, a soldier with more bravery than sense fired on the Yanks with a machine gun and drew the attention of a fighter, which silenced it with one savage burst of gunfire.

Sakei lay by the road as the planes made repeated passes in an arrogantly leisurely and lethal manner. For long minutes there would be relative silence, with only the distant whine of the planes' engines and the cries of the wounded to be heard. Then the screech of the fighters and the cacophonous chatter of machine guns as they sought targets became deafening. At least there were no bombs or rockets. The racks under the planes were empty. They had been dropped on targets elsewhere.

After a while, the planes bored of the game and flew off, or perhaps they were out of ammo. Sakei got to his feet and ran toward the priest's quarters. If Hirohito was dead, Sakei would have failed in his duty and the missing Crown Prince Akihito would be emperor. It could not be!

It wasn't. Sakei found Hirohito in the doorway to his quarters. He was covered with dirt and his glasses were askew, but he seemed unharmed, although obviously shaken. He heard from a noncom that the emperor, on hearing the attacking planes, had virtually flown into a trench to save himself. Sakei was pleased. Let the Son of Heaven know a soldier's fear.

Hirohito dusted himself off and acknowledged Sakei's existence. "Ah, Colonel, another Japanese victory, is it not? Very soon the Yanks will run out of bullets and surrender, won't they? After all, that is Anami's plan, isn't it?"

Sakei bowed respectfully and ignored the sarcasm. This time Hirohito was right. Japan had no roof to deflect the rain of American bombs and bullets. "I am glad you are unharmed."

Hirohito straightened his glasses. "As you should be. What went wrong with your precautions, Colonel?"

Good question, Sakei thought. The obvious culprit was the ass who'd sent that group of soldiers across the field. If he wasn't already killed by the fighters, Sakei would have him shot. He felt only slightly shamed that the men in the field had broken and run. He wondered what he would have done had he seen a plane aiming its guns directly at him.

But the American planes had taken them all by surprise. "It appears, Your Majesty, that the Americans have adopted flying extremely low as a surprise tactic. We shall have to be even more vigilant on your behalf."

Hirohito made a small noise that might have been either a snort or a derisive laugh and disappeared inside his quarters.

"Colonel?"

Sakei turned quickly. He had forgotten the *kempei* officer who'd been cycling down the road to meet him. The man was disheveled and wide-eyed with scarcely controlled fear.

"Captain, I see you too survived our little adventure."

"Happily, yes, Colonel. Do you have a moment to talk now? I did tell you it was a matter of urgency and importance regarding your honored guest."

Sakei had informed the local *kempei* commander that the emperor was under guard at the shrine. It was only logical since the *kempei* would wonder what was going on and expend a lot of effort finding out anyhow. Besides, the *kempei* were allies, however unsavory they sometimes were.

The captain looked around where the numerous dead were being stacked and the wounded were being treated. Blood was everywhere and the sounds of pain filled the air. Sakei looked around as well and grimaced. His battalion had been cruelly punished for one man's mistake.

"What I have to tell you, Colonel, may cause you to wonder whether this raid on the shrine was an opportunistic accident or an attempt by the Americans to assassinate our emperor."

Sakei almost staggered. "What?"

The captain bowed slightly. "Last night we managed to confirm the existence of either a spy or a traitor in this area. I think we should consider the possibility that the emperor's location was given away to our enemies."

Sakei's hand went instinctively to the handle of his sword. Murder the emperor? Why not? The Americans had been guilty of such criminal acts in the past. After all, hadn't they assassinated the revered Admiral Yamamoto by ambushing his plane with their fighters while he was on an inspection mission?

The more he thought of it, the more likely it became. "How?" Sakei demanded.

"We have intercepted what we strongly believe are signals to the Americans that emanate from a clandestine radio in this area. While we were never able to pick up all the transmission, we did record parts and have had them decoded. It was a simple code so it didn't take long to break. They are in English and tell of conditions here on Kyushu."

Sakei nodded grimly. "We must catch that spy and stop him." And I must make other plans for Hirohito, he added to himself. He must become even more stealthy in his actions. The Americans were too strong to confront with strength. He would keep Hirohito alive with cunning.

·

CHAPTER 18

"**W**elcome back to Okinawa, General Monck. We all trust you had a fruitful journey."

"Up yours, Colonel Parker," General Monck said in a low voice that could not be heard by others. Parker's promotion to lieutenant colonel had come through shortly before Monck's officially taking over the regiment. This made Parker the second-in-command.

Parker ignored him. "And how were things on Mount Olympus this time, and aren't you just a little late getting back?"

Monck threw his bag of spare clothing on a table. With the exception of a couple of NCOs who were monitoring radios and pretending not to listen, he was alone with Parker in the regiment's command tent.

"We had to take a detour around a pretty big storm that's out there. In case you hadn't noticed, it's getting cloudy and might just rain."

Monck marveled at the changes only a few days away had wrought. The entire island of Okinawa looked as if it were nothing less than one giant staging and training base for American military might. Here, where his regiment was bivouacked, was a giant tent city, and scores of them were elsewhere on the island. A couple of miles away, an enormous air base was being built near the ruined city of Kadena, with other, similar fields under construction elsewhere. It was incredible and Monck was proud to be a part of it. Even though he had his own share of misgivings, sights such as this made him confident that the United States would prevail against Japan.

"For your information, Parker, not all the gods were at Olympus, otherwise known as Guam. MacArthur deigned not to come. Instead he sent Eichelberger and Krueger, and they met with Nimitz and his staff. When I looked around, I realized that I was one of the lowest-ranking men invited to that conference."

"Did you meet Nimitz?"

Monck smiled. "Yeah, and he's really a pleasant, gentlemanly sort of man. Very easygoing. I even got in a game of horseshoes with him. His staff makes him play each day to keep him relaxed and healthy. Spruance was there too, and he's sort of the same way. Halsey's out blasting the Jap shoreline. Nimitz's staff reflects his attitude. Very friendly and helpful. Not at all like MacArthur's, although Eichelberger and Krueger tried hard to be cooperative, and, in the main, they succeeded." Monck shrugged. "Maybe it was better that MacArthur didn't come. Along with his ego, he would have brought Sutherland and Willoughby, and those two have caused trouble in the past."

Parker pulled out a cigarette and offered one to Monck. They lit up and Monck drew a deep breath. "The invasion is still on for November first. We are designated I Corps reserve. I Corps consists of the 25th, 41st, and 53rd divisions, and we'll be going in on X plus one or two depending on the circumstances. I Corps will be attacking north of Ariake Bay and near a town called Miyazaki. XI Corps will be on I Corps' left and will consist of the First Cav, the Americal Division, and the 43rd Infantry."

"And the marines?" Parker asked.

"They will land to the west of Kagoshima Bay on a spit of land called the Satsuma Peninsula. The V Amphibious Corps consists of the 2nd, 3rd, and 5th Marine divisions. All of this is the Sixth Army and General Krueger commands it, with MacArthur working his magic from the Philippines."

Parker had known some of it as rumors had been rampant for weeks. "Incredible" was all he could think to say as he considered the scope of the coming operation.

Monck chuckled. "Oh, there's more. IX Corps will stage a two-division diversionary thrust towards the island of Shikoku just before X-Day. They have the 81st and 98th divisions. Follow-up forces are the 11th Airborne and the 77th Infantry, and, oh, yes, let's not

forget the 158th Regiment, which will land on a couple of small islands off Kyushu just prior to X-Day."

"Are we still part of the 41st?"

They stepped outside and walked a little ways away from the
tent. The fresh air smelled good. Monck blew a fairly decent smoke
ring that the wind quickly took away. "Who the hell knows. For administrative purposes, I guess so, but General Swift—he's I Corps
commander—made it plain that we could be plugged in anywhere.
By the way, with X-Day only three weeks away, we've got to step up
training even more than we have."

Parker nodded, although privately wondering just how the men
could work harder than they were. "Don't you think we should give
them some rest before we go in?"

"Hell no!" Monck responded vehemently. "I want these people
worked. The last thing I want is for someone to die because we
didn't prepare them well enough when we had the time. I don't
think I could live with myself with that knowledge. And I don't
want them to have too much time on their hands to think about
what's going to happen when they hit Kyushu. They get time off to
go to church on Sunday and they get to see any USO shows that
happen by. Oh, yeah, I heard that Bob Hope will be out here in a
week or so."

Parker whistled. "Wow, I guess we really are important."

Monck couldn't keep from grinning. "Are you being sarcastic?"

"Just a little, General. Did you find out anything else that we
should know about our role and the invasion?"

A gust of rain-tipped wind threatened to take General Monck's
cap, and he had to grab it with his hand to keep it from flying off. "I
found out some more about Kyushu, and none of it is good. Like
we've been told, the island itself is volcanic and rugged, with mountains in the center, and steep hills and deep valleys running all the
way to the coast."

"Mountains?"

"Nothing like the Alps or even the Rockies, but they go up quite
sharply to maybe two thousand feet in the invasion area. We won't
even be landing on a beach per se because there aren't any. There's a

small one in Ariake Bay, but it's not for us. When we get out of our landing craft, we start climbing over that hilly volcanic soil almost right away. Kyushu's so desolate that only about ten percent is under cultivation, and that in a land desperate for food. That fact kind of surprised me. I always thought Japan was one great big rice paddy once you got out of the cities."

Parker shook his head sadly. "Steep hills and valleys means no armor."

"We'll have tank support, but there'll be no massed armor attacks. The difficult terrain also means that many of our units will be cut off from each other while they advance, and coordination will be extremely difficult. We'll be lucky to function in battalion-sized units, much less division or corps."

"Then not working with the 41st is no great loss," Parker mused, and Monck agreed.

Monck looked at the sky. It was getting darker by the moment and the rain was beginning to come down heavier. The two men turned and walked toward the command tent. "You've seen the maps," Monck said. "There aren't very many roads on Kyushu, and those that do exist tend to be sunken, which makes them ready-made ambush sites and strongpoints. Just like here on Okinawa, there'll be a lot of caves and bunkers for the Japs to hide in and for us to root them out of. The valleys that run inland all tend to end in sharp inclines, which will make vehicular traffic almost impossible."

"Marvelous," Parker murmured. "And they've had all these months to prepare for us. Did you get a feel for Jap numbers, or does MacArthur still think it'll be a walkover?"

Monck chuckled grimly. "Without MacArthur gracing us with his presence on Guam, there was a fairly frank exchange of opinions, and it does look like Eichelberger and Krueger have pretty well convinced Mac that his estimates are way too low. A couple of months ago, the guess was maybe one hundred and twenty-five thousand Japs on Kyushu; now the intelligence boys are estimating maybe half a million, with more coming each and every day. The only good news is that most of them are still in the northern portion of the island and having the devil's own time getting to the southern part because of our air superiority. Oh, yeah, they know that we're coming, and it looks like they've figured out exactly where we'll be landing."

"Jesus," Parker gasped. "We're the attacking force and we'll probably be outnumbered."

"That's why we need control of the air and a lot of firepower on the ground. Our troopships will be prime targets for the kamikazes, so we'll be moving out of the transports and onto the landing craft as soon as possible, and before that, we won't get on the transports that'll take us to Japan until the last minute."

"Makes sense, sir. Smaller targets are harder for their planes to hit."

"Agreed, but don't forget that the term *kamikaze* means a helluva lot more than just suicide planes. Nimitz's boys say there'll be a lot of midget-submarine activity, along with manned suicide torpedoes and rockets, and there are at least a dozen Jap destroyers unaccounted for. Hell, they've even got suicide divers who'll be waiting to attach mines to our ships. We've got to figure that all of them will be making suicide attacks against us."

"General, those Jap people are fucking crazy."

They had just reached the tent flap when one of the NCOs burst out, almost running into General Monck. "Jesus, General, we got real bad news."

"What now?"

"Sir," the sergeant almost stammered, "this ain't no rainstorm. Just got word from the navy that it's a full-fledged typhoon and it's even got a name now—Louise. It's gonna hit Okinawa dead on."

Monck and Parker looked at each other, aghast. The 528th was scattered all over Okinawa, engaged in various types of training. They would have to communicate the news as quickly as possible to the disparate units. Thousands of men would have to hide and ride out Typhoon Louise as best they could.

Monck then looked at their frail tent and thought of all the other temporary structures that housed his regiment and its equipment. Tens of thousands of other, similar facilities covered Okinawa. Typhoon Louise had the potential to wipe out much of the American presence on Okinawa.

As if on cue, the wind picked up and shrieked. "All right," said Monck, speaking loudly to be heard over it. "Tell everyone to grab shovels and literally dig in. The hell with the tents and supplies. They can be replaced. Everyone is to save their asses and start right now!"

CHAPTER 19

*F*irst Sergeant Mackensen told the more than two hundred assembled men of A Company in Okinawa that he had just found the dead Jap in a nearby fold of the earth where the man had died.

At Captain Ruger's orders, the company gathered in a large circle around the cadaver. The Japanese soldier had a strangely withered, mummy-like look. Quite some time ago, he'd been burned to death, probably by a flamethrower. His bones were only partly covered by charred flesh, and most of his left leg was missing. A helmet covered the top of his head, and the corpse smiled at them through a half dozen teeth.

They were near what the Japs had called the Shuri Defense Line. When the Americans had invaded, the Japanese had retreated to the hilly southern third of the island to make their defensive stand, and the Shuri Line, anchored on what were now the ruins of Shuri Castle, had cost both sides dearly.

Captain Ruger strode up to Mackensen, who nodded and stepped away. Ruger glanced up at the darkening sky. Shit, Ruger thought, his men were all going to get wet. Paul Morrell caught the glance as well and shivered slightly. He was exhausted.

"All right," said Ruger. "Did everybody get a good look at the little son of a bitch? That's a Jap lying there, and one of the best kind—a dead one. Somebody toasted his ass good, didn't they? But look at him. You know they've got shitty rifles and bad tactics, but this joker wouldn't give up, would he? No, he fought with that shitty rifle of his and died with it. I wonder how many Americans he killed before somebody saw where he was shooting from and got him."

Paul watched in fascination. The lesson was ghastly, but it had the company's complete attention. Only a few months before, that Japanese soldier had been trying to kill Americans, and dead or not, that man was one of the enemy.

In the weeks of training since they'd arrived on Okinawa, Paul's platoon, the company, the entire regiment, had worked hard to replace skills lost over months of inactivity, and to acquire those they never really had. They'd exercised and marched early each day, then spent the afternoons and evenings in weapons training and small-unit tactics. They'd gotten better, and Ruger had managed to get rid of those who were unable to cope with the demands of training.

But that's what it had been, training. At least until now. The presence of a real dead Jap changed everything. Before them lay the enemy as well as the brutal reality of death.

Ruger's eyes swept the assemblage. "And just because he's dead, don't think he's forgotten how to kill. The Japs have a nasty habit of booby-trapping their dead comrades in hope that some stupid GI will come along to take a souvenir, like that helmet for instance. Look good on a wall, wouldn't it? Or maybe something nice for the missus like a gold filling, or maybe a dried ear, or maybe one of those shitty rifles or a real good pistol. Well, if they've booby-trapped the corpse, and they likely have, you've got to be real careful." He turned to his first sergeant. "Sergeant Mackensen, show us what to do."

"First," said Mackensen, "all you people step farther away." There was a shuffling as two hundred plus men complied. "Now you'll notice that I very carefully tied a rope around his one remaining leg. I'm gonna step back and pull on it real hard. If he's trapped, it'll trigger whatever he's hiding."

With that, Mackensen walked a couple of paces away from the cadaver, lay flat on the ground, and yanked the rope. There was a split second of stillness, then a flash of light and the crash of a grenade exploding, sending bones and pieces of dead Jap into the air. Several of the men got parts of Jap on them, and a couple of them started to gag.

Mackensen got to his feet and saluted Ruger. "Captain, the fucking Jap is now well and truly dead."

Ruger nodded. "Very good, First Sergeant. Carry on with training."

As he said that, it began to rain, and the already strong wind started to pick up in power. They had no real rain gear with them, so Paul started to form them up for more work. If it rained, they were going to get wet and that was that. After all, how often did they call off a war because of rain? He wondered how their tents were holding up in what was rapidly becoming a downpour. Captain Ruger, who was only a few feet away, seemed unperturbed.

A PFC handed a walkie-talkie to Ruger, who listened attentively and then appeared stunned by what he'd heard. "Everybody take cover," he yelled. "This is a typhoon." Ruger then sent runners out to the other platoons and ran out himself, saying that he didn't trust their radios to get through in the rapidly growing storm.

Typhoon? What the hell does one do when caught on an Okinawan hill in a typhoon? Paul wondered. "Dig in," he yelled to the men, who were as puzzled as he was. "Get to just below the crest of this hill and start digging in for protection against the wind. Push the dirt up the hill and form a bunker in front of you."

"Why?" asked a soldier, and Paul debated letting him drown.

"Because, Private Haines, a typhoon is just like a hurricane. That means a ton of rainwater is going to land on us and whatever we dig in is going to be full pretty quick. Push the dirt up front so you don't get washed away. Now shut up and dig!"

Paul checked on his men as they dug frantically into dirt that quickly turned into mud. The wind had picked up and was slashing at them. "Keep your helmets on. There's gonna be stuff flying around and you don't want to get hit."

"Like the stuff we left where we bivouacked, Lieutenant?" one of his men yelled, and a couple of others chuckled at the thought.

"That's right!" Already Paul had to cup his hands and holler to be heard. "So keep your heads down." He then grabbed a couple of men who were earnestly digging too far down the hill. When they protested, he told them they had to watch out for flash floods as well as wind. Chastened, they moved farther up the slope and began anew.

Paul helped two of his men dig a hole in the ground and push an earthen berm before them. To his surprise it worked fairly well, although the torrential rain quickly filled their shelter and made life miserable for them. Miserable, he kept reminding them, but safe.

"Look at that," one of them yelled. Paul looked up and saw a piece of canvas fly overhead.

"One of our tents." Paul grinned. "Probably mine with all my dirty laundry in it. We're not in Kansas anymore," he said in reference to the movie *The Wizard of Oz*, "but our gear will soon be."

The wind threatened to rip their helmets off and they had to hold them down. Sand and spray whipped around their heads, and as they cowered, they lost track of time. All they knew was that it had gotten even darker than before and that it was probably night. The wind developed a keening, shrieking sound like that of a tormented animal.

During a brief lull, Paul slithered out of his foxhole and crawled around to see if his men were okay. Except for a couple of cuts and bruises, no one was hurt. Bellying his way back to his shelter, he almost ran into First Sergeant Mackensen, who was also crawling about in the mud.

"Don't bother saluting," Paul said.

Mackensen, who rarely deviated from a stern expression, looked at him funny for a minute then smiled slightly. "Wasn't planning on it, Lieutenant. Captain wants to know how you're doing."

Captain Ruger was probably out on his belly checking on his other platoons. "We're fine, top. We'll be all right. How's everybody else?"

"So far so good."

"Great. By the way, that was a damn good dog-and-pony show you and the captain put on."

Mackensen had started to crawl back but stopped. "What do you mean?"

"I mean that it was an impressive display, blowing up that Jap and all that. But I think it was more than a coincidence that you just happened to find that body and that it just happened to be booby-trapped at just the right time for our men to get shocked and serious about war."

Mackensen put on a look of mock hurt. Then he actually chuckled. "Captain said you'd figure it out. Buddy of mine found the Jap a while back and was driving around the island with it on the front fender of his jeep like it was a dead deer. I took it from him and we've had it hidden until the right time. The real bitch was fixing the hand grenade to that fucker. He kept falling apart and we had to tape him back together."

The wind roared again, Mackensen nodded and departed for the dubious comfort of his own hole in the ground, while Paul crawled to his. By the time he got there, the wind was raging harder than it ever had, and the two others had to drag him into the hole, which caused his head to go under the muddy water.

"You okay, Lieutenant?" Both men were laughing as Paul emerged from his ducking, and he joined in even though he was cold, wet, miserable, and scared.

"Did either of you two volunteer for this shit?" he asked.

"Nah"—they grinned—"we all got drafted too, sir."

A good-sized piece of debris tumbled by. It looked like a piece of wood from a house. Had he been standing, it could have impaled him. Paul wondered just what the hell the rest of the island looked like.

After what seemed like an eternity, the wind abated to where it was simply savage, and the rain became merely a torrent. Considering themselves safe, the men crawled out of their water-filled burrows and stood up. It was getting lighter, and a check of his watch told Paul that it was almost dawn. Again a nose count was taken and he was more than gratified to find that everyone was safe and, except for cuts and bumps, no one was seriously hurt.

Paul waved his sergeants over. They all looked so sodden and despondent he had to chuckle. After a moment's hesitation, they joined him in a spate of nervous laughter. They had passed the test. They were alive. They had handled that bitch, Typhoon Louise.

The passing of the storm brought General Monck and his staff from their trenches. This time it was appallingly easy to look around and see for a great distance as the typhoon had swept the area clean of anything but bare ground. Where once there had been a great city of tents and an army preparing to attack Japan, there was nothing more than a barren plain on which large numbers of men were emerging. Everything they owned was gone, and they were reduced to standing and looking about in confusion.

"Parker," Monck said hoarsely. "Where the hell is my regiment?"

Parker's left eye was swollen nearly shut. He'd been struck across the head by a pot from someone's field kitchen. "Sir, if we're safe, then there's a real good chance they are too."

"We've got to reach them, get in contact with them. Jesus, they're sure to have injured and we've got to get them medical help."

Parker took a look at where there had once been a first-class radio operation. Nothing. There was no way of contacting their separated units, and sending runners wasn't a good idea because the runners wouldn't know where to find the scattered regiment.

"We'll do our best, General."

Monck gave Parker's shoulder a reassuring squeeze. "I know you will. I'll go and throw some general-like weight around and see if I can scrounge up some fresh radio gear from someone. You organize what men we have here and start salvage and cleanup."

Parker snorted. "Salvage? Ain't nothing to salvage, sir."

Monck agreed with that observation. "Well then, gather what flammable debris you can and see if you can get some fires going. It's not all that warm and we don't want these men coming down with pneumonia. Get them dried out and under some kind of cover. If you can," he added softly.

Lt. Col. Don Parker threw him a salute and took off to gather heads. Brig. Gen. John Monck looked again at the moonscape that had been an impressive military facility only a few hours earlier.

It was October 9, 1945, and in only three weeks the U.S. forces on Okinawa were to commence attacking and land on the Japanese island of Kyushu. With what? Monck thought harshly.

▪

CHAPTER 20

*T*onight was the night, Dennis Chambers decided. He could no longer live with the thought of two Jap planes and four Jap airmen being so close to him. He would have to do something about it. He knew he wasn't being terribly logical, but he was also driven to distraction by the bags of rice that the four men had stashed in their tent. If he could only get ahold of that food, he stood a chance of lasting for months, and perhaps the war would be over by then.

While the weather was still mild, the night air had a definite chill, and he could visualize his source of vegetation and insects literally drying up. If that happened and he had nothing to fall back on, he'd starve.

Desperately trying to be quiet, he crawled over the crest of the hill and down through the grasses and small evergreens to within a few yards of where the two pilots and the two mechanics sat facing each other. They had not lit a fire. The glow of fires might attract unwelcome visitors from the sky, but the Japanese had cooked and eaten during the day, and the scent of the cooked food was almost overwhelming to Dennis.

The four Japanese were jabbering on about something that Dennis couldn't understand. At first he thought it was a dialect that his limited knowledge of Japanese didn't allow him to comprehend. But then it dawned on him and he thought that his foray might not be as risky as he had first thought. The four Japs weren't speaking an unknown tongue; they were shit-faced drunk.

He crawled to a point that was almost insolently close to them. They had several bottles of what looked like American whiskey that they passed around and swallowed with abandon. Obviously they felt they would not be called upon to fly this night. He chuckled as he realized he could stand up and they wouldn't even notice him in their alcoholic stupor. Dennis's only fear was that one of them would fall over him on his way to relieve himself. He grasped the sharpened piece of metal that was his only weapon and waited.

After a couple of hours, the drinking bout ended and the four men staggered to sleeping mats that had been laid on the ground. As they snored loudly and occasionally belched or made other noises in their sleep, Dennis crawled up to the closest of the four. Cautiously, he took the piece of metal from his belt and, grasping it as firmly as he could, leaned over the sleeping enemy. Then, with strength and quickness he'd forgotten he had, he slashed across the Jap's throat. The man's eyes opened and he convulsed, but made no sound other than a gurgle as his blood spouted out all over the two of them. The first Jap was dead.

Dennis looked at the others and saw no sign of their awakening. Then he checked his victim. The dead man's eyes were wide-open and looked to the sky in disbelief. The Jap had bled profusely on Dennis, and the sticky feel of the liquid sickened him.

He steeled himself to his task and crawled to the next mat. Again, the makeshift knife slashed and blood poured out. This time, however, the second victim's death throes included a wild swing of his arm that hit Dennis across the face and knocked him back. Dennis tried to get up, but the world began to swim and he realized he was hurt and at the end of his strength. He tried to will himself to stay conscious but it was futile and he sagged to his knees.

As darkness enveloped him, he saw the silhouette of another Japanese soldier standing over him and he groaned. Somehow he had miscounted. There were five, not four. Where the hell had the fifth man been hiding? He could only hope they would kill him quickly and not torture him to death as he knew he deserved from them.

Shit, thought Joe Nomura as he looked over the prone body of an emaciated white man wearing the ragged remains of an air force uniform. He had to be either a downed pilot or a captured crewman. What a helluva fool to try something like this. The guy was obviously too weak to have finished the task even if he hadn't gotten bashed in the head by the man he'd just killed.

Joe had also been stalking the little Jap air base when he'd caught sight of someone else trying to skulk through the trees. When he'd figured out what the other man was up to, he'd been aghast. Not until he'd gotten much closer did he realize that the assassin was an American.

And, Joe thought grimly, one who was in bad shape as well as a whole lot of trouble.

Joe moved toward the two remaining Japanese, who still slept deeply and drunkenly. He drew his knife and, far more expertly than Dennis, killed the third Jap. The fourth was lying with his throat covered, so Joe sheathed his knife and brought the heel of his hand down on the back of the man's neck in a vicious chop. He waited a few seconds before checking for a pulse and found none. The money he'd spent for karate lessons as a kid had finally paid off.

Now what? This slaughter hadn't been in Joe's plans, but it was done and he'd better cover his ass or the *kempei* would be all over the area once it was discovered. He thought for a moment and then smiled.

First, he dragged the unconscious Dennis Chambers away from the area and well into the trees. Then he placed the four corpses around the planes and then pulled off much of the camouflage. It mainly consisted of evergreen boughs and moved easily even for a man with one arm. Within minutes, the planes were open to view from the sky.

Good, he thought. The next task was to take those precious bags of rice. He carried them in his one arm up over the hill and to presumed safety. Then he returned and scouted around a little and found what he was looking for—cans of gasoline. After all, didn't a plane need gas to fly? He set the containers under the planes and rigged a fuse out of cloth.

By the time he was done, he could see the hint of false dawn off in the east. Soon the sky would be filled with searching hunters. Well, he'd give them something to find.

Joe made certain that the still unconscious Chambers—he had checked his dog tags in the growing light and now knew his name—was still safe and even pulled him farther back along with the food sacks. One last look at the Japanese camp brought a new discovery—

several unopened bottles of Johnnie Walker Red. How the hell did four dumb Japs get good Scotch on a hillside in Kyushu? Who cared? he answered, but there was no need for the liquor to go to waste. He lit the fuse. It would take a couple of minutes for the flames to reach the gas. He tucked the bottles under his arm and ran up the hill.

Joe had just crossed over the crest when he heard the whump of an explosion quickly followed by a second. He turned and saw the flickering glow of flames over the hill. It was time to really put some distance between himself and that fire.

A familiar growling noise stopped him in his tracks and he looked up with a grin on his face. The first plane merely flew low over the fire to see what was causing it. A moment later, three more swept over the flames with their machine guns blazing. This caused more fires and explosions as the ammunition for the planes, along with other gasoline stores, went up. Now Joe felt much safer. With only a little luck, everyone would think that the four Japanese were victims of either their own stupidity or the dumb luck of the Americans.

Jesus Christ, Joe Nomura thought in admiration, if only the police at home could arrive as quickly as the planes had. He chuckled and wondered just how his new companion would react to having his life saved by a one-armed Jap. Then he realized something else. He, a Japanese American, had just killed two of his brethren. What he found most interesting was that he felt no remorse. They weren't his cousins; they were the enemy. Fuck 'em.

■

CHAPTER 21

Col. Tadashi Sakei forced himself to wait outside the local police station near Nagasaki while the local representatives of the *kempei* carried out their interrogations.

Normally, *kempei* questionings were carried out with some delicacy and subtlety, and over time, acknowledging that fear of pain and the dark unknown was often a greater motivator to confess than pain itself.

However, time was of the essence, and any recalcitrance on the part of those being questioned was being met with blows from fists, boots, and clubs. He noted that one enterprising young officer was getting some results by using lit cigarettes and burning matches jammed into sensitive parts of the suspect's anatomy, while another was carving chunks of skin off living flesh. As the interrogations went on, the *kempei* were becoming even more creative in their endeavors.

It was incredible that so much had gone wrong so quickly.

From all that had happened, it was simple to conclude that someone had betrayed Japan and that the bombing of the shrine where Hirohito was hidden was no random act.

The first thing they had to do was to find the traitor. Thus the *kempei* had arrested almost a score of men and women who were suspected of having pacifist tendencies. Sakei was relieved to note that most of them were Korean, and, therefore, neither Japanese nor trustworthy. He fervently hoped that the traitor would prove to be a Korean. He would be shamed if any true Japanese turned out to be the traitor.

The lieutenant in charge of the questioning came out of the small building they were using and walked up to Sakei. The lieutenant's arms were covered with blood, along with pieces of flesh and clumps of hair.

"What progress, Lieutenant? We must get on with this."

The lieutenant wiped his sticky hands with a rag. "Two more have confessed to being the traitor, but neither can tell me where the radio is. That means that they and the others were lying in their confessions to avoid the pain. We are continuing our efforts to extract the truth, but I am not confident that any of these people know anything at all. The traitor could have been one of those who already died under questioning, but I doubt that."

"Dammit." Sakei and the lieutenant returned to the building. This meant the traitor was still on the loose.

Sakei entered the building and was immediately assailed by the stench of blood and other body fluids. He looked about him and saw that half a dozen men and women had their hands tied behind them and were hung by their wrists from the roof beams with their feet just tantalizing inches off the floor. This dislocated their shoulders and made every part of their bodies vulnerable to assault.

They were naked and rivers of blood ran down their bodies from bruises, burns, and other open wounds. In a couple of cases Sakei could see where broken bones had split the surface of their skin. He could easily understand where people might confess to the most heinous of crimes if only to stop the agonies being inflicted on them, even if it brought on a swifter death.

Dead bodies were heaped in a corner. These looked at him through vacant eyes, at least the ones whose eyes hadn't been gouged out, and screamed soundlessly at him through gaping mouths where teeth had all been beaten out with hammers. One woman's breasts were bloody stumps, and severed fingers and toes were on the floor.

"You're right, Lieutenant, if they cannot give us the location of the radio, then they are nothing."

The *kempei* lieutenant bowed. "I will find more suspects, Colonel. We will find the traitor."

"Do that. Keep up the good work. In the meantime I will make other arrangements for the safety of our emperor."

The lieutenant beamed at the compliment. "Yes, Colonel. Do you have any special wishes for these people?" He gestured to the remaining prisoners.

"When you are done, kill them and dispose of the bodies where people can see what happens to those who are even suspected of treason."

The lieutenant grinned and saluted. Colonel Sakei left the building and walked the half mile down the dirt road to the compound where Hirohito was quartered.

He found the Son of Heaven well guarded in a cell. He was sitting quietly on the edge of his cot and reading a book. When he saw Sakei, Hirohito put down the book and stared at him.

"What now, Colonel, have you come to play chess with me?"

"No, Your Majesty."

"Why not? Are you afraid you will lose? You will lose, you know, just as you always have. You will lose everything, even Japan, through your foolishness."

Sakei held his temper in check. "Because of us, Majesty, Japan will live."

Hirohito smiled innocently. "Ah, yes. We will live, won't we? Just like when the bombs came and killed so many of your men. And you so foolishly believe a traitor has given away this location when you've got an entire battalion prancing around and making this little place look important to the American pilots. Yes, you are doing a marvelous job of keeping us alive. Very soon, you and all those with you will have succeeded so well that we will all be dead."

Sakei had to acknowledge that part of what Hirohito was saying was correct. It did not take five hundred men to guard the near-sighted and inoffensive Hirohito. It was one of several points that would immediately be corrected. "I will keep you alive, Majesty. We are moving you to a place of much greater safety. One that even the Americans will not dare to bomb."

Hirohito laughed tonelessly. "I doubt such a place exists on this planet, and certainly not in Japan."

Now it was Sakei's turn to smile. "It does, sir. Thanks to the Americans' strange sense of honor, we will find safety in a hospital that is closer to Nagasaki. The Americans will never bomb a hospital that boldly carries the sign of the Red Cross on its roof."

Sakei stood and called for a guard to assist the emperor in gathering his meager possessions.

CHAPTER 22

DETROIT

*D*ebbie had an open invitation to work in the furniture store and help Mr. Ginsberg with his bookkeeping. She did so during the fall whenever she had the time or needed the money. Thus, she didn't really particularly notice when no one called out to her and said hello as she entered the building that Saturday morning. She wasn't expected and Mr. G. and his sales staff of two were probably having a meeting, which, on a slow Saturday, frequently meant analyzing the weekend's football games. With soldiers returning to athletics, no one knew who had good teams or bad, but the consensus was that the collegiate reign of West Point and the Naval Academy was just about over.

She entered the back offices and hung up her coat. Then she heard a strange sound coming from Mr. G.'s personal office. The door was closed, which was unusual. Mr. G. had a thing about keeping it open so he could see what was happening. Curious, she tapped lightly before opening it. Mr. G. was seated behind his desk. He was slumped over and held his head in his hands. The normal disarray she teased him about was all over the floor, as if it had been swept there from his desk, which, for once, was almost bare.

Mr. G. looked up and she could see that he had been crying. For once she wished she had called before coming in. "Mr. G.? Are you okay?" God, what a dumb thing to say, she thought; of course he wasn't okay.

He looked at her for a moment. His eyes were pools of deepest sadness and, to her surprise, seemed to be tinged with rage. "Nothing is okay. Tell me, were the others afraid to enter, or were you not aware?"

Debbie took a seat in the wooden chair across from him. Aware of what? she wondered. "I just came in to do a little work. There was no one outside so I just walked in."

Ginsberg nodded. To her he looked as if he had aged a decade since she had last seen him only a few days earlier. "My faithful staff is doubtless across the street drinking coffee and waiting for me to calm down. A few minutes ago I was quite emotional. Do you wish to know why?"

"Yes," Debbie said timidly.

Mr. G. held a batch of papers in his hand. "I finally got these this morning. They came from a friend of mine in the International Red Cross in France. He's been trying to track down the family my wife and I had in Europe. You will notice, dear Debbie, that I used the past tense."

Debbie cringed. "I heard you."

"Twenty-one of our relatives were alive in Germany and Poland as of a few years ago. Some on the German side, my side, were imprisoned before the war, while those on my wife's side, in Poland, we had hoped were refugees who maybe had fled to Russia. Do you know how many are left?"

"No, sir."

"Four," he said in a rasping voice. "Four out of twenty-one. The ones who went to Buchenwald died a long time ago, only we were never informed. Notifying next of kin of dead Jews was not a Nazi priority. As near as my friend can tell, the people in camps like Buchenwald were worked very hard, fed very little, and finally died of malnutrition or any of the hundreds of diseases that will strike down a weakened body. If they were unable to work for their keep, they were beaten, sometimes beaten to death.

"My wife's people who lived in Poland were swept up by the Germans after the invasion and taken to a place in Poland the Germans called Auschwitz. Do you know what went on there?"

Debbie could only repeat herself. "No, sir."

She'd heard the stories, but, like most people, she'd found them too terrible to be true.

"My friend referred to it as a death factory that may have swallowed millions of victims, mainly Jews, and spat out only their ashes. When the inmates first entered the camp, the healthy were separated from the weak—like the proverbial wheat from the chaff—by some Nazi who had appointed himself God. The weak were stripped of their clothing and valuables and sent into what they were told were showers. When they were all together, they were gassed from the showers and died. Do you know what the healthy Jews had to do?"

Debbie shook her head.

"They had to get rid of the bodies. But first they plundered them for eyeglasses, gold fillings, nice hair, and anything else that might help Hitler. The clothing the dead left behind, even though much was just rags, was sent to German families who had lost possessions because of the bombing."

The thought of it sickened her. Paul had written to her of some of it. He'd seen a couple of the smaller camps and had told of emaciated Jewish refugees wandering Europe. She'd read other accounts in *Time* and elsewhere, but they were as if she were reading fiction. It couldn't happen to her or to someone she knew. Now she knew she'd been horribly wrong.

"But," Mr. Ginsberg sighed, "six survived."

"I thought you said four?"

"Six, and that is the cruelest irony. There were two others who made it through the hells of Auschwitz. They were Polish Jews, a brother and sister in their early twenties. When they returned to the village they'd lived in, the nice Catholic Poles beat them to death for having the temerity to try to reclaim the property that was once theirs. The Russians are in control in Poland, and they have no wish to prosecute anyone for the harmless act of killing Jews. Now that almost all the Jews in Europe are dead, no one cares."

Debbie sagged. She was both Catholic and Polish, and Mr. G. knew that. "I'm sorry. Do you want me to leave?"

He ignored her comment. "What frightens me, Debbie, is that I'm learning to hate after all these years of trying to be a good Jew and not make waves. The war is over but the killing goes on. Now I am convinced that it will never stop for Jews so long as we have to live with non-Jews." He caught the hurt look on her face but did not back off. "I know what others say about me, and the fact of your working here. They say I'm not a bad man even though I'm a Jew, don't they?"

Debbie recalled some of her parents' comments about Jews. Some of their comments were quite harsh. Jews had killed Christ. Jews cheated. Jews were kikes with funny noses. "What about the four?" she asked.

"Three young men and one young woman. The two men are from my wife's side, and the others, a brother and a sister, from mine. The two from my wife's side have already made it to Palestine, while the others are in internment camps in France. The young woman, by the way, was forced to be a prostitute for the German soldiers, even though sexual relations between Jews and non-Jews was forbidden according to Nazi law. Tell me, what is the difference between a concentration camp and an internment camp? Nothing. If you are inside, surrounded by barbed wire, and you don't have the freedom to leave, there is no difference at all."

"What are you going to do?"

"Do?" He glared at her and she realized she had never seen Mr. Ginsberg so angry. "Do? I'm going to get the two in France out of those goddamned camps and over here if they wish. They can't get to Palestine because the British are afraid of offending the Arabs so they won't let any more Jews in, and they certainly won't be safe if they try to return to their homes. No, I will try to bring them here. Then I'm going to work for a separate state for my people, and the hell with the gentiles and the Arabs and anyone who stands in our way."

Debbie stood as well. "Do you want me to leave?" she repeated.

Mr. G. nodded sadly. "I think it would be best." She put on her coat and was headed for the door when he interrupted her. "Debbie, please give me a little time to get over the worst of this."

She smiled slightly. "Of course."

"Good," he sighed. "I will call you, and very soon. I am very fond of you and would not wish to lose your friendship. I also think I will need your help with the paperwork to bring my people over here.

And I will continue to pray for your Paul's safe return. Now, on your way out, would you please get those two fools from across the street and tell them to start selling furniture. They are Jews too, thereby proving that even a Jew can be a fool, and I will wish to talk with them about my plans."

■

CHAPTER 23

Bound hand and foot and blindfolded, Chambers woke up, helpless and immobile. His worst fears had come true; he had been recaptured by the Japanese. He moaned in fear and he heard a slight rustling.

"Listen to me and be quiet," a low, deep voice said, speaking almost into his ear. "You're wrapped up like this for your own protection. There are Jap soldiers only a couple of hundred yards from here, and neither of us wants to draw their attention, do we? Stay still. Do you understand that?"

Dennis nodded and tried to grunt a yes through the gag. Then he realized that the voice had spoken English. Hell, was he hallucinating? Or was he a prisoner and this was all part of some devious Japanese trick? His mind whirled in confusion.

After a period of further silence, he heard, perhaps felt, the presence of the other man. "Okay, Mr. Chambers, nothing has changed. You are still in very great danger and I will not hesitate to leave you here if you are so stupid as to do anything to draw attention to yourself. For that matter, I will leave you if we are discovered even if it isn't your fault. Is that clearly understood?"

"Umph," Dennis grunted, and nodded vigorously. He was delighted at the sound of the other man's voice. The accent was clearly American. That meant that his captor was another escaped prisoner and not a Japanese.

"You are dumber than shit, you know," the other man said as he removed the gag. "You should never have taken on those four Japs in your weakened condition, no matter how drunk they were and no matter how desperate your situation might have been. If I hadn't been right nearby and wondering what the hell was going on, you'd be dead by now. They'd have found you and chopped you into little bits of living flesh for killing those two guys."

"Water," Dennis rasped. When a canteen was held to his lips, he gurgled and swallowed. After a moment, his voice returned enough to speak. "What about the blindfold?"

"It comes off when I think you're ready for it to come off."

That didn't make sense to Dennis. "Ready for what? You're an American, aren't you? Take the damn thing off me."

That brought a chuckle. "Yeah, I'm American, but maybe not what you expected in the way of a fellow American. It's not exactly like I'm mom and apple pie."

"When did you escape?"

There was a pause and Dennis heard the other man take a deep breath. He was making a decision. "I didn't escape, Mr. Chambers. I came here by submarine. And I'm not in the military in the strictest sense, I'm with the OSS."

The man was a spy and didn't want his face to be seen. That made sense. If Dennis was discovered, he couldn't possibly describe the other man if he hadn't seen him. Of course he wondered just how a white man could be an effective spy in the land of people whose skin was yellow.

Then the answer hit Dennis like a blow to the stomach, and it was his turn to take a deep breath. "Where're you from?" he asked, switching to his brand of halting Japanese.

"Honolulu" came the answer. The other man sounded amused.

"Were you in the army?"

"Yep. For a while, anyhow."

Dennis smiled. "Bet it was the 442nd, wasn't it?"

"Very good, Mr. Chambers. Now do you understand why I didn't want you to see me right away? It would have scared the hell out of you to wake up and find a real live Jap staring you in the face. You might have started screaming and brought us some unwanted company."

With that Joe removed the blindfold. Dennis blinked and realized it was evening. He wondered how long he'd been out. Then he looked at the one-armed man in the Japanese army uniform who sat across from him. "Jesus Christ."

"Actually, the name is Joe Nomura, although many people do make that mistake. It's my Christlike demeanor."

"You rescued me, didn't you?"

"Right again."

"What did you do with the other two men?"

Nomura paused. "Thanks to you, I had to kill them, Mr. Chambers. I finished what you so foolishly started." He took out a knife and sliced through Dennis's bonds. Dennis wondered if Nomura had killed them with the same knife he was so casually using to free him.

"One man I stabbed and the other I hit on the neck with the side of my hand. If you're not aware of it, it's an ancient Japanese art called karate. Then I stole their food and weapons, which is what you probably had in mind, and then set fire to the planes. A few minutes later, a couple of our navy hotshots flew overhead and strafed the site and probably took credit for my kills." Joe looked at Dennis and saw the other man looking at him curiously. "Oh, how could I kill my fellow Japs? Is that what's bothering you?"

"Something like that."

"Easy. I'm not a Jap. I'm an American. I crossed that bridge a long time ago. Even though I've lived here in Japan for a while, I was born in the U.S. It wasn't an easy decision and it was a long time coming, but I think I've made it correctly. These people here are just too fucking weird for my taste. Tell me, you got any German ancestors?"

"A couple," Dennis replied. "Yeah. You're right, fuck 'em."

Joe Nomura said he had an errand to run. He had to learn some more about a bunch of Japanese soldiers who were down in the valley. Before he disappeared into the deepening night, he offered Dennis a bowl of rice, which he ate voraciously.

Joe left Dennis with a pistol, a 7mm Japanese Nambu, which looked curiously like a German Luger. Joe explained that it was an officer's gun and it was not for protection. Dennis was to stay hidden in the trees and shrubs and wait for Joe's return. On the off chance that he was discovered, or that a Japanese patrol was about to stumble on him, Joe was to try to disappear into the woods. If he did not get away, he was to stick the gun in his mouth and blow his brains out.

"I think," Joe said, "you would find that preferable to what they would do if they captured you. And the gun jams, so don't even think of wasting shots shooting at them. One other thing. I trusted you with the knowledge of my existence. Believe me when I say I did that very reluctantly. I am much more important alive than you are, is that clearly understood?"

"Yes."

How could Dennis argue with any of that logic? He fondled the pistol and wondered if he had the willpower to kill himself. Yet, even with the fear of death far from removed, he felt a lot better. He was no longer alone.

It didn't even bother Dennis that Nomura had made it clear that he, and not Dennis, was in total charge of this two-man operation. For the first time in a while, Dennis Chambers began to think it really possible that he would survive this ordeal.

CHAPTER 24

Harry Truman sat on a plain wooden chair and looked about. "Tell me, General Marshall, did you know this room existed?"

As always, Marshall answered truthfully, no matter how much it discomfited the still new president. "Yes, sir. I've known about it since it was put in, even been here a few times, but most people, even those pretty high up, have no need to know about it."

They were in the White House map room on the ground level of the White House. It was directly across the hall from the elevator that went to the president's private quarters. The walls of the room were covered with maps, many of them from the National Geographic Society, and the windows had been covered with dark paper to provide its occupants with a degree of privacy. Normally it was staffed by officers whose job it was to keep up-to-date the symbols on the maps that showed the progress of the war. For the duration of this meeting between himself and Marshall, Truman had chased the staff out.

"It was almost two weeks after I'd become president that I learned of this place," Truman mused. "FDR would take the elevator to this level and wheel himself in almost daily and be able to keep track of things. Imagine, it was going on in the White House for almost four years and most people, myself included, were wholly unaware it existed. Makes sense that FDR would have something like this, though. I wonder how many other secrets I still don't know about."

"No more, I would hope. Certainly nothing major," Marshall said truthfully.

Truman swiveled in the chair. "Now, tell me about that damned typhoon."

"And about the atomic bomb, sir, and not much of the news I've got is good news."

Truman laughed, which startled Marshall. "It never is, General, it never is, and no one can accuse you of being a fair-weather sycophant—no pun intended. Well, give me the truth. I can stand it."

The typhoon had done extensive damage on Okinawa. The resulting injuries and loss of life were small, but a great deal of the equipment being gathered on and around Okinawa was destroyed or seriously damaged. Literally hundreds of aircraft were demolished and many others damaged. Large numbers of valuable landing craft were either sunk or damaged. The larger ships had been able to get to sea and ride out the storm without too much difficulty, although a large number of carrier planes were destroyed or damaged. Mother Nature had handed the navy a devastating defeat.

The men on Okinawa were without equipment, and many didn't even have a complete uniform to wear. Everything they owned was blown out to sea. Even though most of the staging for the invasion was in the Philippines and elsewhere, the need to refurbish and replace what was lost on Okinawa would definitely delay the invasion of Japan.

Supplies stockpiled to replace those lost in the invasion would have to be used to resupply the half-naked men on Okinawa. The invasion would be delayed, perhaps as long as a month.

"November fifteenth," Truman said. "Sooner if you can do it."

While the fighting would doubtless be raging during the Christmas season, the president didn't want an invasion too close to that date, Marshall knew. He would expedite the resupply of the forces on Okinawa even if it meant accepting the risk of running short at some time during the campaign.

"Now, do you have any other bad news for me?"

"Sir, it is highly unlikely that we will use atomic bombs during or after the invasion."

"What now?" This was too much. Were there any uses for that weapon?

"Sir, we no longer believe it is a viable tactical weapon for use against Japan in either Olympic or Coronet."

Truman looked at Marshall in disbelief. "Why?" he asked simply.

"Mr. President, the radiation threat is too great to be ignored. We had naïvely thought that we could use A-bombs to blast our way through Jap frontline defenses and push our men on into the interior of Kyushu and elsewhere. Now it turns out that our boys would not be able to go through those areas because of lingering radiation, which is still causing people in Japan to sicken and die. Further, the mushroom cloud itself is an uncontrollable variable that could easily sweep over our men and ships, causing great harm, even deaths. The prevailing winds over Kyushu blow from the north to the south in the winter. Therefore, any atomic cloud would be swept over the beaches and out to sea, and possibly over our fleet. Our men would be contaminated with falling radioactive dust, rain, and debris. The ships can simply be hosed down by properly dressed personnel, but the men on the beaches would have no such option.

"Sir, the scientists are going to detonate at least a couple of our bombs and make controlled experiments regarding radiation. We simply need to know more about it before we continue. On the other hand, if the Japanese are so foolish as to mass their forces inland, then we will bomb them, but those are the only circumstances I can foresee in which we would use an atomic bomb."

The comment about the drifting mushroom cloud brought Truman back to grim and nearly forgotten memories of gas warfare in World War I. Back then a sudden change in wind direction could sweep a lethal cloud of gas back to its senders, rather than on to the enemy, and with devastating and unintended consequences.

"I understand what you're saying, General, but are you certain of the danger? After all, wasn't it just a while ago that everyone was so certain that radiation would dissipate quickly?"

"Yes, sir, but now we have more and better information. Our sources are from additional analysis of the area around Alamogordo where the first bomb was exploded, continued intercepted pleas for medical help from Japanese dealing with the problem, messages from neutral diplomats confirming the continuing radiation-related casualties, and, I'm pleased to say, information from an OSS operative we've managed to land on Kyushu."

Truman was intrigued by the last point. "You don't say? I thought both MacArthur and Nimitz didn't want anything to do with the OSS?"

"When confronted with the reality that only the OSS had someone who could infiltrate Japan, Admiral Nimitz changed his mind. I'm not certain MacArthur's been informed."

Truman smiled. "Probably better that he not be."

"Yes, sir. The OSS got a radio response from their man a couple of days ago. They'd just about given him up for lost after the sub sent to deposit him never returned and was presumed lost. He's been wandering about the Nagasaki area and making solid observations."

"How the hell is he getting away with that?" Truman puzzled, then it dawned on him. "Hell, he's a Jap, isn't he?"

"He's an American," Marshall corrected stiffly.

Truman flushed. "That's what I meant. A Japanese American. Good for him."

"Mr. President, Admiral Leahy and others are not unhappy that we may have no further use for the atomic bomb. They've felt all along that it is an immoral weapon that should never have been used on a civilian target, and that Christian nations should never wage war on civilians, whether nuclear or conventional. They feel we should never intentionally allow ourselves to sink to the level of the barbarians lest we become ones ourselves. I believe Admiral Leahy even used the word 'unchivalrous' in connection with the bomb."

Truman privately wondered just what about modern war Leahy actually considered chivalrous.

"General Marshall, I respect the opinions of Leahy and others, and I personally deplore the carnage the bombs have wrought. But we will use any weapons we have that will help end this war, General. I will not concern myself with what might be construed as being chivalrous."

"I understand, sir."

"I want this war over as soon as possible and with as few American casualties as possible."

Truman excused himself. He had a splitting headache and wanted to lie down. Then he wanted to make himself a stiff drink.

•

CHAPTER 25

Paul Morrell's new fatigue uniform itched. After all the training he and the others had gone through before the typhoon, he was simply unused to the feel of something new. At least, he thought grimly, it stood a chance of not wearing out before the time came to actually land on Japan. He just hoped he'd last as long as the fatigues.

And that time, they were all convinced, was going to come soon, real soon. The army had made Herculean efforts to replace all their missing gear and had largely succeeded. Everywhere he looked, he could see nothing but new material—uniforms, vehicles, tents, and the miscellany of other supplies that an army needs. In a way, the typhoon had done them all a favor by forcing the army to replace worn gear. It had been astonishing how fast it had happened too. In only a couple of days, they were partially refitted and were completely reequipped within a week and a half. It made Paul wonder just how great were the warehouses and resources that could perform such a task so quickly and so efficiently.

Captain Ruger's company had gathered on a hill at the southernmost tip of Okinawa. It was becoming difficult to realize that a war had been fought there only a couple of short months before. Shell craters were being covered by grasses and young shrubs as nature sought to take back what was rightfully hers from the destructive interlopers. In a few years, visitors might have a hard time finding places where their sons had fought and died.

But not yet. Nature had not succeeded in entirely covering man's devastating tracks. In many places the walls of destroyed houses and flattened villages stood as stark reminders to the enormous conflict. Wrecked vehicles of all kinds, including a surprising number of tanks, lay about in disarray. This time, there were no Japanese bodies.

Captain Ruger stood on a rock to look over his now lean and grim-faced company. "Do you know where we are, men?"

The question was rhetorical and no one answered. For a moment, Paul was afraid of a smart-ass comment from one of his men, but none materialized. This was too obviously a place of agony, and the ground on which they stood had soaked up American blood as well as Japanese.

"This," Ruger continued, "is the spot where the last Japanese soldiers on Okinawa died. They were out of ammunition, starving, and many of them were sick or wounded, but they still fought on. They would not surrender."

The men understood. If the Japanese would let themselves be killed instead of surrendering on a crummy place like Okinawa, what the hell would they do on Kyushu? It was a sobering thought.

"Men, there are some who say the only reason the Japs all died is because they couldn't retreat any farther, and that, for them, this was the end of their world."

Paul looked down the hill where a deceptively calm Pacific sent low waves crashing against the rocks of the shore. The last Japs on Okinawa had died on a point of land that was directed south, and not even north toward Japan. Each agonizing moment and step had taken them farther away from their homeland. He wondered what their last thoughts were. Had they been proud and defiant at the end, or had they been too sick and scared even to think at all? What the hell would he think of under similar circumstances?

Ruger held up a Japanese rifle. It was the Arisaka Model 38. It had a bolt action, a permanent magazine, and a five-round clip. It was not considered equivalent to the M1 Garand or the M1 carbine. The Garand was a semiautomatic, while the new version of the carbine could fire full-automatic. The Garand had an eight-round clip and the carbine a fifteen. A number of Americans were still armed with Thompson submachine guns, which had twenty-round clips. The infamous "tommy gun" had been only slightly modified from the Al Capone days for use by the army. Each squad had at least one Browning automatic rifle in its arsenal, and the BAR was almost the equivalent of a machine gun. The Japanese were outgunned.

By comparison, the Japanese Arisaka was so poorly made that

it even rattled when carried. In the right hands, however, it was deadly.

Ruger waved the rifle around so that all could see it clearly. Paul wondered whose souvenir it was. "Think of it," Ruger shouted. "They were even willing to die with only this piece of shit to protect them, but"—he paused for effect—"die they did." He gestured to a lanky buck sergeant who had been taking this in with bemused silence. The sergeant, a stranger to the company, had a large white bandage over his left ear and seemed to have a trembling in his left hand.

Ruger gestured the sergeant forward. "Men, this is Sergeant Gleason. He will tell you a few things about this place and the Japanese."

Sergeant Gleason shuffled his feet. He looked about twenty-two and was obviously uncomfortable addressing a large body of men. Finally, he grinned tentatively. "Your first sergeant talked me into coming out here and seeing if I could help you fellas. Actually, he said he'd rip my fucking other ear off if I didn't show up, and I kinda believed him since he was my drill sergeant in basic a few years ago."

The rumble of nervous laughter seemed to give Gleason some confidence. "Fellas, I spent a month fighting for this god-awful part of God's earth, and I lost a lot of friends. I also lost my ear, and I was kind of fond of that too. I'm going to go home in a little bit, but you guys are going to have to take over from people like me. Now, some of what I'm going to tell you already know, but don't be pissed off. I'm just trying to help.

"When I arrived here, my platoon had thirty-five men and I was a PFC. When we pulled out, there was just eight of us. I was a sergeant and was in charge of the platoon because everybody else was dead or badly wounded. The ear was infected and I was going to lose it and some of my hearing, but I didn't know that at the time. It doesn't matter anyhow. I'm just goddamn glad to be getting the hell off Okinawa.

"Guys, I just want to remind you how the Japs fight. They don't have any air cover to call in and help them like we do, and they really don't have any artillery, so by rights it shouldn't even be a fair fight. With all our firepower, we should be able to blast their asses right out of our way and walk into Tokyo. Only thing is, they don't know that and they won't cooperate. What they like to do is lay low, take whatever beating they have to from our guns and planes, and then when we're right up close, start fighting. What I'm saying is, they like to wait until we're too close to them to call in air or artillery for fear of hitting ourselves. Then they fight like motherfuckers."

Gleason mentally inventoried the weapons among the assembled men. "I sure as hell am glad that someone has some sense and has gotten you boys a lot more BARs and Thompsons than normal. You're gonna need a lot of short-range firepower when you fight them bastards up close. And don't forget to take all the ammo you can possibly carry because some of the little yellow fucks will stay hidden until you pass by and then try to pick off people carrying supplies up to the lines. When you fight the Japs, there ain't no safety in the rear, so don't close your eyes and don't take nothing for granted.

"And when you shoot them, don't just shoot them once. Do it a dozen times if you have to, 'cause they're like snakes and won't die. You cut off the head of a snake and it'll still try to bite you, and the Japs are just like fucking snakes." Gleason had turned pale and the trembling had spread to his other hand. "You can blow off their arms and legs and they'll still crawl up to you with a grenade in their mouth." His voice had become strident and it was chillingly apparent that he was recalling a specific incident.

Second Lieutenant Marcelli, a recent addition to the unit, was standing by Paul. "Jesus," Marcelli said, "I wonder what the poor son of a bitch dreams of at night."

Paul nodded silently. He wondered what his own dreams would be like if he ever made it back to Michigan.

Mackensen put his hand on Gleason's shoulder, whispered something to the young sergeant. Gleason nodded, paused, and regained some control of himself. "Like I said, I was here, so this place has some real memories. Over there"—he waved with his arm—"is what they're now calling the Cave of the Virgins. You know how it got its name?"

Some did. Paul had heard the rumor, but, as before, no one dared to answer.

Gleason wiped his forehead. He had begun sweating profusely and it was far from warm out. "There were maybe eighty Jap nurses in there, all young women, and a lot of them real pretty. They all killed themselves in that cave rather than be taken alive by Americans. The little fools were convinced we were going to rape and kill them, and then eat their dead bodies." Gleason shuddered. "I went into the cave and saw them. They were all lyin' there with their eyes wide-open and deader'n shit for no reason. Some of them weren't even sixteen."

For a moment it looked as if Sergeant Gleason wasn't going to say anything more. Then he pointed to a place on the hill where they were assembled. A large pile of rocks looked as if they had been freshly gathered and placed there.

"Behind them rocks," Gleason added, "was another cave. This one didn't have no virgins in it, just Jap soldiers. Maybe there was some civilians farther back, but I never saw them. The Japs fired at us from the mouth of the cave and we shot in. There used to be an overhang, so our artillery and planes couldn't get at it, although they tried like hell. When we got close enough, we used flamethrowers, but they just went farther back in the cave and came back out when we stopped to see if they were dead. After a while, we gave up shooting at them and dynamited the overhang so that it fell into the mouth of the cave and sealed it up. End of Japs, end of problem."

Paul gasped. The Japs had been buried alive! Everyone in the company with even the slightest hint of claustrophobia felt sickened at the prospect of being sealed in a cave with nothing to do but wait in the total darkness for the oxygen to run out. Paul wondered whether he would have killed himself or would have gone mad first if he had been sealed in a cave for all eternity.

Gleason stepped over to the pile and patted a large rock. "Who knows, maybe some of them are still alive in there. We don't know how deep those caves are, and how much air there might be. Maybe they can sorta hear us talking about them. Maybe they're digging their way out right now after living on the flesh of their dead comrades and drinking their blood for their thirst."

The men looked nervously at the ground as if expecting skeletal hands to emerge and grab them.

"Sergeant Gleason," Ruger asked, "how many would you say were in this cave?"

Gleason shrugged. "Couldn't tell at all. Only saw the ones who were shooting at us. Could've been a few, could've been hundreds."

"And were there other caves around here, Sergeant?"

Gleason nodded. "Lotsa caves, sir. Caves all over this fucking place and a lot of Japs now buried in them too, sir."

Captain Ruger dismissed Sergeant Gleason, who was gently led away by Mackensen. Once again, Ruger climbed on his rock.

"Men, I had Sergeant Gleason tell you his story for a reason. Our training is over, and we're now going back to camp and begin to pack and get organized to ship out. We've only a couple of days left before we're on a boat heading towards Japan. I want you to know I'm proud of you and the effort you've all put in. Let's get moving."

As the men trudged down the hill in a ragged column, Paul knew that he was more afraid of the unknown than he had ever been in his life. When he looked at the faces of his comrades, he could see that same fear reflected in theirs as well.

■

CHAPTER 26

Dennis Chambers reveled in the unaccustomed delight of eating C rations and ignored Joe Nomura's laughing at him.

"If you don't mind," Joe said, "I'll stick with rice. I've had enough of government food to last a while."

Dennis sighed and munched on a cracker. He'd already devoured the meat portion—whatever it was had been a vast improvement on insects and the occasional rodent—and was saving both the chocolate bar and hard candy for dessert. He'd had to drink the instant coffee cold, but it was still wonderful, as was the powdered lemonade, which contained vitamin C. Already he could feel his gums getting better as his mild case of scurvy was defeated.

After the food, maybe the best part of the C-ration package was the toilet paper, although the cigarettes came in a close second. He never was a heavy smoker, but being able to wipe his behind with something soft was an incredible delight.

After only a couple of days, Dennis felt his strength and health truly returning. Joe had helped make a proper shelter against the weather, which had now turned rainy. It wasn't the Waldorf-Astoria, but it was much drier and warmer than what he'd had either in the POW camp or on the hill where he'd first hidden.

Dennis now knew that Joe had no intention of telling him where he went when he disappeared on his patrols, and he'd also not shown Dennis where the radio and other supplies were cached. That was fine. If captured, he couldn't divulge what he didn't know. Dennis did wonder if the Japs would believe his tale, under torture, of a one-armed Japanese American spying on them. He knew that Nomura had laid a good deal of his own safety and future on the line for a man he didn't really know.

For the foreseeable future, Dennis was content to be able to survive. From what Nomura told him and from what he'd heard before being shot down, the invasion of Japan would happen real soon. He would wait for that day and grow strong. He would return to Barb and they would live happily ever after, he thought with a laugh.

"Enough," said Joe. He wiped scraps of food from his face with his hand.

"How 'bout a drink?" asked Dennis.

"When I come back, but you help yourself, okay? Just don't get drunk."

Joe was right. When Dennis had first had a couple of swallows of the Scotch they'd taken from the Jap pilots, it had nearly knocked him out. "I'll wait." He grinned. "I never did like drinking alone."

Dennis again settled into the shrubs to wait. Something was happening down in the nearby camps, and Joe was trying to confirm it. Joe was upset enough that he didn't even mention what it was he'd noticed, although, upon reflection, Dennis thought it likely that it was something else Joe didn't want him to know about. It was, Dennis realized, just another mystery he would have to deal with.

Part Two

THE INVASION PLAN

■

General Anami had been drunk for a while. The other two senior officers, more recently arrived at the command bunker, were still relatively sober. The Americans were coming and it had reached the point where the generals and admirals could not prevent a landing. It would be up to the soldiers and sailors of Nippon to destroy the invaders. In a way it was a relief.

Anami waved his hand to get their attention as they gathered about the table in the safety of the bunker. His gesture was impolite, but the others ignored the breach of etiquette.

"Kyushu," the general said with only the hint of a slur in his voice. "It will be Kyushu. Of that there is no doubt."

General Anami did not necessarily see such confidence in his declaration in the eyes of the others. Admiral Toyoda was openly worried, and Field Marshal Sugiyama looked away when he heard the statement. They were all thinking the same thing: the right decision meant Japan had a chance of ultimate victory, but the wrong one would result in total disaster and an end to the Japan they revered. They had focused on defending the island of Kyushu, but now they had doubts.

"But what if we are wrong," Toyoda wondered aloud. "If the Americans choose to attack elsewhere, such as Korea, Shikoku, or, God forbid, the Kanto Plain outside Tokyo itself, we would be hard-pressed to stop them. Indeed, we would never stop them."

Anami slapped the table with the flat of his hand. The sharp noise made the others wince. "Kyushu. It will only be Kyushu! Nothing else makes sense. We know how the Americans fight. They are cowards who depend on the weight of their supplies to overwhelm us, instead of fighting at close range like warriors should. For this they need bases and air cover. For them to attack Shikoku or the Kanto Plain would be for them to ignore those needs. No, they will not attack Tokyo without supply depots and land-based air cover. Like us, the Americans are out of options."

Anami chuckled. "I recall that the late and revered Admiral Yamamoto liked to play the American game of poker, which he learned during his tour of duty at our embassy in Washington. I also recall that he taught it to us."

Admiral Toyoda smiled at the memory. "I lost a great deal of money to Yamamoto in a vain attempt to master that game."

Anami wondered what the great Yamamoto would have recommended they do in a situation such as this. He had the uncomfortable feeling that Yamamoto, the architect of the attack on Pearl Harbor, would have counseled surrender. Yamamoto was one of a number of commanders who had worn the cloak of Bushido lightly. It was as if his years in the United States had softened him. Perhaps it was better for their sacred cause that Yamamoto lived on only in memory.

Anami sighed. "To use another American saying, we must play the cards we've been dealt. We are in desperate straits, but we still have some good cards in our hand. First, they must come to us and fight on our homelands, which our military will defend with every drop of blood in their veins. Second, we know exactly what they will do and when they will do it."

The others nodded reluctant agreement. Their actions had been based on a briefing by the brilliant Maj. Eizo Hori of the General Staff. Hori, legendary as a result of his earlier assessments of American intentions, had forecasted the attacks on Iwo Jima, Saipan, and Okinawa with stunning clarity. Japan's tragedy was that she'd been unable to do anything to stop them.

This time would be different. Hori had determined that Kyushu, and only Kyushu, would be the target of the first American assault, and that the attack would occur after October, when the typhoon season was considered over. Hori had then traveled to Kyushu and interviewed Lt. Gen. Isamu Yokoyama, the commander of the Sixteenth Military District, which comprised Kyushu. He had then hiked the paths and traveled over the stark beaches of the forbidding island.

Hori concluded that the Americans were going to attack in only three places, and that they would attack more than one of them at a time in an attempt to overwhelm the Japanese defenders. The three places were the west side of the Satsuma Peninsula, Ariake Bay on the east side of Kyushu, and the land south of the city of Miyazaki, which was also on the eastern part of the island. No other places made sense. America's goals would be to establish bases in the bays of Kagoshima and Ariake and use them to launch a final assault on the Kanto Plain. Once lodged on Kyushu, the Americans would be almost impossible to dislodge. Thus, it was absolutely essential that they be defeated before securing bases on Kyushu.

Hori's logic convinced both Anami and Yokoyama, who subsequently developed their plans based on those assessments. Anami and the others had seen nothing to change their minds in the ensuing months. All American efforts hinted at by intelligence sources that allegedly aimed at Formosa or Korea, or anywhere else for that matter, were dismissed as feints. The landings would come on Kyushu, and they would come soon. Already there were reports that large American forces had left the Philippines and that others would soon leave Okinawa.

General Sugiyama sipped his drink. "General Yokoyama has deployed fifty-two thousand men to repel landings on the Satsuma Peninsula, sixty-one thousand men at Miyazaki, and another fifty-five thousand men at Ariake Bay. Altogether he will defend the coast with sixteen infantry divisions plus a number of fixed coastal brigades as a first line of defense. They will be quickly reinforced by four additional infantry divisions and three tank brigades once the exact strength and direction of the American attacks are ascertained."

"Tanks?" Admiral Toyoda queried with a smile and a suppressed giggle. The small and underarmed Japanese tanks were monumentally inferior to their American counterparts. What armor the Japanese army possessed had worked well against the Chinese, who had even less, but the American Sherman tank outclassed anything the

Japanese had, presuming that Japanese tanks could find their way to the battlefield under the watching eyes of American planes.

"Our tanks," Sugiyama responded with a trace of bitterness, "along with other reinforcements, will move at night to places where they can be dug in and hidden. They will then function as relatively stationary defensive weapons."

"Good," said Toyoda in an attempt to mollify the prickly field marshal.

Sugiyama regained his usual boisterous confidence. "There are now more than six hundred thousand men on Kyushu with more arriving daily. The Americans will be crushed."

Anami nodded. "And what about American airpower?" Far too many of the enormous Japanese army on Kyushu were on the northern part. They would have to travel overland to reach the southern portion where the initial battles would take place.

Sugiyama shrugged dismissively. "Airpower has never yet won a war. Their planes will hinder us, but they will not stop us. As we will do with the tanks, we will make every effort to move our infantry at night, and in small groups if they must travel during the day. That way their planes won't see us. It will make it difficult for us to coordinate any large-scale attacks, but again, it will not stop us. Even now our men are swarming over the hills to the south of Kyushu where the decisive battle will be fought. General Yokoyama will have our men form defensive lines and independent strongpoints rather than waste themselves on piecemeal attacks that would be decimated by overwhelming American firepower. While attack may be the preferred method of fighting for the Japanese soldier, I concur with General Yokoyama that a fierce defense would better serve our poor country."

General Anami agreed. It would be far better for the Americans to impale themselves on Japanese defenses than for it to be the other way around. He had no doubt that the Americans would ultimately be able to force themselves through the first line of defenses on Kyushu. It was only intended that they pay a terrible price for the privilege.

"Admiral?" Anami asked as he turned to the senior naval officer.

Toyoda also reflected confidence. "The Americans will bleed

from a million wounds. We have amassed more than ten thousand kamikaze planes, along with a thousand Ohka piloted rockets. That is more than six times what we used with such devastating effect at Okinawa. The pilots have been instructed to leave the picket ships alone and to go for the troopships and carriers only. They are not to squander themselves on unimportant targets like destroyers and other small ships."

They recalled the efforts wasted on the American picket destroyers at Okinawa. It was reputed that one destroyer, the *Laffey*, had been hit by twenty kamikazes, a total waste of effort. Anami wasn't even certain that the *Laffey* had been sunk after all that effort.

"There are," Toyoda announced proudly, "still more than a dozen destroyers and fifty submarines remaining in our fleet. The destroyers will all attack, as will those submarines not in use ferrying soldiers from Korea or currently on other duties. We have more than four hundred midget submarines as well as thousands of smaller craft which have been equipped with mines, bombs, and torpedoes. While many of the men sailing in them are not true kamikazes, all have pledged to press their attacks with vigor."

"Good," said Anami.

Toyoda bowed at the brief compliment. "As Field Marshal Sugiyama has said, our efforts to launch the attacks and to carry them out will be handicapped by the American planes, but not halted. Our aircraft and naval forces are dispersed and well hidden. We had hoped to be able to launch our attacks on their shipping as one overwhelming wave of planes and ships, but the disruptions to our communications will prevent that. Instead, our forces will attack as they receive the orders to do so. This may be a blessing in disguise as the result will be many days of continuous warfare, which will strain and exhaust the Americans at the most critical time of the battle."

It was reality, Anami concluded, and his companions had adapted to it. "General Sugiyama, how about your plans to arm the civilian population?"

Sugiyama flushed slightly. "It has not gone well. There are some units forming, but not in the numbers we expected. We are dismayed by the defeatism within the civilian population. When the bombers come over, more and more civilians are putting out white flags of surrender, as if"—he snorted derisively—"the bombers could see them. There are so many civilians waving white flags that our police have almost given up trying to stop them. General Yokoyama feels they would be a hindrance in battle and I have deferred to his judgment. On the other hand, he is using tens of thousands of civilians to dig defenses, carry supplies overland, and to staff hospitals. What weapons we have are being given to infantry newly arrived from Korea, many of whom have lost so much in escaping from the mainland. Those few civilians who have volunteered to fight are being given bamboo spears and taught how to make Molotov cocktails."

Again, Anami accepted the reality. The bulk of the population of Japan were not warriors, not samurai, and had been shocked and terrified by the devastation the war had brought them. The economic fabric of Japan had been torn apart. People no longer went to work; instead, they spent their time in hiding and almost never emerged. It was up to men like himself to save them.

"The Americans are weak," Anami added softly. "Their economy is in ruins and their army is ready to mutiny. Why else would they cancel the rationing of civilian goods, and why else would they release their best warriors and return them to civilian life? No, the United States is severely weakened and needs only a push before its will to fight disintegrates. Because they have released so many soldiers, we will be fighting their second and third best, many of whom have no combat experience. Their better soldiers have had their fill of us and are running home. These are more reasons why we will win this battle and save Japan!" he added vehemently.

"But what about the Russians?" Sugiyama asked. A quick glance at the map showed that Soviet forces were well south of the Yalu in Korea and were on the verge of taking the city of Pyongyang, while other Red armies were driving into the heart of China. Amphibious forces of the Red Army had taken the Kuril Islands and Sakhalin Island to the north of the island of Hokkaido. Those islands, however, had not been heavily defended. This did not stop the assaults from shocking the Anami government. As a result, additional forces had been sent northward to defend Hokkaido from similar landings. It had also forced the Japanese to reassess their situation with regard to the Soviets.

"The Russians," Anami said with a sneer, "are paying the price of their treachery. Already they are running out of supplies, and a Siberian winter is beginning to blanket them in ice and snow. Do not worry about the Russians. Stalin's frozen and hungry legions are not going to be a factor in the coming battle."

And so much more was going on with Stalin. At Anami's direction, Foreign Minister Hideki Tojo was working wonders with the most subtle of negotiations. With only the slightest good fortune, there would be some unpleasant diplomatic and military surprises for the Americans as the despised Soviets were being extremely cooperative. Anami thought that the Soviets also wanted the Americans to bleed profusely.

Anami took another sip of the cheap, harsh whiskey that was all that remained of what had once been a magnificent supply. But they would be stopped, he swore.

The Decisive Battle would begin shortly. The storm that had swept the Pacific and caused so much damage on Okinawa had delayed the inevitable invasion but not stopped it. Yet, every day the invasion was delayed had brought additional strength and numbers to the defenders of Kyushu. What a magnificent thing it would be, Anami thought, surging with pride, if the typhoon turned out to be yet another divine wind, a true kamikaze.

•

CHAPTER 28

*A*s always, Commander Hashimoto let no hint of any emotion show on his face as he stood in the conning tower of the I-58. Inwardly, he was churning. He wanted to yell at the confused soldiers who had spilled out of the hatches and onto his deck. They looked like fish escaping from a torn net. He wanted them to hurry even faster than they were, for every instant spent on the surface and so close to land was fraught with peril. Even seconds too long could mean death. He silently cursed.

As with the other transits, this too had been a litany of confusion and even horror as one soldier, confined in a submarine that was under the ocean and jammed full of sweating, stinking bodies, had gone mad and been bludgeoned to death. It could not be helped. Ferrying soldiers from Korea to Kyushu by submarine was the only way their arrival could reasonably be assured. The I-58 had made a score of those trips between Korea and Kyushu and, by Hashimoto's count, had delivered more than fifteen hundred frontline soldiers to fight the coming of the Americans.

The routine was simple. The I-58 would surface in the night off the Korean coast and south of the city of Pusan. Small boats would stream out from the shore and deposit as many soldiers as the I-58 could hold. That most were without weapons or other equipment meant that more could be squeezed in. Once loaded, the I-58 would submerge and make the 150-mile journey to Kyushu. Sometimes they would pause at Tshushima Island, a rough midway point in their journey, and surface to clear the air that the presence of so many bodies had fouled. The I-58 had been refitted with a German air-breathing device called a *schnorchel*, but it was barely adequate under normal circumstances, and the additional men simply over-whelmed the *schnorchel*'s abilities.

When they arrived at the night-darkened coast of Kyushu, the soldiers would be off-loaded onto yet another swarm of small boats and taken ashore where they would get new equipment. From there they would be sent southward to stem the anticipated onslaught.

While Hashimoto recognized the need to do this, he resented that his submarine had been forced to act as a transport and not as a weapon. He knew it was as a result of his using two of the precious *kaiten* human torpedoes against that damned American sub. In retro-spect, he realized that he should not have given in to the wails of the young volunteers and should have saved them for a more significant target, such as a carrier, and used conventional torpedoes against the American sub. He had been rebuked for his actions, and the assign-ment as an underwater ferryboat captain had been his punishment.

Thank God, his stint in purgatory was about to end. Or it would as soon as the last of the soldiers stumbled and bumbled their way off his boat and onto the small craft. Thankfully, they were being quiet. While the likelihood of voices carrying over water to where an American patrol boat might be lurking was small, it was not a chance he was prepared to take. The soldiers had been ordered to maintain silence under penalty of death.

Hashimoto saw his lookouts straining, staring into the darkness to try to detect even the slightest hint of motion. If they saw any-thing, the I-58 would submerge immediately, even if that meant that some of the soldiers were lost.

Many of the larger American planes had radar and would, upon registering a contact, drop flares and use searchlights to pin a target. Then they would strafe with machine guns and drop depth charges to sink the target. Since the I-58 was in relatively shallow water, a sudden attack would be fatal, as he could not dive deeply to get away. Hashimoto had a submariner's dread of being submerged so close to the surface as to be visible to an enemy plane.

Hashimoto saw an army officer heading toward the conning tower. It was the commander of the army unit. What the hell did the man want?

"Captain, I wish to thank you for bringing us safely home."

Hashimoto wanted to tell the man to shut up and get the fuck off his ship, but he forced himself to be polite. The officer wheeled and stepped briskly onto the last of the small craft. En route, the officer had told an interesting story. He claimed that he and his men had actually passed safely through the Russian lines on their way to the Pusan area. Most interesting if it was true. But then, the officer was quite young and most likely confused. The Russians were Japan's enemies, and not her allies.

Hashimoto ordered the hatches closed, and the I-58, free of its cargo, turned its nose toward the sea and safety.

"The last time," Hashimoto muttered, and a few heads turned at the sound of his voice. No one dared to ask what he was talking about.

Hashimoto gave the order to dive and went to his cramped cabin, where he sat down at his small desk and examined the piece of paper on which his radio operator had written his new orders. His hands shook slightly as he reread the orders. The I-58 was to proceed with all prudent haste to a position off southern Kyushu. There, American ships were gathering for the invasion. His orders concluded with the simple phrase that he was to attack and destroy any and all targets of opportunity, but with special emphasis on carriers and troop transports.

For the first time in weeks, Hashimoto smiled. The orders had told him he could return to base and get additional supplies if that was necessary. He had thought about it briefly, but decided against it. He was safest under the sea and not alongside a dock at some navy base that was subject to bombing. No, he would proceed directly to the waters off southern Kyushu. He had food and water for several weeks normal cruising and could extend that by cutting back on rations. He had a full complement of Type 95 torpedoes. He did not have any of the distracting *kaiten* on this trip and didn't want them.

Targets of opportunity, the orders said. The I-58 and her sisters were free to roam and kill as they wished. Instead of working as ferries, they were to be sharks, predators of the sea. It was glorious, as was the phrase *targets of opportunity*. It was a submariner's dream and he vowed to live it to the fullest.

■

CHAPTER 29

With more than a thousand men and many tons of their equipment jammed onto the attack transport USS *Luce,* Morrell found it more comfortable to be on the deck than below in their cramped sleeping quarters. In this he was joined by hundreds of others, who, after several days afloat, found the accumulated stenches from belowdecks a little difficult to take.

Several days of puking and sweating had turned the interior of the *Luce* into something of a putrid garbage dump. No lights were permitted on deck, not even cigarettes, and Paul wondered if Jap pilots could really see the ship from the glow of a bunch of cigarettes. Maybe they could, but it probably was an unnecessary precaution. Even solely with starlight, he could see the shapes of other ships in the convoy.

Another, more primal force drove the men to the decks. They approached ever closer to Japan each time the *Luce*'s bow surged into the choppy November waves. They all knew that death might strike at them at any moment, just as it was striking at those who were going before them. Along with the so-far-unseen suicide planes, Japanese submarines were presumed to be nearby, and no one wanted to be inside a ship as it sank into the depths of the Pacific. They would much prefer to take their chances on the cold waters of the ocean, rather than a downward plunge in a seven-thousand-ton steel coffin. Most of the soldiers had decided that the risk of being struck by a kamikaze while on the decks of the *Luce* was the lesser of evils.

Paul shifted his aching buttocks on the cold metal of the deck. There was a chill in the November air, but it wasn't really cold yet. If only he had a pillow or a cushion to sit on, things would really be okay. He reached into his pocket and pulled out his wallet, which he opened to the photo of Debbie. He could barely see her face in the stiffly formal studio picture she'd sent him. The face that looked up at him really wasn't her. It didn't show her laughing, or flashing that silly grin he liked so much, and it didn't capture anything of her personality. It didn't smell at all like her, and it sure as hell didn't feel like her, and the portrait was from the shoulders up so it didn't show any of the slender but delightful body he liked to hold.

But it was the only thing he had to remember her by and it triggered rushes of memories that almost caused tears to well up in his eyes.

"Nice-looking girl, Paul. Gonna marry her?"

It was Captain Ruger. Paul laughed reluctantly, folded his wallet, and put it back in its waterproof pouch. At least he hoped it was waterproof. "I hope so. If I get back, that is." Then he corrected himself. "I mean, when I get back."

Ruger sat down beside him and watched as a couple of soldiers edged by them. Right now their biggest danger came from being stepped on, not from the Japanese.

"I just put my wife and kids' picture away too. It hurts a lot to look at it, but I had to at least one last time. I guess everyone on this slow ship to nowhere feels that same way."

They had spent their last days on Okinawa packing their gear for the journey and spending their empty nights trying to forget about it. In what some felt was a macabre salute to the departing soldiers, there'd been USO shows galore to lighten their emotional burden. Bob Hope did arrive and brought Jerry Colonna and Frances Langford with him. Danny Kaye was there and so was Kate Smith. In just a few days they got more entertainment than many could handle, although that didn't stop some GIs with a warped sense of humor from announcing that Glenn Miller would be appearing at a particular field. This resulted in several hundred men waiting patiently at the designated place for the arrival of a man who had been killed a year earlier over the English Channel.

Finally, they had been taken out to the attack transport *Luce,* where they had, once again, waited. When they did move out to sea, it was to join a vast convoy. Comments were made about being able to walk across the rows and rows of ships all the way to Japan without getting their feet wet.

During the daylight hours they saw the destroyers and other escort ships dipping in and out of the endless lines of transports and herding them like sheepdogs keeping the wolves away.

Then the convoy slowed and almost stopped. Word went through the ship that the invasion had started. This was quickly confirmed by the *Luce*'s captain, who read an announcement to that effect to the soldiers and crew. On hearing it, a few men had cheered, while some others wept. The majority responded in grim, almost prayerful silence. Now any hopes they'd been harboring that they would not have to take part in the ordeal were dashed. Their turn to land on Japanese shores could come at any time.

"You take care of everything like I told you?" Ruger asked.

"I did. I told the men that if something happened to you, I was taking over the company and that Sergeant Collins would be responsible for the platoon. Or if something happened to me, for that matter, it was still Collins. I ran down a complete chain of command involving all the NCOs and made certain they knew just who was next in line."

"How'd they take it?"

Paul laughed softly. "It went okay until the PFCs got into the act and figured out that Private Randolph was the most junior man in the platoon. Randolph then said if he was ever in charge of the platoon, he was taking it and him home right away and fuck the war."

Ruger chuckled in the night. It never ceased to amaze him how men found humor in the darkest of situations. The black humor showed that morale was fairly high. "Good for them. You told them to make wills?"

"Yeah, but most of them didn't. They said it's bad luck to make a will on the eve of a battle. I didn't, either. I rationalized my way out of it by deciding I didn't have anything to leave anyone."

And I really don't, Paul thought grimly. What the hell kind of a mark will I have left on this world if some Jap shoots me? No wife, no kids, nothing. My parents would mourn for me and Debbie would too, but, after a while, life would go on. My parents would go about their own lives, and Debbie would find someone else. God, she would have to. She had a life to lead. At least his parents were older, almost fifty. He had written Debbie and told her not to waste herself on his memory in case he got killed, and that he wanted her to live a life that was full, whether it was with him or not. He'd started to cry while writing it.

"I did write some last letters, though," Paul said. "If worse comes, they'll know that I loved them."

Ruger nodded and Paul realized it was difficult for the other man to speak. Ruger had kids and a wife. Maybe it was better not to have family like that.

Finally, Ruger recovered his voice. "Everyone's writing letters. Are you censoring them?"

"Hell no!" Paul snapped. "I don't want to read what may be their last words. Besides, what kind of secrets could they give away? Dear Mom and Dad, I'm on a transport and we're headed for Japan and—oh, by the way—I'm scared shitless. Sure as hell aren't any secrets in a letter like that, are there?"

Ruger smiled in the darkness. "Agreed, and that's one of the little reasons you're my heir apparent. I actually had to tell young Lieutenant Marcelli to lay off reading the men's letters for just that reason. Let them know they have privacy. I put you in for first lieutenant, but I don't expect you'll get the promotion officially before this is over."

Paul muttered his thanks. "What happens now, Captain? When do we go in?"

Ruger took a deep breath and watched it mist as he exhaled. "Word is that the first waves have been mauled pretty badly, a lot worse than expected. That means we could be landing as early as tomorrow. I guess they're trying to figure out exactly where."

"Jesus." He'd been hoping for a few days, maybe even a week before going ashore.

"Yeah. We all should be getting a good night's rest, but I think that's kind of impossible under the circumstances. I can't imagine anybody able to sleep much this night."

Paul felt his heart race and he tasted a surge of bile. "Whatever you do, don't let them hurry us in on my account."

Ruger stood and looked over the railing. The captain was staring in the direction of Japan, and a distinct glow was now on the horizon. The ship and the entire convoy had been zigzagging, and the motion was enough to cause a standing man to sway, but they were still moving inexorably closer to Japan.

"Is that the battle?" Paul asked in wonderment.

Ruger gripped the railing. The *Luce* had changed course again, and their bodies tilted slightly. Ships always zigzagged now. What had happened to the cruiser *Indianapolis* when she had failed to do so was on the minds of everyone. She'd been sunk with enormous loss of life by one Jap sub.

"It sure ain't the dawn," Ruger said hoarsely. His throat was suddenly dry. "That would arrive from the other direction. Yeah," he said, still in little more than a whisper, "it's the landings. We're moving slowly but still getting closer with every minute."

Paul stood and walked the couple of steps to the railing. Others had seen the strange light in the distance, and the rail was soon lined with silent men straining to look and listen. The light, an orange-reddish glow, seemed to flicker slightly, and the men became aware of a dull, rolling, thundering sound. Guns. They could hear the big guns from the ships.

"Before I saw you sitting here," Ruger said softly, "I went up top as far as I could in this tub and I saw the lights from off in the distance. Funny thing about a ship, you can see for twenty miles, maybe more. I just stared at it until someone from the crew asked me to get down."

"The fires of hell," Paul rasped. Now the quivering light extended for miles in each direction, painting numerous ships in its satanic glow. "How far away from Japan do you figure we are?"

"Maybe fifty miles. Maybe a little less."

Suddenly, light flashed above them, followed by the booming sound of an explosion. In the flaring light of the explosion a plane disintegrated and fell into the sea in flaming pieces, some only a few hundred feet away. Men pointed and yelled at the sight.

"Oh my God," gasped Paul.

"I think we just saw our first suicide attacker, and it looks like one of our planes got him."

The decks of the *Luce* bristled with 20mm and 40mm Oerlikon antiaircraft guns, whose crews strained to see in the night skies. What would have happened if the Jap hadn't been seen by the American pilot? Both men shuddered and concluded that there was no safety on the USS *Luce,* or anywhere else in the world.

Lines of tracers from other ships illuminated the night as gunners sought out targets that neither Paul nor Ruger could see. A helmeted sailor ran by and told the soldiers to get their asses belowdecks. A few complied, but most remained on the deck. They would take their chances where they were.

The *Luce*'s antiaircraft guns added to the angry, deadly chatter. Still, no one could see what the guns were shooting at. Paul and Ruger crouched on the deck. All around them, men removed their boots and some of their clothing in case they were plunged into the water. They could hear yelling and screaming from below.

"Jesus Christ," Ruger yelled, "we'd better get down and try to calm them." He turned and raced toward the sound of the tumult. They didn't want a hysterical mob on their hands.

There was another burst of light. A ship was on fire about a mile away as a kamikaze drew blood. Then another ship was hit as more kamikazes struck home, and both wounded vessels became plumes of flame. What if those ships were full of men like the *Luce*? How many hundreds were dead or wounded in what had to be a pair of charnel houses? He caught the silhouette of a destroyer against the flames as it raced toward one of the stricken ships to pick up survivors.

Oh, God, he moaned again as he headed below to escape the carnage.

CHAPTER 30

.

The young and disturbingly neat *kempei* officer stood at attention, looking elsewhere and avoiding eye contact, but was otherwise undaunted as Col. Tadashi Sakei vented his wrath.

"It is inconceivable that you have been unable to find one radio and one spy with all the resources at your disposal. It is even further inconceivable that you have been taken off the assignment. Is it your commander's intention that the traitor wander about Kyushu until he dies of old age?"

The lieutenant wasn't sure just who was going to die of old age, the spy or his commander, but decided it would be imprudent to ask. "Sir, the invasion in the south has forced us to reassess our priorities in light of our capabilities. There are far too many civilians who wish to surrender, and there have been some desertions from the army."

Sakei was aghast. Weakness from civilians he could understand, but Japanese soldiers running from the enemy? Never! But then he recalled that many of the men now in Japan's army were new soldiers, very young, and not well trained. With that in mind, he concluded that he should not be surprised that many were not imbued with dedication to the code of Bushido.

Sakei shook his head in disgust. "So, you gave up on the spy."

"Not entirely, Colonel. While my captain is of the firm opinion that we will never be able to find the spy with the detection gear we now have, we will not cease looking. But we have given up on using technology to locate the clandestine radio. We will have to wait for him to make a mistake."

Sakei rubbed his forehead. He had a savage headache. There had been many of those lately. "Again, tell me why."

"Colonel, we need three pieces of directional information to locate a transmitter, which is, of course, why the method is called triangulation. One or two will only give us a long line, and the traitor could be broadcasting from anywhere along that line, which could conceivably stretch around the earth. Three sources is an absolute necessity, and we must have them before the spy's radio is moved. We have been able to get one, sometimes two positions, but never three because the hills and valleys block the signal. The roads are so miserable that we cannot get our trucks with the triangulation gear out into the valleys to set up for that third source.

"To be truthful, sir, triangulation works best in an urban environment, not the countryside. The spy transmits in short bursts, rarely more than a couple of minutes each time, and it takes us hours to set up, if we are able to get out into the field in the first place. By then, he is always off the air well before we can establish meaningful contact. He is cunning and never broadcasts from the same location. The best we've been able to do is identify a fifty-square-mile area in which he is operating."

Sakei took a deep breath to control himself. Even though he'd like to strangle the insolent and pompous *kempei* puppy, he was telling the truth. They would find the spy when he made a mistake, and not sooner. He reassured himself with the knowledge that most people in such a situation would make a mistake sooner or later. Sakei could only hope the mistake occurred before the war ended.

"Are you still able to translate his messages?"

The officer beamed, delighted to change the subject. "Indeed, sir. He is still using the very simple code he started with, and we now suspect it's the only one he has. Moreover he is rotating his frequencies on a predictable basis. Again, we think he was given only a few to work with, so we are able to anticipate him and listen to his transmissions.

"Sir, the spy continues to give the Americans information about our food resources, the medical conditions in the area, and the units and numbers of men coming through the area. We think he was a soldier because he uses a soldier's terminology and comments on their condition and weapons rather skillfully. There are those who suspect that the spy is an American from the phrases he uses, but it may be a Japanese citizen who spent some time in the United States."

Sakei agreed with that possibility, although he still wondered at the spy's place of origin. More and more he too had wondered if the spy actually was a Japanese. He recalled that many Japanese had emigrated to the United States in the years and decades past. Could one of them be the spy? he asked the *kempei* lieutenant.

"Yes, Colonel, it could. We believe there are a number of people of Japanese descent working for the Americans. That would tie in with the spy's comments about a submarine that was sunk. We weren't certain whether it brought him, or his supplies, or both. He seems to have picked up an accomplice as well. He informed his contacts that someone was with him by running off a string of numbers. As we now have an index of all American POWs, we were able to identify the numbers as belonging to an American officer we'd thought had been killed in the Nagasaki bombing. He must have survived and then run off into the hills in the ensuing confusion. If so, he was lucky. Mobs have caught other Americans and ripped them to pieces."

The lieutenant added that he thought that the last bit of information was both good and bad news. Bad because he now had two people on the run and two to search for. Two could help each other and stand guard over each other. But the news was also good, because at least one of the two was likely a Caucasian, a white-skinned gaijin. Those few whites who remained free in Japan were diplomats from neutral countries. They were kept near their diplomatic postings in Tokyo, unless they were taken out on a carefully guided venture to see some American atrocity. Thus, any white-skinned American would, as they themselves said, stick out like a sore thumb. The spy would have great difficulty hiding his companion.

Sakei stood and dismissed the lieutenant, who disappeared gratefully. Sakei then walked to a connecting tent where Emperor Hirohito was held.

"Well," said the emperor, "still unable to find your spy?"

"He will be caught," Sakei replied stiffly.

"And the American invasion, what further news on that?"

"It is my understanding that our defenses are holding and that counterattacks are taking place."

Hirohito smiled grimly. "In other words, the Americans have

landed successfully and the Japanese army has been unable to drive them off. General Anami must be proud of what he has brought to Japan."

Sakei did not respond. Hirohito's assessment was correct. The Americans had landed the day before in overwhelming force and were inching their way inland despite brutal losses. The coastal defenses had been breached in many places and would soon be overrun. It was grimly apparent that, in only a few days, far too many Americans would have landed to be dislodged without an enormous effort. He wondered if Japan was capable of that effort. He shook the defeatist thought from his mind.

"Your Majesty, the Americans are paying dearly for the privilege of desecrating our land. As to driving them off, the landings started only yesterday. It will take time to accumulate our army and attack."

"I don't doubt that. I just wonder what good it will do."

So did Sakei, and the thought astounded him. Americans were on Japanese soil, and Japanese soldiers were starting to run. It struck him that his world could be ending.

"Majesty, in the speech you never made to the country—the one in which you counseled surrender?—you used a phrase to the effect that we would have to endure the unendurable. Well, it is General Anami's intent to force the Americans to endure what is not endurable so that they depart our lands and leave us in peace."

"At least the bombings have ceased."

Sakei agreed. Even though the tent compound that housed the emperor was in a clearly marked hospital area, there was always the threat of attack from the air. Sakei had taken great pains to ensure that his now much smaller number of guards dressed like hospital orderlies and that nothing threatening or unusual was apparent from the air. Even so, there was the constant fear of an American pilot making a mistake, an accidental bombing, or some hotheaded Yank just wanting to kill Japs and not caring if it was a hospital in his sights.

Therefore, everyone was thankful that the landings had drawn virtually all the American planes southward to protect their ships and men. Even the giant bombers seemed to have vanished. Both men wondered just how long the relative calm would continue.

Should the American planes return, it would mean that the landings had been so successful that the Americans on the ground no longer needed such constant protection. Sakei tried to visualize the titanic battles taking place just a little more than 150 miles away.

Sakei bowed and left his unrepentant emperor. If the planes returned, it might mean that he would again have to move the emperor to yet another safe place. He did not relish that thought at all. He'd been lucky so far, but how much longer could that luck last?

■

CHAPTER 31

Dark smoke half-obscured the harsh hills of Kyushu from the men who again lined the rails of the *Luce*. Clouds from fires and recent explosions billowed skyward, and the men on the crowded transport could see individual explosions where shells impacted on targets farther inland. Rumblings of man-made thunder, occasionally punctuated by sharper, cracking sounds, buffeted them constantly. It was as if Kyushu were alive and angry.

It had been a sleepless night for the men on the *Luce*. The incipient panic had halted and the men had calmed down. Most then spent the rest of their time mentally trying to prepare for the ordeal ahead. Sardonically, most had decided they would rather face Japanese guns than trust the dubious safety of the *Luce* as the nightlong battle between the kamikazes and the navy had turned more ships into flaming ruins.

When the LCIs hadn't arrived for them by midmorning, the men began to chafe and wonder, even hope that their landing had been canceled. The delays were agonizing.

To a man, they hoped that the daylight hours would be free from more kamikaze attacks, but the white lines in the skies told them otherwise. Above the low clouds, contrails twisted and crossed each other as American planes continued to seek out their suicidal enemy.

Then, suddenly, the guns on a nearby ship would open up at a diving plane. Soldiers would gape and pray as streams of shells sought out the dark blot in the sky that was the Jap plane. A kamikaze who'd made it that far was a survivor who had somehow penetrated the fighter defenses only to face being blown out of the sky by shipborne guns. When a suicide plane was hit, it either exploded into pieces or had a wing ripped off, which caused the plane to cartwheel out of control and into the ocean. When that occurred, the men cheered.

Sometimes, however, an enemy plane got through, and as they waited, another transport took a hit. They watched in horror as flames billowed from the ship. The stricken ship quickly launched lifeboats, and hundreds of soldiers tried to escape the inferno by jumping into the sea. It looked like an anthill that had been disturbed, only those were people, not ants. The *Luce* did not change course. Picking up survivors was the job of the destroyers and their smaller cousins, the destroyer escorts.

"Get me ashore," Paul muttered, and shook as he watched men's heads disappear forever beneath the waves. "Please, God, get me off this ship."

At long last, the landing craft arrived and the men clambered awkwardly down cargo nets. One man screamed and fell into the boat. He grabbed his leg and began to writhe and moan. A medic checked him quickly and turned to Captain Ruger.

"His ankle's broken, Captain. We gotta get him to a hospital ship."

Ruger was coldly furious. "Bullshit. I saw that cowardly little motherfucker let go and fall intentionally. He stays where he is."

The soldier in question was wide-eyed with fear and pain, and the medic was confused. "What do I do with him, sir? I gotta treat him."

Paul had heard of people hurting themselves intentionally to avoid going into combat, even shooting themselves, but he'd never seen it before. He wondered if Ruger was correct in his judgment.

"That sorry son of a bitch is going with us to Japan," Ruger snarled. "When we get there, you drag his ass out onto the ground and leave him there. If he's lucky, somebody'll take pity on him and take him to a field hospital. But there's no way that little shit is going to sleep on a bed with clean sheets while the rest of us are fighting Japs."

That brought an angry growl from the rest of the men, and the LCIs were quickly filled. The injured man whimpered that he didn't want to go, which seemed to confirm Ruger's assessment, but he otherwise stayed quiet.

The LCIs formed a large circle as they waited for all of them to be loaded, and men got sick as they bobbed in the choppy water, and the stink of vomit was added to the scent of fear. Finally, the little boats were lined up with the others that had loaded their human cargo from other transports, and the whole line headed inshore.

As they drew closer to land, Paul peeked over the edge of the boat and looked at Japan. The steep hills seemed to spring directly from the sea. They were scarred and torn, with most of their vegetation blown away or burned off. He could see ruined vehicles and other unidentifiable things that burned fiercely.

As they passed through a line of warships, they tried to identify them. The only one they were certain of was the battleship *West Virginia*. When her sixteen-inch guns fired at some distant target, the blast was deafening, and it was as if the whole ocean quivered like an earthquake. Despite the shaking they took from the sound of the firing, many were cheered by the sight of the old battlewagon pounding Japan. The *West Virginia* had been mauled and sunk at Pearl Harbor and, like most of the others sunk in that catastrophe, had been refloated and given an opportunity to take revenge. The *Wee-Vee,* as she was affectionately known, was happily complying.

"Lookit!" one of the men yelled. Paul followed the soldier's outstretched arm and saw a body floating facedown in the water. Then he saw another, and another. All were Americans. "Aw, Jesus," said someone, who began retching.

"Get your fucking heads down!" yelled the ensign in charge of the LCI as it turned sharply to avoid something. An anonymous voice exclaimed that it was a mine. Bullets clanged against the hull and someone screamed. Paul turned and saw a sailor crumple to the deck. Blood gushed from his massive stomach wound. A medic rushed to help him, but the ensign only glanced briefly at his fallen crewman. His eyes stayed fixed on the dangerous waters and the task of navigating toward the shore.

Sergeant Collins stared at the wounded man. "Jesus, Lieutenant, I thought we owned at least part of this place. What the hell's going on?"

Paul shook his head in disbelief. If the landing forces were still taking small-arms fire a full day after the initial assault, just what had actually been accomplished?

Paul pushed his way through the packed men to the ensign. From the scars on the LCI, she seemed to have made several trips to the Japanese shore. "Is it always this bad?"

Without looking at him, the naval officer laughed harshly. "Bad? Hell, buddy, this trip is a piece of cake. You should've been here yesterday when they threw all kinds of shit at us. I've made four trips in, and this is by far the easiest. I've heard that most of the guys in the first waves were wiped out and that half the people who went ashore yesterday are dead or wounded. If you're real lucky, you guys might even make it onto land before you get killed."

Finally, the ensign glanced down, and Paul saw the ensign was even younger than he was. "The sailor who just got shot is a replacement for another guy who got killed yesterday," the ensign said more gently. "Look to your left."

Paul did as he was told and saw a capsized LCI, and others that were bobbing, half-sunk, in the waves. Some were abandoned and burning, with bodies still in them. The sick-sweet stink of burning flesh was heavy in the air, and Paul gagged.

As they approached the shore, Paul called for all the men to check their gear one last time. A couple of them sank to their knees in prayer while others lowered their heads and moaned. More bullets clattered against the LCI, and a shell landed close by, spraying them with water and metal splinters, but neither caused casualties.

Finally, they felt the landing craft's flat hull scrape against the bottom. The ramp dropped quickly and the men ran through knee-deep water and up onto the steeply rising land. Jesus Christ, Paul thought with horrified disbelief as he clambered uphill, I'm in Japan!

Before the men's headlong rush could slow, a sergeant with an armband that designated him a beachmaster popped out of a foxhole and yelled at them to follow him.

"Move it!" he hollered. "Move fast or you're gonna stay here forever."

The platoon needed no further motivation. The beachmasters owned the landing sites, and regardless of rank they were to be obeyed without any hesitation. The platoon ran like furies where he directed them. Other LCIs had disgorged their human cargoes, and other beachmasters guided their reluctant flocks upward and inland.

Paul ran with his troops toward a series of long, narrow trenches cut in the side of the hill. The beachmaster herded them in. On the way, they saw more dead. The majority had been badly mauled or burned, with parts of bodies strewn about with ghastly abandon.

Paul saw the disconnected head of an American soldier that appeared to be staring at the sky in some amazement. He'd seen the results of violent death in Germany and thought himself somewhat battle-hardened, but this was death on a scale that dwarfed his experiences and threatened to overwhelm his senses.

Inside the trench, Paul got himself under some semblance of control and checked his men. Four were missing.

He turned to the beachmaster sergeant, who was breathing heavily and staring at the glowing end of a cigarette. "Four of my guys are missing, Sarge. Shit, we've just gotten here and I've lost four men!"

The beachmaster shook his head. "Maybe not, Lieutenant. There's a lot of confusion. More'n likely they just got lost or rubbed off onto somebody else's unit. If they're okay, they'll show up. If not"—he shrugged—"then there's nothing you can do about it anyhow."

He offered a smoke, which Paul accepted gratefully. His cigarettes had gotten wet. "Sarge, I thought we owned this place, or at least part of it," Paul commented, unconsciously repeating Collins's earlier comment.

"We thought we did too. But the Japs infiltrated back last night and set up shop with snipers and small mortars. That's why graves registration hasn't cleaned up the beach yet. Ain't no sense in getting killed trying to save a dead body. If we keep our heads down, we're safe from the snipers, and it would take a direct hit on the trench to cause any damage from the mortars. The Japs've got some bigger guns shooting indirect fire on us, but the navy's doing a good job of putting them out of business when they do open up.

"This is bad," the sergeant continued, "but it ain't nothing like yesterday, Lieutenant, nothing like it at all. Yesterday was all flying metal and GIs screaming as guys died. The Japs had troops in bunkers near the water that had to be burned out with flamethrowers. Sometimes a Jap would pop out from behind us and throw a grenade. Lieutenant, this is a walk in the park."

Paul took a deep breath and felt the smoke from the Chesterfield scorch his lungs. It felt good. As he smoked, two of his lost lambs sheepishly reported in. As the beachmaster had guessed, they'd run off the beach with the wrong group of GIs. The other two arrived a couple of moments later, shaken but okay. Paul took another drag on his cigarette.

"How far away's the front?" he asked the beachmaster. After all, the man was a veteran who'd been there a whole day and a night.

The sergeant looked about nervously. "Between ten feet and a mile. Kinda depends on who's counting and measuring. Snipers and infiltrators can be anywhere, so keep your guard up at all times. The big front's about a mile away. You're gonna see it real soon."

Morrell finished the cigarette and threw the butt away. I'm in Japan, he again thought in disbelief. I'm in Japan and thousands of Japanese are going to try and kill me. He looked at his men and saw similar fears reflected on their pale and frightened faces. He had landed and his platoon hadn't yet lost a man. It couldn't continue that way. The devastation in the ocean and on the shores told him that their turn was coming. And all he had to do was survive it.

CHAPTER 32

■

Marshall arrived at the White House with Gen. Omar Bradley in tow. Bradley, who had returned from Europe a few months earlier to take charge of the recently formed Veterans Administration, felt ill at ease in the White House. As a result of his new appointment, he no longer considered himself a full-time military man, and he found the change unsettling. The VA assignment was a chore Bradley had taken on with great reluctance.

Bradley thought it was incongruous to be worried about assimilating returning veterans when a climactic campaign was under way in Japan. Earlier in the year he had led a million and a half men into battle against the Nazis, and he felt he should still be their commander. However, his president had thought otherwise, and the lanky, popular, fifty-two-year-old West Point graduate had complied with the wishes of his commander in chief.

Bradley had grudgingly obeyed. He was also mildly concerned by Marshall's admonition that he should listen rather than comment during the meeting with Truman. It was what he would have done anyhow. Not only was he the junior member of the trio, but he had little knowledge of what was transpiring in the Pacific. He knew the general plans, of course, but not the details.

A few moments later, Admiral Leahy arrived and greeted the others with formal cordiality. He seemed surprised at Bradley's inclusion, which did nothing for Bradley's state of mind.

Truman bade the men to sit around a small table. He waved a piece of paper in their direction. "Gentlemen, I certainly hope you can shed more light on the situation than this imperious little pronouncement from General MacArthur does."

Marshall smiled tightly. The pronouncement had gone out from

MacArthur's headquarters and to all members of the press as well as the White House. It was almost as if the president were included on the distribution list as an afterthought.

The message itself was painfully short: "On the morning of November 10, 1945, American ground forces under the command of General Douglas MacArthur commenced landings at several points on the shores of Kyushu, the southernmost of the four main Japanese home islands. Even though confronting stiff, and at times fanatical, resistance, General MacArthur's armies are pushing steadily inland. With God's blessing and through the bravery of our young men, we pray that the will of the United States will prevail."

Truman laid the paper on the table and looked about in exasperation. "This doesn't tell me a damned thing about the battle. It's a press release, nothing more. It also implies that only the army is fighting and ignores the efforts of the navy and, once again, the marines."

The latter issue was a sore point. The navy was separately commanded by Nimitz and could take care of its own press releases. On the other hand, MacArthur commanded three divisions of marines, who technically belonged to the navy but who were under his control for this campaign. The marines had landed on the southwestern side of the island while the army assaulted the southeastern part, and all were involved in bitter fighting. By implication, MacArthur had snubbed the marines.

He had done this before. Earlier in the war when the various units that had fought for him at Bataan and Corregidor were recommended by him for citations, he had left out the 4th Marine Regiment. The men of the 4th had fought with incredible bravery and had endured terrible casualties before ultimately having to surrender along with the other forces under Wainwright's Philippines command. When questioned, MacArthur had said that the marines already had enough medals. The intentional oversight had been corrected in Washington.

"Typical of that fella MacArthur," Marshall said, using his favorite phrase for MacArthur. It was not a compliment. He'd seen the statement before and concurred with Truman's assessment. "General Krueger is the field commander in charge of the Sixth Army, but you'd never know it from this statement."

"General," snapped Truman, "I really don't care how eccentric MacArthur is, or even if his ego is bigger than mine, just so long as he wins and wins quickly. Unfortunately, this scrap of paper doesn't tell me a damned thing. What is going on in Japan? Are we indeed pushing inland, and what are the costs?"

Marshall grimaced. "The landings are a little more than two days old and there is still an enormous amount of confusion. I can, however, tell you what we do know. At all three main landing sites, some penetrations have been made in the Japanese defenses for distances up to two miles. In other cases we are still stuck near the shore and the Japs are defending their positions furiously. It is going about as we figured. We do not have a beachhead in any depth, and we have not yet established a continuous front from which we can break out from the beachhead. At best that will take several more days."

"Casualties?" Truman asked softly.

"These are not firm figures," Marshall responded, "but we suffered between twenty-five and thirty thousand on the first day with between seven and eight thousand on the second. The first day of an attack such as this is always the worst. If history is our guide, about a third of the casualties will be dead or dying."

Truman moaned softly and looked toward the ceiling. In two days the United States had lost the equivalent of more than two divisions, almost an entire corps. No wonder putting the reserve forces in as soon as possible was urgent. The number of dead and wounded was far in excess of those suffered during the landings at Normandy in June 1944. But then, as he'd been reminded so often, the attacks on Kyushu were much greater in scope.

"MacArthur said the Japs would break," Truman said softly. "Has that happened?"

Marshall shook his head, while Bradley gazed in silence at a map on the wall. "No, sir, and in all fairness to General MacArthur, it is far too early to expect that to happen. There are some signs that the resistance will not be as fanatic as it has been in the past. In a few instances there have been withdrawals, and a small number of Japanese soldiers have actually surrendered. Only a couple of hundred so far, but it's a trickle that might someday become a flood. We think it's attributable to both the war-weariness of the rank and file, as well as to the poor quality of training that the newer conscripts have been getting."

"Lord, I hope so."

"Mr. President," Leahy injected, "are you aware that General MacArthur commands from the heavy cruiser *Augusta,* and that he is off Kyushu?"

Truman smiled tightly. "Yes, Admiral King informed me that the old warhorse had essentially commandeered the cruiser. King wasn't surprised and I agreed with him that there was no reason to deny Mac his ship. We certainly have enough of them. There was no way that MacArthur felt he could fight this battle from the safety of Manila, or even Guam." To their surprise, Truman chuckled. "And I can even see why he insisted on the *Augusta.* After all, it was the ship both FDR and I sailed on when we went to Europe. Hell, if it was good enough for two presidents of the United States, then it might just be okay for General Douglas MacArthur and his friends."

Both generals and Admiral Leahy smiled at the additional reference to MacArthur's monumental ego.

"Like I said," Truman added, "I really don't care how strange he acts and what he needs for his personal comforts just so long as he wins." He turned to Leahy. "Now, did you get anything from Admiral King regarding suicide attacks?"

Leahy would rather that King have delivered the information himself, but the other admiral was now trying to find additional transport shipping to send to the Pacific and had asked Leahy to carry the news. King's absence pointed out the desperate situation the navy was in.

"Mr. President," Leahy began, "over fifty ships have been hit by various types of suicide attacks, which include airplanes, small boats armed with torpedoes and dynamite, suicide midget submarines, manned torpedoes launched from rails that run to the water, and just about anything else they can think of to throw at us. Two of our larger carriers, the *Ticonderoga* and the brand-new *Tarawa,* have been badly damaged and have been pulled out of the battle. They may have to return to the U.S. to be repaired. One escort carrier has been sunk, and five others so badly mauled they are no longer serviceable."

"In just two days?" Truman gasped.

"Yes, sir. The rest of the damage was done almost entirely to our transports. As we feared, the Japs are concentrating on the carriers and the transports, and virtually ignoring the other ships. One troopship was hit by a suicide plane and badly damaged while it still had all its troops on board. There were more than five hundred casualties in that one incident alone, with many dead."

"Awful," Truman said, "just awful. Admiral, why didn't radar pick up the plane?"

"Sir, radar is good but far from perfect. Not all of our ships even have it, and it breaks down a lot. Then, with all the planes that are in the air at all times, the operators get fatigued and overwhelmed with information that can't be deciphered fast enough. With all that going on, they can't determine who is friend and who is foe. Last, the very way radar beams out in its searches leaves gaps. Low-flying planes will often get through and must be spotted visually."

Truman nodded bitterly. Yet another military marvel was proving itself to be astonishingly fallible. "If we've lost so many, how about the Japs?"

Marshall spoke. "We are confident that the preinvasion bombing and shelling killed or wounded large numbers. While the day of invasion, X-Day, probably cost us more than them, the Japs are paying for it now and will continue to do so in the long run."

Truman nodded. "And how long can the Japs keep it up?"

Marshall looked to see if Leahy wanted to add anything. The admiral did not. "Probably for quite some time. They appear to have more troops on Kyushu than we thought they did, and they continue to be able to feed more into the battle. They are coming across the mountains of central Kyushu in numerous but widely dispersed small groups that are virtually impossible to see by air, much less hit. There are a score of these rough trails and almost twenty thousand men a day can make it overland from northern Kyushu to the battle area."

"And," Leahy injected, "we are dead certain they are still able to bring reinforcements from both Korea and the main island of Honshu. They are using submarines as transports from Korea, and our intelligence estimates say they can bring over about two thousand men each day that way. During bad weather, which is getting more and more frequent as winter gets closer, they are attempting surface runs with troopships.

"Additionally, the straits between Honshu and Kyushu are only a mile wide at their narrowest, which means small boats can swarm across at night, take casualties from mines and planes, and still land a lot of men. During bad weather they are virtually unstoppable because they can't be seen."

"What about using our surface ships?" Truman asked.

"Sir," Leahy said, "using surface ships in the waters north of Kyushu or in the straits makes them terribly vulnerable to attacks by kamikazes. We have some of our own subs looking in the area, but bad weather hinders them as well."

"Mr. President," Marshall added, "through radio intercepts and our source on the ground, we've identified a number of divisions now on Kyushu as those that had been manning the defenses outside Tokyo. This supports our contention that the war will be won or lost for the Japanese on Kyushu. This is consistent with their doctrine of fighting the one Decisive Battle that will give them victory. But there is something very disturbing going on."

Truman looked at Marshall. The whole thing was disturbing. What else could be going wrong? "And?"

"Sir, it looks like some of the Japanese units coming across from Korea are passing through Russian defense lines to get there."

Truman sat bolt upright. "What?"

Marshall walked to a map of China and Korea. "When the Reds came in, in August, they launched a two-pronged attack. One quickly headed south into Korea, where it has stalled around the city of Seoul. This was no surprise to us. Northern Korea is really just an extension of Siberia. In a short while the weather will turn miserable and everything will freeze. The Russians will soon have a devil of a time keeping their very large army supplied and fueled over the totally inadequate Trans-Siberian Railway.

"The second prong headed south through Manchuria and into China to help Chiang and Mao Tse-tung fight the Japs there. Chiang has been complaining that the Russians are helping Mao fight the Chinese Nationalists rather than the Japs, but we've all felt it was Chiang exaggerating again."

To some, Chiang was highly unloved and considered capable of many duplicities to get additional American material help, which would then be stolen or used to fight the Communists and not the Japanese. It stood to reason that the Russian Communists would be far more helpful to the Chinese Communists than they would to the Nationalists, who were foes of the Communists.

"Go on," said Truman.

"Sir, it may just be the vastness of China and Manchuria that is permitting bypassed Japanese units to filter through the Russian armies, but I believe it is something that should be watched carefully."

Truman said it would be, rose, and dismissed the meeting. Leahy left separately, while Marshall and Bradley drove off together. As their staff car headed down Constitution Avenue in the direction of Arlington, the two generals rode in silence. Finally, Bradley broke the spell.

"General Marshall, why did you have me attend that meeting?"

Marshall turned away and did not answer.

Bradley persisted, "General, you are never a man to waste time, either yours or anyone else's. While it was most interesting, it has nothing whatsoever to do with my new duties at the Veterans Administration. Therefore, what was the reason?"

Marshall's face was grim. "General Bradley, what did you think of that fella MacArthur's announcement? Did he state a case for his normally overwhelming sense of moral superiority that would end in total and unequivocal victory for him and for us?"

Bradley thought back over the precise words Mac had used. He hadn't tried to memorize the message, but he felt he recalled the sense of the short document.

"No," Bradley responded quietly, "it was less than his usual splendid rhetoric, and there were some big ifs implied in it. If I recall correctly, the gist of it was that he prayed for victory, but did not guarantee it."

"Exactly. General MacArthur started out this summer by saying the invasion of Kyushu would be a cakewalk, and that the Japs would run and quit. Now he's saying we should win, but we just might not. He's finally admitting there are a lot more Japs on Kyushu than anyone dared admit to him, and that the situation could be quite grave. Tell me, General Bradley, what's the largest army Mac's ever commanded?"

The question puzzled Bradley. "Maybe half a million in the Philippines last year. No, the Philippine campaign was smaller than that. Maybe three hundred thousand."

"Yes, and now he has more than twice that. And don't forget he's sixty-five years old, the same age as I am. It's the time where most people are thinking of retirement, not commanding vast armies in major campaigns. God knows I wonder if I could do what he is trying to do."

Marshall grimaced in distaste. "Also, he thinks both Ike and I hate him because of the things he's said about us earlier in our careers. As a result, he thinks I left him and his army out to dry in Bataan in 1942. I am more and more convinced that MacArthur thinks everyone in Washington and the Pentagon is out to get him. I can't prove it, but I wonder if the man's paranoid."

"I'm curious," Bradley said. "I know he referred to Ike as the best clerk he'd ever had, but what about you?"

Marshall chuckled briefly. "He said I'd never rise to anything higher than a regimental command. Now, of course, I've got five stars like he does, and he's under my command. Therefore, he thinks I'm out to humiliate him in a quest for revenge."

Bradley smiled. He'd heard the story before, but only through the rumor mill. "That makes him a lousy judge of character, but do you really think he thinks you're out for him?"

Marshall nodded grimly. "Yes, and from 1942 on."

Bradley whistled tunelessly. "And for that reason you think he thinks you've set him up to fail? You're making it sound like we've indeed got an aging paranoid who's in over his head and commanding the American army that just invaded Japan."

Marshall nodded. Bradley sank back in his seat. "Good grief, General, but just where do I come in?"

Marshall looked at him grimly. "General Bradley, I want you to do only the minimum necessary work at the VA. For the next couple of weeks, I want you to learn as much as you can about Operations Downfall and Olympic. The implications are obvious. If MacArthur falters or collapses from the strain, and I feel both are very possible, we'll need someone to step in and take over."

Gen. Omar Bradley looked out the window at the passing Washington scene. They had crossed the Arlington Bridge and were headed toward the Pentagon. Bradley felt as if a tremendous weight had landed on his shoulders and then slid down to the pit of his stomach. He had wanted to be rid of the Veterans Administration assignment and now it seemed he might be relieved of it. But what on earth might he get in return?

Part Three

THE WAVES
ON KYUSHU

•

CHAPTER 33

The angry bark of a rifle sent scores of soldiers sprawling on the ground. "Sniper!" someone yelled, and a fusillade of bullets, this time from American guns, filled the air. There was silence and then someone screamed for a medic.

Lt. Paul Morrell raised himself to his hands and knees and tried to see what had happened. They had been climbing a heavily shrubbed but not particularly steep hill near Miyazaki in Kyushu, and the men had been moving out in skirmish formation when the shot had been fired.

There was motion to Paul's left so he slithered over in that direction. Other prone soldiers grudgingly moved out of his way.

"Over here, Lieutenant." It was Wills, the medic.

There was more firing and Sergeant Collins profanely called for the men to stop. Paul got up and ran hunched over, expecting every second to be shot by the sniper. He made it safely to where Wills was working on a soldier who lay on his back. Paul threw himself down beside the two men.

It was Haskins, a young PFC about twenty. His throat looked as if it had exploded, and Wills was frantically trying to stop the blood that was gushing out over both of them. Paul tried not to look at the ripped and torn cartilage that was exposed just beneath the young man's chin. Haskins's mouth was flapping and it looked as if he was trying to say something; he couldn't, except for a low gurgling. Haskins's eyes fixed on Paul, silently imploring him to get him out of the mess he found himself in.

Paul looked at the medic, who shook his head. "I gave him morphine. A lot of it." A few seconds later, Haskins's eyes glazed over and he stopped breathing. "Nothing I could do, sir," Wills said, and he began to gather up his gear.

"You did your best," Paul said, conscious of the emptiness of the comment.

Wills didn't respond. Nothing would be said about the overdose of morphine that had hastened Haskins's death. Many of the soldiers carried extra morphine to put either themselves or a buddy out of misery in the event of an awful wound. It was something else the people at home didn't know about.

Haskins was the platoon's first fatality since landing on Kyushu almost a week earlier. A couple men had been wounded, but none killed. They'd been fortunate. The powers that directed their lives had kept their battalion as a regimental reserve until earlier in the day. Thus, they'd left reserve status and moved up to the front only a few hours earlier.

Paul moved a few feet away from the dead soldier and sat down in the dirt. He really didn't know Haskins well at all. He'd been a quiet kid who just did what he had to and pretty much stayed out of trouble. He'd been a late arrival to the company and had replaced one of the earlier men who'd been a total screwup. Now, because he was more competent than the dud whose place he'd taken, he was lying dead on the ground with his throat ripped out.

Sergeant Collins flopped down beside Paul. "We got the sniper, sir. Wanna see?"

Paul realized that he did want to see the Jap who'd killed Haskins. "Yeah."

Collins led him up the hill about a hundred yards to where a couple of men stared at the ground. A body lay half out of a hole. The upper torso, riddled with bullets, barely looked human. Leaves and branches jutted from the webbing of the Jap's helmet, part of his camouflage. The man's rifle lay beside him.

Collins kicked at the corpse and it slid back into its hole. "He wasn't very smart. He was pretty well hidden and should have waited until we passed. Then he could have hopped out and shot a couple of us before we got him. I think he panicked."

Wonderful, Paul thought, and shuddered. He hoped none of the

Jap soldiers had the balls to wait while the army had passed by and over them.

Captain Ruger approached and found him deep in thought. "Shake it, Paul. You lost a man. It was your first and it won't be your last."

"I know, Captain. We lost our first American and we just killed our first Jap. That's one for one. Tell me, how many Japs are there on this stinking island?"

"A lot," Ruger said.

"Yeah, just a few minutes on the line and we've got a dead kid. Now I've got to write a letter to his family telling them that he was brave and died both instantly and painlessly, when we all know he was scared to death for several agonizing minutes and flopping like a fish. And all the while he was trying to say something through a hole in his neck that was so big you could stick your fist in it."

Ruger eyed Paul coldly. "You gonna be okay? You've got a right to be upset, but I don't need my second-in-command collapsing on me."

"I won't collapse," Paul said grimly. "This never happened to me, not even when I was in Germany. Of course, the war was almost over so even the krauts were concentrating on staying alive. I had a couple of guys hurt, but it was mainly their own fault. What the hell did Haskins do to get killed like that?"

"He was born," Ruger said, and grasped Paul's shoulder. "Look at the bright side. We took the hill. Only thing, there's another hill right after this, and another one after that."

Paul stood and slung his carbine over his shoulder. "Yeah, and this is supposed to be the gentle part of the terrain around here. What the hell are we gonna do when the ground gets really difficult? You and I both know that there'll be more than one sniper on the next one."

They both turned toward the north. Hill after hill grimly rose in serrated splendor, like so many sword blades waiting to slash them. They were not hills, Paul realized, they were weapons in the Japanese arsenal, and every one of them would have to be disarmed.

CHAPTER 34

*I*t had been Comdr. Mochitsura Hashimoto's fond hope that the submarine I-58 would be able to sneak out and around the flank of the American invasion fleet, then attack transports and carriers through what had to be its more vulnerable rear. After all, wouldn't the eyes, ears, and guns of the Americans be pointed toward Japan and not back in the direction from which they'd come? He admitted to himself that this might be a futile wish, but it was the course he would pursue.

First, the Imperial Navy's submarine command had changed their minds and radioed that he should indeed carry the disliked *kaiten* human torpedoes on his sub when he attacked the American fleet. He had complied without protest. If ever the *kaiten* were going to prove themselves useful, this would be the time.

This necessitated a delay while he sailed to the hidden supply facility and had the four human-piloted torpedoes attached to the deck of the I-58. His sub could have carried six of the strange things, but the specially adapted torpedoes were in short supply. There were more than enough human volunteers to ride them to their doom, but the American raids had severely affected Japan's ability to manufacture the weapons.

Along with torpedoes, Hashimoto thought ruefully, everything else was in short supply. When he asked for supplies, all he received was a litany of unavailable items, including fuel. He was able to top off his tanks, but a harried supply officer informed him that there were no more fuel reserves. So, this would likely be his last cruise. If that proved to be the case, he could end his part in this dreadful war and return home with honor satisfied.

What really dashed his hope for a rearward assault was even more significant than the delays required for the installation of the *kaiten*. The utter vastness of the American fleet precluded any attempt to flank it. His executive officer had bitterly surmised that it would be necessary to sail to Australia to find the American flank. As with many a bitter jest, it held a nugget of truth. The numbers of enemy warships off the coast of Kyushu defied counting. There were more American battleships and carriers off Kyushu than the Japanese navy had ever dreamed of having in their fleet, and they were accompanied by vast hordes of smaller cruisers and destroyers. Truly, the American ability to manufacture weapons had tragically been underestimated by the Japanese government. Even though he would fight bravely, Hashimoto knew that his efforts, even if successful beyond his dreams, would be meaningless when compared with the size of the American fleet.

He hoped that his fellow submariners would have the same type of success that he planned on for the I-58. Cumulatively, perhaps they could affect the outcome of the war. Hashimoto had no delusions regarding the ultimate end to the conflict: Japan was doomed to lose. All he could do was what he'd been ordered to, and that was to help cause so much damage to the Americans that they would negotiate a better peace for Japan. It seemed foolish to him. An earlier peace might have found the Americans in a more forgiving mood. Now they would truly be vindictive.

The I-58 approached the American armada frontally, but submerged and with great stealth. Although Hashimoto's main concern was detection by American sonar, he felt that he still had some advantages. For one thing, the sheer volume of shipping made for inconsistent and cluttered sonar readings as hundreds of ships' screws churned the water and, he hoped, sent confusing information to the sonar operators.

Sonar was a devilish weapon. Ultrasonic waves were radiated out by the sending ship and, when they bounced off an object in the water, announced to the world that a submarine might be calling. At first it was thought that sonar would spell the end of submarine warfare. It had not. Sonar, like radar, was a good but imperfect weapon, with many ways it could be fooled by a cunning submariner, and Hashimoto counted on these imperfections to help him.

The volcanic continental shelf that surrounded Japan extended well out into the Pacific and was as hilly and rugged as the islands it surrounded. This meant that the I-58 could skulk about on the ocean bottom and hide among the irregularities in the ocean floor when her captain felt she might be threatened by surface enemies. A submarine lying inert on the bottom was invisible to sonar.

Periodically, however, the I-58 had come to periscope depth to refresh her air through the snorkel, and to see whether she had made it past the defending American warships through the simple expedient of having them wash over the I-58 as they closed in on Kyushu.

But this had not yet happened. Each time the I-58's periscope had poked above the waves, Hashimoto had seen long rows of destroyers and other antisubmarine craft several miles in the distance. This portion of the American fleet showed no indication that it would be closing on Kyushu anytime soon, and any attempt to penetrate the lines of destroyers would be suicidal.

Commander Hashimoto had no doubts that he would probably soon die for Japan, but he wanted his sacrifice to be worthwhile. He had four of the precious *kaiten* and twenty-four standard Type 95 torpedoes ready to be fired. His orders had been specific—he was to only attack carriers and transports. Other ships were to be left alone.

While he recognized the order as militarily essential, it was also irksome. Although depressed by what he saw as the inevitable outcome of the war, Hashimoto still had a warrior's lust to kill other warships, and while he definitely considered a carrier a warship, he did not extend that title to the fat and sluggish transports. He would have liked nothing more than to loose a spread of torpedoes at the several destroyers currently in his vision. He would sink them as he had the American cruiser *Indianapolis*. The *Indianapolis* had gone down with great loss of life, a fact that saddened him deeply.

He ordered down periscope and stepped away. It was almost dawn and it was no longer difficult to see the enemy ships. He did not dare have the periscope visible for more than a few seconds at a time in the daylight lest some eagle-eyed American lookout see its small ripples running contrary to the wind and the sea.

Lt. Sakuo Yokochi, his second-in-command, looked at him in dismay. "Still nothing, Captain?"

Hashimoto wanted to snap at the man for his foolish question, but merely glared at him until Yokochi turned away. It was so frustrating. There had to be a way through the wall of defenders. The American destroyers were like bees protecting the precious honey in a hive.

A distant rumbling sound rolled over the sub and rocked it, causing some of his men to gasp in surprise. Someone was being fired upon, and Hashimoto concluded that the target was probably one of the numerous midget submarines that were also trying to sink American ships. The Americans were alerted and it would now be a time of great peril for the I-58.

He was about to order the I-58 back down to the bottom when a thought struck him and he smiled. It was indeed a time of great peril, but might it not be a time of great opportunity as well?

"Up periscope," he ordered, and enjoyed seeing the dismay on Yokochi's face. Lieutenant Yokochi was a fool and the type of man who would never had made it to the rank of lieutenant had there not been so many casualties in the navy.

Hashimoto stared through the lens as additional explosions vibrated along the I-58's hull. Someone was getting heavily depth-charged. He felt a momentary twinge of regret for the agonies of his unknown countrymen, but he was more concerned by the possibility that this was his chance to penetrate the American destroyer screen.

He looked at the American destroyers and smiled. Like predators moving in for the kill, the warships were streaking away from the I-58. Two Fletcher-class destroyers positively raced past his view in their haste to join in the fun of the final attack. The result was a gap in their lines. It would only exist for a while, but it did exist at this moment.

"Ha!" he exulted, and ordered the still submerged I-58 toward the gap at flank speed. He ignored the sharp intake of breath from his officers, especially Yokochi. He ordered the periscope down and stood by it with his arms folded across his chest. If any of the American ships did detect him underneath the water with their sonar, the I-58 could be doomed.

Minutes of waiting stretched into eternity. The American line of warships had been only a couple of miles away. He calculated time and speed; they were right where the Americans had been. If his gamble was successful, they would now proceed without incident into the heart of the hive and steal the honey. Hashimoto decided he liked the analogy.

If they'd been detected, or if one of the American ships that had left station realized that a mistake had been made and returned to its place, then the I-58 would likely be located and destroyed.

Further minutes crept by and he willed himself to relax, but not show his surging emotions. The men of the I-58 must believe that their captain had everything under control at all times. Beside him, Yokochi had checked his watch and figured it out as well. He smiled timidly at his captain, who chose not to acknowledge it.

They were past the defenses. Now they were in the heart of the American fleet. It would be full daylight in a little while. Once again the I-58 would lie on the bottom and wait for darkness to return. This time, however, when night fell, the sub would be the hunter and not the hunted. This night Hashimoto would be the predator.

CHAPTER 35

THE USS AUGUSTA,
SOUTH OF KYUSHU

Seaman Tim Jardine rubbed his burning eyes and leaned against the mount of the 40mm antiaircraft gun that was his battle station on the *Augusta*. He was supposed to be resting while others scanned the darkened sea and skies for signs of the Japanese. Everyone on board the nine-thousand-ton heavy cruiser was tired from days of being at their battle stations. It was so bad Tim wondered if they would be capable of fighting if a Jap plane did manage to find them. All he and the others really wanted was to go to sleep and the hell with the Japs.

At least they were able to let some of the men rest and doze while the others watched and waited through the night. He wished he could have a cigarette, but orders were to keep everything as dark as possible.

Jardine caught the shadow of motion behind him and froze. At the last possible second he recognized the famous silhouette and snapped to attention. He was about to salute when Gen. Douglas MacArthur swept by him, unseeing and apparently deep in thought.

Jardine turned to his mates and hissed, "Hey! You guys see that? It was MacArthur, his royal self."

"You mean Dugout Doug in the flesh?" chuckled Carl Haverman, one of Jardine's buddies in the gun mount. A couple of the others laughed softly as well.

Jardine looked at the disappearing figure as MacArthur headed toward the bow of the cruiser. "Shit, I hope he didn't hear you. I got this thing about not insulting five-star generals. Piss one of them off and he can really make your life miserable."

Haverman snorted. "I don't care if he hears us or not. What the hell can he do to us, huh? Hell, he's the reason we're here, ain't he? If it weren't for him fucking up so badly in the Philippines and all over the ocean, we'd all be home by now."

Jardine looked to see if anyone else had heard Haverman's comments. He was particularly concerned that the ensign on duty didn't take offense, but that young man was hunched over in his chair and snoring deeply.

MacArthur was considered a hero by some for his actions, and a bum by others. There was little middle ground. Either you admired the man or you thought he was scum. Jardine tended to admire him, feeling that people didn't get to five-star rank on charm alone. He rubbed his eyes again and tried to rest. In a little while it would be his turn to look into the night and try to differentiate between twinkling stars and a Jap fighter.

Alone on the bow of the *Augusta*, Douglas MacArthur gripped the rail and tried to peer through the night toward Japan. Only the slight glint of starlight off his West Point ring of the class of 1903 was visible.

Although an older man who needed glasses to read, his hearing was excellent and he had heard Haverman's comment calling him Dugout Doug. He had heard it a thousand times before and even seen it in print. It wasn't fair. None of the disasters of late 1941 and early '42 were his fault.

President Franklin Delano Roosevelt had put him in an impossible position, then blamed him when the Japanese had swarmed over the Philippines and caused the surrenders of Bataan and Corregidor along with tens of thousands of American and Philippine troops. Gen. Douglas MacArthur also held the rank of field marshal in the Philippine army. He had wanted to stay with his men of both nations and fight alongside them, perhaps die with them.

Roosevelt would have none of it. There had been too great a risk that MacArthur would have been captured instead of killed, then displayed as a trophy by the Japs. Instead, Roosevelt had ordered

MacArthur to escape to Australia. MacArthur had reluctantly complied and, along with his wife and young son, taken the danger-filled trek across the southern Pacific.

Only when he arrived at Australia did he understand Roosevelt's treachery as augmented by his other enemy, General Marshall. MacArthur's understanding was that he would retain control over the army in the Philippines, but Marshall placed Lt. Gen. Jonathan Wainwright in command. Wainwright had surrendered, not MacArthur. MacArthur had wanted Wainwright to fight on, but Wainwright had received permission from Marshall to surrender not only Bataan and Corregidor, but all of the Philippines. It was outrageous. Some of the land and soldiers surrendered hadn't been threatened and could have held out as armed enclaves for quite some time, perhaps until being reinforced.

Of course, as he later found out, there were to be no reinforcements. Roosevelt had decreed that Nazi Germany was the primary threat to America and that the Pacific war could wait. Instead of an army, MacArthur had been given only handfuls of units and dribbles of reinforcements with which to launch limited and bloody offensives. Even so, he had persevered and won island after island and battle after battle, culminating in the liberation of the Philippines in 1944 and now, the ultimate, the invasion of Japan herself.

For that he was still castigated by some in his army, and by members of the press as Dugout Doug. Worse, what should have been his hour of triumph was rapidly becoming very, very hollow. Vital information had been withheld from him regarding true Japanese numbers and strength on Kyushu. He and his staff hadn't gotten true figures until far too late to change their plans. Thus, his army was now slogging and clawing its way inch by bloody inch into Japan instead of advancing triumphantly through its cities.

Some told him that it was his own staff's fault that he'd been misled, but MacArthur rejected that. Generals Willoughby and Sutherland had been with him through thick and thin, and while they certainly made some human mistakes, they were loyal to him and that was that.

He let go of the rail and began to pace back and forth across the narrow bow of the cruiser. Above him, the three eight-inch guns of the forward turret glowered protection for him as he reviewed the combat situation.

The marines on the west of Kyushu had reached the high ground between their landing sites and the deep waters of Kagoshima Bay. They could now look down into the large, sheltered anchorage, but they had not yet forced the west gate to the bay, and the Japs had dug in to prevent that. To deny Kagoshima Bay to the United States, the Japs only had to hold one side of the gate.

To the east, the two army corps were nowhere near their objectives. Only a few small towns had fallen, and the American navy was still unable to use Ariake Bay. Until Ariake Bay was taken, there could be no port or airfields developed. Without a port, there could be no massive reinforcements of men and equipment. Take Ariake and the army could leapfrog into Kagoshima Bay and join up with the marines. Without it, they were forced to live like vagabonds and depend on what was stored on the hundreds of support ships that waited in giant convoys just off Kyushu. It was not an efficient way to run a campaign and had to change soon.

MacArthur wondered how much of it was Krueger's fault. Certainly, Lt. Gen. Walter Krueger was a solid professional soldier, although perhaps a bit unimaginative. The men under Krueger's command seemed to lack a zest for battle and were getting bogged down at the smallest obstacle. Should he replace Krueger with Eichelberger? He would think on it. Eichelberger had wanted the task, but MacArthur had insisted on Krueger having his turn. Now he wondered if he had been too hasty in appointing Krueger over Eichelberger.

The casualties had been appalling. Instead of breaking and collapsing, the Japanese had fought like the devil in most places and showed no sign of changing, although some second-rate units and individual soldiers had given up. How the insidious General Marshall must enjoy seeing MacArthur's battle reports and realizing that all was not going as well as he had predicted.

Marshall now had Truman's ear just as he'd had Roosevelt's, and that situation bore watching. Truman was such an intellectual lightweight that Marshall was bound to dominate him. MacArthur did have to give Marshall his due; he had a keener mind than MacArthur had thought and had used it to his utmost advantage.

At least MacArthur had managed to keep the invasion both an all-American show and an all-white-American war. He had withstood pressure from Roosevelt and then Truman to incorporate three divisions of British Commonwealth troops into his army. Great Britain had offered them, but he had withstood it. The three divisions—one each from Australia, Britain, and Canada—would have been a logistical nightmare to keep in the field. Unlike the European theater, where there were ports and occupied landmasses where vast and differing kinds of supplies could be stored, all of his men would have to live for some time off what was on the ships. MacArthur had rightly convinced Marshall that he didn't have the resources to supply the Commonwealth troops with their own ammunition, food, and weapons. Therefore, the three Commonwealth divisions had to change to American tactics and equipment if they were to join the battle.

With neither the time nor the resources to do this, the British had backed off, although they were beginning to switch over to American gear in anticipation of the second phase of the battle for Japan—Operation Coronet, the invasion of Honshu. This MacArthur could accept. When Coronet occurred, there would be supply depots on Kyushu, and the logistical problem would be over.

As to minority soldiers, MacArthur simply didn't think they would fight well. Roosevelt, doubtless egged on by his aggravating wife, Eleanor, had felt they should be incorporated into the army as fighting men, instead of supply soldiers and laborers, which was their normal use. Truman now supported this incredible idea as well, to MacArthur's astonishment. MacArthur felt that he could understand the political logic and the urgency to widen the population base from which the soldiers were drawn, but he could not permit this to happen to the detriment of his army. Negroes, while fine fellows in their own way, were simply not cut out to be warriors. He had put his foot down before and would do it again. There would be no Negroes in the front lines in the invasion of Japan.

Of course, and MacArthur smiled at the thought, if Eisenhower wanted them in Europe and if that freed up white soldiers to fight in Japan, well, that was fine by him. MacArthur recalled Ike as being a fine chief of staff for him, but he now was one of Marshall's boys and, therefore, part of the cabal against him.

It further pleased MacArthur that he had kept the despised Office of Strategic Services, the OSS, out of his area of operations. He'd heard that they'd done well in Europe, but doubted it. He despised amateurs and that's all they were. Imagine, they'd wanted to use some of his several hundred nisei translators as espionage agents and spies to be inserted into Japan. No, he'd answered. Once there, it was too likely they'd go over to the Japanese side. Let his nisei stay in Australia where they could be watched.

If the OSS, through the navy, wished to send in Japanese Americans, then let them find their own qualified people and run the risk of losing them. He would not help the navy. MacArthur had heard reports that the OSS had managed to land one man, who had done some good, and were following up with others, but they would not use his tame Japanese in the ensuing battles.

Douglas MacArthur was not afraid of the outcome of combat. He accepted that he was far braver than most men. It was not that he was without fear; indeed, he knew it and despised what it could do to a man. But he was able to control it, even conquer it.

Bravery was something that came quite naturally to MacArthur. He'd first seen combat during the 1914 punitive expedition to Vera Cruz, Mexico, where he'd pistoled at least a half dozen Mexican soldiers. He'd been nominated for the Medal of Honor, but denied it because his one-man patrol hadn't been authorized. It had been the first in a long line of personal affronts against him by bureaucrats in Washington. Later, he'd been decorated in World War I and had, of course, been unperturbable under fire several times during the current conflict. Thus, it galled him mightily when people cast doubts on his manhood and courage. He'd thought of personally berating the sailor, but decided it would be useless. Let them judge him on the basis of the victory that would surely come.

MacArthur looked out on one of the several destroyers escorting the *Augusta*. The heavy cruiser was the center of its own small task force, and his presence on her caused four additional warships to be detailed to protect both him and the *Augusta*. Someday soon, one of his political enemies would make comments about that, but American ships no longer traveled alone. The catastrophic sinking of the *Indianapolis* was too fresh on everyone's mind. Even if he hadn't been on board the cruiser, she would not be alone.

MacArthur had heard muted criticism regarding his choosing the *Augusta* in the first place. The whispers said that he wanted the *Augusta* because two presidents had sailed on her. What foolishness! He'd selected the *Augusta* because it had been configured to handle an admiral's staff, which meant it could house his. Admiral Nimitz had suggested they share the resources of Nimitz's command ship, the *Wasatch*. MacArthur, while appreciating the gesture, had demurred. He'd feared that his presence on the *Wasatch* would look as if he were under Nimitz's command when the command was actually shared by the two men.

On the other hand, there was no reason for the *Augusta* to be so far from Japan. They were a full hundred miles behind the fleet, which itself stretched for scores of miles, and this was not what he'd had in mind when he'd voiced the wish to be closer to the battlefields. He would tell Admiral Nimitz it was essential that the *Augusta* move much closer to Japan.

MacArthur thought and smiled. He would direct that the *Augusta* be stationed off Ariake Bay; thus, when circumstances permitted, he would be ready to go ashore on Japanese soil at the first opportunity. Wouldn't Gen. George Catlett Marshall like that!

MacArthur chuckled deeply at the picture. Some damn Republicans had contacted him about a presidential candidacy in 1948 against what they presumed would be that country nitwit, Harry Truman. A triumphal entry onto Japanese territory would help that cause, and the cause of America, immensely.

Now, if the Japanese army would only cooperate and begin to shatter. He sighed and bit down on the stem of his unlit corncob pipe. It was incredible that the Japs were still fighting. They had few weapons, fewer supplies, rudimentary organization, primitive communications, and poor leaders. He had to give the Japanese soldier a warrior's credit for being personally quite brave, but they would ultimately be defeated. Then General of the Army Douglas MacArthur would have his revenge, both on the Japanese and on the coterie of enemies conspiring against him in Washington. Yes, he thought, and smiled again, it would be a pleasant time.

■

CHAPTER 36

Joe Nomura walked slowly and disconsolately down the dirt path that cut through the overgrown field. He was upset and frustrated. American armies were fighting desperately 150 miles south of him and he had done nothing lately to help them. He had continued his periodic reports, but there had been nothing new to report for a while.

There was still little food for the civilian population, and medicine was in even shorter supply. He had told his listeners that the average Japanese civilian was on the verge of starvation and disease and wanted the war to end, even if it meant surrender. He sometimes wondered if anyone important was actually getting his messages, or whether he was sending them into an electronic mine shaft.

The Japanese people had lost horribly in terms of their homes, their livelihoods, and the lives of their loved ones. The devastation of their cities, even those not atom-bombed, was virtually total. Work and travel were impossible. They cursed the American planes that flew overhead and bombed their homes and few remaining factories with almost contemptuous ease. In one way, the American invasion was a blessing for the Japanese civilians as it continued to siphon off large numbers of American warplanes.

The civilians he saw were sick at heart and discontented with the Anami government, which persisted in fighting a war they saw no way of winning. Strangely, this discontent did not reflect in a dislike for the vanished emperor. Virtually no one in Japan had ever heard Hirohito speak, so no one noticed his absence from the public forum. However, they did understand that Anami was in charge and that the military and the *kempei* backed Anami. Even with his own Japanese background Joe found it hard to understand their fatalism, but the civilians accepted the situation.

Joe had reported that large numbers of Japanese soldiers continued to infiltrate from north Kyushu to the south after either being shipped by submarine from Korea or having navigated the narrow straits between Honshu and Kyushu in swarms of small boats. He'd identified several major units originally stationed around Tokyo as having been switched to Kyushu, including several Imperial Guard divisions. It confirmed his opinion that Japan's major effort would be on Kyushu. He hadn't reported his opinion. Let the generals figure that out for themselves. He thought it was so obvious that they wouldn't need help from a lowly field operative to draw that conclusion.

Gathering this data had required little in the way of effort. The soldiers he'd met on the trail were more than happy to chatter like magpies when they'd met up with him. After all, he was one of them, wasn't he? Nomura's tattered uniform and missing arm were more than enough to induce the soldiers to tell him everything they knew. It was inconceivable that he could be anything other than what he looked like—an honored Japanese war veteran.

But what had he done lately? Joe wanted to do something that would really help the men who were fighting and dying for him. At least Dennis Chambers was still alive, feeling well, kicking and bitching. Chambers was as frustrated as he was. Living the life of a virtual hermit on a Kyushu mountaintop was driving Chambers nuts as well. An air force pilot, not a recluse, he too wanted to do something.

When they'd heard of the landings, the two men had discussed the possibility of working their way south and into the American lines. This they'd quickly discarded as an improbable accomplishment. Dennis's white skin would mark him as an enemy to the Japanese, and he'd be shot on sight if he was lucky. Then, Joe's yellow skin would draw fire from every American who saw him, and they'd ask questions later. They'd reluctantly decided they were much better staying where they were and not trying to get through the combatants. If the Japs surrendered, then they would decide how to deliver themselves to the proper authorities.

What really worried both men was that the war would develop into a prolonged stalemate, causing them to stay in hiding indefinitely in northern Kyushu. Equally frightening was the thought that the fighting would work its way northward and wash over them. This would cause the same difficulties as trying to get through the lines in the first place.

It wasn't fair, but what the hell else was new? Then he saw the bicycle lying on its side on the edge of the path. He grinned as he saw that no rider was around. If it was abandoned and rideable, it would beat the hell out of walking all over Kyushu in search of information to send back to mama in the States.

Joe grabbed the handlebars, righted it, and worked the pedals. It was dirty and battered, but the tires had air and it otherwise looked all right. Finally, he might be more useful. He would take the bike back to where Dennis was hidden and they'd discuss it over a shot of their dwindling supply of whiskey.

The bicycle was painted brown, which meant that it belonged to the military or at least had at some time in its past. This didn't worry him. With the desperate shortage of fuel, bicycles were everywhere, and many had belonged to the military. A brown bicycle would draw no attention, particularly since it would be ridden by a one-armed vet.

As he turned the bike around and began to pedal awkwardly, he saw something sticking out of the tall grass alongside the path. It was a leg.

"Hello, hello," he said softly, then grimaced as he realized he'd accidentally spoken in English. He hadn't made that mistake in a while, not even with Chambers.

Joe got off the bike and walked over to where the body lay facedown. The man wore the uniform of a captain in the Japanese secret police, the *kempei*. Joe knelt down and checked for a pulse even though the body was cold and graying. The captain of the secret police was dead. Joe rolled the corpse on its back and saw a massive indentation in its skull.

With no other evidence, he concluded that the Jap officer had crashed his bike and fractured his skull in the fall. A little checking showed a rock near where he'd first found the bike that had what looked like dry bloodstains on it. The officer had probably crawled the few feet away from the accident before dying.

So now what to do? he wondered. Joe grinned and rifled the man's pockets, finding identification papers and money, along with a ring of keys. Joe took the corpse by one foot and dragged it farther into the underbrush. There, he stripped off the uniform and boots. After hesitating only a second, he took the dead man's underwear, leaving the body naked and unidentifiable. If he wasn't found in a couple of days, he'd be bloated and half-eaten by bugs. The *kempei* officer would become just another dead body in a country that was filled with corpses.

All the while he did this, Joe kept looking up and down the path to see if anyone else was coming. No one did and Joe wasn't surprised. Other than the army, or refugees on the main paths leading farther north, everyone tried to stay near the refugee camps, where there was at least a little food. A lot of people had also made the passage across to Honshu to get away from the fighting. He thought the civilian population of Kyushu was half what it had been when he'd first landed.

Joe made a bag out of the dead man's pants, slung the improvised sack over his shoulder, and remounted the bike. As he pedaled down the path, his spirits were uplifted. He had absolutely no idea what he might do with the *kempei* uniform, but he had at least done something. Or maybe the beginning of something. Maybe he and Dennis could work on the uniform and make it fit him. It was a shame that the dead Jap was such a plump little shit. It would make alterations that much more difficult. But not impossible, he exulted, not impossible at all.

•

CHAPTER 37

The U.S. Army's I Corps headquarters was in a badly damaged brick building in the small port city of Miyazaki. The shattered windows were covered with wood, and it was ringed by grim-faced American sentries. Even though the town was considered secure, no one was taking chances on suicide attacks.

After meeting briefly with the commander of the 41st Infantry Division, Brig. Gen. John Monck walked out into the shattered streets and up to his chief of staff, Colonel Parker. As they walked, their four-man security detail formed a loose perimeter around them. Monck hating having them, but, like the situation at I Corps, it was better to be safe than sorry. More than one senior officer had already been killed by Jap snipers.

Parker was his usual almost insolent self. "Well, what new tidings did they give you, General? Will the war be over by Christmas? The way the Japs are still fighting, the only way that could occur would be for us to surrender to them."

Monck sighed. He was exhausted and not really in the mood for Parker's often snide comments. As usual, though, he said nothing. Parker was far too valuable to him for him to be put off by his attitude. Besides, Parker was so often right.

"Parker, Major General Doe says we are doing a fine job and that we should keep up the good work. We are to continue plugging our way north, killing Japs and climbing hills as we go. Before you say anything, let me agree with you. It isn't much in the way of grand strategy, or innovative tactics, but then, there isn't much we can be strategic or innovative about in this campaign. At this point, this is nothing more than a slugging match."

Parker raised his hands briefly in mock surrender. "What about our casualties? Did General Doe have any comment there?"

Monck shook his head sadly. "When I told Doe we had taken eighty dead and more than two hundred wounded in less than a week of actual fighting, he didn't seem unduly disturbed or impressed. When I reminded him that it was about eight percent of my regiment, he just shrugged and said he'd see what he could do about getting us some replacements."

"God," Parker muttered. Both men could do the arithmetic. At the rate they were losing men and without replacements, the regiment would cease to exist in a relatively short while. They both knew that the dead and wounded had all been incurred in what news releases referred to as "minor skirmishes." The entire battle for Kyushu so far consisted of hundreds of such minor skirmishes.

"General, what'll we do when the Japs counterattack in strength as they must? Did General Doe have anything to say about that? And what about Swift?" Parker asked, referring to Maj. Gen. Innis Swift, who commanded I Corps.

"Swift wasn't there. He's off conferring with Krueger, who's probably getting more orders from Mac. Krueger, by the way, has finally gotten his headquarters ashore. He's set up shop on a hill just off Ariake Bay. Look, don't be so harsh on Doe, or Swift, for that matter. Everybody's taking it on the chin from the Japs, and some of the people who started fighting before we did are in even worse shape."

"I know, I know," Parker said. "It just seems like such a waste. What did he say about us getting better artillery support?"

The U.S. Army possessed virtually total air and artillery superiority, but had been unable to knock out very many of the numerous Japanese strongpoints. While they had gotten a high percentage of them, the better-sited and stronger Japanese positions remained impervious to bombing and indirect artillery fire. What was needed was close-in firepower that could shoot right down the throat of a bunker or cave. Artillery could plow up the ground nearby, but the hidden and dug-in Japs remained impervious to anything but the fortuitous direct hit on a gun embrasure. Ultimately, it was then necessary for the infantry to root them out, and this was wasting lives.

"Doe understands. He's trying to get some tanks and mountain howitzers assigned to forward units."

"Great. I just hope it occurs soon."

Monck agreed. He looked around and saw they were not headed back to their jeeps. "Colonel, just where the hell are you taking me?"

"To this dismal excuse for a town's waterfront, General. There're a couple of things I thought you'd like to see."

Monck allowed himself to be led to the shore, where low waves sloshed among a number of small and ruined wooden fishing ships. Some of them clearly showed bullet holes where they'd been strafed by low-flying aircraft. Their broken remains were either on the beach or in the shallow water. The livelihood of Miyazaki had been smashed, which might be one of the reasons there were so few people in the firebombed town. With the exception of a few old men and women, the civilian population appeared to have fled, doubtless to the north.

A number of them, however, must be dead, killed in the attacks that sank their ships and leveled their buildings. The air was filled with the lingering stench of rotting flesh. It was nothing new and they almost took it as normal, along with the scent of smoke from countless still-smoldering fires. They had been breathing the stink of decay since the moment they had landed. Fresh, clean air was an almost forgotten memory.

"Look, General."

Monck followed where Parker was pointing. "What the hell is that?" Monck asked as he stared at a small wooden boat about ten feet long that was lying on its side on the beach. It had an extremely low freeboard and a single seat in the back. The whole thing, with the exception of where the seat was, was covered by wooden decking. It reminded him of a kayak.

Parker walked over and towered over it, and it almost looked like a child's toy. "That, General, is a suicide boat that never made it out to sea. There are a lot of them around here. The front of the damned thing is supposed to be stuffed with explosives, and the driver sits in the rear with his legs covered by the decking. Then it scoots out into the water, and he tries to ram one of our ships. At that point the whole thing is supposed to blow up, taking the Jap to the Happy

Hunting Ground or wherever dead Japs go, and sending the unlucky target ship to the bottom. There was a small outboard motor, but it looks like someone liberated it since I saw it a few minutes ago."

Monck tried to imagine going out to sea in such a frail craft, with waves crashing around and over it, and knowing that death was the only goal. The little boat pointed out the alienness of the Japanese way of fighting, and the desperation that made them such formidable enemies.

Parker wasn't through with his tour. He led Monck a ways down the waterfront to where a set of railroad tracks led directly into the water.

"This one's really something else, sir." They followed the tracks less than a hundred yards inland, to where a cave had been dug into a low hill. Inside, a long tubular shape rested on a flat handcar.

"General, this is one of their human torpedoes. They call it a *kaiten*. The intelligence boys were all over it since they thought all the *kaiten* were launched from ships. Now they know the Japs can send them down tracks like this, and into the water, from anyplace along the coast of Japan. Intelligence is particularly concerned that some of these bastards will be launched at us from the confines of Ariake and Kagoshima bays where the bigger ships won't have so much freedom to maneuver and escape."

"What happened to this one?"

"There were a couple of dead Japs lying around a little earlier, and one of them was probably the pilot. My guess is that a near miss from a bomb killed them. Maybe the same thing happened to the guys who were supposed to man the little boats. Who cares, just so long as they never got launched."

"Good," Monck muttered as he thought about the ships lying off-shore. A number of them could be seen from where he was standing. Human torpedoes came in several types and had effective ranges that began with several thousand yards and went up to several miles. Again it was appalling to think of someone riding a torpedo as if it were a horse and sending it crashing into the hull of a ship.

Monck shook his head and thought of the men who were fighting and dying at sea, and then of his own men, who were clawing their way up each hill they confronted. Like most soldiers, he had often been jealous of the navy and that their war was relatively clean. It seemed to have just gotten a whole lot dirtier.

"Parker, just what the hell have we gotten ourselves into?"

He had no answer. Monck gestured to their guards and they began the journey back to their regiment.

Platoon Sgt. Frank Collins slithered down the steep and rain-slicked hill oblivious to the light but constant rain. His clothing and the soft flesh underneath were cut where the small, wet rocks that jutted from the volcanic soil had sliced at him. He ignored them all. His only urge was to make himself one with the hateful ground and thus not be seen by the guns on the hill above him.

The thought that some Jap was looking down at him and aiming either his cannon or machine gun at him made him whimper with fear. With every jerky motion of his arms and legs, he prayed that he would be allowed to make another. He tried desperately to stay within the folds of the hill, but he had that nightmare feeling that scores of slanty eyes were glaring at him and laughing at his slow, painful progress to shelter.

Mud-covered and exhausted, he slipped into a small ravine and felt a surge of relief. He was safe. At least for the moment. Collins sucked a few lungfuls of air and moved over to Lieutenant Morrell, who looked at him with concern.

"You okay?" Paul asked.

"Other than scared shitless, Lieutenant, I'm just fine, thank you." Morrell offered Sergeant Collins his canteen, and Collins accepted it gratefully. The water, warm and rancid, tasted undeservedly delicious. Not even the purification tablets could rob it of its taste. Collins took a dirty rag from his pocket and wiped sweat and cold mist from his face. "I want to take up another line of work, sir."

"Don't we all, Sarge. Now, what'd you see up there?"

The platoon's advance up the fairly steep hill was halted by a brief cannonade and the staccato crackle of Japanese machine guns. They'd dropped where they were, then scrambled downhill for cover and dug in as the previously unseen cannon again fired from a bunker about two-thirds of the way up the hill. At that point, they realized the Jap gunners had them pinned down. They could not advance and they couldn't retreat without exposing themselves to additional casualties.

First they'd called on artillery support, which hadn't been effective. The rain obscured their spotter's vision and the maps of the area were inaccurate. With logic firmly on their side, the regiment's artillery was reluctant to loose a heavy barrage on the Jap position when American soldiers were only a couple of hundred yards away. As a result, only a few rounds had been fired onto the hill, and none had shut down the Jap gun.

Air cover was equally unavailable because of the layer of mist that touched the top of the hill. The planes would not fly and bomb blindly either. The platoon was on its own. They'd plunked a few mortar rounds at the Jap position, but these had merely churned up some dirt.

Then Sergeant Collins had made his solitary patrol.

"Sir, it's a standard Jap bunker setup. There's one main fortification and at least three machine-gun nests connected to it by zigzagging trenches. There may be a fourth on the other side of the hill, but I kinda doubt it. For once artillery did help out, at least a little. They nailed the nest directly in front of the main bunker. Ain't nothin' left but smoke and dead Japs. However, the big bunker and the two light machine guns flanking it are operating just fine, thank you."

Paul nodded. The Jap complex had been well hidden, and had the enemy gunners showed any fire discipline at all, the platoon would have walked right up to it and been slaughtered. As it was, they'd still been hurt. Jap light machine guns had thirty-shot clips, and he considered them the equivalent of an American Browning automatic rifle, or BAR, and not a true machine gun, which was belt-fed. Even so, they could be quite lethal and were helping to keep the platoon pinned down.

"How're my guys?" Collins asked.

"Holcomb took a bullet through the hand that ripped off at least three fingers," Paul answered, thinking of the grisly mess of tendons and flesh that was Holcomb's hand. "He's okay, but in shock. Keye was shot in the thigh and lost a lot of blood before someone got a tourniquet on him. Unless we can get them to the rear sometime soon, they may not make it."

Both men understood. The healthy could wait in wet misery for darkness and then make their escape, but the wounded needed help immediately.

Paul sighed. "What's in the bunker?"

"Jap tank."

"A what?" said Paul, astonished. Since landing on Kyushu, no one had seen a Jap tank. For that matter, they'd seen precious few American ones.

Collins grinned through his fatigue. "Yessir, it's a real live Jap tank, and she's dug in hull-down in the bunker and covered with dirt and logs. Nothing but a direct hit is going to knock her out, and there's damn little of her poking out from the bunker besides her big gun."

It was commonly accepted that Jap tanks were small, thinly armored, and carried a small-caliber cannon. Thus, they were no match for American M4 Shermans, or even the lighter M24 Chaffees. But even a small-caliber cannon was more than Paul's platoon had.

However, that was not his main problem. He had two men who might die if he didn't get them some help, and he might lose still more men if he tried to move them back. There was only one answer. He would not sacrifice additional men for his wounded. They would have to wait until darkness or until help came.

"Sir," Collins asked, "you get through to the captain?"

"Yeah. He's got his own problems but said he'd try to get us out of this mess." The rest of the company was one hill over and had their own problems with Japanese guns. The irregular folds of ground had separated their platoon from the rest of the company. For that matter, Paul thought, they were pretty well separated from the rest of the army. He had the damnedest feeling that he and his platoon were all alone on Kyushu.

Collins risked a quick look at the top of the hill, where the mist now seemed even thicker. "Too bad we can't get a napalm strike on them. Armor or no, that'd cook their goose, literally, and settle things real fast. It's a shame the flyboys don't like to run into mountains when they bomb in the rain."

They gave no thought to sending a man up with a flamethrower. They had one, but he'd be an easy target for the Japs.

With that, they settled down to wait for help or night, whichever came first. As time ground on, they dug in deeper and were able to put substantial mounds of earth between themselves and the machine guns, while the Jap cannon remained ominously silent. It occurred to Paul that the entire platoon had been stopped by fewer than a dozen Japanese.

At first Paul didn't notice the grinding, whining, growling sound in the distance, but as it grew louder, he realized that something big was getting close. Then he and the others grinned hugely as an M4 Sherman tank breasted the hill behind them and descended gracelessly, sliding the last few feet into the ravine where they were hidden. The tank commander positioned the Sherman between them and the Jap guns, and Paul cautiously moved over to the driver's hatch, which opened a crack.

"You guys call for a tank?" came a voice from inside the dull brown armored vehicle.

Paul grinned. "Damned right."

The hatch opened wider and a man with dark, curly hair stuck his upper body out. There was grease on his face. "I'm Staff Sergeant Joey Orlando and this is my tank. How can I help?"

Paul quickly explained the situation with the Jap tank and the machine guns. As if on cue, the Jap tank fired a round that landed farther down the ravine, and one of the machine guns fired a burst that did nothing but make everyone wince. The Japs had seen the American tank and weren't happy.

Orlando grunted. "I make that a thirty-seven-millimeter gun, which tells me that it's a Jap Model 95. She's got two machine guns in her as well, but they're probably useless with them dug in like that. The Model 95 is a dinky piece of shit with thin armor. I've got her outgunned with my seventy-six millimeter. If I can get a clear shot at her, one of my rounds'll go through her like shit through a goose."

"Be my guest," Paul offered. "You going straight up the hill?"

"Naw, and I can't afford to get in a shooting match with that pig. I've only got twenty rounds left. I wanna flank her, and I want some infantry to protect me from any little yellow assholes coming out of holes with grenades or Molotov cocktails. This might be a better tank than the Jap, but she will burn real fast under the right conditions, and I don't want to lose a tread to that thirty-seven of theirs, either. That happens and I gotta sit there and wait for nightfall just like you were. No, I wanna take her in the side or rear. That'll also give me a chance to find a safe way up that hill where my tank won't get stuck or slide back. Who's gonna lead the troops going with me?"

Paul shrugged. "I guess I am."

Sergeant Orlando smiled openly. "Good. I know too damn many officers who would volunteer their mother rather than go up that hill."

"Sergeant Orlando, I am not thrilled at the thought."

"Lieutenant, I'm not either. Y'know there were four tanks in my platoon yesterday? One blew an engine and is being fixed, while another got blown up by a crazy Jap with a bottle full of gas and all five guys in it got burned to death. Then the fourth rolled down one of these hills and rolled over. Nobody got killed in that one, but everybody has broken bones and a couple of my friends may never walk again. So, if you don't mind, I'm a little leery of this place and am gonna take it as cautious as I can."

Paul nodded. "We'll take good care of you, Sergeant."

"Then let's go." Orlando closed the hatch. A moment later, the Sherman rumbled out of the ravine and moved toward the platoon's left flank. Paul, a half dozen riflemen, and one man with the flamethrower scrambled alongside and struggled to keep the tank between themselves and the Japanese on the hill.

Paul had ordered Collins and the rest of the platoon to move up around the right flank and keep the second machine gun occupied. He presumed the cannon in the bunker would concentrate its fire on Sergeant Orlando's hulking tank when it was visible.

They got to where the Jap tank couldn't see the infantry well and started up the hill. The wet ground made the climb difficult for the tank, and a couple of times Paul thought that Sergeant Orlando would say he couldn't make it. But Orlando was both skilled and persistent and they kept inching upward. The flanking Japanese machine gun opened up and bullets rattled harmlessly off the Sherman's turret, while the Jap tank's cannon fired sporadically to no effect. Sergeant Orlando's tank returned fire with the machine gun in her hull, hitting nothing but keeping the Jap gunners' heads down.

The infantrymen stayed in the shadow of the tank and kept an eye out for anything that looked like a camouflaged hole from where a Jap might emerge. Nothing stirred and the men gained confidence as they climbed farther up the hill.

The Americans drew closer until they could see the tip of the barrel of the machine gun as it spewed out its hate. Paul tried not to think of what might be going through the gunners' minds as they saw the American tank approaching. They had to know they were doomed. Why didn't they retreat? What the hell was wrong with these people?

Just as Paul was beginning to wonder when Orlando would use his main gun, he was rocked back by the sound and concussion of the Sherman's 76mm cannon firing. An instant later, the Japanese machine gun disappeared in a cloud of smoke and a shower of rocks.

Safer now, but still moving carefully, the men spread out and advanced on the smoking nest. When they looked in, they saw the shredded remains of what might have been four or five Japs. With all the pieces of smoking flesh lying about, it was hard to be exact.

The Sherman's hatch opened and Orlando looked down on his handiwork. "Not bad," he reasoned. "One shot is all it took."

"Yeah," said Paul. "Now all we got to do is get that buried tank."

Orlando closed the hatch and the Sherman started up again, this time veering for the higher ground above and behind the bunker. Paul understood immediately. Orlando was going to hit the Jap from behind. The way the bunker had been laid out, it probably lacked a firing port in the rear. This meant the Jap would be blind and helpless as they advanced down on it.

Orlando drove the Sherman up the hill to where he was above the bunker and within a hundred feet of it. Paul gripped his rifle tightly and found it hard to comprehend that live Japs were just a few feet from him.

"Get ready," Orlando yelled through the cracked hatch, "and get your men spread out, Lieutenant."

Seconds later, the Sherman's gun fired, then fired again shortly after. When the dust and smoke cleared, they could see the rear of the enemy tank where the shelling had blown away the back of the bunker. One more shot and the Jap tank shuddered and began to smoke. The soldier with the flamethrower ran to the hulk and fired a stream of liquid fire onto the Jap tank, where it stuck to the exposed metal and began to blaze with an insane fury.

"Migod," Paul said as he recoiled from the suddenness of the flamethrower and the heat it was generating. Within a few seconds the Jap tank began to rumble and then it exploded, filling the hill with a small fireworks display as ammunition and fuel blew up. Last, there was one big explosion and the turret of the Jap tank flew through the remaining earthen cover and several feet into the air before coming to a rest a little ways down the hill, where it lay like a child's broken toy.

Paul heard an animal howling and realized it was coming from his throat as he and the others cheered their little victory. The Sherman's hatch opened again and Sergeant Orlando climbed out and shook Paul's hand. "Hot damn," Orlando said, laughing. "My first time in combat and I got me a Jap tank."

"Excellent!" Paul exulted. "Now what about that other machine-gun nest?"

As he said that, Sergeant Collins ran up to them from the other side of the bunker. "Gone, sir. They saw what happened to their buddies and bailed out."

"Look out!" Paul exclaimed, wide-eyed, and fired in Orlando's direction.

A lone Japanese gunner clutched his heart and fell.

"Guess not all of them," Collins said. "We'll do a clean sweep."

Thanks to Orlando's tank, Paul's men had taken the hill, wiped out a bunker with a tank in it, destroyed a machine gun nest, and done it with no additional casualties. Better, they'd caused some Japs to break and run away, which they rarely did.

Now he could send his wounded back to the rear without fear of more casualties, and they could get medical care. "Staff Sergeant Orlando, you and yours got anyplace in particular to go right now?"

Orlando shrugged. "Home, but they won't let me. Why?"

"I think we work well together. You want to stick around?"

"And be your mascot, sir?" Orlando grinned infectiously. "Sounds good to me. Besides, I owe you."

Laughter rang out, a welcome and rare sound.

CHAPTER 39

KYUSHU,
EAST OF NAGASAKI

*O*SS field operative Joe Nomura performed an awkward pirouette in front of the small fire, bowed, and laughed at the thought of a *kempei* officer behaving in such a manner. Dennis Chambers smiled and shook his head at the incongruous sight.

"Dammit, Joe, you look real enough to scare anyone when you just stand there in that toy-soldier outfit, but the shitty little dance you did kind of kills the effect."

Nomura laughed. "I never could dance, that's why. How does the uniform look without the arm?"

"Hell, it looks great, particularly without your arm. It makes you look sinister, like some old-time warrior who's survived a hundred battles and come back a war-wise hero. You'd make a tremendous samurai."

Joe took the compliment with a smile. After a number of false starts and experiments while the two men taught themselves the art of sewing, they'd successfully cut the dead *kempei* captain's uniform down to where it fit Joe fairly well. It wasn't perfect, but both men felt it would pass casual observation as most uniforms worn by the Japanese military were even more ragged and ill-fitting than they usually were.

Unlike Germany's Gestapo, who had their own distinctive uniforms, *kempei* officers wore the standard Japanese officer's uniform, but with a distinctive armband displaying the Japanese characters *ken* and *hei,* which translated as "law soldier." Usually, as in this case, the characters were black on white, and they made the wearer of them a minor god with enormous power over other people's lives and well-being.

According to his papers, the dead soldier, Capt. Shozo Onichi, had commanded a *buntai,* or section, in the area. Based on Onichi's rank, the two men guessed that a section would be about a hundred men. Logic also said these would be scattered about Onichi's area of control, which they presumed to be fairly large, but that the men would know who Onichi was and what he looked like. This meant that impersonating Onichi was out of the question. Joe would have to use another identity if he was to wander around in the uniform.

Kempei officers carried a sword and a pistol. Joe kept the pistol but discarded any thought of carrying the sword. For one thing, a one-armed swordsman looked out of place, and for another, the sword had been made especially for Onichi and had been engraved with his name. Joe's possession of it would be extremely difficult to explain.

"Okay, buddy, now what?" Dennis asked. "What're you gonna do? Halloween was months ago."

Joe checked the fit of the tunic. What he was planning frankly scared the hell out of him. "Dennis, I am going to ride that bike into the nearest village or camp and find the *kempei* field office there. After that, I'm going to make it up as I go along and see what I can turn up."

Dennis shook his head in mock dismay. "That's what I was afraid you were going to say."

Joe grinned. "Who knows, this could be the opportunity of a lifetime." Or the end of a lifetime, he didn't add. Joe wasn't certain why he was going through with this idea, only that the opportunity was too good to pass up.

"What if someone recognizes you?" Dennis asked. "After all, you've been wandering the area for some weeks as a shot-up veteran. How'll you explain yourself?"

Joe shook his head. "Won't have to. I'm the secret police, Japan's Gestapo, remember? Even if somebody should make the connection, they wouldn't dare ask me about it. Hell, I could shoot them on the spot for their insolence. Nah, they know that *kempei* often go around in plain clothes so they can spy on people. They'd probably think I was the biggest prick alive and then wonder what they might have said to me that would come back to haunt them and get them thrown in prison."

"How long do you think you'll be gone and what should I do about it?" Dennis asked almost plaintively. He was in no hurry to be left alone again. He also regretted that their carefully hoarded supply of liquor was all used up. He could see where he could need a drink if Joe left him alone for any period of time.

"A couple of days, maybe less, maybe more. But I do want you to move away from here. If things go wrong for me, it could be real dangerous for you." Joe looked farther up the wooded hillside and across the valley. "Go up there, or someplace else where you can keep an eye on this camp. You pick the spot so I won't know it and won't be able to tell anyone no matter what they do. You see me come back alone, wait until you're sure it's okay. You see me being followed, or Jap soldiers around me, you run like hell. Oh, yeah, don't forget to take the pistol and don't hesitate to use it on yourself if it looks like you're going to be taken."

Dennis nodded glumly. He was just getting used to the idea that he and Joe might make it through this thing. He had again started to dream and plan of life with Barb back in California when he finally came home to her. Now Joe Nomura's actions stood a good chance of wrecking those plans.

But Chambers had a sense of duty and honor as well, and he understood what Joe was doing and why. It was just that he didn't particularly have to like it. It was one thing to wander through Japanese camps as an innocuous and invisible refugee, but it was completely different to be an officer in the *kempei,* one of the elite in the Japanese military. It was sort of like sticking your head in the proverbial lion's mouth. He knew Joe to be resourceful and intelligent, along with ruthless, and he could only hope that those talents and traits would be enough to see him through.

.

CHAPTER 40

KYUSHU,
NORTH OF ARIAKE BAY

Sgt. Yuji Yokota and Ens. Keizo Ikeda had reached an accommodation concerning their personal differences. After all, with only the two of them remaining at the clandestine base, it made no sense to argue, and it was now obvious to Ikeda that the mechanic sergeant was doing everything he could to ready the plane for its final glorious flight. Keizo acknowledged that it was not Yokota's fault that the other five planes at their hidden base had managed to take off as ordered and fulfill their destiny as kamikazes.

He was wrong, of course. Yokota had been stalling, hoping to delay his transfer back to the army once Ikeda had departed. Yokota had no intention of dying if he could avoid it. He did understand the ensign's motives. Ikeda's family had been destroyed by American bombers and the boy wanted revenge. Yokota disagreed with him, but he respected the young officer's sense of grief and loss. Yokota wondered how he'd react to the loss of his own family. It was an academic question as he had no family. The army had been his family and he was more than ready to disown it.

Thus, as the next day dragged on and the plane was not ready as promised, neither man lost patience with the other. To his dismay, Yokota found there were real problems with the plane that he had great trouble fixing. Finally, well after his estimated completion time, Yokota put down his tools, wiped his face with a greasy rag, stood, and bowed before Ikeda, who was genuinely surprised at the gesture.

"It will fly, sir."

Ikeda beamed in relief. At last. "Thank you, Sergeant."

"Sir, it will not, however, fly very well. Despite everything I've done, and for reasons I do not understand, the plane simply will not fly very high."

Ikeda's face clouded. This was not good. Standard tactics called for a kamikaze to dive out of the obscuring sun and plummet onto a target. This tactic also drastically increased the speed of the plane, which then reduced the likelihood of its being shot down. "What do you recommend?"

Yokota was surprised that the officer, particularly a young pup such as Ikeda, would ask his opinion. "Sir, there is no choice. You must stay well beneath a thousand feet at all times."

Ikeda thought quickly; he would stay well below the thousand-foot figure. Instead of diving from the sun, he would skim the earth. If he could not hide in the clouds, he would seek shelter in the trees and the folds of the hills of Kyushu. It would be extremely difficult flying, but he could do it.

"Will you take off at dawn?" Yokota asked, recalling Ikeda's remark that he wished to be one with the sun. This day was almost over and it would be dark in a little while.

Ikeda smiled. It was curiously beatific. "If the plane is fueled, I will fly now, Sergeant. I've seen enough sunrises."

Yokota disagreed with that as well, as he wished to see many more sunrises, but he helped Ikeda with the final preparations. A few minutes later, the old plane, laden with explosives and tins of carefully hoarded extra gasoline to aid in its immolation, lumbered down the grass runway. The engine ran roughly and it didn't look as if the plane would gain enough speed to become airborne. Yet somehow it did, and the small craft began to curl its way around the nearby hills.

As the old wood-and-cloth plane departed, Sergeant Yokota wished the young ensign a successful encounter with the U.S. Navy and a peaceful eternity. Then he stripped off his uniform and anything else that marked him as a soldier.

In the plane, Ikeda exulted. He was on his way. As he kept tight control of his erratic steed, he concluded that a low-level night attack might give him an advantage. Coming in low and slow, he might not be noticed until it was too late. Also, the plane was a dark gray. He began to like the idea even better than that of diving out of the sky.

Beneath him, the ground sped by. Even though it was night, he could still see signs of habitation, and sometimes people paused to look up at him as he came upon them so quickly that they could not run and hide. In the distance he could see the flashes and glows that were the battle for Japan's future. He was surprised. The fighting was much closer than he thought.

Then he was over the battlefield. It was marked by the continuing flicker of small-arms fire in both directions, and then he was past and over the American lines. Again, flying low was an advantage. Even though occasional tracers reached out their glowing fingers to pluck him from the sky, he was beyond them before the gunners had a chance to react to him. He thought it amazing that he could actually see American tanks and trucks, along with tents and other facilities as he swept overhead. The Americans made no effort to shelter themselves.

In the distance he saw the flat darkness of the ocean. But before he reached that, he flew over some American supply dumps and saw the immenseness of them. Then he viewed an airfield under construction, followed by yet another one, which already had a handful of planes parked along the runway. If the Americans were confident enough of their position to build airfields, even small ones, then things were truly dire for Japan. He prayed that his effort would help.

Soon he was over the dark waters of Ariake Bay and headed out toward the vastness of the ocean. A couple of American destroyers were anchored just offshore and fired at him with no effect. They could barely see him in the night and were afraid of hitting each other as he flew just over the waves between them.

Ikeda regained some altitude and scanned the area, but saw no tankers or large transports that would be worthy targets, only smaller craft that seemed to scatter beneath him. Again he exulted; they were afraid of him. "Banzai!" he shrieked to the wind.

Satisfied that there was nothing in the bay whose sinking would fulfill his sense of destiny, Ikeda pressed on toward the open sea. As before, his orders were to attack carriers or large transports and to ignore smaller ships, even warships. Only in the case of dire necessity was he to deviate from his orders.

As he flew on, the plane's unreliable engine started skipping. Perhaps the poor-quality fuel was clogging it, or maybe Yokota wasn't quite the mechanic he thought he was. Either way, it didn't matter. His time in the air was now limited, and unless he wished to crash uselessly into the sea, he had better find a target, any target.

Ikeda flew on and prayed. He could not die unfulfilled. He had to find a ship. It was difficult to stay airborne, and soon his altitude fell to under a hundred feet. He could almost feel the waves reaching out to doom his quest. Then, in the distance, he saw a slim, dark shape on the water with an even larger one behind it. American ships, but what type were they? He laughed. Whatever they were, they would have to do.

Ikeda turned his struggling plane toward the larger of the two ships. As it drew closer, the larger ship took on shape and identity as a warship. It had massive turrets and a superstructure that was now taller than the height at which he was flying. Ikeda hoped that it was a battleship. That would be a fine ending to his life.

Bullets and shells reached out toward him from both enemy warships, but it was too late and he flew through them as if protected by a magician's spell. As the American ship filled his view, he closed his eyes and thought of his family.

.

CHAPTER 41

Seaman 1st Class Tim Jardine felt that he was now living almost all his life within ten feet of the antiaircraft guns that pointed out into the chill night. He comforted himself by realizing that it could have been a whole lot worse. At least some of the maddening restrictions on their behavior and movement had been relaxed. In a way it was funny. The closer they got to Japan, the less edgy the brass had gotten about the possibility of enemy attacks. Maybe they were getting used to it.

It did seem that fewer Jap planes were flying, and it was logical that the Japs had to run out of suicide pilots someday. After all, a kamikaze didn't make many return flights if he set out to kill himself.

Jardine and the other men in the gun mount had also concluded that their officer, Ensign Hollowell, was a pretty good guy, even if he was an officer and young and inexperienced at that. For one thing, he had devised a better way of rotating men at the guns that kept them fresher during the night. He also wasn't a prick when it came to keeping things neat and shipshape in the area. If the navy wanted the guns manned all the time, then certain things had to be considered less important than others. The turret and its occupants may have looked a little casual, but they were ready to fight.

But the best thing about Hollowell was that he was always hungry and had a great habit of getting food and Cokes for the men. Jardine bit into a sandwich and decided that if feeding people made them like you, then Hollowell was going to be very popular.

Haverman handed Jardine his binoculars and stretched his shoulders. They ached from the strain of peering out into the darkness of the night. "Here, your turn."

"Thanks," Jardine said as he settled the straps over his helmet. "Keep an eye out for MacArthur, he was walking around a little while ago."

Haverman grunted but did not make any disparaging comments about their important guest. MacArthur's nocturnal habit of pacing the ship alone was an old story by now. Just about everyone had seen him, although no one spoke to him. MacArthur just wanted to be alone to think, and who could blame him? The invasion was a month old and the Japs were still hanging in there with no signs of their giving up. Jardine shuddered at the thought of the hell the men on Kyushu were going through. Thank God he'd been drafted into the navy.

Jardine looked through the powerful glasses. As usual, there was nothing. Then a star twinkled and went out. What the hell? He checked where the star was and it returned.

"Dammit," he muttered.

"What is it?" Ensign Hollowell asked.

"I'm not certain, but there may be something out there, just over the horizon. I'm kinda certain I saw some motion low in the sky."

Hollowell made a quick phone call. A moment later he hung up. "Lieutenant Greene says there's nothing on radar, so, if it's a plane, it's way the hell out there. The darkness may be playing tricks on you. Greene thinks it might be a bird."

"Okay, sir," Jardine said, but he didn't feel comfortable. He had that gut feeling that whatever he saw was fairly close, and it sure as hell didn't strike him as a bird. Wrong sort of motion, although he had to admit that he hadn't seen all that much. It was just a sense that it wasn't a bird.

So why hadn't radar latched onto it? If it was a plane and was close by, it should have. But where was it written that radar was perfect? The more he thought about what he hadn't quite seen, the more uncomfortable he became.

Oh, hell, maybe he was just a little tense being so much closer to Japan than they had been a few days ago. They'd all been surprised when the five-ship unit had changed its routine and moved well north of their original position. Now, instead of being behind the fleet, they were just within the navy's defensive perimeter. Then he laughed to himself. Like, how did he know that they really were closer? There had never been any land in sight to prove to them that they were actually any nearer Japan than they had been before. Maybe it was all a big joke and they'd wake up tomorrow off San Francisco.

Then he saw it again. It was dark and just a few feet above the waves, and it looked like some weird bird of prey. But it wasn't a bird. It was definitely a plane and it was close, very damn close and coming at them. He yelled and the antiaircraft battery came alive. Ensign Hollowell saw the dark shape and hollered out the range but not the order to open fire.

There was a second's hesitation. What if it was an American plane? Was the *Augusta*'s floatplane out on some damn fool errand? Hollowell sure as hell didn't want to shoot down an American plane.

At that moment, the portside destroyer opened fire, and searchlights lit up the sky. Instead of helping, it blinded the men in the *Augusta*.

"Dammit," snarled Jardine as he tried to blink away the sudden loss of night vision.

"Can you see it?" screamed Hollowell.

"No!" Jardine could see nothing except light streaks across his eyes. Then it was in front of him. "Yes!" he yelled back. The guns opened up at the dark plane that was dreadfully close and still only a few feet above the water. Streams of tracers laced the sky, but none seemed to hit the plane that was now only a hundred yards away and closing in with horrifying quickness.

"It's going to hit us!" Haverman moaned, and covered his head. The plane was headed right for them. Then, at the last second, the plane was struck by a shell and shuddered. It seemed to rise up higher by a few feet and flew right over Jardine's head. It was so close that he saw the landing gear above him. With a roar it crashed into one of the eight-inch bow turrets. Explosions and flames racked the bow of the ship, hurling Jardine to the deck. He screamed in fear and confusion as the cloud of burning gasoline swept above them, showering him with flaming debris. Frantically, he pounded at the host of little fires that had started around him until they were out. Only then did he realize that he had burned his hands.

Behind him, damage-control parties rushed toward them and their hoses sent water hurling onto the major fires. Secondary streams doused Jardine's gun mount and ended any fear of their ammunition exploding. Jardine heard others moaning in pain and realized that, other than his hands, which had begun to blister, he wasn't badly hurt. He whimpered at the joy of it. The goddamn kamikaze, and that's what it had to have been, had tried to kill him, but had failed. He was still lying facedown, with debris on top of him. He had to have a lot of bruises, but all of his limbs seemed to be functioning.

Ensign Hollowell lurched to his feet. The right side of his face was all red and one eye was closed. "Sound off," he ordered, and the men complied, identifying themselves. Everyone was alive, but a couple were injured. Haverman said he thought his leg was broken, and that seemed to be the worst of it, presuming that Jardine's burns weren't too bad. Maybe he could get a trip back to the States out of it?

"I think I'm okay," Jardine responded, "but there's a bunch of crap on my back." He didn't want to move. The debris wasn't all that heavy, but there might be an unexploded shell or something else that might hurt him if he moved it himself. "Somebody check it out, please."

Ensign Hollowell staggered to him and pulled some things off him. Then he looked down. "Aw, shit," Hollowell said, and started gagging. "It's an arm."

Jardine shrieked and jerked away, causing the limb to flop down on the deck where he stared at it in shock and revulsion. The arm had been ripped off at the shoulder and was badly burned. "Ain't one of our guys," Jardine finally said. "Thank God." Somebody had been ripped apart, but it wasn't one of his buddies in the gun mount. He was being heartless, but so what? He was alive and the other guy wasn't and that's all there was. "Hey, maybe it belongs to that Jap pilot?"

Hollowell looked at the severed arm in the light of the still burning gasoline. Damage control had brought the fire under control and there were no more explosions, but flames still flickered in a score of places.

"There's a ring on the hand," Hollowell muttered, and willed himself to examine the ghastly thing further. "Oh, Christ have mercy," he whispered as he turned the charred hand over and examined the ring. "Oh, Lord."

"What is it, sir?" Jardine asked. What the hell was so important about a ring? He looked at it more closely, shocked to recognize a West Point ring, class of 1903.

CHAPTER 42

*P*resident Harry Truman's demeanor reflected the shock and sadness of the entire nation. For all his faults, MacArthur had somehow been considered immortal, and his death had been a severe blow to the nation's collective spirit.

"I want a full military funeral for the man, and that includes his body lying in state in the Capitol Rotunda. If his widow will permit it, General MacArthur will be buried in Arlington with absolutely the fullest military honors possible. Like him or not, the man was a legend who died for his nation, and we will not permit his memory to be forgotten."

Marshall and Leahy nodded. For a nation that was still grieving the loss of FDR, the announcement of the death of Gen. Douglas MacArthur in a kamikaze attack on the cruiser *Augusta* was too much to bear.

"For reasons I will never comprehend, I don't believe he ever liked me," Truman continued, "but I can't hold that against him. Hell, if every man who disliked me stood in a line, that line would likely circle the earth at least a couple of times. What is important is that he is the highest-ranking American killed in this or any other war, and he will be given what he deserves, a military funeral that includes a parade to Arlington."

Marshall nodded. Deaths of ranking officers in combat were rare in modern warfare. Maj. Gen. Maurice Rose, commander of the 3rd Armored Division, had been killed in Europe, and Lt. Gen. Simon Bolivar Buckner, the commander of the Tenth Army on Okinawa, had been killed by Japanese artillery on the last day of the fighting on that island. Other generals, such as Wainwright and Sharp, had been captured in the Philippines, but no one even approaching Mac-Arthur's five-star rank had even been scratched.

As they discussed an outline for the funeral, Truman realized that the death of MacArthur removed a strong Republican candidate for the presidency in '48. Realistically, that only left New York's Tom Dewey as a threat to his election as president in his own right.

Truman hated himself for thinking of partisan politics at a time like this, but he'd been at it for so long it was impossible not to. At least MacArthur's tragic end had deflected questions regarding Japan's so-called list of prisoners they'd received from a Swedish emissary. He'd promised a response to it as soon as the people at the Pentagon had finished examining it, and a lot of parents and wives were getting angry and frustrated at the length of time it was taking.

Truman shook his head. It was all so futile. "What were the total casualties on the *Augusta*?"

Leahy responded, "Besides MacArthur, ten killed and seventy-two wounded. All of the dead and most of the seriously wounded were in the forward turret which was directly hit by the plane. The men in that turret were burned by the gasoline from the plane. Fortunately, the ammunition in the *Augusta*'s turret did not explode, so she'll be back on station fairly shortly. The majority of the other wounded are light to moderately so and will return to duty within a couple of weeks."

"All right," Truman sighed, "just bring MacArthur's body home as soon as possible."

As a result of the explosion and fire, little had been found of Douglas MacArthur's mortal remains. The largest portion identifiable as his was his right arm, and that only because the hand wore his West Point ring. Other body parts had been found but were too badly damaged to determine whether they were his or somebody else's. Ironically, more of the Jap pilot's body had been found strapped in the cockpit of the wreckage of his plane than had been found of Mac-Arthur's. The navy had even identified the Jap before burying him at sea. Sometime in the future, some scholar or military historian might want to find out more about the otherwise insignificant man who had struck down General of the Army Douglas MacArthur.

"General MacArthur was a most difficult man," Truman added. "He was pompous, obstinate, arrogant, and a genius. But most of all, he was ours. Like I said, he gets a funeral almost befitting a head of state."

"Sir," Marshall said, "this may be distasteful, but, whether we wish to or not, we must quickly appoint a successor to MacArthur."

"Anybody in mind?" Truman had no doubts that Marshall already had an heir designated for MacArthur's position. Marshall was always a number of steps ahead of everyone else when it came to planning, which made him without peer in his position.

"Mr. President, I wish to appoint General Omar Bradley to succeed General Douglas MacArthur."

"A good choice, General Marshall, but why him in particular?"

Marshall was prepared. "Sir, while only the Sixth Army under General Krueger is currently active in Kyushu, the First and Eighth armies are preparing to invade Honshu, near Tokyo. Put together, you have an army group, and General Bradley has extensive experience at that command level having led one in Europe."

Truman had read his mind. "What about yourself?"

Marshall smiled. "Other than the fact that you wouldn't let me go, I have to admit that I can serve the war effort better here in Washington than I could over there."

Truman concurred but was insistent. "Then what about Patton, or Eichelberger, or even General Krueger, for that matter?"

"Sir, General Patton is the wrong type of commander for this war. The very aggressiveness that made him successful against the Nazis would hinder him in Japan. Kyushu represents a grinding type of assault and not the war of motion and maneuver that is Patton's specialty. I'm afraid the result would be still more casualties and little gained from it.

"Generals Eichelberger and Krueger are fine men, but they suffer from two flaws. First, neither has commanded at the army group level, and it is not time to experiment or train someone. Second, neither Eichelberger nor Krueger are reconizable names to the American public. The death of MacArthur is a terrible shock, and in order to keep the confidence of the American public, that shock must be countered by naming someone of great stature and high regard to replace him. By all aspects, General Omar Bradley is the best—no, the only—choice."

"Agreed," Truman said softly. Marshall was right on both counts, particularly the second. Marshall's political acumen and sense of what the nation wanted did not surprise him. It reinforced his opinion that Marshall might be an excellent replacement for Byrnes at State. Byrnes's health had begun to fail, and at sixty-six he wasn't getting any younger. Hell, Truman snorted, who was?

"Sir, I've included General Bradley on everything about Olympic and the subsequent plans for Coronet for more than a month now. He is as well prepared as he possibly could be."

Truman was surprised and wondered why he felt that way. Marshall was always doing these things. The man was incredible. "And why, may I ask, did you presume to do that?"

"Mr. President, I had no idea that General MacArthur would be killed. I did, however, have serious concerns that he might not be physically or emotionally up to the monumental task before him. I was worried that he might have problems that would require him to be replaced very quickly, and I made certain that General Bradley was well groomed to succeed him in the event that occurred."

Truman smiled. "God, you are a coldhearted bastard. But I'm damned glad you're on our side and not theirs, and I'm even more glad you did what you did, distasteful though I find it."

"General Bradley found it distasteful as well, but I prevailed on his sense of duty and he agreed to spend his time boning up on Downfall. I am confident that he is as knowledgeable as he could be without actually being there."

"When can he be ready to leave for Japan?"

Marshall checked his watch. "General Bradley is packed and ready to depart at a moment's notice. Planes are ready to begin relaying him across the country and then across the Pacific. If all goes well, he could be with Nimitz on Guam or Okinawa in twenty-four to thirty-six hours."

Truman was pleased. "Where is he now? I would like to make an announcement of his appointment, and he should be standing beside me when I do it."

Marshall again smiled. "Sir, he's waiting in the next room."

■

CHAPTER 43

Joe Nomura pedaled carefully through the narrow and littered streets of the squalid camp. It wasn't easy to maneuver the bike with only one arm, and the dirt paths between the hundreds of tents were filled with hordes of displaced humanity. The areas between the rough living quarters were strewn with trash, a most un-Japanese phenomenon. To Joe it meant that the fabric of Japanese civilization was unraveling.

It amused him to watch the reactions on the faces of the Japanese civilians. Their eyes immediately went to the *kempei* armband and they moved out of the way as quickly as possible to let him pass. Don't stop here, they silently told him. No one wanted to be on the *kempei* shit list, he decided. From what he'd heard about the *kempei*'s more recent methods of punishment and extracting information, he couldn't blame them. The *kempei* had not always been overly brutal, but the desperation of the times was driving them to it.

Joe found a policeman and harshly ordered him to direct him to the *kempei* field office. Joe had almost asked him politely, but recalled that Japanese officers habitually treated those of lesser rank and stature with cold contempt. His rudeness was expected and in keeping with his position.

The *kempei* office in Camp 10 was a wooden structure that might once have been the house of someone fairly well-to-do. As such, it was one of the few real buildings in the area with a roof, and it did not surprise him that the *kempei* had taken it over for themselves. Everything else in the camp was tents or hovels largely made of debris. A disturbing number of people were living out in the open, and the weather was definitely cooling. He pitied them. With bad weather accompanying chronic food shortages, many would succumb to illness in the weeks and months ahead if the war continued.

He laid his bike against a wall, confident it would not be touched by the people watching him, and tried the door to the house. It opened easily and he entered. An oil lamp was on a table and he lit it with one of the matches that lay beside it. There was no electricity in the camp.

The room contained several file cabinets, a desk with a typewriter, and several chairs. A telephone hung on the wall, and when he tried it, there was no dial tone or the voice of an operator. A shortwave radio by another wall was set on one of his frequencies, which he did not consider comforting. A hand-crank generator connected to another bicycle powered it.

The cabinets were locked, but he found that he had the key to them, along with the key to the desk drawers. In the desk he found what he wanted—blank *kempei* identity cards.

Humming contentedly, he set up the typewriter and tried to recall what his mother had taught him about typing Japanese characters. After a few mistakes, he managed to give himself an official *kempei* identity card, using his own name, Jochi Nomura. His OSS handlers had mentioned in passing that, since it was so easy to forget an alias, an agent should use his own name whenever possible. Why not, when no knew him from Adam anyhow?

Joe had just signed the card in the name of the regional commander and put it away in the wallet that had once belonged to the late Captain Onichi when the outside door opened and a young private entered. The man stared and blinked at him for a second and snapped to attention.

Joe took the initiative. "Why was no one here?" he demanded. "Do you always leave the office and official files in such a manner? Is there no sense of security here?"

"Sir," the private stammered, "there are only two of us and my corporal was out investigating an incident when I received word of a disloyal act occurring. Someone had put up a white flag and I did not feel I could wait for his return before tearing it down."

Good, Joe thought, only two people at this little station. "I presume that you resolved it satisfactorily," he said haughtily.

"Yes, sir. The man who put up the flag was identified by his neighbors and beaten thoroughly."

"Very good," Joe said, and the private relaxed. The unknown captain was not going to punish him. "Where is Captain Onichi? I was expecting to find him here."

"Sir, I have not seen him in a couple of weeks. This is a very small station and he spends very little time here. You will more than likely find him at Camp Seven." The private pointed to a map. It showed that Camp 7 was about ten miles farther away and to the west.

"Indeed. Why would he be there? Is Camp Seven all that much larger or more important than Camp Ten?"

The private looked puzzled. "Sir, the camp is about the same size as this is, and I'm not certain about the reason he spends his time there."

Joe thought that the fat little captain whose body was rotting in a field was either getting laid or fed at Camp 7. Maybe even both, but he was curious at the look in the private's eyes and the tentative tone of his voice. Joe decided to probe a little more about the late Onichi's actions.

"Then tell me what it is you are not certain about."

Now the private was definitely uncomfortable. "Sir, it's only a rumor, but I have heard it said that there may be a very important member of the government under guard in the hospital at the camp."

Joe was intrigued and wondered who it was. More important, was it information that was worth forwarding to his handlers. "Really? What makes you think that?"

The private clearly wished he were elsewhere. This was the longest conversation he'd ever had with an officer. Even shorter ones had usually resulted in his being punched. He was deathly afraid he'd make a mistake and be punished.

"Sir, one of my fellow soldiers went there once with Captain Onichi. There is an area of the medical compound that is restricted and protected by soldiers of the Imperial Guard, who are commanded by a guards colonel. The soldiers are disguised as hospital workers and allow no one in or out of the restricted area without the colonel's permission."

Interesting, Joe thought. Disguised as hospital workers, they could not be identified as soldiers from the air and thus compromise whatever they were doing. Why were they going to all that effort, and whom were they protecting? "And you believe that your captain should be there now?"

"Yes, sir," the soldier responded eagerly. Perhaps the unknown officer would leave right now if he was encouraged. "Captain Onichi and the guards colonel are working very hard together to capture the spy who is active in the area."

"I know," Joe lied glibly, although his heart was racing. The private had just confirmed that the radio setting was no coincidence. "That is why I am here. Catching the spy is very important."

The private was even more eager to please. "Perhaps you would like to see the latest radio intercepts we got from the spy? We get copies of what we don't hear ourselves so that they will help us catch him."

Joe would indeed like to see them, and the private got them. As he read the partial transcripts of his messages to the OSS, Joe congratulated himself on not telling the outside world what he was doing. As he'd suspected, the Japanese were reading and decoding his messages, and any reference to his being disguised as a one-armed *kempei* officer would have meant his doom. He still had an ace up his sleeve in the form of another way of sending a coded message, but he'd been told to save it for something truly important, as any code could be broken over time. He would use the second method as a last and desperate resort when there would not be enough time for the Japs to decipher it.

Then he wondered. Why would the guards colonel and the late Captain Onichi be so concerned about the actions of the spy? Why would they consider one spy such a threat to whatever it was they were doing? Whom or what did they have at Camp 7 that they were so desperate to hide? Joe had the nagging feeling that whoever was in seclusion at Camp 7 was more important than the average wounded general or admiral.

Joe walked over to the map and checked the coordinates. If he left immediately, he could be in Camp 7 in a little while.

CHAPTER 44

YUSHU,
REFUGEE CAMP 7

Joe Nomura stood at attention in the tent that served as a command post and tried to analyze the man he'd just reported to. Col. Tadashi Sakei was a strong and dominating presence, but seemed to be on the edge of an emotional cliff. The colonel's left eye twitched and he looked exhausted, almost haggard, as he questioned Joe about his background. Something was clearly bothering the colonel.

Joe wondered what pressures the man was under. Camp 7 was almost a mirror image of Camp 10, where he'd gotten the phony identification that Colonel Sakei had insisted on seeing and examining carefully. This in itself was unusual. The uniform and the armband had so far been more than sufficient to ensure cooperation. No one had asked for proof that he was a *kempei* officer, and he had begun to wonder if he had wasted his time by forging the document. Now he knew it was time well spent as the hawk-eyed colonel stared at the piece of paper.

But why the concern and the elaborate disguise? Camp 7 was crowded and dirty, filled with thousands of confused and frightened civilians who lived in disorganized and shabby clusters. The focal point of the camp was the hospital in which Nomura now stood. Sakei wore a medic's jacket over his uniform and immediately insisted that Joe do the same. There had been no explanation for this behavior except the obvious one—Sakei wanted no one flying overhead to detect soldiers on duty in what was otherwise a civilian hospital. Why? Why the hell were armed soldiers disguised as orderlies guarding a small tent complex?

Sakei finally returned Joe's identification. "Be seated, Captain Nomura." When Joe complied, Sakei went on, "Tell me, where is Onichi? He was supposed to report to me yesterday."

"I don't know, sir. He hasn't been seen in several days." True enough, Joe thought. Even if he was found now, no one would be able to recognize him. "It is possible that he could have been killed or wounded by an American plane."

"Or he could have run off and tried to save himself. I hope this doesn't offend you, Captain, but Onichi did not strike me as a strong-willed person. Certainly he did not have your combat experience. Where did you say you lost your arm?"

"Guadalcanal. I was wounded in the early fighting and was fortunate to be evacuated." He managed to look sad as he said that as if in memory of lost friends. The vast majority of the Japanese sent to fight the Americans on Guadalcanal were dead and rotting in the jungle. The Japanese navy had performed marvels in getting at least some of them off, but many thousands did not make it.

Sakei examined a fingernail. "How were you evacuated? Destroyer or submarine?"

Joe wondered, Is he trying to trip me? "Colonel, I really don't recall. My arm was badly infected, gangrenous, and I was heavily sedated. My only recollection of the entire trip is that of pipes overhead. I have no idea whether they were from a submarine or a destroyer. To be honest, sir, I really don't care."

To his surprise, Sakei laughed. The nonanswer seemed to satisfy him. "Someday you'll have to find out which it was and thank them properly. And now, what is your reason for being here in Camp Seven?"

"Sir, I was directed to work with Captain Onichi and you regarding the American spy and the radio broadcasts that we've intercepted."

Sakei registered surprise. "Why do you think he's an American?"

Oops, Joe thought. Shouldn't have said that. "Sir, it's the opinion of those who've read his reports, which are in English. The speech patterns are distinctively American."

"Ah," said Sakei. "Do you speak English, Captain?"

"Yes, sir, and quite well if I might say so."

"And do you agree with that assessment?"

Joe took a deep breath. "Sir, I believe it is either an American or someone who has spent a great deal of time in the United States."

"Is he of Japanese descent, in your opinion?"

Joe hoped Sakei's next question wasn't whether the spy had only one arm. "Possibly, but not necessarily," he answered, forcing himself to be calm and dispassionate in what amounted to a discussion of himself. "The spy, and we do think there is only one although he is traveling with an escaped POW, could be another escaped prisoner, or even a pilot who crashed and has managed to escape detection. Either alternative would raise the question of how the spy got his radio. Therefore, it is most likely someone who was landed by submarine or small boat. In that case it does not necessarily follow that the person would be Japanese. Someone who is stealthy, good at disguises, or perhaps just extremely bold might get away with what he's doing."

Sakei took a cigarette from his jacket pocket and offered one to Joe, who took it gratefully. It was a Chesterfield and he wondered how Sakei had gotten it this late in the game. Probably off a POW, or even a body.

"Captain Nomura, I want you to continue looking for the spy. I don't think Onichi will ever turn up, and I want you to work directly with me. Is that a problem?"

"No, sir."

"Good. Do you understand why I am so concerned about this one spy?"

"No, sir, I am not. I do presume that it has something to do with the presence of you and your men in this compound and the fact that you are disguised as medics." Joe decided to add another truthful statement to his story. "At Camp Ten, I read Onichi's files and they made reference to someone of importance being in this hospital. Again, I presume that is the reason."

Sakei looked at him thoughtfully. "Captain, do you play chess?"

Joe blinked in surprise. "A little. Truthfully, I haven't played in years." Joe recalled being taught by a thirtyish schoolteacher who'd been on vacation one summer when he was seventeen. She'd also taught him some amazing new sexual adventures that had been much more interesting than chess.

"Are you intimidated by extremely important people, Captain?"

"I don't think so, sir. I respect them, of course, but I am not intimidated to the point where I am unable to function properly."

"Good. Somehow I did not think that a veteran who'd faced death in the jungles of Guadalcanal would be incapable of thought or action in the presence of a high-ranking personage. The individual we are protecting is an extremely important member of the royal family. Let's just say he is not fully behind the current war effort and is being kept out of the public eye for his own good as well as that of Japan."

"I see," Joe said thoughtfully. Who the hell was it? One of the princes? Hirohito had two brothers and a son.

"The gentleman is bored and is constantly after me to play chess with him. While playing, he harangues me with reasons why we should quit the war. If he were a lesser personage, I would beat him with my fists as well as at chess. He is but a mediocre player, and I am confident you would be able to hold your own with him as well as refute his misplaced logic, or at least not be affected by it."

Joe allowed himself a smile. "I share that confidence, sir, but how will it affect my search for the spy?"

"You will have to do both, Captain. I will give you a small traveling chess set that I have. Please refresh yourself and practice. If you would like, I will play you and give you some pointers."

Joe smiled ingratiatingly. "At this time I do not think I would be a worthy opponent for an infant. I will, however, take you up on your challenge in a couple of days."

Sakei laughed. "It is good to be with a soldier. You have no idea how weak Onichi was. He was so squeamish during interrogations of civilian suspects that he had to turn them over to his underlings. He did not know that a few painful and necessarily brutal deaths were but a small price to pay for victory."

Joe took the small case with the chess set, saluted, and left. He hated chess, but if he was going to find out what was going on in Camp 7 and determine whether it was important enough to report, then he would play the damn game. But Sakei's comments about interrogating suspects surprised him. The *kempei* in Japan rarely physically abused Japanese citizens. They might kick or punch someone, but Sakei had strongly implied brutal torture. The *kempei* preferred more subtle methods of intimidation to inspire terror.

So what then was so important that people had to die for it? Who the hell was the haggard Colonel Sakei trying to protect? Who could be so important? Then it dawned on him. Sakei hadn't been referring to one of the princes or even the crown prince when he said it was one of the royal family. The man in the hospital was Hirohito himself!

■

CHAPTER 45

"**M**arine, you die!"

Lt. Paul Morrell nudged Sergeant Collins. "Maybe we should tell him we're U.S. Army and not marines."

Collins coughed deeply and spat on the ground. Like most of the men, the chill air had given him a bad cold. "Let'm die happy, sir. If he wants to think we're marines, it's just fine by me. I'm just a little surprised he pronounced his *r* so well. Don't they have difficulty since it's not in their alphabet?"

Once again, they lay prone on a hill and faced upward at a Japanese strongpoint. This one was a cave that had been pounded by artillery without destroying it or killing the occupants. The machine-gun fire from its narrow opening had stalled the advance, and the ground leading to it was too steep for Sergeant Orlando's tank to negotiate. Attempts to burn them out with a standard infantry flamethrower had also been futile. They were less than a hundred yards away from the cave and the inhabitants had started yelling at them in bad English.

"You die like MacArthur!"

One of the men near Paul asked, "Should we yell back, sir?"

"Don't let me stop you."

Morrell checked the shadows on the ground. In a few minutes it would be night and the advantages would shift, but to whom? Maybe he could get some men close enough in the dark to throw in a satchel charge and blow up the cave entrance. He thought back to the lecture on Okinawa and shuddered at the thought of people, even Jap soldiers who had it coming, being buried alive. He hadn't had to do that yet, but it looked as if the time was coming.

On the other hand, there was the distinct possibility that the Japs in the cave were working up enough nerve for a banzai attack, which would end it all and take them out in a blaze of fanatic glory. If that was the case, he didn't want his men out of the holes they'd dug when it occurred. They'd wait awhile.

The sky darkened and the cloud layer made it even more gloomy and difficult to see. Paul checked by radio with Captain Ruger and was told that mortars with flares were ready for firing. Paul and Ruger wished they weren't so damned close to the cave. As always, the Japs had waited until the platoon was on top of them before revealing their existence. Once again, he had wounded to care for.

"MacArthur dead! You dead too!"

"How the hell do they know these things?" Sergeant Collins wondered. "They get a newspaper in there or something?"

"Beats me," Paul answered. "You have any thoughts as to how many of them are in that cave?"

"I gotta guess at least ten or so, but not too many more. Goddamn cave just doesn't look that big."

That was close enough to what Paul was figuring. Not that many Japs, but they were so damn close to them. If only the flamethrower had killed them, but it hadn't. Maybe the cave was deep enough for the Japs to hide in and save oxygen, which also meant that there might be more Japs inside than they thought. Or maybe the enemy had built baffles or walls within the cave that the fire from the flamethrower could not negotiate its way past. It hadn't taken long for the Japs on Kyushu to figure out that a flamethrower's stream could be deflected by a wall of rocks and that the persons behind the barrier would be reasonably safe as long as their air held out.

"I want a flare," Paul ordered. A few seconds later, the hillside was illuminated with a harsh, artificial light that floated down to the earth, where it gradually faded away. There were no Japs under it.

"Nimitz eat shit!"

"Nimitz's a sailor," Paul found himself saying. "What'd you expect?" That got more laughter from those who heard it, causing Paul to wonder again just how men could find humor in such deadly circumstances. The resiliency of both himself and the men under his command was incredible.

"Banzai!"

They froze. Was there motion by the cave? Paul called for another flare. It revealed nothing.

"Banzai!" The voice was a lament and a scream. A frightening call to arms.

"Sergeant," Paul said, "you know what the hell they're doing?"

Collins was chewing gum nervously. "I think they're working up the nerve to come out. Probably liquored all to shit as well."

"Banzai! Banzai!"

"Flare," Paul ordered, and again the lights came on. Still no Japs.

Then, just as the light faded, Japanese soldiers spilled out of the cave like ants erupting from a disturbed colony. In an instant of shocking clarity, Paul could see that only a couple of the dozen or so Japanese running at them had rifles. Most carried grenades and ran toward them with their mouths wide-open and screaming incoherently. In front of them, one man, obviously their leader, waved a sword and exhorted them on.

"Fire!" Paul screamed. "More flares!"

Rifle and BAR fire rippled down the American line. Japs were hit, tumbled, and jerked about. Within seconds, a half dozen were down and writhing on the ground, but another handful had made it through. More gunfire erupted and additional enemy soldiers thrashed and twitched and rolled downhill. They were dead, but their momentum carried them forward.

A couple of them were still unhit. The officer with the sword was nowhere to be seen, but two men with grenades in each hand were almost on them. Then there was one. He stopped a few yards in front of them and hurled both grenades just as his body was ripped to bloody pieces by a score of bullets.

One grenade exploded harmlessly in front of them, but Paul watched in horror as the second grenade arced through the air toward the soldiers to his left. First, he heard screams of panic, then a loud *PHUMP!* and finally a call for a medic.

While the rest of the platoon continued to shoot the fallen Japanese to make sure they were dead, Paul raced to where the cry for a medic continued with rising intensity. He leaped into a ditch where two previously wounded men looked on in shock at the body of their medic, Corporal Wills. Wills lay facedown with his arms stretched out. Blood and gore saturated the ground on all sides around his abdomen. Sickened by what he knew he would find, Paul turned the man over.

Wills's body from the chest cavity to the hips had been hollowed out as if a giant scoop had spooned out his body organs. Paul could see his heart along with his spinal cord and hip bones. The heart twitched a couple of times and stopped. Wills's face bore a look of surprise. Paul turned away and vomited while the two wounded men began to whimper. He returned Wills to his facedown position and the whimpering stopped.

When he could finally speak, Paul asked the two wounded men what had happened. One spoke while the other nodded agreement. "Sir, the grenade rolled in and Wills jumped on it. Maybe he thought he could throw it out, but there wasn't time. He jumped on it and it blew him all to shit."

A second medic arrived, and a shaken Paul Morrell left the site to find Captain Ruger. Collins told him Ruger had arrived and was at the Jap cave. Paul climbed the darkened, body-cluttered ground to the cave mouth. He flinched as someone emerged from the cave and into the night. It was Ruger.

"Try not to shoot me, Mr. Morrell."

Paul's left hand had started shaking. "Sorry, sir."

"The cave is empty. A couple of dead bodies, but nothing else." Ruger ignored Paul's nervous reaction to the fight. "The place wasn't booby-trapped and they left nothing useful. Just some ammo cases and a few bottles of what looks like home-brewed whiskey. The filthy swine drank everything before they attacked and didn't leave a damn thing for us. Good job stopping them, Paul. That was a helluva fight."

Paul disagreed. "One of them got through and killed Wills. I had thirty men on line and they couldn't stop a dozen Nips who were at point-blank range."

"Couldn't be helped, and you're being too hard on yourself and them. The Japs were running downhill and had only a little ways to go. Your men didn't have time to choose targets, so I'll bet most of your men, those who fired, all hit the same targets. Hell, that officer

with the sword probably got shot a hundred times. I'll bet everybody
wanted a chunk of his skinny yellow ass."

Paul recalled how only a few had gone down in the first fusillade.
"Yeah. But what do you mean 'those who fired'? Everybody shot,
didn't they?"

Ruger laughed. "In a situation like that I'll bet half your boys
were so shocked shitless by the sight of real live Japs running down
their throats that they couldn't shoot at all. Either that or they fired
so wildly they stood a better chance of hitting the moon than they
did the bad guys. Tell me, how many of them did you kill with that
popgun of yours?"

Paul thought for a second, and the answer stunned him. "I was so
scared of the Japs, and so busy yelling for someone to shoot them
along with calling for more flares, that I never did a thing with my
carbine. I might as well have left it at home."

"That's what I mean, Paul. And your boys probably did better
than most would've. After all, we're veterans now."

There was no sarcasm in Ruger's comments. Once again, hours
of boredom had been followed by seconds of sheer terror. Some soldiers had done well, others poorly. All had behaved normally.

"Captain, I want Wills decorated," Paul said, and explained that
the young medic had thrown himself on the grenade in an apparent
effort to save the other two men.

"You sure he actually fell on it intentionally?" Ruger asked. "Maybe
he just stumbled trying to throw it away or while trying to get out of
there himself?"

"Two men will testify that he made no effort to save his own life,
even if he could, and that he jumped on the grenade to save his men."

Ruger started the walk down the hill. Paul saw that he was carrying the Jap officer's sheathed samurai sword. "What're you going to
do with that thing, Captain?"

Ruger paused and waved it awkwardly with one hand. The long,
single-edged blade was designed to be gripped with two hands. "Keep
it as a trophy for the company. If I left it here, some rear-echelon asshole would pick it up and send it home as a souvenir of his bravery.
These things are individually made and may have belonged to that

Jap's family for generations, maybe longer. If I can, I'll try to get it back to his relatives after the war is over. If not, I'll keep it or give it to a museum. The Jap was a brave man. Incredibly stupid, but brave."

"So was Wills, sir. Brave that is, not stupid."

"So put him in for something, Paul. How 'bout the Distinguished Service Cross?"

Paul could see Wills's mutilated body and the eternal look of surprise on his young face. Wills had been one of the good guys in the platoon, although Paul now thought of just about all of them as good guys. "No, sir, let's go all the way. Let's put Wills in for the Medal of Honor."

Ruger thought for a moment. Politicians and senior officers getting honors for just being in the vicinity of the shooting, and not for doing anything even remotely heroic. What Wills had done on a bleak hill on Kyushu definitely deserved to be remembered.

"Yeah," Ruger answered softly, "let's do it."

Paul felt better. Wills's death would have some reason for occurring. "And another thing, Captain. You'd might want to stop waving that sword around. Some Jap sniper's likely to get a little pissed at you for having it instead of the original owner."

He laughed out loud when Ruger quickly dropped the sword down to his leg and looked nervously about.

CHAPTER 46

KOREA,
NORTH OF THE HAN RIVER

Light feathers of icy snow whipped the barren hill overlooking the frosty brown waters of the Han River. A few miles to the west was the ruined city of Seoul. It could only be seen as a distant and still-smoking blur on the horizon, but it marked the only part of Korea south of the muddy and ice-swollen Han River currently occupied by Soviet forces.

To Marshal Aleksandr Vasilevsky, commander in chief of the Red Army's Far Eastern Forces, the city of Seoul and the Han River line constituted only a temporary halt in the inexorable advance of the Soviet forces against the Japanese armies. That the halt was essential and commanded by Moscow did not affect his opinion that it was temporary.

On August 9, 1945, the same day the Americans dropped the second nuclear bomb, on Nagasaki, a million and a half Soviet soldiers and airmen had surged into Manchuria and then on into Korea and China. Organized into three army fronts—the Trans-Baikal, the First Far Eastern, and the Second Far Eastern—they consisted of eighty infantry and armored divisions, which contained five thousand armored vehicles and twenty-six thousand guns and mortars along with a fleet of five thousand planes. This overwhelming and battle-hardened force was hurled at the Japanese, who were pitifully short of manpower and modern weapons.

With few exceptions, Japanese forces confronting them had already been depleted by the need to transfer so many frontline soldiers back to Japan and had been swept aside or bypassed. Japanese airpower was nonexistent, and Japanese armor was laughably inadequate against the Soviet T-34, the finest tank in the world. The vaunted Japanese soldier had no chance to stand and fight against Soviet armor and firepower. In the face of the ferocious Soviet onslaught and far away from home, many Japanese units had crumbled and run, making the code of Bushido a joke. Within a few weeks, Manchuria, northern Korea, and northern China had been overrun with only moderate losses to the Red Army attackers.

On orders from the Stavka, the Soviet military's high command and in reality the word of Joseph Stalin, Vasilevsky had diverted forces from the drive on Korea to concentrate on the efforts in China. The Korean peninsula was an apple that could be plucked at any time, while the opportunity to take China from the Japanese, and to help the Chinese Red Army at the same time, was too great to be ignored.

It also mattered that the tenuous Soviet supply line from west of the Urals to Manchuria was overloaded and could not sustain Vasilevsky's entire army with food, fuel, and ammunition. When the Siberian winter closed down roads and rail lines, choices had to be made as to which areas would be supported by the limited resources, and sustaining operations in China was the choice.

Vasilevsky had halted his operations in Korea while focusing his efforts in China and had been pleased with the results. Beijing and Shanghai had fallen along with a number of other major cities, and the Soviets still drove southward.

But now, as he watched the columns of antlike figures cross the pontoon bridges of the Han River, Marshal Aleksandr Vasilevsky was no longer quite so pleased with his success. That was because Lazar Kaganovich stood beside him on the frozen hill overlooking the Han. Kaganovich was the deputy premier of the Soviet Union, theoretically second only to Joseph Stalin.

The fifty-year-old Vasilevsky had originally been a czarist officer and had, before that, even studied for the priesthood. Both occurred before the Revolution, which, when it came, he endorsed with fervor. With his background, along with his tendency to be cultured rather than affect the crudeness of so many other Soviet officers, Vasilevsky had never felt comfortable in the inner circles of the Soviet hierarchy.

Even though Stalin himself had once considered taking holy orders, Vasilevsky was still concerned that his relatively elitist background might come back to haunt him. He had worked closely with Stalin and knew that he had the power of death at his whim. Vasilevsky's command at the far end of the Soviet empire pleased him because it meant he was far from the reaches of Joseph Stalin and the murderous intrigues of the Soviet empire.

However, Lazar Kaganovich's presence on the Korean hill meant that Stalin had reached out to him. To some people, the huge but cadaverous-looking Kaganovich personified evil. Years earlier, he had delivered his own teenage daughter to be seduced by Stalin, then permitted his own brother to be executed. Kaganovich had further demonstrated his loyalty to Stalin when he orchestrated the death by starvation of the millions of prosperous farmers, the kulaks, whose continuing prosperity insulted the egalitarian ideals of communism. As deputy premier to a man who kept everything to himself, Kaganovich's main role was to be Stalin's executioner.

"Does the sight please you?" Kaganovich asked.

Vasilevsky wondered how any man could permit Stalin to fuck his own daughter, murder his brother, and still work for him. Kaganovich's degree of devotion to Stalin was frightening.

"Indeed it does, comrade, as does anything Comrade Stalin wishes."

"Some might say that we are letting the Japanese get away," he said, gesturing to the columns of Japanese infantry that moved across the bridges in plain sight and under scores of silent Soviet guns.

Vasilevsky recognized the clumsy probe and deflected it. "Anyone who felt that way would be disloyal. Comrade Stalin knows what he is doing and has proven that many times over."

"Good. Even though we all felt you would understand and comply, it was considered important enough that I come here to bring you the message in person."

"I understand." Vasilevsky also understood that the penalty for hesitation in complying with Stalin's order would have been a bullet to the brain from Kaganovich's pistol. It had been widely rumored that Stalin had gotten Kaganovich's daughter pregnant as a result of the seduction. Vasilevsky wondered what had happened to the unfortunate girl and her bastard child. He doubted that either still lived.

Yet, despite his personal and unrevealed misgivings, Vasilevsky had to admire the audacity of the new situation. Kaganovich's message was that Stalin had reached a secret accord with the Japanese government. Under it, the Red armies in Korea would halt in place and safe passage through the Russian lines would be granted to the Japanese forces in China and other parts of Asia. The results of the agreement were below Vasilevsky. Long lines of Japanese soldiers, including many taken prisoner in the preceding battles, were crossing over the Han and back into Japanese control.

"Comrade Kaganovich, how long do you think the secret of the accord will endure?"

Kaganovich's laugh was a sharp cackle. "Long enough for many tens of thousands of Japanese to escape to Korea, and long enough for us to tilt the balance of the war of liberation against the corrupt Chiang Kai-shek regime in the favor of Mao Tse-tung's Marxist forces. Then, like Poland and eastern Germany, we will present the United States with a fait accompli which they can only undo by force of arms. They will not fight for China any more than they will for Poland or any other country we desire to control."

"Do we care what ultimately happens to the Japanese crossing our lines? Have we made further arrangements to get them to Japan itself?"

"We care nothing about them," Kaganovich snarled. "Once the stinking yellow shits are across the Han, they are Japan's problem. Let the Americans bomb them to pieces when they try to cross the straits to Honshu and Kyushu. But those that do make it to their home islands will go on fighting and further weaken the United States by the casualties they will inevitably inflict. This is all part of Comrade Stalin's grand plan. He is delighted when the capitalist nations such as Japan, Germany, Great Britain, and the United States fight each other. Each battle between them weakens them all and makes the ultimate victory of communism that much more likely to occur soon.

"Japan," Kaganovich continued, "cannot win this war no matter what awful weapons she decides to use. All she can do is make her defeat and destruction all the more absolute. At the same time, she will drag the United States down with her. After a while, we shall take over the remainder of Korea and excise the Japanese army with as much difficulty as I would have squeezing a ripe yellow pimple. Then we will be in a position to take over Japan itself once the Americans are through exacting their revenge."

Vasilevsky shivered and it wasn't from the cold. What if the American reaction to this betrayal by Russia was not what Stalin predicted. The Americans had the atomic bomb. Would they use it in revenge against the Soviet Union? He shivered again. If that occurred, millions would be slaughtered and the fighting might go on forever. What kind of world might be left for the descendants of Lenin's cause to inherit?

CHAPTER 47

KADENA, OKINAWA

Adm. Chester Nimitz greeted Gen. Omar Bradley with his usual casual cordiality. Bradley had been about to salute the five-star Nimitz when he found his hand grasped firmly and shaken by the admiral.

"Good to see you, General." Nimitz's smile was wide and sincere. It was easy for Bradley to respond in kind.

Bradley had been in the air in a miscellany of transports and bombers for what seemed an eternity and had not, other than for catnaps, had much sleep in the last couple of days. Arrival at the Okinawan air base had energized him. Overflying the island, now an even vaster military camp than it had been prior to the invasion of Kyushu, he had been reminded of the vast accumulation of men and matériel in England just before the Normandy landings. Better yet, the affable Nimitz seemed genuinely pleased to have him here to take over control of the suddenly leaderless army and its accumulating woes.

They walked briskly to a hangar that Nimitz had converted into an instant meeting area. Bradley had flown with only a few lower-ranking aides, and Nimitz, seeing that his own staff outnumbered and outranked Bradley's, sent most of his men away. Such tact and concern were typical of Nimitz, and Bradley wondered if MacArthur had ever appreciated it.

"Before we get started," Nimitz said, "this is for you." He held out a small package, which a puzzled Bradley took and opened. Inside were two sets of five stars. "I just got word a couple of hours ago that you've been promoted," Nimitz continued. "This is an extra set of mine. I'd be honored if you'd wear them."

Bradley's face flushed with embarrassment and pleasure. He grinned and cheerfully allowed that he'd be deeply honored to accept them. Nimitz pinned them on him while the handful of aides applauded, and the two men sat on comfortable chairs that faced each other. There was no table and Bradley commented that there was nothing between them. The two men realized that Bradley's promotion meant a continuation of the divided command structure: Bradley would command on land, while Nimitz commanded at sea. Each had his own substantial air arm. The command issue remained touchy. Cooperation would be required.

"General Bradley, where do you intend to exercise command?"

Bradley had given that a lot of thought on the flights over. "I've sent orders that MacArthur's staff is to move to Okinawa immediately. The Philippines are just too far away from the war. Lord, in Europe I thought a hundred miles behind the lines was a long ways, but the Philippines are thousands of miles from Japan. I can't command from that far away. As there is no real central point where land forces for the next phase of the operation are gathering, there's no reason not to be closer."

Nimitz chuckled. "The concept of distance is radically different in the Pacific. Are you keeping all of Mac's staff?"

The question was a careful reference to the problems Nimitz and his people had had dealing with MacArthur's arrogant chief of staff, Gen. Richard K. Sutherland, and the arguments over intelligence estimates with his intelligence expert, Gen. Charles A. Willoughby.

"Willoughby and Sutherland are gone. Willoughby was wounded in the attack on the *Augusta,* and I'm having Sutherland reassigned stateside. As to the rest of his staff, I don't think it's wise to change too many horses in midstream, so I'm just going to keep his people for the time being and see how they work out. If people need replacing, it will be done on an individual basis. I'm not planning any housecleaning. Willoughby and Sutherland will be replaced by their immediate subordinates, although I am bringing Matt Ridgway in from Europe with an open-ended assignment to assist me."

"Makes sense." Nimitz did not add that Willoughby and Sutherland's absence might improve the army's willingness to accept intelligence estimates from sources other than their own. The choice of

Lt. Gen. Matthew Ridgway as an apparent liaison to serve where needed was wise as well. The fifty-year-old Ridgway had distinguished himself in the European theater and would be well placed to step in if any field commander faltered.

"Mac's staff should be arriving in a steady stream over the next several days," Bradley said. "I can't imagine they'll all be thrilled to leave the relative comforts of Manila for the tents and huts of Okinawa, but I think it best."

Nimitz smiled at the thought of some of Mac's staff actually having to rough it a little. So far, he was pleased with the army's new commander. Bradley was living up to his reputation for common sense and plain dealing.

"Admiral, in a little while I plan on visiting Krueger on Kyushu, along with Eichelberger and Hodges, and getting some real up-to-date information on the army. But what about the navy's situation?"

Nimitz sighed. "We have suffered more losses at the hands of the Japs than we did in any battle or campaign all throughout the war. The kamikaze aircraft in particular have been devastating. We haven't lost any major ships—no battleships, fleet carriers, or heavy cruisers—but a score of small carriers have been sunk along with a number of light cruisers and destroyers. At least a hundred transports have gone to the bottom, which is causing real problems in supplying the army. Many, many ships, including an additional number of transports as well as the largest warships in our fleet, have been struck and damaged to some degree. A number of them have had to leave Japanese waters for repair.

"We are fairly safe here on Okinawa, but the ships off Kyushu live in fear twenty-four hours a day. The attack on the *Augusta* seems to have energized the Japs. From a manpower standpoint, the navy's suffered more than thirty thousand casualties with half of them killed, and many of the wounded very seriously so. Our only hope is that the Japs will soon run out of planes and suicide boats."

"How many of their planes have been shot down?" Bradley asked, recalling that the Japs had an estimated ten to twelve thousand planes when the invasion started.

Nimitz laughed. "If you believe my pilots and gunners, then all of them and at least twice over. Realistically, we may have shot down five thousand, but more than eight hundred have struck their targets. Based on intelligence estimates and message intercepts, another thousand or so never got near the fleet and crashed because of mechanical problems or other defects. However, a good estimate is that there are somewhere between three and six thousand planes still waiting in Japan for us. Good news is that we seem to have the submarine threat under control, and other types of suicide craft—small boats, divers, and such—have been pretty well eliminated. All that remains are the darned planes."

To Bradley it sounded as if the navy was taking a beating. Yet the fleet was still close to Kyushu and naval planes continued to fly close cover for the men on the ground. If the navy gave up, it would be impossible for the men on the ground to sustain their slow but steady advances. The kamikazes would also be free to find targets of opportunity on Kyushu, with supply and fuel depots being particularly vulnerable.

"Admiral, I understand that you made an offer to share the facilities on the command ship *Wasatch* with General MacArthur, and he, uh, did not think it appropriate."

Nimitz grinned at the memory of it. MacArthur had been polite but there was no misinterpreting his feelings that he would be subordinate to Nimitz if he and his staff were on the *Wasatch*. "That's one way of putting it," Nimitz said drily.

"Well, if the offer still stands, I'd like to take you up on it and move myself and a few key people onto the *Wasatch*."

Nimitz beamed. "That would be excellent!" The two cocommanders could talk to each other face-to-face and solve problems without being separated by thousands of miles of ocean. Sometimes Nimitz wondered how America's army and navy had done as well as they had with the prevailing arrangements.

"Say, General Bradley," Nimitz said teasingly. "May I presume you'll be our guest for dinner and possibly permit us to celebrate your well-deserved promotion in a traditional manner? Alcoholic beverages may be forbidden on ship, but it appears that we are on land at the moment."

"Delighted, Admiral. And when I am on board the *Wasatch,* I'll be certain to designate a portion of it army territory so we can get around that little prohibition."

Better and better, Nimitz thought. "And one other thing. Do you play horseshoes?"

Horseshoes, which Nimitz loved, had been prescribed for him as a means of alleviating the stress of his position. "Admiral Nimitz, I would be delighted to take you on in horseshoes."

CHAPTER 48

THE STRAITS BETWEEN
HONSHU AND KYUSHU

On a normal evening, the rugged coastal hills of the nearby island of Kyushu would have been plainly visible from the equally harsh coast of Honshu. But this, Field Marshal Shunroku Hata mused happily, was not an ordinary evening. This was a wonderful evening. It was one of those nights when the marriage of the cold wind from the north and the warm sea from the south had turned the night air into a dense fog that would last for many hours.

If he was shrouded in the fog, the American bombers and fighters would be blind to his actions. All along the shore, a mighty host had assembled, and its crossing of the mile-wide straits separating the larger island of Honshu from the smaller island of Kyushu would be a military triumph that would ring through Japanese history. Hata mentally compared it with Hannibal's crossing the Alps against the Romans. In this case, it would be the arrogant and supposedly invincible Americans who would be shocked to find that the battle-torn army on Kyushu had been so stunningly reinforced by two fresh and well-equipped infantry divisions.

For weeks he had planned, hoarded, and hid his thousands of men in places along or near the coast. Patiently, he had waited for the right weather conditions that would ensure that the two reinforced divisions of infantry would be able to cross that maddeningly narrow body of water without great harm.

Along with men, Field Marshal Hata had used his skills and power to accumulate hundreds of small boats that could hold anywhere between ten and fifty soldiers each. They were filling with men and would soon rush across the straits. There they would unload their human cargo and return for another trip. Hata's staff had felt it would take only two or three trips to complete the transfer. Thanks to the weather, it would all occur this one evening. The two divisions, thirty thousand men, would be safely across and inland on Kyushu before the weather changed. They would swarm the narrow straits like locusts crossing a field.

Japanese weather forecasters along northern Honshu and Korea were confident that the bad weather would hold at least throughout the night. Hata laughed silently at the term *bad weather*. He considered it marvelous weather. Some other day he would appreciate the sun and the blue sky; tonight he adored the gloom and fog. If the kamikazes were the divine wind, then tonight was the night of the divine mist.

The sixty-six-year-old Field Marshal Hata was in overall command of three area armies: the Sixteenth on Kyushu, which was currently fighting the Americans; the Fifteenth, which was based on the part of Honshu facing Kyushu; and the small Fifth Area Army, which was based on the northernmost island of Hokkaido. While the Sixteenth and Fifteenth faced the Americans, the Fifth looked nervously across the waters toward Sakhalin and Siberia, where the Soviets lurked.

At least he did not have to worry about the Red Army at this time. He had been assured that the Soviets would not move against Hokkaido or anywhere else. This enabled him to strip garrisons and exchange units without fear of the Russians stabbing him in the back.

The Russians might be a threat in the future, but the immediate problem was the American invaders, and an additional force of thirty thousand men might be enough to tip the scales in the favor of Japan.

The signal was given. As far as his limited vision would allow him, Hata could see hundreds of men pushing off into small boats while their comrades cheered them on, exhorting them to move more swiftly so they could make the journey themselves. It was glorious and made him think of a medieval pageant as the little boats disappeared into the fog.

Under normal circumstances, having so many men gathered in ranks along the beaches would have been suicidal, an invitation to the Americans to bomb and strafe, but this night the mist cloaked them. Hata's two divisions would go ashore and head inland, skirting the radioactive ruins of Kokura as they began their trek to the front lines.

"Banzai!" someone yelled, and a thousand nearby throats repeated the cry. Hata's chest nearly burst with pride and an unbidden tear swelled in his eye. These were good troops, the best Japan had left, and they would stop the Americans.

Field Marshal Hata walked the rocky beach, letting his men see him. They saluted and cheered him, and he saluted back with an uncharacteristic broad smile on his face. He knew it pleased them to know that he shared the night with them. Not many generals, much less field marshals, got this close to the men who would die for them. Hata knew it would further inspire the brave young soldiers in their fight for Japan's survival.

He checked his watch. It had been more than an hour, and the first wave should be across the straits. He received confirmation of this from a radioman, who said that many were already unloading and the men were heading inland. Some of the swifter boats had already made it back to Honshu and were loading again. He squinted out into the dark waters and wished he could see more clearly.

And then he could.

There was no mist. For a fraction of a second, he could see every small craft that bobbed on the waves and the dark columns of infantry beyond that snaked into the hills of Kyushu. Then a light brighter than a thousand suns washed across him, baking him. A second later, a shock wave blasted across the straits and blew his charred body into a thousand pieces. The shock wave continued up the hills of Kyushu and Honshu, draining the life from many of those who had not been killed by the fire of the initial blast.

Those who survived the heat and shock wave watched in agony as the evil-looking mushroom cloud lifted toward the heavens. At its base, a massive tidal wave formed and hurled itself onto the land, washing away further thousands of those who had lived through the first seconds of the explosion and dragging their bodies down to the sea.

When it was over, few remained to tell of the catastrophe, and most of those who did live were sickened and later killed by the rain of radioactive water and debris that blanketed the area. Had more been alive when this deadly torrent occurred, the deaths from radiation poisoning would have been greater. As it was, only a handful were left to sicken and die.

As the angry wave receded back into the churning straits, the mist soon returned and covered the water. If someone had walked into the scene and not known the truth, it would have appeared peaceful and serene with only a moderate rain falling to mar the night. No one would have believed that the thirty thousand men of the Japanese 81st and 214th Infantry Divisions had been there and then ceased to exist.

CHAPTER 49

MIYAKONOJO, KYUSHU

It seemed like a miracle, or maybe several miracles, 1st Lt. Paul Morrell thought. Their ordeal at the front was over, at least for a while. The entire regiment had been rotated out of line for rest and refit and sent to a camp near the undistinguished town of Miyakonojo, about fifty miles inland, while some other poor slobs took over the thankless task of climbing hills the Japs didn't want them to.

As an example of their new status as temporarily rear-echelon, they'd had the opportunity to wash their uniforms and shower. An astonishing amount of dirt had run off Paul's body, and he was surprised at how skinny he'd become. He weighed himself and found that he'd lost fifteen pounds and that his body was mottled with bruises and laced by scratches. He looked at himself in a mirror and saw a gaunt-looking stranger with deep-sunk and fatigued eyes. What the hell had happened to the young man he'd once been? He wondered if he could ever go back to his prior life.

They ate hot meals topped off with a dessert of cold ice cream, and so what if they ran out of chocolate—everything was delicious. They had cots in tents that actually kept out the wind and the rain. Paul vowed that he would never again think of a tent as a primitive place to live. Compared with the previous weeks of living in rain, mud, and squalor, a tent was luxury beyond compare. The Waldorf-Astoria in New York would not have been better, he thought. Then he laughed at himself. Of course it would be better.

Even more civilizing was the presence of good, cold American beer. Paul clutched several bottles to his chest and stepped outside. Despite the chill, he and most of the others found it relaxing to be in the open air to smoke, drink, and just wallow in the wondrous fact of their being alive and well. A number of guys were still indoors playing cards or just sleeping, but it was exquisite to be outside and able to walk upright without fear. Although artillery rumbled in the distance, the air was free of the stench of death and the smell of sulfur from exploding shells. For once, the air they breathed was actually fresh.

Weapons were stacked in their tents, but they all still wore the steel pots that had protected their skulls since the landing. About a third of the men who had landed with the regiment were dead or wounded. They'd paid a helluva price for a beer and a warm place to sleep.

Paul walked past a group of enlisted men who were sprawled on the chill ground. "Hiya, Lieutenant," said Weaver, a PFC from Chicago. Weaver had been slightly wounded but had declined a chance to go to the rear earlier. By declining to go, he had probably screwed up his chance for a Purple Heart. Paul made a mental note to see if he could do something about that.

"Hi yourself," Paul said, grinning, ignoring that none of them had made any effort to come to attention. It was not the time to be tight on military formality. Now was a reminder that it really was a citizen army, with few professional or career soldiers. First Sergeant Mackensen was the only one he could think of, although some would doubtless want to remain in the service after the war ended. If, that is, the war ever ended.

"Got a question for you, sir," Weaver said.

Paul stopped. "Okay."

"Do you think they should have drafted Frank Sinatra like they did Joe Louis?"

Paul laughed. "I have a question for you—who the hell cares?"

Weaver pretended to be hurt. "We do, sir. Every day we come up with a topic to discuss, and Sinatra's draft status is today's issue of deepest concern. Hell, sir, it helps keep our minds out of the war."

Makes sense, Paul thought. Keep the agony at bay with silliness. "What other questions have you come up with?"

Weaver belched and almost dropped his beer. As it was, he spilled some and it sloshed over his leg. He didn't seem to notice. "Well, sir, yesterday we discussed whether or not Judy Garland fucked the Tin Man, and the day before we decided that smoking really was good for you and wouldn't stunt your growth."

"Heavy stuff." Paul laughed. "What's the consensus on Sinatra?"

Weaver looked at the others, who nodded for him to continue. "Well, we think we're better off without him. We think he's so skinny someone would have to carry his gear for him. Also, I don't think he sings that great anyhow and won't last, despite what my little sister writes about him. She just loves his skinny little dago ass. By the way, last week we decided that Scarlett O'Hara probably was a lousy lay. We still wonder, though, whether Jap pussy is slanted sideways like their eyes are. Guess we'll have to find that out ourselves, although none of us are so horny yet that we'll screw someone who actually eats raw fish."

"You will be soon," Paul told them solemnly. "Keep up the good work, men."

He walked past where Sergeant Collins, First Sergeant Mackensen, and several others were relaxing as well. Collins had a silly grin on his face while Mackensen's eyes were blank. Sweet dreams, Paul thought. Sergeant Orlando, owner of the M4 Sherman that had proven its worth a dozen times, brushed by him on his way to join the group.

"Sorry, Lieutenant, but this is the NCO club. Officers' country is two trees and five rocks over to your left."

Paul slapped him on the shoulder and told him where he could drive his tank and then spin the turret. All the rules were relaxed, at least for the time being, and it was good, damn good, to be alive.

Just about two trees and five rocks over, Paul found Captain Ruger, Lieutenant Marcelli, and Lieutenant Bergen sitting on the ground. Lieutenant Kinski, he recalled, was resting from a bout of near pneumonia. Kinski was a new guy who'd replaced Houle, who'd been killed a week before.

"Siddown," Ruger ordered, and Paul happily complied. He squatted on the ground and took a long pull of beer. Each of the others had a beer in his hand and a couple more in the pockets of his jacket. "Ammunition," Ruger added, and patted a full bottle. "Never want to run out of fuckin' ammo."

Paul sprawled on the ground and looked up at the sky. "What now, brave captain?"

Marcelli answered, "Live for today. There may not be a tomorrow."

Ruger cuffed him on the arm. "God, that's dismal. We're getting out of here. All of us! Even Kinski, when he gets over his case of the sniffles."

Paul thought such fond hopes were the alcohol talking. Unless the war ended soon, they'd have to return to the fighting and take their share of casualties once more. Paul wondered just how many times a man could be shot at before the bullet with his name on it was fired. He decided to change the subject.

"Okay, Captain, we go home. Then what?"

"Gotta get home real fast and get out of the army so I can make a lot of money while I can. The Depression was ended by the war, but it sure as hell is coming back. Roosevelt might have fixed it for a little bit, but this Truman character ain't smart enough to keep the wolves from returning. I was poor before and I ain't gonna be poor again."

Ruger finished a bottle and threw it angrily into the darkness, where it landed with a dull thud. "That's what I hate about being here. All the people who were in the army are getting out and getting all the good jobs and all the good women. Thank God I got a good woman waiting for me, at least that's one thing I won't have to worry about. But by the time we get discharged, there won't be shit left in the way of jobs, and the Depression will come back in all its ugliness."

Marcelli handed Ruger a fresh bottle. "Some people say that the economy won't go belly-up. They say there's so much pent-up demand for goods that a boom economy will last a long time. I read an article about that in a *Collier's* I found," Marcelli added brightly.

"So, how you gonna solve the problem, Captain?" Paul asked.

"Real estate," Ruger answered quickly. "Nobody's built any houses in years, and there isn't that much room left to build in the cities, and, besides, most city houses are small and cramped. People who have money are going to want something better than the little homes their parents had and will be moving out into the countryside. Hell, a lot of them are still living with their parents in those lit-tle houses. I'm going to buy vacant land and build houses on it."

Paul wondered how that ambition jibed with his earlier state-ment that the economy would go to hell, but decided not to pursue it with the inebriated captain. However, he was intrigued by the comment that no homes had been built since the war started. No cars had been made, so it made sense that other aspects of the econ-omy had frozen in place as well. If so, it meant that a lot of people did indeed have a lot of money to spend. Large plots of vacant land outside of the city might be a good idea for an investment. All he had to do was get home and get his hands on some money. He had a col-lege degree, liberal arts, and it was time to put it to use.

"I just want a job, any job," muttered Lieutenant Bergen. "My dad had a farm in Kansas and lost it all."

Ruger raised an eyebrow. "I thought you were from New York?"

"I am now. We moved there and lived with relatives and tried to find work. There wasn't much there either."

Paul thought of his almost privileged background. At times his parents had been worried about money, but they had never been des-titute. He had seen people begging in the streets and sifting through other people's trash for thrown-away treasures, but, even during the worst of times, he had never thought it could happen to him. Now he was beginning to realize just how fortunate he'd been and just how much he had taken it for granted.

Weaver's comments about Sinatra and his being skinny might have been about the Depression as well. He'd known of a lot of guys who'd failed their preinduction physicals simply because they weren't healthy enough to be soldiers. There was nothing apparently wrong with them, but years of poor eating had damaged them phys-ically. He wondered if they would live shorter lives as a result. He laughed. Hell, they might live a lot longer than he would. After all, the Japs weren't shooting at them.

"Here's to MacArthur." Bergen raised his beer and slopped some onto his chest. "Shit," he said, and wiped it off awkwardly.

"Fuck MacArthur," Marcelli snarled. "If he'd done this right, we wouldn't be here. We'd have won already. He's dead and good rid-dance."

Captain Ruger coughed and fumbled for a cigarette. "You think Bradley'll do better?"

"Couldn't do worse," Marcelli answered.

Paul wondered about that as well. He knew of Bradley from his reputation in Europe and felt they'd gotten a top-notch man to replace MacArthur. Bradley would do a good, solid job and not place his men in unnecessary jeopardy. But, of course, much of what occured would depend on the Japanese, who had, so far, proven damned uncooperative.

They talked and drank until they ran out of beer. Then they sent Lieutenant Bergen—he was the junior officer present as well as the most sober—back for more, which they polished off. Finally it was time to return to their tents and the luxury of sleeping on cots instead of the ground. They would wallow in the ability to sleep in until the headaches that were going to occur from their drinking wore off. The MP guards around the camp would protect them from any Jap snipers or infiltrators. All they had to do was rest and build up their strength for the next round of fighting.

As Paul staggered into his tent and stripped down to his Skivvies, he wondered just what life would be like when he got back home. He wondered what Debbie's reaction would be when he finally got back to her. In a way, he felt guilty. It'd been a while since he'd had the time and the opportunity to even think of her, much less write her. Their mail hadn't caught up with them so he didn't know if she had written lately or not. He closed his eyes and conjured up a vision of her face. She seemed to smile at him and then he was asleep.

CHAPTER 50

ARIAKE BAY, KYUSHU

Men stiffened to attention as the four-seater R5A helicopter lowered itself awkwardly onto the ground. When the rotors stopped their insane whirling, Lt. Gen. Robert Eichelberger saluted General of the Army Omar Bradley as Bradley emerged gingerly from the ungainly machine.

"Welcome to paradise," Eichelberger said as Bradley returned the salute. The two men then shook hands warmly. "Did you enjoy your helicopter ride?"

"Incredible machine. I knew we had them, but this is the first time I've ridden in one. And it was a fine idea having me ferried out from the *Wasatch* in it. How many others are there and what are we using them for besides limos for generals?"

Eichelberger laughed. "We have nearly a hundred in total, although many are smaller than the one you rode in. We use them for courier service because the roads here are nonexistent, and you'll be pleased to know that we are using choppers for medical rescues and evacuations. Of course, the wounded have to be heavily sedated or they'll go into shock from the realization of what they're flying in."

"Wonderful," Bradley said sincerely. The care of his wounded was always a primary concern.

"We first used them in the jungles of Burma a year or so ago, and under the circumstances, it was a logical thing to do here. We've also outfitted some choppers with rockets and machine guns and have had a little success with them as gun platforms. Unfortunately, they're so damned vulnerable to almost any kind of gunfire that we've put that idea on the back burner. Pretty soon I'm confident that someone will come up with a helicopter that's larger and will be armored enough to stand small-arms fire."

"Good idea," Bradley said as they walked toward the miscellany of huts and tents that were the headquarters buildings of the American army in Kyushu.

Bradley halted. "Is the air force here?"

"Yes, sir. Per your instructions, you'll talk with LeMay alone, and then with Krueger, Hodges, and myself tomorrow."

"Good." What he had to say to Maj. Gen. Curtis LeMay would best be said in private. The air corps was a young service, and Curtis LeMay, at thirty-nine, was a very young general who was brilliant, hard-driving, and innovative. His idea to strip the B-29s of machine guns so they'd be lighter and then fly low-level bombing runs on the Japanese had worked brilliantly. Many Japanese cities had been reduced to flaming rubble with few losses to the B-29 fleet. As recently appointed commander of the Twentieth Air Force, LeMay was the senior air corps officer in the Pacific.

Sometimes, however, LeMay's aggressiveness caused others to question his judgment.

Bradley entered the hut Eichelberger indicated. LeMay, a burly man, stood and snapped to attention. Bradley gestured for him to sit down.

When both were comfortable, Bradley began, "General LeMay, you have a reputation for directness. I want some straight answers to some simple questions. First, who ordered the atom bombing of the straits between Honshu and Kyushu?"

"I did," LeMay answered without hesitation.

"On who else's orders?"

"President Truman's."

Bradley hid his surprise. Marshall had radioed him that the bombing had come as a complete surprise to Truman. This meant that LeMay had liberally interpreted his orders. Or disobeyed them. "Clarify that for me, General."

LeMay's eyes registered mild surprise. "General, following Hiroshima and Nagasaki, we then bombed Kokura. Washington was informed that there were no other targets remaining in Japan that were worthy of an atomic bombing, even though one city, Niigata, did remain from the original list of four. I did not quite agree with the decision, but complied. However, we were able to continue fire-bombing cities and other targets with conventional bombs, and it was clearly understood that atomic bombs could be utilized in the future against targets that were purely military in nature."

"And the straits bombing fit this description?"

"It did absolutely. Two divisions of infantry were out in the open and packed together like little yellow sardines. We bombed them and we killed all of them."

"What about civilian casualties? I was led to believe that Jap refugees crossed the other way from Kyushu to Honshu."

"Could've been some, but I doubt that. Our eavesdroppers said that the Jap army had grabbed everything that floated for this effort. There would have been damn few civilians, if any, out on the water that night. Besides, who cares? There isn't a target in the world that's one hundred percent military. Civilians have been getting in the way since man invented the club, and that's just too bad for them."

"What about our POWs?" Bradley asked. "Were any of them in the area as hostages?"

"Possibly, although probably not. This was a secret move on the part of the Japs so they wouldn't broadcast the fact that our boys were out there as hostages. It would give away their little scheme. And if any of our guys were killed by the bomb, then it was the fault of the Japs for putting them there instead of in proper camps. Sorry, but it wouldn't be the first time Americans were killed by our own bombs. You do know that a couple of dozen were killed at Nagasaki, don't you?"

Bradley concurred grimly. Japanese usage of Allied prisoners in military and industrial work was contrary to international law and had caused a number of tragic casualties. "General LeMay, are you aware that many of the world's countries are calling us butchers and barbarians for dropping yet another atomic bomb?"

LeMay laughed harshly. He started to take a cigar from his shirt pocket and then thought better of it. "General Bradley, that's bull-shit and you know it. Hell, I've killed ten times as many Japs, civilian and military, with conventional weapons as I have with nukes. And don't let them snow you with that crap about radiation. As I see it, anything that kills Japs, whether today or next month or even the next century, is fine by me."

LeMay again grabbed for that elusive cigar and retreated. He was not certain what Bradley's reaction would be to his smoking it. "What the hell do those people want, General? Should we go back to crossbows? Nah, the more we kill, the sooner this war ends and the killing stops. Then we can get prepared for the next one against the Russians. The commies are going to be a helluva lot harder to fight than the Japs."

No argument there, Bradley thought. He too felt that the Russians were the real threat to a peaceful future. "General, don't you think it would have been appropriate to inform your commanding officer of your intentions to bomb the straits?"

"General Bradley, the opportunity came up quickly and we didn't think we'd be able to communicate with you and explain the situation in time. We know the Japs are trying to pick up our broadcasts, and we were afraid they'd realize we were up to something. We also thought you'd approve, even if after the fact."

Bradley leaned back in his chair and glared. "You're right about my approving it. I would have. It's the best possible use of a terrible weapon. But the rest of what you said is pure crap. You don't just throw on a nuclear mission just like that and take off in ten minutes. You've been listening to the Japs planning this thing from the beginning, at least days and perhaps weeks, and decided a long time ago that getting me, or whoever else might have replaced MacArthur, angry was a risk worth taking. You weren't going to take the chance of being turned down, were you?"

LeMay shrugged unconcernedly. "Guilty. I got a war to win and Japs to kill. Screw it, sir, it was a target handmade for an atomic bomb. Conventional bombing would have been worthless because of the bad weather. With an atomic bomb, the bombardier only needed to drop the damn thing in the general vicinity of the straits and accuracy wouldn't matter one damn bit. Colonel Tibbets commands the squadron that's dropped all the atomic bombs and he flew the plane himself, and they managed to drop it right on the bull's-eye. The dumb Japs didn't know that the mist hung only a couple of hundred feet above the water so the bombardier had some recognizable mountains to use as aiming points. We bagged ourselves two full divisions and one field marshal. Not a bad night's work if you ask me, although the scientists say that the mist actually held down deaths from the flash."

Damned if LeMay doesn't remind me of Patton, Bradley thought with some satisfaction. He and Patton had once been friends until it was necessary for Bradley to rein him in once too often. He would try to avoid that problem with the belligerent LeMay.

"General LeMay, do you want that third star?"

The question surprised the young general. "Hell yes."

"Good. Now the way to do it is to keep from surprising me. You will not, repeat *not,* use any nuclear weapons in the future without my express permission. Had you told me of your plan for bombing the straits, I would have heard you out, asked some of the questions I've raised today, and then very likely approved. Thus armed I would not have felt like a fool when Truman asked me about the bombing. Whatever authority you feel you might have had from Truman, Marshall, MacArthur, or God Almighty no longer exists. Until and if the air corps becomes a separate service, it is still part of the army, and the army reports to me. Is that clear?"

"Perfectly." LeMay looked surprised and chastened.

"Do you have any plans for A-bombs pending now?"

"None whatsoever, although we are still looking for anything fat and juicy like the straits."

"Good." Bradley relaxed. The situation was under control. LeMay might be overly aggressive, but he was ambitious and ethical and would follow direct and succinct orders. He would not jeopardize a chance at that third star. One question nagged at Bradley. "Tell me, what would Tibbets have done if he could not have found the target in the mist? He could not have returned to Tinian."

LeMay was horrified at the thought. "Hell no! Nobody's gonna try and land a bomber with an atom bomb on it, or any other kind of bomb for that matter, at a base of mine if I can help it. No, sir, he was to drop it in the ocean if he had to. If it was already armed, then it would go off and he would kill a lot of fishes but that's all. Better he kills fishes than the damn thing explodes when he lands at Tinian and we lose a perfectly good base and a helluva lot of good guys."

Made sense, Bradley thought, although the very idea of discarding one of their precious atomic bombs was jarring after all the effort that had gone into developing them. "What about the navy?" Bradley teased. "Any concern that you might cause damage to them if you'd had to ditch the bomb?"

LeMay grinned evilly. "Screw the navy. Nah, sir, they would have been warned."

Bradley laughed and rose. "General LeMay, please go back to killing Japs, and for God's sake, smoke that darn cigar."

CHAPTER 51

THE PACIFIC, SOUTH OF
TANEGA-SHIMA ISLAND

*T*he ocean floor is far from flat. Its undulating hills and valleys of varying sizes and depths generally reflect the land it surrounds. Japan, a hilly and mountainous collection of islands, is encircled by a submerged continuation of herself. Thus, a submarine lying in hiding on the ocean floor on the Japanese continental shelf was rarely a stable and level platform.

The I-58 was down at the bow and tilted slightly to starboard as she lay silently on the bottom. This made any normal function such as standing, walking, or sitting awkward at best. One couldn't even lie down properly under the circumstances, and this made sleeping difficult. Exhaustion on the sub was a common result.

But, hidden as they were in a submerged crevasse, they were safe from detection. Sonar probes couldn't find them. Commander Hashimoto again reviewed his successes and his failures. On the positive side of the ledger were the sinkings of two freighters and an American warship that might have been a light cruiser or a destroyer. Which it was he didn't know. It had attacked him so quickly while he was lining up another freighter that his only concern was to sink it quickly and get away. Identifying it was irrelevant.

On the negative side, three fairly undistinguished ships were all he had to show for a combat cruise in which he had hoped for fat pickings once he had penetrated the American destroyer screen. Despite his best efforts, it hadn't worked out that way. Even though hundreds of American transports and scores of carriers were in the area, the vastness of the North Pacific worked to hide them. Then, when he did find a group of potential targets, the wolfish and snarling destroyers were always present. He had attacked on occasion, but the counterattacks by the destroyers had forced him to hide, and the men of the I-58 did not press the attacks to their conclusions.

At least he had gotten rid of the *kaiten*. The last remaining suicide-torpedo pilot had ridden his chariot to glory and death the previous day. Whether he had hit the freighter they'd targeted, Hashimoto didn't know. He and the crew of the I-58 rather doubted it as there had been no explosions rumbling in the distant ocean. With profound sadness, he imagined the *kaiten* spiraling downward in the sea's darkness to oblivion. What a waste. He hoped the eager young fool had died quickly.

One other time, the I-58 had been forced to make an emergency descent when a pair of American destroyers had angrily charged on his periscope. He thought they'd been directed to him by an airplane that had seen the I-58's shape underneath the waves. At least his unloved executive officer had finally served a purpose, if not in life then in death. The man had been killed in an earlier depth charge attack when an explosion hurled him against a pipe, cracking his skull. Afterward, his body had been kept in cold storage. When the depth charges got too close for comfort, the cadaver was stuffed into a torpedo tube and released upward with some debris. It had convinced the destroyers that the I-58 had been killed and they had departed.

Hashimoto checked his position. He was fifty miles south of the island of Tanega-Shima, which itself was south of Kyushu. Tanega-Shima was not a safe haven as it had been occupied by the American 158th Regimental Combat Team since early November, several days before the main assault on Kyushu.

Hashimoto had intended to stay closer to Kyushu, but American destroyers and a lack of good targets had caused him to stalk his prey ever farther away from Japan proper.

Enough, he decided. They had rested here a sufficient length of time. "Periscope depth," he ordered, and the boat slowly rose toward the surface. As it left the mud of the undersea ravine, the I-58 stabilized and Hashimoto was able to stand and walk properly.

"Anything?" he asked the men whose ears and listening devices strained for the sound of the turning screws of a hostile ship.

Neither he nor the others detected any ominous noises. This did not necessarily mean they were safe. A destroyer could be lying silently on the surface and waiting for him to betray himself, or an American search plane with radar might detect his periscope as it lifted above the waves and drop bombs on his head. As a precaution, his ascent was slow and he would raise his periscope with great caution.

Finally, Hashimoto ordered up periscope and began a visual search. He swiveled in a full three-sixty and saw no sign of danger, or targets for that matter. Dammit, he cursed. Where were all the American ships?

Then he blinked. A smudge was on the horizon. Yes, the light was good and there was definitely something there, actually just below the horizon. He calculated distance and speed and concluded that it was a large ship. Perhaps it was the carrier that had been denied him. Incredibly, the ship seemed to be alone. Could the Americans be repeating the mistake that had cost them the *Indianapolis*? He found that hard to believe, but the evidence of his eyes was too compelling.

Then the grim truth hit him as he reworked his calculations. The distant ship was moving slightly away from him and at a speed in excess of thirty knots. The I-58 could do nine knots submerged and just over twenty on the surface. He would never catch her, and he wasn't even close to being in range for one of the dozen torpedoes he had remaining. While the torpedoes could speed toward an enemy at forty-five knots, their range was only two and a half miles. He wished for the larger torpedo that once flew from Japan's now sunken surface ships. Their range was more than twelve miles. Even with that, he conceded grudgingly, the attempt would have been futile as the target was more than twelve miles out.

"Ah," he said suddenly, and the others looked at him. "The target is turning," he announced with a tight smile, and there were gasps of surprise.

The target was zigzagging and one of her movements was bringing her closer to the I-58. But how close? he wondered. Would he be able to fire his torpedoes at her, or would she just tantalize him with her presence and then race away?

Hashimoto ordered down periscope and directed the sub's full submerged speed toward where he thought the target was headed. And then he waited. If fate was with him, the target ship would be drawn close. If not, then he would swallow his anger and seek another.

Half an hour later, he again looked through the periscope. The target was markedly closer and still moving at great speed. Perhaps that was why she was alone. She could move more swiftly than any escorts. Better, she truly was a great ship. The dazzle camouflage painting on her hull and upper works broke up her design so he could not determine what she was, although she lacked the boxy shape of a carrier. She was, however, simply the largest ship he had ever seen.

Then it dawned on him. The massive target drawing closer to him was an ocean liner, probably the *Queen Mary* or the *Queen Elizabeth*. The leviathans had sped across the Atlantic Ocean with passengers in peacetime and now carried soldiers, but he had never before seen one. He knew they'd made numerous solo Atlantic crossings without incident because they had almost twice the speed of a submarine and were much faster than most surface warships. Traveling in a convoy had been deemed much more of a danger than cruising alone. Yes, that's what it must be, and she was coming toward his position like a greyhound. Hashimoto plotted a new course to intercept her, one that presumed she would not change again. He feared that she would turn away before she came into range, but he had to make the effort. He peered through the periscope until his head ached but he couldn't stop looking. More minutes crawled by, and now the great ship was almost within range of the I-58's arsenal. The target was plotted and all four bow tubes were ready.

No! Hashimoto slapped at the periscope in fury. She was starting her turn. He wanted to scream. But then he smiled. She was so big that turning quickly was physically impossible. Soon her drift had carried her well within range, and she had presented him with virtually her whole length to shoot at. She had come close enough that, with the periscope telescope at full zoom, he could see dots that were people on her deck.

"Fire tubes one through four," he ordered. His voice was incredibly calm even though he wanted to exult aloud with the ecstasy of success. The Japanese torpedoes were superb and would do their work.

The submarine rocked in the water as four torpedoes, each with almost nine hundred pounds of high explosives, surged outward and underwater at speeds many automobiles couldn't reach on land.

Hashimoto's eyes stayed glued to the scene. As the seconds counted off, he saw an antiaircraft gun on the ship fire tracers toward him. Either the periscope or the torpedo tracks had been sighted, but it was too late for the liner to do anything but continue her inexorable starboard turn.

The first torpedo struck near the bow on the port side and was followed in quick succession by three more as explosions took in nearly the entire length of the giant ship. Her continued forward motion caused the ocean to surge through the gaping holes in the target's hull. The liner was literally driving herself into the sea.

The forward tubes were reloaded with incredible haste. "Fire one and two."

Again the submarine rocked as nearly a ton of death raced toward the stricken target. These torpedoes too exploded on the port side, and with the accumulation of wounds, the ship began to roll sickeningly on her side.

Then Hashimoto knew horror. The ship's decks were black with humanity. Thousands of men were on the target, moving and swirling like people in a crowded Tokyo street, and they were all trying to escape the dying ocean queen at once. The ship continued to roll on her side with astonishing swiftness. It was like watching a child's toy in a pond. Nothing that mighty should die so quickly, but she did.

Minutes later she had turned completely on her side. Scores of men stood helpless on her exposed hull as it bobbed and wallowed in the water. She shook them off her slippery hull like a dog sheds itself of water. Then her bow slid into the water, and her stern, with her propellers still spinning in obedience to her last instructions, followed until there was only gurgling white water where the great liner had been. On board the I-58, they could hear the creaking and groaning sound of the giant metal ship breaking up in its descent to the bottom. Hashimoto thought he could hear the death screams of those trapped belowdecks for her final ride.

A stunned Hashimoto looked on the sea where the ship had been. The handful of lifeboats and rafts were jammed with humanity. The sea was covered with dark dots that each represented the head of a desperate swimmer. The water wasn't frigid, but the men in the water wouldn't last long. He briefly contemplated surfacing and trying to rescue some of them, or even giving them his own rafts, but thought better of it. There were just too many and the danger was too great. There had been more than enough time for the ship to have gotten off a distress call, hadn't there? Help for the dead queen had to be on the way, wasn't it?

But what if there wasn't? The Americans hadn't missed his earlier kill, the *Indianapolis,* for several days after the sinking. What if this was a repeat of that incident? This was war and they were the foe. The I-58 had hurt the enemy of Japan and hurt him badly. Hashimoto still had a handful of torpedoes left and more targets to seek out before trying to sneak back to Japan.

But the sight of so many men thrown into the ocean sickened Hashimoto. He stopped looking through the periscope and pressed his forehead against the cold metal of the tube.

"Down periscope," he ordered, and gave a course that would take them away from this place of death. He grieved for the men he'd just killed. Hashimoto would continue the war, but he was now sick of the killing. The feeling had been growing in his soul for some time. He would report his success to Tokyo, but would take no joy in it. The joy he had felt at finding such a target had disappeared.

Then Hashimoto knew what he would do. The Americans were looking and listening for Japanese subs. He would radio his report in such a way that they would know exactly where to look for the survivors of the dead queen. Perhaps that way he could live with himself in a future world.

■

CHAPTER 52

President Harry Truman buried his face in his hands and would have wept if it would have done any good. The other man in the office, Gen. George C. Marshall, bit his lower lip and waited for the tirade he expected and in some way felt he deserved. But it didn't come.

"Why?" Truman asked softly. "Why on earth was the *Queen Elizabeth* sailing alone to Japan? Why weren't there any escorts with her?"

Marshall lowered his head sadly. Admiral Leahy or King ought to have been answering Truman, but Leahy had emotionally collapsed as a result of the sinking, as well as being in disfavor with Truman because of his increasingly pacifist views, while King was trying to coordinate the continuing but increasingly futile search efforts for survivors.

"Both the *Queen Elizabeth* and the *Queen Mary* have been leased to us by Britain's Cunard Line and neither has ever sailed with an escort. They are so fast that most warships simply couldn't keep up with them, and they certainly were able to outrace any submarine. They've made numerous trips across the Atlantic to England and made them without any U-boat attacks, and with even greater numbers of GIs on board. The U-boats were always a much greater menace to shipping than any submarines the Japanese sent out." Marshall didn't add that both he and King thought that virtually all the Jap submarines had been sunk.

"So what happened this time? Did we just run out of luck?"

"It appears that the *Queen Elizabeth* was guilty of nothing more than stumbling on a waiting Jap I-boat." He added that there would be no further solitary sailings. The fully laden *Queen Mary* had been recalled to San Francisco. "After all is said and done, bad luck and a mechanical problem with the ship's sonar may be the answer."

"And, after all is said and done," Truman said, unconsciously mimicking Marshall, "how many young Americans are dead?"

Marshall started to answer, but his voice broke with pent-up emotion. He took a deep breath and tried again. "There were just over fourteen thousand unassigned army replacements on the ship. While rescue efforts are still continuing, we have picked up only a little more than two thousand of them, and a lot of them are in pretty bad shape. Admirals Nimitz and King hold out little hope that we will find more than a few more men alive. Rescue ships have plucked several hundred bodies from the waters and will continue that aspect of the recovery effort."

Truman winced. "And if it wasn't for the broadcast from the Jap sub, we wouldn't have yet missed her, would we?"

The killer of the *Queen Elizabeth* had been identified through his broadcast report as Comdr. Mochitsura Hashimoto and the sub as the I-58. Hashimoto and the I-58 had destroyed the *Indianapolis* only a few months earlier in circumstances that were chillingly similar.

"General, is this Hashimoto a war criminal?" Truman asked. "Can we promise the American public the satisfaction of a hanging in return for this disaster?"

Marshall again wished that a naval officer was present to respond. "The *Queen Elizabeth* was a legitimate target and he was under no compulsion to warn her, or do anything else that might have endangered himself. His actions were similar to what many of our own submariners are doing in their actions against Japanese shipping. In fact, Hashimoto may have saved a lot of lives by broadcasting his triumph in the clear, without any encoding. He gave the precise location of the sinking, which was highly unusual. Since the *Queen Elizabeth*'s radio was knocked out within minutes of being hit, that transmission was our only real knowledge of where to begin looking."

Truman had wondered about that as well. "Do you think he did that on purpose to help us get those boys out of the water, or was he trying to show off and rub it in?"

"I don't know. Although rather unlikely, it is just possible that he was trying to save lives by the time he sent his message. If the war ever ends, we might have a chance to ask him."

Truman stood and looked out the window behind his desk. "I'm curious. England had any number of ports where a liner full of soldiers could disembark troops, while we don't yet hold a single good-sized Japanese port. Just where on earth was the *Queen Elizabeth* going to dock and unload all those troops?"

"She was going to reach a point off Japan where she would be surrounded by a horde of destroyers to protect her. LSTs and other smaller craft would swarm around her, and men would disembark directly onto them. As Nimitz's boys had it planned and rehearsed, the *Queen Elizabeth* would be emptied in a few hours and be back on her way to Hawaii or California."

But it hadn't gone as planned and almost twelve thousand American boys had been drowned. So far, they'd managed to keep news of the catastrophe out of the newspapers and off the radio. Just how much longer this could keep up was debatable. A few days was the best guess. With the earlier crises of the war behind them, many reporters and correspondents were openly chafing against what they felt was unnecessary government censorship. Several papers had already announced that they would no longer abide by censorship rules, and the attorney general had told Truman that there really wasn't much the government could do about it. Prosecuting newspapers would be politically disastrous and might not result in a favorable verdict in the courts.

A few days, Truman thought. Just a few days and then the world would know that twelve thousand GIs had died not in battle but in getting there. That it was nearly Christmas would make it even more devastating. The atom bomb had killed thirty thousand Jap soldiers a few days earlier, and a conventional torpedo had just killed twelve thousand Americans in what the Japanese were sure to call justifiable revenge. Where was the justice? What the hell use was it to have superweapons when the enemy's old ones worked so damnably well?

CHAPTER 53

KYUSHU, CAMP 7

Joe Nomura was about to lose the chess match to the Son of Heaven.

"Check!" he said in an undeniable tone of gloating.

Joe bowed and smiled. "You win, Your Majesty. Would you like another game?"

Hirohito laughed again. "No, beating you four times in a row is enough. You try hard and are improving, but you really aren't a very good player."

"It's been years since I had the opportunity to play, sir." And that was in Hawaii, dammit!

"I know," the emperor said gently. "I did not mean to make fun of you. I enjoy playing chess with you and I enjoy having you to talk with. You are so much less a radical than the good colonel, my jailer." Joe was genuinely surprised. "Oh, I know you are a member of the *kempei,* which means you should be a fanatic like Sakei, but I see in your eyes that you are wearied by the war."

"I think everyone is, Your Majesty." It was a good, safe answer.

"Of course, but there is a great deal of disagreement over what to do about it. You are aware, are you not, that I am here because I agreed to surrender to the Americans?"

"Yes."

"Anami and the others who took over are afraid that the Americans will destroy Japanese culture. I disagree. I feel that surrender is the only way to preserve it, and there are many who agree with me. Tell me, Captain, what do you see in this camp, and when you leave here and walk through the countryside? Do you see a culture being preserved, or do you see dirty and starving people eating roots and dying of cold? And when you listen to military reports, do you hear that the Americans have been driven from Kyushu or that their planes have stopped bombing our few remaining cities?

"No! Captain, I believe that it is men like Anami and his puppet Colonel Sakei who will destroy Japan if they are not stopped. It is they who threaten the continued existence of Japanese culture, and not your emperor."

Joe said nothing. Even though his few sessions with Hirohito had been cordial, one did not argue with one's emperor. Nor did one agree with him too promptly. There was the concern that he was being tested, but for what? Silence was the best course.

"I understand, Captain, that you will neither say nor do anything that will put you in any jeopardy, and I applaud both your tact and your restraint. Yet again your eyes betray you. You wish you could say something, but don't know how or what to say, do you?"

Joe smiled. "Your Majesty is quite wise."

"And perceptive."

Joe did not disagree. Where the hell was this going? he wondered.

"Someday you may have to make some difficult, even agonizing decisions, Captain. You may have to decide where your true loyalty lies. Is it to Anami and Sakei, or is it to Japan and your emperor? My duty lies in ending this war as quickly as possible and by using any means available. I feel that I could have been the instrument of peace. I pray that it is not too late for me."

Hirohito clapped his hands. "Go now. Think about what I have said and what is the evidence of your eyes, your mind, and your heart. I know you will make the decision that is best for Japan."

Almost in shock, Joe stood and bowed. He left the compound hastily and rode his bike out into the countryside. What the hell was Hirohito saying? It sounded as if he wanted Joe's help to spring him from his prison, and the more he thought about Hirohito's words, the more he became convinced that his assumption was correct.

Now what? Jesus. Just when he thought he had a handle on things, someone went and changed the damned rules. He had to get back to camp and contact his handlers. Maybe it was time to break into the new code? He was only to use it as a last resort because, after that, there was no other. Maybe he should try to use the old one without compromising himself. He'd have to talk to Dennis. Dennis was damned clever and would help come up with something.

With a jolt that nearly caused him to fall off the bike, he realized that he might have it within his power to end the whole war if he could get Hirohito out of his confinement and into the hands of other people who thought the way he did.

CHAPTER 54

Ernest Bevin was Great Britain's secretary of state for foreign affairs in the relatively new government of Prime Minister Clement Attlee. It seemed poignant and significant to President Truman that the heads of both the world's greatest democracies had fallen within a couple of months of each other. Franklin Roosevelt had died of a massive stroke, while Winston Churchill had been replaced by a Labour government that the British people felt was better qualified to lead them through the coming peace.

Of the three world leaders who'd forged the wartime alliance against the Nazis, only Joseph Stalin remained.

"Mr. President, I have come on a mission of great urgency, and it is imperative that we be able to speak frankly and candidly, even though that will require the stating of some unpleasant truths." Bevin chuckled. "Indeed. First let me say that I come as the representative of a country, Great Britain, that is your only true friend on this earth."

Byrnes responded quizzically, "I'm delighted that you reaffirm our alliance, but why do you state that you are our only true friend?"

Bevin nodded. "Because France, under the insufferable Charles de Gaulle, is going its own arrogant way, and the other European countries are too devastated to provide anything beyond lip-service support to you as allies. In Asia, Chiang's China is tottering and claims to be your ally for the sole reason that you provide Chiang with the material resources to fight the Japanese and the Communists. Russia, of course, is betraying you routinely."

There was overwhelming evidence that the Russians were fighting only the Chinese Nationalists, while permitting hundreds of thousands of Japanese soldiers to trek through Soviet lines to Korea, where the Japanese tried to slip them into either Honshu or Kyushu.

"I spoke with Ambassador Gromyko this morning in person," Truman said, "and with Molotov by phone. Both men flatly deny any complicity in the fact that the Japs are getting through to Korea. When I showed Gromyko proof that Russian ships were actually ferrying Japs to Korea, they professed shock and said it must be the actions of a deviant local commander."

Bevin arched an eyebrow. "Did you believe them?"

"Hell no, and I let Gromyko have it with both barrels." Truman laughed bitterly. "When I tried to scold Molotov, the son of a bitch hung up on me. Deviant local commander, my foot. Nobody in the Soviet Union even goes to the john without Stalin's specific permission."

Bevin relaxed slightly. "Do you accept that China is lost?"

"I don't see how it could be otherwise," Truman answered. "I've met with some congressmen who are supporters of Chiang Kai-shek and they've yelled at me that we have to do something, anything, to help Chiang, but nobody knows what that something or anything might be. Yes, Mr. Bevin, China is lost no matter what the so-called China Lobby in Congress says and wishes."

"Mr. President, distasteful though that may be, it helps bring me to the reason for my visit. The Russians are moving down the coast of China and taking over the land held by the Japanese, which includes all the major coastal cities."

Byrnes nodded. "But how does that affect Great Britain?"

"Hong Kong," Bevin stated simply.

"I see," said Marshall. "You want your empire back and you wish us to help you get it."

"Not totally," Bevin corrected. "England is emotionally, physically, and economically ruined by this war. What my government has to do for her people is to end the war as quickly as possible so that we can begin to recover before recovery is impossible. Our army and navy must be brought home and the enormous expenditure in war material must be pared down."

"And how does Hong Kong fit in this picture?" Truman asked.

"It is much more than a symbol of empire. I know that your nation hates the thought of colonial empires and has made it emphatic that you are not going to fight to reestablish European colonies, but Hong Kong is unique. It is a British city-state, albeit with a large Chinese population, that is both a symbol to my country and a place where a great number of British prisoners, civilian and military, are being detained."

Truman understood and conceded that point. "The safety of our prisoners in Japanese hands is a grave concern."

"Then you were as horrified as we were about the massacre in Kagoshima," Bevin said.

U.S. Marines had finally stormed Kagoshima City in bloody house-to-house fighting. After slogging through the charred ruins of the town, they'd found more than two hundred Allied prisoners of war who'd systematically been murdered by the Japanese before they themselves committed suicide. The prisoners' hands had been tied behind their backs and they had been beheaded.

"We have to get our prisoners back," Bevin said. "The Japs have seven or eight Dutch or Commonwealth prisoners for every one American in captivity. While we have liberated some helpless wretches in our drive through Burma, the vast majority remain in very brutal Jap hands. You were truly fortunate in that you rescued so many in the Philippines, but you know full well just how terribly they'd been treated."

Only now were the truths of the Bataan Death March and the atrocities at the Philippine camps such as Cabanatuan being accurately assessed. The kindest camps were those where the inmates were merely overworked, beaten, and starved. At others, these were combined with torture, hideous experiments, and ritual murder. Lt. Gen. Masaharu Homma had commanded the Japs in the Philippines at the time of Bataan and was one of the leading candidates to be hanged after the war. Gen. Tomoyuki Yamashita, who currently led the ragged remnants of the Japanese army in the hills of Luzon, was another.

"So what do you want?" Truman asked.

"As I stated, Hong Kong. We wish your support in taking it. I'll be candid. If we do not get it, we may have to consider making a separate peace with the Japanese. It is that important to us."

"Just how do you plan to use our support to take the city?" General Marshall asked.

"At their current pace, we estimate that the Russians will be in Hong Kong in four months, six at the latest. The Soviet thrust does seem to be running out of steam, but it is still pushing southward.

"We wish to detach our task force from your Pacific fleet and use it to support a relief expedition. That Royal Navy force includes four battleships, five carriers, and a number of cruisers and destroyers. We also have three divisions training to invade Honshu as part of Operation Coronet. We need American transports to take those three divisions to Hong Kong and help land them in sufficient time to retake the city and forestall its takeover by the Communists. Let's be honest, gentlemen. America neither needs nor particularly wants Great Britain's participation in the coming invasion."

"General MacArthur may not have wanted your help," Marshall said, "but General Bradley absolutely does. And I know that your small but heavily armored carriers are almost impervious to Japanese kamikaze attacks, which makes them immensely valuable at this time."

"When?" Truman asked, cutting off Marshall.

"In sixty days. Ninety at the most. If the Reds get wind of our intentions, they will expedite their march down the coast. We must get there first and leave the Russians outside Hong Kong."

Marshall was concerned. "Mr. President, we are planning the invasion of Honshu in a little more than three months. Because of the losses we've taken from the kamikazes and weather, we have barely enough transports now to complete our plans. If we skim off enough to take three divisions and their supplies to Hong Kong, I don't think they can be back to their staging areas in time. The invasion will have to be postponed."

"Or accelerated," Truman said softly, and watched as Marshall's face registered astonishment. "Here is what we will do," Truman said, turning back to Bevin. "General Marshall and General Bradley will determine whether we can land on Honshu sooner rather than later and free up the shipping. I agree with you, the war must be ended. The United States is growing wearier of this war far more quickly than I ever dreamed."

News of the existence of a list of prisoners had caused many relatives of missing Americans to hope for the best. Some had marched in the streets in favor of an end to the war. So far, they were a vocal minority, but Truman knew that another disaster like the *Queen Elizabeth* or the massacre at Kagoshima would increase their numbers to where they would be a force to be reckoned with.

Truman leaned forward and smiled in Bevin's face. "Now let's discuss the price of our cooperation."

Bevin laughed. "What do you want?"

"Britain will immediately support the idea of a homeland for Jews in Palestine and begin to act on that support."

Bevin pretended surprise. He had expected this sort of quid pro quo. "That is contrary to our current policy and will outrage the Arabs."

Truman smiled. "I don't give a damn about the Arabs. Congressional elections are coming in less than a year and presidential elections in two years after that. I wish to be reelected and so do you. My party represents an international focus, while the Republicans still harbor a large number of isolationists. Think about it. Who is more likely to be present with you in Europe to confront the Russians: Tom Dewey or me? The Republicans are against communism and Dewey is fairly forward-thinking, but other Republicans, Vandenberg for instance, would rather fight the Reds on the coasts of New Jersey. I am certain you would rather we confront them on the Elbe in Germany.

"Mr. Bevin, there are very few Arabs in America, and those who are here aren't particularly political, but there are many, many Jews. American Jews normally vote for my party, the Democrats. Giving in to the legitimate aspirations of European Jews for a homeland and keeping your earlier promises about it being in Palestine will help me get elected in '48. It's just that simple. You want Hong Kong and I want Palestine. If you agree, we will assist you in three months, not sooner. That might just give us time to invade Honshu and swing a sufficient number of transports south with your warships. Do we have an agreement?"

Bevin calculated his losses. The hell with both the Jews and the Arabs, he thought. More than either, Britain needed Hong Kong, and three months should be more than sufficient time. Even though most Englishmen knew that the days of empire were over, they wanted England to be the country making the decisions and setting the terms that would free her colonies. Fortunately, it was a myth that Great Britain was economically dependent on places such as Hong Kong and India. She wasn't.

Bevin conceded. "All right, but there are many Jews who do not wish to go to Palestine and instead wish to come to America. These you will take. Also, the opening of Palestine to Jewish immigration must be done in such a way that the Arabs will see your country as pushing and bullying us into doing it and thereby hate the United States and not us. We are dependent on their oil and need their goodwill to make it back economically. You may never be able to get petroleum from the Arabs in the future, however."

"That's acceptable," Truman said. In the world of politics, forever never occurred. Regardless of the rhetoric and the passion, today's enemies could easily become tomorrow's allies and vice versa. "The Arabs can keep their damned oil. We have more than enough for our needs."

CHAPTER 55

KYUSHU,
NORTH OF MIYAKONOJO

*T*he commander of 528th's 1st Battalion, Maj. Jimmy Lee Redwald, was a little too flamboyant in his dress and mannerisms for Brig. Gen. John Monck's personal taste. Redwald casually ignored the unwritten prohibition on looking too much like an officer while in a combat area. His fatigues were always clean and pressed, and his boots shined. Since Redwald didn't have the rank to have anyone available as a valet, Monck presumed that the major did the laundry and spit-shining himself. Monck could think of several better ways to spend an evening.

Redwald also kept his major's insignia on the front of his helmet, although he did not use the shiny brass that would have drawn sniper fire from all across Japan. The major was infatuated with what he'd heard and read about the hard-driving George Patton in Europe. On occasion, Monck had reminded Redwald that Patton operated farther behind the front lines than a mere major did and was less likely to draw enemy fire. That little fact did not appear to impress the lanky Oklahoman.

On the positive side, Major Redwald's battalion was well run and the men seemed to respect their commander while tolerating his attempt at being colorful with quiet amusement. On balance, there were a lot worse officers and not that many better.

What the hell, Monck thought as he, Parker, Redwald, and Monck's driver drove toward Redwald's command post with their guard vehicles ahead and behind them. If being a show-off works for

Redwald, who cares. "Jimmy Lee, who's this boy you're putting up for the Medal?"

"Didn't you get my report, General?"

"Of course I did and it reads quite well. But they all do, don't they? I know what it says, but what does it mean? Did he really dive on that grenade to save others, or was it some kind of fluke? As much as I'd like to have a Medal of Honor awarded to one of my men, the Medal's a precious thing and I want to know what's right before I endorse the report and send it on to division."

Monck's endorsement was but one of many steps before a Medal of Honor could be awarded to the dead medic, while a lack of an approval would kill it.

"I've been wondering that same thing since Ruger forwarded Lieutenant Morrell's report to me with his endorsement," Redwald said. "All I can say is no one really knows what went on in that poor boy's mind when he saw that grenade lying in front of him. Was he really trying to save his men or did he think he could smother it and save himself? Maybe he just plain stumbled while trying to get out of the way and fell on it despite himself. I really don't know and no one else does either. The only thing I do know is that the Wills boy is dead and two wounded men aren't, and all as a result of his actions. Ask the two wounded boys and they'll say Wills was Jesus Christ himself."

Monck agreed silently with Redwald's assessment. Neither officer would speak of another fact, that having a Medal of Honor winner under their command would mean an honor to the unit and some would rub off on Wills's superiors all the way up the chain of command.

"You gonna approve it, General?" Redwald asked hopefully.

"I don't know." Monck wasn't going to recommend something he didn't believe in. "Wills's going to get something, but I don't know just what. You know as well as I do that it might get knocked down to a Distinguished Service Cross or a Silver Star before the whole process is over. Both of them are high honors, but neither one is the Medal. Parker, what do you think?"

Parker ignored the talk and looked instead at the surrounding desolation. The area they were driving through had been heavily fought over, and a multitude of shell craters made the terrain look like a moonscape. At least the dead had been picked up. American graves registration had interred U.S. dead in temporary cemeteries, while Japanese dead had been buried in mass graves or plowed over where they'd fallen.

As on most of occupied Kyushu, no Japanese civilians were around, which was prudent on their part. Even civilians stood a good chance of being shot on sight. There had been enough suicide attacks on the part of old men, women, and even children to justify the quick response by the GIs. The few Japanese who did remain on southern Kyushu were housed in camps.

"Personally," Parker finally answered, "I'm glad I don't have to make that decision."

Monck grinned. "Thanks for your help."

"What's really important," Parker continued, "is why the shiny major in the front seat hasn't been shot at by the Japs. I mean, he is so clean he glistens."

Redwald laughed. The teasing was old hat. "Just trying to set an example for my men."

The jeep lurched through a large shell hole in the dirt road, then made a wide turn to avoid another one. They were less than a mile behind the slowly advancing front lines and traveling conditions were primitive at best. What few roads there were had been chewed up by the war. In many areas, supplies had to be hand-hauled up to the front, which further slowed the regiment's advance.

The situation was the same for the rest of the invasion force. Requests for mules had gone out and would be filled. Mules had been used with considerable success in Italy and in other rugged areas, but the need for them had not been anticipated in Kyushu, which was becoming more and more reminiscent of a World War I battlefield instead of a modern World War II killing ground.

In Monck's opinion, the lack of mules was just another after-the-fact screwup. A great big book would someday be written about what could have been done better in Kyushu. By that time, of course, it would be too late for the participants.

The jeep came to a virtual stop as they inched their way past a large pile of loose rubble. Suddenly the pile exploded and a demonic screech filled the air. Monck was paralyzed by the apparition that emerged through the dirt and dust. It was a Japanese soldier, his mouth wide with his scream, and a samurai sword gripped with both hands. With incredible quickness, he brought it up from his waist to over his head and swung it expertly.

With a near-silent swish it sliced off Redwald's head, sending it flying through the air to land on the ground with a dull thud. He swung again. Monck threw himself out of the jeep and the blade clanged against the metal side of the vehicle. Parker had scrambled out the other side, but the driver was trapped and had started to scream. Monck fumbled for his pistol, pointed it at the Jap, and pulled the trigger. Nothing. He had forgotten to remove the safety.

The Japanese soldier again shrieked his fury and the sound was recognizable as "Banzai." Just as he was about to kill the driver, one of the guards from the rear jeep ran up, jammed a Thompson sub-machine gun into the Jap's chest, and fired a burst that shredded their attacker's torso. He howled and fell backward. The GI stood over him and fired another burst, which further pulverized his body, sending flesh and bone spraying through the air.

Monck checked the driver, who was shaken and sobbing but otherwise okay. Parker was on his feet and unhurt, although almost equally shocked. The blood on Monck's uniform had come from Redwald's headless body, which still sat primly in the front seat beside the driver, who had begun vomiting over the other side.

Good idea, Monck thought. His own stomach was heaving at the grisly sight. He looked over to where Redwald's head lay faceup. Incredibly, it looked as if he was smiling.

"Parker," Monck gasped, "what the hell just happened? I thought this place was safe?"

Colonel Parker lit a cigarette with trembling hands. "Ain't nothing safe on this island, General. I think that was one of what our boys're calling spider men. Those are suicide soldiers who dig into the ground and cover themselves up. Then they wait until the fighting has passed by and attack targets of opportunity like one of those trap-door spiders back home in Arizona." He took a deep drag and it seemed to steady him. "Y'know, I think he went after Redwald and not you or me because Redwald looked more like a senior officer than we do."

"Helluva price to pay for clean living," Monck muttered, but he agreed with Parker's assessment. Redwald was dead and they were not because Redwald looked the part of an officer more than they did.

Monck's guards had finished searching the dead Jap's body. They were eager to drag the corpse out of sight so they could see if he had any gold fillings. It was a despicable habit, but if the frontline troops didn't get a crack at the fillings, then some rear-echelon jerk would pry them out. Monck tolerated pulling gold fillings, but drew the line at cutting off ears or penises and drying them for use as an obscene necklace.

According to the dead Jap's papers, he was an officer and about forty years old. In that case, Monck wondered, where the hell were the rest of the guy's troops? Maybe they were all dead and he was the last of the Mohicans and determined to join them. If so, he'd just got his wish.

CHAPTER 56

SHIBUSHI, ARIAKE BAY, KYUSHU

Gen. Omar Bradley ducked his head as he and Eichelberger entered the dugout headquarters of the U.S. Sixth Army on Kyushu. Along with the stale air and the heavy overlay of cigarette smoke, Bradley noticed the pathetic attempts at Christmas decorations. A few ribbons and some Christmas-tree balls hung on a local fir do not a holiday make, he thought ruefully. Another Christmas would be spent with American soldiers killing the enemy and dying in turn. What a lousy world it sometimes was.

In the distance, antiaircraft guns crumped into the sky, and the people in the dugout complex looked nervously at each other.

Bradley turned to General Krueger. "Should we get to a shelter?" The roof over their heads was camouflaged canvas.

Krueger looked worn-out. His eyes were dark-ringed and his face sagged. "No, at least not yet."

Bradley accepted the decision. As a result of the army and marine advances, some Japanese kamikaze attacks had shifted to ground targets. High on their list were fuel dumps and anything that looked like a supply depot. The army had lost a large amount of its fuel and ammunition reserves in the attacks.

Nor were places like Sixth Army headquarters immune. This was the reason for the highly visible and well-defended headquarters complex that was a couple of miles away and totally empty of working personnel. It had drawn Jap suicide planes the way honey draws bees, while the real headquarters, half-buried and well hidden, remained unmolested.

Bradley took a seat by the makeshift conference table. "General Marshall wishes this offensive wrapped up as soon as possible so we can concentrate on the second phase of the operation."

At sixty-four, Lt. Gen. Walter Krueger now looked eighty. He was known as a meticulous planner, an instructor, and a man who worked mightily to keep casualties down. Now he was haunted by failing in that goal.

"General Bradley," Krueger said slowly, the fatigue evident in his voice, "we're moving inland and up the island as fast as we can. If we try to push harder against Jap resistance, we'll only stack up more dead and wounded. Just like on Okinawa, it sometimes takes days to clear a cave complex on one small hill only to find another one a few hundred yards away. This is not the type of fighting that can be rushed."

Bradley stepped to a wall map that showed the line of American advance. A little more than one quarter of Kyushu was in American hands. The line of American battle symbols ran from just north of Sendai on the west coast and looped across the island to a point halfway along the east coast between Miyazaki and Nobeoka. Kagoshima and the dormant volcano that dominated the city had been taken, as had Mt. Kirishima in the middle of the island. Artificial harbors were under construction in Kagoshima and Ariake bays, while more than a dozen small airfields were in operation.

Land areas taken included those optimistically labeled the Ariake, Miyazaki, and, on the other side of the island, the Kushikino "plains." Other areas were labeled "corridors," as if they formed an easy path to the interior of Kyushu. Plains and corridors they might have appeared on maps, and the land might actually have been more gentle than that in the interior, but it was still rugged. By moving through those alleged plains and corridors, the army and marines had been rewarded by confronting even more difficult and arduous terrain. It hardly seemed fair, Bradley thought.

"General Krueger," Bradley said, "the original plans called for us to take only the southern third of Kyushu, and I believe we have pretty much accomplished what we set out to do. Ariake Bay is ours, as is Kagoshima Bay. Our ships are using both shelters and will use them even more if only the kamikazes would stop coming over."

As if to punctuate the comment, something exploded a few miles away.

"Gentlemen, the president is under tremendous pressure to finish this war. He is under additional pressure to support British operations along the China coast in conjunction with the liberation of Hong Kong. He has committed to supporting the British with transports and landing craft in three months."

"No!" General Eichelberger blurted. "That'll mean a delay in our attack on Tokyo."

Bradley smiled grimly. "It is now almost Christmas and it is just over three months before Operation Coronet, the invasion of Tokyo, is scheduled to take place. I want that attack accelerated. Gentlemen, I want this battle on Kyushu wound down so that all our resources can be directed towards Honshu and Tokyo. I want our boys ashore on the Kanto Plain and driving towards the Imperial Palace as soon as is humanly possible. We cannot delay Coronet; therefore we must accelerate it."

"But what will I do for an army?" Eichelberger asked softly. It was a reminder to Bradley that he and the absent Hodges were scheduled to be field commanders for Coronet as Krueger was for the smaller Olympic. "Surely you don't expect to use the men now on Kyushu?"

"That's correct, I do not. Along with their presence being needed here, they are far too worn-out for further offensive operations. No, they are to stay here."

"Thank God," said Krueger, who could finally see an end to his horrors. "But Bob's right. What will he use for an army? The invasion of Honshu will use an additional fourteen divisions in the initial phase alone. Half those boys are either en route or not even formed up."

Bradley smiled tightly. "Then we'll use the half we got. Gentlemen, I've been coordinating with Nimitz and the Pentagon on the status of the Japanese army defending Tokyo. What had once been estimated at eighteen infantry and two armored divisions has been reduced to less than half that, and many of those remaining soldiers are nothing but untrained warm bodies in uniforms. They are recent conscripts who've had no training whatsoever and don't possess much in the way of weapons. Our air force has been pounding anything they see, so there has to be further erosion in their ability to fight.

"Bob, Walt, I don't think the Japs have anything left near Tokyo to fight with. I agree with intelligence estimates that there will be little resistance to an invasion of Honshu."

Bradley saw the disbelief on their faces. They'd heard much the same thing from MacArthur earlier in the year, and it had proven horribly, tragically wrong. But Bradley also saw a glimmer of hope that this would end the terrible fighting. This was information that had come from several sources, and not just MacArthur's pet intelligence coordinators who had been deemed infallible by their late commander.

Bradley moved away from the map. "The battle lines are almost static and we are playing into their hands. The harder we push against their defenses, the more men we lose. This battle for Kyushu is nothing more than a rehash of Verdun in the last war, or Stalingrad in this one, where one side tried to make the other side bleed itself to death. We can't continue fighting and losing men at this rate."

"All right," admitted Eichelberger. "We can't. So what's Walt to do while Hodges and I try to pull an army out of thin air?"

"First of all, Bob," Bradley said, "your army isn't coming out of the air. It'll be coming from the Philippines, California, Hawaii, and Europe. It'll be close, but I'll guarantee you at least two marine and ten army divisions, along with at least one armored brigade, for the invasion."

Eichelberger nodded. "If you're right about the state of the Jap army, it'll do. In fact, it'll more than do."

Bradley turned to Krueger. "Walt, you may have the most difficult part. Any reinforcements and replacements not already landed here are now going to go to Bob. You'll have to make do with what you have."

Krueger shrugged. "I kinda guessed as much. If it'll help end this thing, I'm game. As if I had a choice." He grinned for the first time.

"Good," said Bradley. "One thing I am very afraid of is a major

Jap counterattack. If they detect that we've slowed down and eased off on the pressure, I'm convinced they'll try one. I want you to keep up a minimum level of pressure to keep their attention focused on Kyushu."

Eichelberger arched an eyebrow. "A counterattack? Do you really think the Japs are up to that? We've hit them pretty hard, Brad. They've taken a lot of casualties, probably a lot more than we have."

Bradley seated himself and leaned back in the chair. "Just about a year ago I was in Europe and we were all counting out the German army. They were dead, we said, defeated and destroyed. Then the Germans found a weak spot in the Ardennes and we wound up fighting the bloodiest battle in the history of the United States, at least until this one.

"Against all odds, the Nazis managed one last attack, one last hurrah, and just when we thought they couldn't. We were caught preparing our own plans as if they didn't have any of their own. Are you aware that our latest intelligence estimates are that the Japs still have more than half a million men on Kyushu?"

"I know," said Krueger. "We kill them and they keep replacing them with fresh bodies from Korea and Honshu. Maybe they aren't top-notch soldiers, but they're still fighting. Damned Reds are helping them too. We think we've caused a quarter of a million Jap dead or wounded, but they keep making good the losses."

"Truman will take care of the Russians," Bradley commented hopefully, "but you've got to watch out for the Japs. If the Battle of the Bulge is any guide, they will wait for an extended period of rotten weather when our air forces are grounded and attack then. Unfortunately, they are still getting good weather information from stations in Korea and even from Manchuria. Since the winter storms flow down from up there, they will have several days' advance notice. So will we, of course. Nimitz has already put a number of navy weather experts on ships and has them in the Sea of Japan off Korea and Honshu."

"Good," both other generals muttered in near unison.

"General Krueger, I want your boys to be ready to circle the wagons—and I mean that almost literally—when Nimitz gives the signal that the weather is ripe for the Japs to attack. If nothing comes of it, that'll be fine by me, but I'd rather have a false alarm, even a number of them, than a rehash of the Bulge, where two regiments of the 106th Division were forced to surrender. I don't want to even think of additional American troops being captured by the Japs. I don't care how you do it, but there will be no weak places for the Japs to exploit if and when they do attack."

"What about atom bombs?" Eichelberger queried.

"There won't be a place for them on the battlefield that I envision if the Japs do attack us." Mentally, Bradley hedged the statement. If a suitable target was found far enough from the battle lines, he would consider it.

The door to the room burst open. "Incoming!" yelled a sergeant. "Jap planes on a dead line towards us."

"Shit," said Krueger as the men raced in undignified haste down an earthen corridor to the reinforced shelter. "I guess our little secret's out. I was really starting to get fond of this hole."

•

CHAPTER 57

TOKYO

Relations between senior officers of the Japanese army and the navy were generally formal at best. The rivalry was historically intense. Each had its own priorities and each was bitterly jealous of the other, even to the point of orchestrating assassinations in the decades prior to the war.

The army had argued against the southward push of the navy that had brought the United States and Great Britain into the war. At the time of Pearl Harbor the Japanese army was fully involved in a major land war with China—one it had started without seeking government approval—and wished to finish that war before starting any new adventures.

Within a year of the attack on Pearl Harbor, the Imperial Japanese Army could only sit and seethe in impotent fury as the Imperial Japanese Navy lost battle after battle and watch in frustration as enemy warships drew ever closer to Japan.

As 1945 drew to a close, only the army remained to defend Japan, and the naval officers who'd been so proud and smug the years before were scarcely tolerated pariahs whose rash efforts had failed the empire. While the navy licked its wounds and tallied its losses, the army had gone on the offensive in China and pushed the Chinese Nationalists southward, forcing the American air forces to evacuate bases from which they'd been bombing the home islands. As a result, many army officers now looked down on their naval counterparts. The army had always felt that Japan's true adversary was the Soviet Union, and it had galled the generals to have to make peace, however temporary, with Stalin, who had broken it that summer.

In this hostile environment, the unique friendship between Lt. Gen. Masaharu Homma and Vice Admiral Jisaburo Ozawa somehow first developed, then flourished. Both were in their late fifties, and each had experienced glory and despair. Both men had pragmatic feelings about the war and felt that it had to be concluded quickly before Japan disappeared.

They also thought that the code of Bushido, which required fighting to the death, was nonsense in the current circumstances. Homma, who had served two terms as liaison with the British army, was well aware of the fighting capabilities and the industrial might of the West. Ozawa had seen that might in more recent action. He had watched in agony as ship after ship of his fleet sank as a result of the hammer blows inflicted by the overwhelmingly powerful Americans.

In 1941, Homma had commanded the Fourteenth Japanese Area Army in the invasion of the Philippines. He had succeeded, but had paid a terrible price for the victory. Instead of the quick and easy conquest that intelligence estimates had promised, the American and Philippine soldiers had fought bravely and held out for months longer than anticipated. The defense of Bataan and Corregidor had upset the Japanese timetable for conquest, and Homma, upon ultimate completion of his task, had been returned to Japan and left in administrative limbo.

Homma was further stung that the Americans had blamed him for the Death March and other atrocities committed by his subordinates. He had ordered that prisoners be treated fairly, but these orders had been ignored. Homma accepted the blame. Morally, he felt responsible. He had conquered a nation but had lost his career.

Ozawa, on the other hand, had merely lost his fleet. Highly regarded and respected, he had been an early proponent of airpower and had skillfully led his carriers in combat until the last of them was overwhelmed in the climactic Battle of Leyte Gulf. A quiet and basically humble man, he knew there was nothing more useless than an admiral without a fleet, and he no longer had a single major surface ship, much less a fleet.

Each man understood the other and their relationship grew. Had the government of General Anami been aware of it, it might have expressed disapproval. But the Anami government had many other and more compelling problems to resolve than to worry about two old officers getting together for drinks and idle conversation.

General Homma's vivacious and tiny wife, Fujito, beamed happily as she answered the door and admitted the admiral. She bowed and took Ozawa's soggy hat and raincoat, then departed to let the admiral and her husband have their talk.

"Your journey here was uninterrupted?" Homma inquired.

"Safe enough," Ozawa replied. "One innocuous car is not going to attract an attack."

Both men knew it was not quite that simple. With fuel rationing so strict that civilian car usage was virtually nonexistent, American pilots had easily concluded that any car or truck on the road was a legitimate military target. Ozawa had been both prudent and lucky. He did not burden his host with the fact that he and his driver had twice bolted from the vehicle during his ten-mile journey out of fear that he had been sighted by Yank planes. He had wiped most of the mud from his uniform trousers from his having hid in a ditch. Homma was too tactful to comment on the stains.

"You are fortunate," Ozawa commented, "that you live far enough away from Tokyo proper to be relatively free of the bombers and the fires." Ozawa's own small house had gone up in flames during a bombing. He now lived with relatives.

Homma nodded. His home in exile was only twenty miles from the Imperial Palace, but it might as well have been a thousand miles from the source of power. At least until recently.

After tea was drunk and the amenities observed, Homma brought out some rice brandy that a local entrepreneur had made. If not good, it was at least potent. Ozawa smacked his lips in appreciation, then leaned forward and smiled slyly. "Should I congratulate you or offer condolences, my friend?"

Homma chuckled. "A little of both would be in order."

As a result of the death of Field Marshal Hata in the latest nuclear bombing, the army commands had been reorganized. General Homma had been recalled from exile and given command of the Twelfth Area Army, which encompassed Tokyo and most of the area surrounding it.

"At least you have an army," Ozawa said softly. "While I have no surface ships at all. The last destroyer was sunk a couple of days ago. A few submarines remain, but the enormous American fleet is largely unmolested. My trips to headquarters are little more than exercises in futility."

"Good friend," Homma replied, "the truth is that my situation is as bad as yours. The Twelfth Area Army largely exists on paper and in the confused mind of General Anami. Once it consisted of eighteen infantry and two armored divisions, but it now lists but eight infantry and one armored, and these are but terribly depleted shadows of themselves. The other divisions have been sent to the slaughterhouse in Kyushu, while the remaining units have been stripped by transfers and then pounded to pieces by the ever-present American planes. I doubt that I could field fifty thousand trained men and twenty tanks. My soldiers cower in their bunkers all over the Kanto Plain. It would be virtually impossible for me to assemble them into a true fighting force under the circumstances. For all intents and purposes, Tokyo is undefended by the Japanese army."

Ozawa was shocked. "I had no idea it was so bad."

"Nor did I. Until my recent appointment, I was uninformed of the situation. It is the same elsewhere on the home islands. The Fifth Army on Hokkaido has been reduced from five divisions to two, the Eleventh north of here from six divisions to one, the Thirteenth to my south from six to two, and the Fifteenth, which is adjacent to Kyushu, from eight to three. Large numbers of civilian militia have been formed, but they are unarmed and untrained. They will be useless when the Americans come."

"Is it possible that they won't come?" Ozawa asked hopefully, even though he knew the dreaded answer.

"They will come. It is only a matter of time. Anami thinks otherwise of course. He feels that the recent slowdown in American operations on Kyushu means they have been defeated, or at least so bloodied that they have no will to continue. Anami feels the time is ripe for a counterattack that will drive the Americans back into the ocean. Another Decisive Battle, he says, and the war will be won to the extent that we can have a negotiated peace with honor."

Ozawa laughed in derision. "A Decisive Battle? Just how many of those will we fight? Pearl Harbor was a Decisive Battle, as were Midway, Leyte, a number of others. Leyte Gulf was supposed to be the battle that ended the war and it almost did. We lost what was left of our navy in it! What a fool he is to believe in that discredited doctrine!"

As the smaller nation, Japan had always looked for a way to deliver a knockout blow against the overwhelming might of the Americans. The naval war had been predicated on sucking the American fleet into a decisive battle with the Japanese fleet off Japan that would end in an overwhelming victory for Japan. It was a shame the Americans hadn't cooperated, Ozawa thought ruefully.

Homma poured a little more brandy. "Major Hori, who has been so successful in anticipating American actions, told Anami the Americans have not been defeated. Instead, Hori feels they have taken all they require of Kyushu for use as a staging area and are now preparing to invade south of Tokyo. For the first time, Anami disagreed with Hori and sent him away after a tongue-lashing. I agree with Hori. The Americans will invade Honshu and will do it soon."

A plane flew low over the house, and the frail structure began to shake. Both men looked at each other as they recognized the now distinctive growl of an American P-51. It was so symbolic of their total helplessness that an American fighter could gaze down on them from only a few hundred feet and nothing could be done about it.

"Admiral, so many of the fine young men we've sent to Kyushu have been killed or wounded in the fighting, while many others never even made it to the cursed island. It is a closely guarded secret, but only about half the men sent on the journey ever arrive. The American planes kill them en route or sink their boats in the straits. The same is happening with the men we are trying to bring from Korea. The slaughter of the young is incredible. An entire generation of Japanese men is being destroyed. If we do not end this, we will be like France was after the last war. Emasculated."

Ozawa thought for a moment. There was something he had to say, but it had to be said carefully. "In your opinion, is the military situation hopeless?"

"Yes."

"Is nothing going right for us?"

"Well, the Americans haven't quite figured it out, but with our hidden airstrips on Kyushu just a few miles behind the front lines, suicide attacks are no longer as necessary as they had been. The planes can actually load up with bombs and return without too much difficulty. Many now fly but a few feet off the ground, bomb, and return to their hideouts. American supplies are in such abundance that it is virtually impossible for even the most inexperienced pilot to miss dropping a bomb on something important. Our fliers will not resume actual suicide attacks until the counterattack, which will not come until the weather grounds the American planes."

"But what about the secret weapons? Are they but rumors?"

Homma shook his head. "Some of them are real, but may bring more harm to Japan than to the Americans. We have quantities of poison gas and plague germs to use against them, but I fear for American retaliation, which could utterly destroy what little remains of Japan."

Gas? Germs? Ozawa was appalled. What kind of war was Anami waging? Ozawa's voice nearly broke in despair. "Is there nothing we can do?"

Homma laughed harshly and took the leap of faith that Ozawa was with him. "Are you suggesting a coup?"

"Why not? That's how Anami came to power, isn't it? It would be justice to turn the tables on that drunken buffoon."

"Indeed, but Anami has the emperor and claims to speak for him. As long as that is the case, any coup would be ignored. Besides, Anami has surrounded himself with those loyal to him and they are not under my command. He is very careful and trusts very few in the army. Myself, I am watched very closely when I am near his headquarters. I believe I was chosen for my current assignment because I was available, not out of any great confidence in my abilities or in my loyalty."

Interesting, thought Ozawa. "Where is the emperor? We've heard rumors, but what is the truth?"

"The emperor is at some undisclosed place on Kyushu. Incredibly, he was sent there before the invasion because it was deemed safer than Tokyo. It is now considered too dangerous to try and bring him back."

"Amazing," the admiral commented. "So we will continue to fight until the last young man is dead and until the Americans have stormed the Imperial Palace. But what if we found the emperor and he announced a desire for peace?"

"Then much would be changed, my friend. Perhaps what remains of Japan could even be saved."

They spoke for a while longer, this time of families and friends, many of them recently dead. Much later, the admiral departed and Homma fervently wished him a safe journey.

Homma went to his bedroom, undressed, and lay down on his back on the sleeping mat. Fujito came and knelt beside him. She was his second wife and younger than he. She was one person who had brought stability to his otherwise wild and erratic youth. She was priceless to him. Without her, he would have wound up an irresponsible and drunken fool.

"Did it go well?" she asked as she ran her hands down his muscular chest.

"Very well," he said with a smile as he enjoyed the gentle touch of her hands. He knew full well that she had been listening all the time. "The good admiral understands everything. I believe I have planted a seed, although there may have already been one present. We will now have to see what grows."

Fujito's hands roamed lower. "Ah." She giggled softly. "I have found something that is growing already!"

Homma laughed. She slipped off her robe, then swung her slender, naked body over his and led him into her. He was strong tonight and she moaned happily and reveled in each powerful upward thrust. The inaction of the previous years had almost driven him to despair and sometimes sapped his manhood. He was a tiger, not a domestic animal to be kept penned. His new command and its challenges were so much better for both of them. Fujito had sublime confidence in her general. If anyone could solve Japan's terrible dilemma, she was confident that her husband could.

CHAPTER 58

KYUSHU,
NORTH OF MIYAKANOJO

When Captain Ruger had dictated what Paul Morrell referred to as his "last will and testament" while on the troopship off Kyushu, both had thought that the personnel changes in it would occur after his being killed or wounded. Promotion had not been a thought.

The killing of Major Redwald, their battalion commander, had changed that. Ruger had been promoted to the temporary rank of major, and Paul was given Ruger's old command, although not the rank of captain. First lieutenant was a common enough rank for an inexperienced company commander. In the absence of any other available junior officers, Sergeant Collins assumed command of Paul's old platoon. Sergeant Orlando continued to provide support with his tank.

Both Paul and Major Ruger had made it clear that they didn't want to break in any rookie second lieutenants at this stage of the battle. Paul in particular found that amusing. Only a few months earlier he had been the unwanted and untested rookie. Now he was considered experienced and part of the old guard.

First Sergeant Mackensen put down the field phone. "Lieutenant, there's a problem with Lieutenant Marcelli. I think you'd better go over."

Paul swore softly and scrambled out of his foxhole and through the light cover of brush to where the second platoon was dug in. Mackensen and a radioman followed close behind.

The company had been back in the lines for several days after their all too brief respite. Little had changed in their absence, although a cockamamy rumor said that they were to seize some good defensive ground and hold on until the Japs starved to death.

Bullshit. They had continued to inch up increasingly steep hills and fight their way through strong Jap positions. Paul had lost track of the date. Was it Christmas yet? If so, he thought as he stumbled on a rock and almost lost his helmet, how would Santa find him? At least he'd gotten some mail and managed to send some good letters off to Debbie. Thank God he could count on her.

"Over here, Lieutenant," one of Marcelli's soldiers yelled.

Paul covered the last few yards to where a small group of men clustered about a large lump that lay in a foxhole. It was Marcelli. He was facedown and still, but his chest moved from the effort of breathing.

"What happened to him?" Paul asked. The men shrugged and moved off. They didn't want to know.

Mackensen slid into the hole and tried to move Marcelli. He was curled up in a fetal position and unresponsive. The stink of feces and urine wafted up from the hole. Lieutenant Marcelli had fouled himself.

When Mackensen moved Marcelli's head, his eyes were squinched shut as if daring the world to make him look. Mackensen tried to straighten him out, but he returned to his curled-up ball position like a preformed rubber toy. It was ghastly to look at. This creature looked nothing like the eager young officer who was Paul's friend.

"He's shell-shocked, Lieutenant," Mackensen announced softly. "He's gone someplace else, the lucky bastard."

Paul slid down beside the lieutenant, shook him gently, and patted him on the cheek. "Jerry, can you hear me?" he whispered in Marcelli's ear. "Jerry, c'mon, buddy. We got a job to do and I need you. Help me out this one time and we'll all get to go home."

He heard a low moan and saw a thin line of drool starting to run down Marcelli's chin. Seeing a man like that was even more awful than seeing one wounded by a bullet or shrapnel. Bullet wounds you could bandage, but what the hell did you do when a man's mind snapped? No wonder the other soldiers didn't want to hang around. They were afraid it was contagious. It wasn't, of course, but each man knew that he had his own breaking point. They just didn't want to be reminded of it. Paul had to get rid of Marcelli before his condition played havoc with the rest of the company's morale.

Paul snapped at his radioman, "Get a medic up here with a stretcher. I want him out of here right now." The operator gulped and sent the message.

Paul found a blanket and covered Marcelli. He wanted to keep him warm, but he also didn't want anyone else staring at him as if he were some kind of freak. "Well, First Sergeant, what do you think happened?"

Mackensen shrugged. He didn't understand weakness, and in his world, battle fatigue or shell shock qualified as weakness. He knew it occurred and was sympathetic to those it hit, but he had no idea why it happened.

"Beats me, sir. We both saw him yesterday and he was fine. A little nervous, maybe, but that's not unusual out here."

No, Paul sighed, not unusual at all in a land where everything, even the earth and the trees, was hostile. Shell shock was getting more and more common, although this was the first case he'd seen in the company. There would be more as there was only so much that the human psyche and soul could take.

With the exception of the few days in the rear, they'd been in combat almost every day since landing more than a month ago. The company had suffered more than seventy casualties and had received only a dozen fresh-faced young replacements, who'd been unprepared for the horrors confronting them. As a result, a high percentage of the innocent and clean-uniformed replacements had themselves gone down. What saddened Paul the most was that few knew who the dead and wounded replacements were. No one wanted to make friends with someone who was likely to die. They were stuck with the people they'd begun with in the company, but they didn't have to open their hearts and souls to anyone else. Why compound problems with the burden of grief when someone was lost.

The stretcher-bearers came and got Marcelli strapped down and carried away. For a moment, the young lieutenant had opened his eyes, and Paul had been struck by the total blankness behind them. Wherever Marcelli's mind was, it wasn't in this world. As he disappeared down the hill, Paul wished him peace, although he feared that Marcelli would become like one of those World War I veterans he'd once seen at a government hospital. They'd lived there for decades, utterly unaware and comprehending nothing. He'd been twelve at the time, and the scene had given him nightmares.

Paul shuddered and wondered when he would break. Then he wondered if his mind hadn't already gone. Perhaps this whole thing was just a nightmare? Maybe all he had to do was close his eyes and it would all go away? Maybe he could will himself home with his head cradled between Deb's breasts while she kissed his forehead and told him everything was okay.

Yeah, sure, and all he had to do was click his heels and he'd be in Kansas with Dorothy and Toto.

Mackensen was looking at him funny. Had he been babbling out loud? "Any orders, sir?"

"Yeah," said Paul grimly. "Let's go kill some fucking Japs and get this over with."

CHAPTER 59

OKINAWA

OSS agent Johnson didn't like working alone after all the time spent with Peters. The two men had established a rapport that was almost the same as two brains working in tandem, or perhaps being married, as some of the other OSS personnel teased. Teamwork was especially important because the puzzle he was working on wouldn't cooperate and divulge its solution. Thus, he was tickled when his partner in crime, Peters, walked through the door of their hut and hung his wet coat on a hook. Peters had caught the flu and had been on sick call for a couple of days. He still looked like shit, but Johnson had missed him.

Johnson looked down at the piece of paper whose meaning had been eluding him. "Got a very cryptic message from Nomura that I don't understand. Instead of using the emergency code, he's using a message within a message, only I don't know what it is. It's gotta be obvious, but not to me right now."

Peters knew what he meant. Sometimes messages were like crossword puzzles. Where one person might be stymied, a second would see the solution immediately. Johnson handed him the paper and Peters read the elusive message verbatim: "Sound of tall construction machinery adjacent. Cooperation expected from chief operator in moving it from the premises."

"What the hell?" Peters said.

Johnson laughed. "Now I don't feel so bad. It's been driving me nuts since it came in a few hours ago."

Peters thought hard. What did the phrase *tall construction machinery* really mean? Intuitively, he knew those words were the key to the solution. They also knew that it must have been extremely important for Joe to have sent the information in such a manner. Yet it was still not important enough for Nomura to have used the emergency code. He was still saving that.

"Quick, list all the types of tall construction machinery you can think of," Peters ordered.

"Derrick, crane, steam shovel, hoist, windlass? Hell, I don't know. There's probably others I can't think of."

Something clicked in Peters's mind. An involuntary shiver went down his spine. He was afraid of the way his thoughts were proceeding. "Would *voice* be a synonym for *sound*?"

"Sure, are you onto something?"

"Yeah. Or maybe I am. Substitute *voice* for *sound* and *crane* for *tall construction machinery* and you have 'voice of the crane is adjacent.' "

Johnson's jaw dropped. "Voice of the Crane is one of Hirohito's titles. Jesus, is Nomura telling us that he is in direct contact with the emperor?"

Peters nodded. "It's hard to believe, but I think he is. And if I'm right on that count, he's also telling us that Hirohito wants to get out of wherever he is and we're expected to help."

"Hoo, boy," Johnson whistled. "This is way too big for us to handle. We better bring some brass on board with this. Do we tell Washington?"

"No," Peters said reluctantly, "For the time being, I think we'd better keep this right here on Okinawa. I don't want this secret to leave this island just yet. Besides, if our assessment is full of crap, I don't want that news off Okinawa either."

PETERS AND JOHNSON stood at attention as Lt. Gen. Matthew Ridgway entered the small conference room. Both agents were dressed in army uniforms, but without any indications of rank. Ridgway's crisp, strong-jawed appearance reinforced the impression of a can-do type of leader. He looked younger than his fifty years and had only recently transferred in from the European theater, where, as a major general, he had commanded the XVIII Airborne Corps, which had included the 82nd and 101st Airborne divisions in the Battle of the

Bulge, and the earlier and ill-fated Operation Market Garden. Ridgway's third star was only a few months old. He held no specific command; instead, he functioned as a troubleshooter for Gen. Omar Bradley. His presence was taken by Johnson and Peters as a good omen.

Ridgway took a seat and directed the others to do likewise. "Where's Hirohito and just why do you think we can snatch him away from his own people?" he snapped.

Peters answered, "He's being held by Anami's people in northern Kyushu. I don't know exactly where and our agent declined to give specifics. It's far too risky for him to divulge that he has that knowledge as we are fairly certain the Japs are picking up a lot of what he's sending and decoding it by now."

Ridgway grunted. "And you really believe your man is in contact with him?"

The general had their brief written report, but wanted to hear their answers verbally. Their fear that it would be laughed away was already dissipating. They had hoped to see either Bradley or Nimitz, but this conference with Ridgway meant that at least someone at the top thought it was worth pursuing.

"The message from Nomura is necessarily cryptic," Peters continued, "but we strongly believe that is the gist of it. Our agent has located Hirohito, who is likely a prisoner, and the emperor wants out of his captors' hands so he can bring peace."

"Why?"

It was Johnson's turn. "Intelligence analysis says the emperor was never that strong an advocate for war against America and was more than ready to surrender after Hiroshima and Nagasaki. The subsequent overthrow of the Japanese government by Anami and his cohorts had nothing to do with Hirohito except to put him in personal jeopardy."

Ridgway shook his head. It was almost too incredible to believe. "And we're supposed to accept that this Nomura character of yours has landed on Japan, wandered around for months, somehow become Hirohito's best friend, and, as a result, the emperor will let us take him off Kyushu and out to an American warship? You know a few people on Bradley's and Nimitz's staffs think you guys are either drunk or hallucinating? Worse, there's the serious possibility that you've misread the message, or that the whole thing is a trap to kill anyone who tries to liberate Hirohito. For all we know, this Nomura character has either been captured and tortured or he's become a turncoat."

Johnson persisted, "General, Mr. Nomura has proven himself very resourceful. We do not believe he has been captured or is sending messages under any duress. There were key words to use and ways of phrasing things that would have tipped us off if that was the case. No, I believe he is dealing with Hirohito and that Hirohito wants to get somewhere so he can really and finally end this war. What we need is your approval and assistance in getting them out."

Ridgway cupped his chin thoughtfully. "I'm curious, gentlemen, just how had you planned on extracting Nomura in the first place when the time was right?"

"By submarine, sir," Peters answered. Inwardly, he exulted. Ridgway was still listening to them. He hadn't laughed them out of the office. "We were going to get him out the same way he got in. Only when the boat that landed him was sunk, we didn't think the navy would let us have another one."

"So you essentially wrote him off after that."

"Yes, sir. To be brutally frank, we wrote him off even before that," Johnson added with candor. "We thought he'd last maybe a week or so and really never expected to have to pull him off under any circumstances. We gave him some plans, but they were more like placebos to make him feel good. We never expected him to do this well or last all this time. We really thought he'd have been caught or killed a long time ago. What he's done for us has been nothing short of incredible."

"So I've heard." Ridgway had read the reports from Nomura and what was now a small but efficient cadre of other Japanese-American OSS agents operating on Honshu. When the book about these activities was written, he'd decided, it would be a helluva bestseller.

Ridgway took a deep breath and made a decision. "All right, we'll do it. First off, we need to insert some people in there to do some real operational planning. How do we get that message to him without tipping off Jap eavesdroppers?"

Peters handed Ridgway a typed sheet of paper. "This is part of his placebo, only we referred to it as a menu. It's a list of possible extraction locations, dates, and an equivalent alphanumeric code. All we have to do is tell him to designate the best time and place from his copy of the list, and you can send in what I presume will be an advance party."

"Very good." Ridgway grinned. God, if he could pull this off, he would go down in the history books as the general who ended the most miserable war in American history and saved many thousands of American lives. So too would this Nomura character, who must have a real set of balls to be doing what he was doing. Ridgway had long since decided he'd like to meet Nomura. Bradley and Nimitz had said he'd have to wait in line.

Ridgway chuckled. "Admiral Nimitz told Bradley that there was a new era dawning regarding cooperation between the army and the navy. I have a few thoughts on how to help out your Mr. Nomura and test the good admiral's sincerity at the same time. Gentlemen," he said, grinning, "I think the next few days are going to be very, very interesting."

CHAPTER 60

KYUSHU, CAMP 7

Emperor Hirohito moved his rook, pausing before removing his hand. Once he let go of the piece, the move would stand. Until then, it was tentative and reversible. Finally he let go and smiled. "I believe you are in check, Captain Nomura."

Nomura sagged. Damn, he was getting so close to winning. "Indeed I am, Your Majesty."

"A shame. For a while there I thought you were really improving, but then you made a couple of moves that disproved my theory. Unless, of course, your mind is not on your game."

Nomura smiled. "You are correct, sir. Many things are distracting me. With regrets, sir, it is truly difficult to concentrate."

"I understand, Captain. Chess in the midst of a war for survival must seem like a trivial enterprise. Now then, what solutions do you propose to my dilemma?"

Nomura took a deep breath. This was the moment he'd been both anticipating and dreading. To divulge anything would be to brand himself as either a traitor or a spy. If he had misunderstood what Hirohito wanted, or if Hirohito had changed his mind, he would place himself in mortal danger simply by opening his mouth. All or nothing, he decided.

"Sir. Arrangements that I would not wish to comment on are being made to free you. When that time occurs, you will be able to make any announcement you wish regarding your opposition to the war. Hopefully, the result will be the honorable surrender of Japan."

"Colonel Sakei and his soldiers will not surrender me to the opposition without a struggle."

"I know."

Hirohito looked saddened. He fully understood that men would die in the effort to free him. The blame was Anami's, and not his own. Anami, the man he had once thought of as a friend, had caused his imprisonment and continued the war, causing the deaths of so many tens of thousands. So what if a few more died? In a macabre way, it would be an investment, and the profit reaped would be the continuation of Japan. He accepted that.

"Captain, when I am, ah, freed from here, it cannot be to another prison cell, not even a highly gilded one."

"I understand." Nomura hoped the people in Washington understood that as well.

"Do you? Wherever I wind up, it must be as the emperor of Japan, the spiritual and constitutional leader of a sovereign nation that wishes an honorable peace with the United States. Any attempt to use me or to show me off as a trophy will backfire and result in my removal from the throne by the warlords. This could even occur in absentia."

Nomura nodded his understanding. He was almost too surprised to speak. Was the emperor signaling that he understood that the Americans would take him, and that he would not be rescued by another group of Japanese? Nomura did not think he had given any hint of that.

"Captain, would you do me a favor?"

"Certainly, Majesty."

"Please remove your tunic and shirt."

Confused, Nomura stood and did as requested.

"It is as I thought," Hirohito said. "You are an American."

"What?"

"Don't deny it, Captain. Look at your vaccination. You were vaccinated on the arm. Japanese are vaccinated on the hip."

Nomura's mind whirled. Should he try to deny it and say he had received his shots while in the United States or something like that? After all, he had already told Hirohito that he'd traveled widely. But if the emperor believed he was an American and voiced his opinion to Sakei, then Nomura was doomed. Who would take his word against that of an emperor, even an imprisoned one?

"Well?" the emperor asked. "Do you admit it?"

Nomura bowed his head. "Yes."

"When did you plan to tell me?"

"I had no idea, Your Majesty. Maybe not until the last minute, sir, when it would be too late to do anything about it."

Hirohito looked pained. "I suspected that would be the case. I understand your logic and I accept it. I have no idea how you will accomplish this and do not wish to know. You are an incredibly brave and resourceful man, Captain. You have fooled Colonel Sakei, who, however, sees what he wishes to see. Put on your clothing before someone comes in, and we shall play another game. It is well that we do something while we talk."

Nomura again did as requested. "How did you suspect, sir?"

"A number of small things, nothing significant taken individually, but collectively they become relevant. Most of the people I deal with are members of the extended royal family or the military hierarchy, and I am used to the manner in which they defer to me. You, however, portrayed yourself as an ordinary officer without Imperial connections. You were properly subservient, except at those times when your wish to win at chess overpowered your discretion. No ordinary Japanese would have behaved like you did. At first I put it down to my own ignorance of ordinary Japanese, but then I more closely watched the behavior of the others in Sakei's detachment. Prisoner or no, they think of me as a god, and your eyes tell me that you think otherwise.

"Then, on realizing that the so-called spy was still on the loose, I began to put two and two together. I also thought it unlikely that a true *kempei* officer would be so easily suborned. Tell me, did you kill the man whose uniform you wear?"

"He was dead already. A traffic accident."

"Amazing. In the midst of a war we still have traffic accidents."

"Sir, you said Sakei sees what he wishes. Are you confident of that?"

Hirohito pushed a few pieces around the board and Nomura did likewise. "Yes, Captain. Like his leader, Anami, he is blinded from the truth. You wear the uniform of a Japanese officer and say you are his ally. Therefore, he believes you. It is almost inconceivable to him that an officer could betray his nation. Continue acting as you have and keep telling him that Japan is winning, and the poor deluded man will think you are a staunch ally."

Hirohito sighed deeply and for a moment Nomura thought he was in pain. "When I became emperor in 1926, I named my reign *showa,* which means 'enlightened peace.' I never thought it would come to this. This war must be concluded."

Joe Nomura bowed in deepest respect. "It will end, sir."

"Captain," Hirohito said sternly, "I meant what I said about not being treated as a prisoner. If my people perceive that I am in shackles or held against my will, they will disown me, and all my efforts will come to naught. You must make your superiors understand that."

"I will, sir." Nomura had no idea if he could accomplish that. He only hoped that his superiors would figure it out for themselves.

"One other thing, Captain."

"Sir?"

Hirohito smiled briefly. "You gave in far too easily. I have no idea how or where the ordinary Japanese people are vaccinated."

CHAPTER 61

As he stepped out into the cold and damp December air, Truman waved to the onlookers and began his morning walk. The streets of Washington were busy with vehicular and pedestrian traffic. Dressed in suit, overcoat, and snap-brim hat, Truman made it an almost daily ritual that delighted spectators almost as much as it tickled him.

As he moved out briskly at a pace that would daunt a soldier, Secret Service agents took up their places around the president while a gaggle of reporters and the just plain curious trailed behind. In all, the ad hoc parade consisted of about fifty people. It amused Truman that so many of the older print and radio reporters had declined to even try to keep up with him. Now it was the young pups such as Brinkley, Sevareid, and Rooney who tried to keep pace with a man who knew he was in excellent physical condition and proved it with astonishing frequency. It tickled Truman that the heavy boozers and incessant smokers among the journalists had all been walked into the ground.

Today he had exited the White House on Pennsylvania Avenue. He would walk down Fifteenth Street to where it rejoined Pennsylvania and then to the Capitol, loop around to Independence Avenue, and finally back to the White House by way of Seventeenth Street. It was several solid miles of walking and it would feel good. Somehow life always became easier when he managed to get in some exercise.

"Mr. President, any further comment on the prisoner of war lists?"

One of the more unusual aspects of Truman's daily walks was that the reporters keeping up with him could ask him any questions they wished. Of course, he didn't have to answer, or, if he did, he could frame the answer any way he wished. Harry Truman had long ago figured out that the question-and-answer game could be worked both ways.

"As I've said, boys," he responded solemnly, "the list is a cruel delusion and only goes to show what a hard and unreasonable foe we're fighting. It sickened me when they listed as living so many young men we knew were dead. That it gave false hopes to people back home was a terrible thing for the Japanese to do."

The list had been given by the Japanese to the Swedish embassy, who had turned it over to the Reuters News Agency. It contained the names of people who were known to have died in the campaigns or had already been liberated and appeared to presume that no one had died in Japanese camps. Many other names were suspected of being fictitious.

"As to the young men they've put in jeopardy by placing them in danger areas," Truman continued, "well, the rules of war say they are responsible for our men's safety. If they do not make a reasonable effort to protect the Allied servicemen they have as prisoners, then they are criminally liable."

He didn't add that the condition of those who would be liberated was likely to be ghastly at best.

"Mr. President, there are rumors that the British are working on a separate peace with the Japs. How would that affect the war?"

Truman returned a friendly wave from a black woman standing by the curb. "The war in the Pacific is an almost all-American effort. If the Brits do decide it is in their best interests to make peace, then there's nothing we can do to stop it."

However, Truman knew it was highly unlikely. The British needed American help to get to Hong Kong, and the Japanese there had already reached an accommodation with the Russians and didn't need one with the British. A local truce with the commandant at Hong Kong was possible, but nothing that would end the alliance with the United States.

"What about the revolts in the Holy Land? Is it true that we'll be sending troops to help the English keep order?"

Truman shook his head. "They haven't asked for our help yet, although I might look favorably on such a request. We cannot have

Muslims and Jews killing each other. It is inconceivable to me that survivors of the Holocaust cannot find peace in the Holy Land."

The announcement that Britain was going to open up Jewish immigration to Palestine had caused an unexpectedly serious explosion among the indigenous Muslim population. Hundreds had been killed in rioting, and the cities of the Holy Land were burning. Anti-American sentiment in Arab countries was at an all-time high.

In Palestine itself, British forces were hard-pressed to keep order, and there were indications they favored the Muslims anyhow. Truman had already decided that the British might be getting help from American forces now in Europe whether they wanted it or not.

"What's being done to stop the Russians?"

Good question, Truman thought. He avoided a direct answer by laughing and making small talk with a startled group of passersby. In fact, the Soviets were taking over everywhere their tanks were parked. Poland was gone, and East Germany was occupied as was part of Austria. Hungary and Czechoslovakia were tottering, while Bulgaria and Romania were already solidly allied with Stalin. Only in Greece had the Reds been halted, and there appeared to be a curious situation developing in Yugoslavia as the Yugoslavs under Tito seemed to be marching to a different Communist drummer.

The reporter persisted, "Sir, what additional is going to be done to help Chiang?"

This one he could answer. "We are continuing to send him supplies. Short of sending him troops, which we are not in a position to do, there is little else that can be done. He's going to have to fight his battle himself."

The reporter nodded and took notes. Truman had intentionally confirmed the obvious—China was going Communist and there wasn't a damn thing anybody could do about it. Even the most aggravating of the congressmen in the China Lobby now accepted that fact, although their public pronouncements said otherwise.

"Mr. President, what about the rumors of Jap peace feelers? Is there anything to them?"

"No," he snapped. "There are no true peace feelers. Any so-called peace feelers are the same as before the Anami coup in August. That is, they are from well-intentioned Japanese civilians, mainly low-ranking diplomats who are stationed in Europe. They personally wish peace but have no control or influence over the actions of their military government."

Truman was personally convinced that most of the people in Japan were heartily sick of the war. If only they could be reached, he thought, but he was convinced it was hopeless. The Anami government controlled the military, and the military controlled Japan.

"Mr. President, when will we invade Honshu?"

Truman laughed heartily. The reporter flushed and grinned back. "Do you really expect me to answer that question?" Truman said.

"No, sir, but would you comment on the progress of the fighting on Kyushu?"

Truman paused again to shake a few hands. A tourist took his picture with a Kodak. "Any fighting is awful, and this is extremely hard, particularly since the war should have ended months ago. However, our boys are continuing to make progress."

"Do you anticipate a Japanese surrender?"

"We anticipated one last August. Remember, we had one in hand and Anami's thugs snatched it away."

A reporter half ran to get close by. Truman could see that the boy's face was flushed. The puppy wouldn't last more than a block or two. "Can you comment on the pressure from the Vatican to negotiate a peace rather than holding out for unconditional surrender?"

Now let's see who's paying attention, Truman thought. "We will never negotiate with the Anami government."

The reporter took quick notes. Truman looked behind him to where a couple of the more experienced reporters were looking at him quizzically. Yes, they knew that news was often made by what was not said, and the president of the United States had just not said a mouthful.

Before anybody could elaborate, the disorganized entourage turned onto Independence Avenue and were suddenly confronted by a group of several hundred women who blocked the road ahead. As the Secret Service tightened their protective cordon around Truman, he saw that many of the women were carrying signs and placards. END THE WAR NOW some said, while others read BRING OUR BOYS HOME or END THE KILLING TODAY. He was particularly stunned by one placard naming him as a murderer of American youth.

The women themselves looked nothing like the unwashed, hairy, and wild-eyed radicals who normally marched and protested whatever they felt was wrong with the world. These were all white women, middle class and well dressed, and many looked at him grimly. He could read expressions of anger, frustration, and, to his horror, contempt. He involuntarily recoiled from the depths of their passion while flashbulbs popped and photographers immortalized the event.

Truman was hustled down a side street by the Secret Service and then into the backseat of a trailing car. He brushed off the apologies from the chief agent. The chief said he'd known of a small demonstration in front of the Capitol, but had thought nothing of it as there were almost always demonstrations of some kind. But this one had quickly become unusually large and particularly vocal.

When Truman returned to his office, he checked with Jim Byrnes and found that similar demonstrations were taking place in a number of cities across the nation, and that the demonstrators were primarily women, tens of thousands of women. Truman was shocked. It was almost unheard-of for a large portion of the "normal" population to be against an American war. He poured himself a whiskey and water and another for Byrnes.

"Jim, what the devil's going on? Why are they blaming me instead of the Japs?"

Byrnes took a quick swallow. "I think we're gonna be catching real hell from now on. People are tired of the war and sickened by the casualties. This week it's the women protesting. Next week it'll be their husbands. Good Lord, what'll happen if this spreads to the young men and they stop showing up for military service? Hell, they know we can't prosecute everyone."

Truman thought Byrnes was overreacting and said so. American boys would always do the right thing about their obligation to serve when called. But he also recalled that there had been riots over the military draft during the Civil War, and that the world war in 1918 had not been fully supported by the American public. The attack on Pearl Harbor in 1941 had galvanized a confused nation and unified it as it had never been before. Now it looked as if small rips in the fabric of unity were beginning to develop. What on earth would he do if large numbers of young men actually decided not to show up for induction?

Truman put down his glass. He had to find a way to end the war. "Jimmy, I seem to recall you wanted this job yourself at one time?"

Byrnes helped himself to some more whiskey. "I believe you've been grossly misinformed, sir. Nobody in his right mind would want to be president."

"True." Truman laughed.

Truman knew that Byrnes's statement was facetious. In 1944, Byrnes had campaigned hard for the vice-presidential nomination, but Roosevelt's slight and almost uncaring nod had given it to Truman instead. As a result, Truman was stuck with the job.

Now, Truman had to deal with the real concerns that were developing. Only a few months ago, a Gallup poll had said that fully 90 percent of the public supported forcing Japan to an unconditional surrender. But that was no longer the case. The polls still showed a majority wanted unconditional surrender, but that number was declining. Truman mistrusted polls, but he acknowledged that a trend was occurring. If the wives and mothers of America were turning against him, what did it mean for the nation's future?

CHAPTER 62

.

KYUSHU,
NEAR MIYAKONOJO

The flat, sharp crack of the nearby rifle shot sent everyone sprawling in the cold, wet dirt. Paul's first reaction as he hugged the ground was that someone's rifle had gone off accidentally. With everyone running around with loaded weapons it was a constant worry, and he determined to find out who it was and have Mackensen rip him a new asshole. They'd lost enough good men to the Japs without anyone having to worry about being shot by their own men. So far, he'd managed to avoid having that sort of tragedy and planned to keep it that way.

Then, in the second it took for those thoughts to clear his mind, he realized that the sound of the gun said it was not one of theirs. By now the noise made by a Garand or a carbine was a familiar, even friendly and reassuring one, and the shot that had sent them all scurrying was alien. A Jap had taken a shot at them and he had been close by. And, unless he was a magician who could move through the woods in silence, the sniper was still there.

The men now hiding on the ground made no sounds. Fire control was excellent. No one was blazing away at shadows, thus giving away their position or endangering others. Paul broke out into a sweat as he realized that the Jap could not be more than a few score feet away, if that far. Lie still, he told himself. Any kind of motion in the low shrubs and trees might attract the sniper's attention.

But where the hell was he? That Jap had to give them a clue as to his whereabouts, didn't he? They couldn't lie on the ground forever.

Of course, if you were shot, forever began immediately. This thought made lying still on the ground look very much like the right thing to do.

Again Paul's company was on a steep hillside and attempting to seize the high ground. This particular hill was heavy with bushes and some surprisingly tall conifer trees that reminded a couple of the men of northern California. As they had advanced northward and into the interior of Kyushu, the type of foliage had changed from the palms and banyans of the south to the more familiar pines and beeches. Even the trees that would normally drop their leaves retained them, although they were brown and lifeless.

It was another hill that was too steep for Orlando's tank to climb even if it had been available. The Sherman was in the rear for long-overdue maintenance. The infantry would have to solve the problems themselves.

CRACK!

The sniper fired again and Paul flinched. He closed his mouth and nearly bit dirt as he tried to hide. This time there was no doubt. The son of a bitch was almost on top of him. There was no cry for help so it appeared the Jap had again missed his target. Either that, Paul thought ruefully, or he had killed his victim instantly and silently. Speculation didn't matter; the sniper had to be taken out.

Paul shifted his body with almost glacial slowness. He would make no sudden motions that would attract the enemy. After what seemed like an eternity, he had rolled onto on his back with his carbine on his chest. He looked upward through the trees and tried to figure out which one hid one Jap sniper.

He could see nothing. The trees were all thick and blotted out the sun. Yet the sniper had to be in a tree, and that tree was damned near to him.

Click.

Paul froze. Oh, Jesus, he thought. The sound had come from almost directly above him, and it was a bullet being chambered in a rifle. The sniper was going to shoot. He squinted and stared at a cluster of limbs about thirty feet above him. Was it the Jap or were his eyes fooling him? The cluster of branches could be a platform hiding the sniper or they could be a perfectly natural accumulation of fallen debris. If he fired at it and was wrong, he would have given away his position to the sniper, and that sort of mistake could be fatal. He stared at the branches and willed the Jap to do something to give himself away.

A stick slowly moved by the branches and began to project out. As Paul watched in fascination, he realized that he was looking at the barrel of a rifle. He shrieked and fired his carbine on full automatic until the clip was empty. The sound deafened him for an instant. Leaves and twigs exploded from the trunk of the tree and the camouflaged firing platform.

Then there was silence.

"Who fired?" yelled Mackensen.

"I did," Paul answered hoarsely.

Mackensen was beside him. "You get him?"

Paul gestured upward. The obscuring branches had come off the tree, and what remained had taken on a distinctly human form as it dangled facedown. It was limp and lifeless, but human. Then whatever had been holding the body to the tree came loose and the Jap commenced a fall to the ground, his body hitting several limbs that slowed his descent.

The body landed only a few feet away from Paul and Mackensen. A second later the Arisaka rifle clattered down beside its owner. Several of Paul's soldiers had emerged from their refuges and looked at the Jap, who was now sprawled awkwardly on the ground.

Mackensen moved to check him out. "Be careful," Paul said.

"Hell, sir"—Mackensen grinned—"if that fall didn't make him go off, nothing will. I really don't think he's booby-trapped." He inserted a booted foot under the man's armpit and rolled him over on his back. Paul gagged. One of his shots had ripped off the man's jaw, while others had ripped open his chest and stomach.

Humming idly, Mackensen went through the Jap's pockets and pulled out his papers. There was nothing terribly exciting. He announced that the Jap was an enlisted man in a unit they already knew they were fighting.

Mackensen straightened up and handed the papers to Paul. "I don't read their shit all that well, sir, but I think this says he's seventeen years old. He also wasn't that good a shot since he didn't hit nothing."

There was a snapshot of an older couple who were probably the dead man's parents and another of a young girl dressed in a demure kimono. It chilled Paul. He had a picture like that in his wallet and he visualized some Jap soldiers looking at it and commenting crudely. He wondered what they would have thought of Debbie's photo. Would they have laughed at his parents the way his men were now doing with the Jap's and make noises about whether they wanted to fuck the girlfriend? Probably, Paul decided.

There was some Japanese paper money as well, and he gave it to the soldiers. It was worthless, but everyone wanted some to send home as a souvenir.

Paul looked more closely at the corpse. Mackensen had said he was seventeen, just about the same age as Debbie's brother. He was small and frail and looked more like thirteen than seventeen. Most Japs were smaller than Americans, but this man couldn't have been more than five feet tall and probably didn't weigh more than a hundred pounds.

Then Paul noticed how unhealthily thin the dead man was. He was almost emaciated and Paul made a note to pass that fact on to battalion. The only bodies they'd seen lately had been badly burned or shredded, which made it impossible to estimate their overall health. If everyone in the Japanese army was as hungry-looking as this sorry cadaver, then the Japanese supply system had completely broken down.

Hell, just last night Paul and his men had eaten a hot chicken dinner from a mobile field kitchen. When was the last time the Jap'd had a full meal? Weeks, he guessed, and it was probably boiled rice. If the Jap army was starving, that was good news.

Paul checked the man's equipment. The uniform was worn thin and in tatters. It was a far cry from what he and the others were wearing. It was still above freezing, but the air was damp and chill, just what his mother referred to as perfect pneumonia weather. This poor Jap must have been freezing, which might have thrown off his aim.

The slowdown in the American advance had permitted rear-echelon units to move closer to the front, and the men had actually been able to warm up in a tent with a portable stove the other day. Paul wondered when the dead boy had last been warm.

The young man's footwear was as bad as the rest of his gear. The soles of his boots had worn through and been replaced by pieces of wood. Paul looked at his own combat boots and wet-weather gear. He was dry and fairly comfortable. How the hell had the dead boy even been able to function? Again, it was information to send back to battalion.

A couple of men had checked the Jap's mouth and pronounced in disgust that there were no gold fillings. Paul felt a queasiness in his gut and walked away. He found refuge behind a bush and puked everything that was in his stomach, including what might have been left of that hot chicken dinner. He heaved until his stomach hurt and then his body shook. He had just killed a man and the reaction had set in.

Finally, he got control of himself and rejoined his men. Mackensen looked at him sympathetically. "You okay, sir?"

Paul chose to lie. "I'm fine."

"Your first?"

Paul took a mouthful of water from a canteen, swirled it around his mouth to cleanse it of the taste of bile, then spat it out. "Yeah. It shows, doesn't it?" He was slightly ashamed of his reaction in front of the rocklike first sergeant.

"Well, sir, that puts you one up on me," the first sergeant said with undisguised admiration. "That was damned good shooting and great hunting."

Paul thought Mackensen was kidding. His first sergeant had to have killed scores of the enemy. But then, who knew whether you actually killed or not? Many times Paul's men had blazed away at an unseen enemy, or in the general direction where they thought the Japs were. The results were impersonal and generally unknown. This type of killing was unique. The only other times they'd actually seen the Japs they'd killed were during that banzai charge and when they'd taken out that bunkered-in tank.

"Thanks, top," Paul said, and managed a grin. "That means a lot coming from you." He saw looks of undisguised admiration on the others in the area. 1st Lt. Paul Morrell was a killer. Killer Morrell had blown a Jap's ass out of a tree and saved their lives. With the GIs' sense of exaggeration, he knew the legend would grow and have him shooting a score of Japs out of a score of trees and with only six bullets. Well, the only life he was certain he'd saved was his own.

Paul recalled Ruger's comment about his not firing during that earlier Jap attack and how upset he'd been to realize it. Now, not only had he fired his carbine, but he'd killed with it. He would not, however, tell anyone that this was the first time he had actually fired his weapon in anger. Killer Morrell. He decided he sort of liked it. More important, if it gave his men more confidence in his abilities, then it was all to the good. All he had to do now was make sure he deserved that confidence.

Part Four

RESOLUTIONS

·

CHAPTER 63

SOUTH OF KYUSHU, THE POLISH POPE

Maj. Stan Kutchinski was furious. For the second time in the last three missions, an engine was acting up and he would have to abort the bombing run. As he looked down at the gray-black ocean almost twenty thousand feet below him, he cursed another missed opportunity. This should have been his sixteenth mission, but an oil leak in one of the B-29's four engines had changed all that.

Earlier in the war, he would have pressed on along with the other bombers in his command since the B-29 could easily fly with three, or even two, engines. But orders were orders, and in the case of mechanical failure, he was to turn back. It wasn't something he could hide, as the problem forced him to shut down one engine. Thus, he had turned back to base and relinquished command of the other bombers to his number two.

Kutchinski wasn't concerned about being considered a coward for aborting the mission. The twenty-five-year-old major had seen enough aerial combat to satisfy any requirement for bravery. Instead, he was upset about missing a chance to rack up another score toward getting to go home. As a means of pacifying rebellious young officers who wanted out of the war, the military had reinstated the policy of rotating bomber crews back to the States after twenty-five combat missions. Today would have been sixteen if his plane, the *Polish Pope,* hadn't decided to act up.

With sixteen in, he would have needed only nine more, and that would only have taken a few weeks, a month at the most. Back home, he might have been discharged and given the opportunity to latch onto one of the civilian airlines. Kutchinski was convinced that air travel was the thing of the future, and he wanted on board an airline as quickly as possible. At the worst, he would have been given a military job training other pilots and would still have had time to make contacts with the airlines.

Aborting bombing missions because of mechanical failure wasn't done because there was so much danger from the Japanese planes and guns. In fact, the runs weren't particularly dangerous at all anymore. Jap interceptors were almost nonexistent, although the occasional kamikaze would try to ram a B-29, and Japanese antiaircraft guns had been battered into mush by other bombers.

But mechanical failure was a solid reason to abort because of the possibility of having to bail out over Japan, where there was the overwhelming likelihood that they would be killed out of hand by the angry Japs. Kutchinski and his men had heard too many tales of Americans being literally ripped to pieces by Jap mobs. Sometimes he wondered if he could blame the Japs. On previous missions they had flown over the Kyushu battlefields and seen the clouds of smoke reaching thousands of feet into the sky from the blackened and ruined land. What was occurring below in that tragic inferno was scarcely imaginable. Then they thanked the gods that had permitted them to join the air force rather than the godforsaken infantry.

Kutchinski's real fear was that there'd be a general stand-down because of a lack of targets before he could reach twenty-five missions, and he'd wind up being stuck in the military for the rest of eternity. No matter how the pie was cut, there were now too many planes and too few targets. Today they were to have bombed a valley where the Japs might be hiding some soldiers. A valley? What the hell kind of a target was a valley? Then he'd decided that it would have been a good one if it had helped him get to that magic number twenty-five.

"Major?"

It was Sgt. Tom Franks, the belly gunner, calling on the intercom. "What is it?"

"Ship on the water below us."

Kutchinski grinned. "That's where ships are supposed to be, Sergeant." Like the others on the *Polish Pope,* Franks was an original member of the close-knit crew, and none of them thought too much of military discipline when they were in the air and away from the base.

"I know that, Major sir, but I've been watching this one through my binocs and it looks like a sub. Aren't they supposed to be underwater?"

"Except when they're not," Kutchinski said. "What's so interesting about this one?"

Franks paused. "I don't believe it's one of ours."

Kutchinski turned the controls over to his copilot and went down the middle of the plane to the underslung glass bubble that housed the belly gun. Franks handed him his binoculars. They were high powered and unauthorized. Franks had won them in a poker game a couple of weeks earlier.

"Take a look," Franks invited.

Kutchinski took the binoculars and focused them. It was difficult because the plane was bouncing slightly and there were irregularities in the glass bubble, but he finally managed to get a good look. Yes, it was a ship, and, yes, it was a submarine. It was hard to tell its speed from their height, but the small wake indicated it was moving slowly. Kutchinski agreed with Frank's assessment that the sub indeed looked strange. He switched on the intercom and told the copilot to descend to ten thousand and circle the vessel.

"She'll see us and dive if she's a Jap," Franks complained.

"Better that than drop a load of bombs on one of ours."

"Ain't ours, Major," Franks insisted.

Kutchinski hoped it was a Jap. He had never bombed a ship and hated to abort the mission with a full load. In a few moments he was going to have to dump the bomber's load into the ocean. Now maybe, just maybe, he might have a useful target.

Kutchinski was well aware that no bomber had likely yet sunk a moving warship. Despite pilots' claims to the contrary, it was just too difficult to hit a moving target from a great height. The ship below had too much time to gauge the fall of the bombs and simply turn away. That there was really no such thing as precision bombing was another factor.

Despite new Norden bomb sights, most bombs didn't land any-where near their intended target. Norden bomb sights didn't take into account the nervousness of the operator, where a single sec-ond's misjudgment could send a bomb early or late to its destination, winds that could shift even the largest bomb in its flight, and air tur-bulence that jarred the plane and spoiled the calmest bombardier's aim. These and the fact that bombers could still be fired at during some aspects of their run all conspired to send bombs off target.

But what if it was a Jap sub and there was something wrong with her? She was clearer now and her silhouette was definitely strange. Their radioman signaled Guam that they had a possible enemy sub sighting and were trying to verify. Guam told them to be careful.

Maybe the *Polish Pope*'s luck would change. After the two earlier aborts, some wiseasses were saying it was because of the plane's name. There had never been a Polish pope, Kutchinski was told, and there never would be. The name was a jinx. Even Father Girardelli, the Catholic chaplain, had suggested he change it. The priest had also assured him that the papacy was reserved for deserving Italians and had gotten a little angry when Kutchinski had told him there was no such thing as a deserving Italian.

"He's shooting at us!" yelled Franks.

"He surely is," Kutchinski said happily as tracers arced from the sub toward their plane. That settled it. The sub was a Jap. He bounded to the pilot's seat and took over command of the plane. And she's not diving, he thought with glee. Maybe she can't, he thought. Such a shame.

He decided he would not try to hit the sub directly, but came at her bow-on at one thousand feet. If a bomb dropped even near a ship, the pressure would cause the sub's hull to buckle and send her down as effectively as if he had dropped one straight down her con-ning tower. He ordered the nose gunners to spray the decks of the sub with .50-caliber machine-gun fire as they approached. It wouldn't be accurate, but it might make those on her deck keep their heads down for a critical second while they bombed.

For an instant before the bombs dropped, he saw figures running about the deck of the sub and jumping into the water. Then the plane flew over and peeled away. Kutchinski saw nothing but heard the tail gunner whoop with joy. He banked the plane in a tight turn and saw the waters around the sub had been whipped into a froth as a dozen five-hundred-pound bombs exploded around her. As expected, none hit, but they caused a pressure surge that lifted the sub out of the water and laid her on her side. She began to take water and settle.

"Anybody taking pictures?" Kutchinski hollered. An affirmative reply came from two of his men who never flew without their cameras.

Franks hollered that he could see that several hull plates were damaged. "She's ruptured like my uncle Harry, Major. She's done for!"

"My sympathies to your uncle Harry," Kutchinski yelled over the intercom. He then directed his radio operator to notify the navy that there might be debris that could provide intelligence, along with the possibility that some Japs had survived the onslaught. Through his own binoculars he thought he could see heads in the water.

As the men on the *Polish Pope* circled and watched, the stricken sub sank beneath the waves, breaking in half just before she slid from view. It occurred to Kutchinski that damned few men had been able to get off, and he wondered what was going on in that sinking ship as it descended to the bottom of the Pacific. He decided he didn't really want to know.

•

CHAPTER 64

SOUTH OF KYUSHU, THE I-58

omdr. Mochitsura Hashimoto vomited oily water and grasped for a piece of floating debris. The dying submarine I-58 had sent a torrent of matériel upward as she sank to the bottom, and much of it now floated near him. If he could stay afloat for a while, he might not yet die. That he was still alive in the first place hinted that he might not yet have been chosen to die this day.

He wiped his eyes and squinted. The oil and the salt from the water had blurred his vision. A life preserver bobbed a few feet in front of him and he struggled into it. Relieved of the need to use all his strength swimming, he looked about him. The I-58 was indeed gone, as if there had been a doubt. He hollered and a scattering of voices answered.

In a few minutes he had gathered up the survivors of the sinking. Counting himself, there were eight men. Eight men out of the entire crew. A couple were wounded, but would survive if he could get them out of the chill waters in a reasonable amount of time. He didn't think there were sharks this far north, but he quickly concluded that sharks were the least of their problems. The cold would get them in a few hours at most.

They fashioned a raft of sorts out of the remains of the sub and clambered on board. They had no food or water, but at least they were alive. They were the lucky ones.

Luck, however, could be good or bad. It had been good luck that the I-58 had evaded destruction for so long. They had used the last of their torpedoes and were attempting a passage back to Japan when, bad luck, the bow fins had suddenly stuck in a position that gradually drove them toward the surface. But perhaps that had been good luck? Had they jammed in the downward position, the I-58 would slowly have descended to the bottom of the ocean, where it would have laid forever while the men died of oxygen loss if the depths didn't crush the sub's hull.

Hashimoto shuddered at the thought. He had thought they were far enough away from the American warships and ordered an immediate surfacing to see if the damaged fins could be fixed. He feared daylight surfacing, but there had been no choice.

It had been bad luck that the American plane had spotted them. Even then he did not think the danger was immediate. The plane, a bomber, had circled them and was obviously puzzled at their behavior and uncertain of their nationality. The damage to the bow fins would only take a few minutes to fix, and then they could dive from the vulture's sight.

It had been stupidity, not bad luck, that doomed them when the machine gunner on the conning tower had fired at the bomber. Not only was the bomber out of range, but it gave away the game. When the bomber came in with its guns blazing, Hashimoto had been forced into the water with most of the men who now sat with him on the raft. He and the others had just made it back onto the deck of the sub when the bombs had exploded, killing the I-58. That they were not in the water, good luck, had saved them. Water does not compress so the pressure of the explosions on their bodies in the water would have squashed the life from them.

"Captain," said one of the sailors, pointing toward the horizon. Two ships were approaching. This time there was no puzzlement. They were American, and in only a few moments, he identified them as destroyers.

The only remaining officer was Ensign Naha, a young man Hashimoto didn't really know. Ensigns were best seen and not heard. Naha stood up shakily on the raft.

"We must not be taken," he announced.

"What do you propose?" Hashimoto asked. The ensign bowed respectfully and knelt down to keep his balance. "Do we have weapons to use on the Americans?" Hashimoto asked.

A quick check showed there were none, not even a pocketknife. "I believe it is our fate to be captured," Hashimoto said. He wondered whether that would be good luck or bad. Regardless, it would happen.

"I will not surrender," yelled Naha. Before anyone could stop him, he jumped into the water and disappeared. In a few seconds, some bubbles popped onto the surface. They were all that remained of Ensign Naha, and the sight of yet another wasted life saddened Hashimoto. He realized that a decision he had always thought impossible was now imminent.

"Captain?" asked one of the sailors through blueing lips. "Shall we follow him? Give us your orders."

The destroyers were much closer and had paired off, one on either side of the huddled group. In a few moments they would be on top of them. It occurred to Hashimoto that the Americans could only have been a mile or so over the horizon. Luck again?

"My orders are that we live."

"They will shoot us," the sailor wailed.

"Not if we show them we are harmless. Strip," Hashimoto ordered. He and the six other men peeled off their clothes. He'd heard that the Americans were concerned about Japanese hiding grenades in their clothing and on their bodies. Nakedness, however degrading under the circumstances, might show them otherwise.

"Everything," he commanded, and in a few seconds they were all naked and shivering from fear as well as the cold.

With exquisite seamanship, one of the destroyers placed itself virtually alongside the raft. "Do you surrender?" someone asked in terrible Japanese.

"We surrender," Hashimoto responded slowly but clearly. He hoped that the American understood him. "I am an officer and you have my word on it."

Getting on board the destroyer was tricky. Netting was lowered, but a couple of the men were too numbed from the cold to hold on. The Americans dropped ropes and hauled up the Japanese like cargo.

Hashimoto, as the officer in charge, was the last and managed to climb the net.

Finally he stood, dripping and naked on the deck of the American warship. He was surrounded by at least a score of armed men. Submachine guns were leveled at them as if the seven cold, miserable, and naked Japanese would try to take over the destroyer.

They are afraid of us, Hashimoto realized. They are terrified. They outnumber us and outgun us, yet we are to them the stuff of nightmares.

Hashimoto picked out a man who was obviously an officer, perhaps even the captain. Hashimoto's English was extremely limited, but he felt compelled to say something.

Bowing with as much dignity as he could manage under the circumstances, he said, "Surrender. We surrender. We fight no more."

·

CHAPTER 65

Secretary of State Jim Byrnes and Undersecretary Joseph Grew joined General Marshall and President Truman in the Oval Office. The meeting had been called at the request of Marshall, who immediately told them that Magic and other sources confirmed that the Japanese were planning to use gas and biological weapons.

The news visibly upset Byrnes. "Not poison gas. Not at this stage of the game."

Truman was deeply concerned, but took the news calmly. "General, I gather you can verify this."

"Sir, they've had a gas and biological warfare program based in Manchuria for a number of years."

"Go on," Truman ordered.

"Gentlemen," Marshall began, "one Lt. Gen. Shiro Ishii was in charge of what the Japs referred to as Unit 731, and it was located near Harbin, Manchuria. I believe it was situated there well before the war started, so it's had time to grow and develop with relative secrecy. The unit was in charge of virtually all of Japan's research into poison gas and germ warfare. Ishii is rumored to have authorized the use of gas and germs on Chinese villages a few years ago as well as performed medical experiments on prisoners of war."

Byrnes glared. "Sadistic bastards."

"Agreed," said Marshall. "They may have attempted germ warfare against the British in Burma, and it is possible that they attempted to spread plague germs among U.S. troops on Saipan. Mercifully, the sub bringing it in was sunk, but some evidence did drift ashore."

Truman shook his head. "How successful would you gauge Japan's program to be, General?"

"Very successful. The key would be the fact that Ishii rose in rank from major to lieutenant general in only a few years. Without success, he would not have been promoted. Ishii and some of his staff are back in Japan. This means that the Russians let them pass through. They doubtless brought additional quantities of their inventory."

Truman seethed. "And now they can send waves of poison gas against our boys."

"Not exactly," Marshall answered. "I do not believe they have huge supplies of gas, but if they do use gas, it will more likely be in the form of artillery shells or bombs attached to kamikaze planes. That would be far more accurate and nowhere as dangerous to the senders as the old method was."

In the First World War, gas had been released from containers and blown by the wind across to the enemy's trenches. One real problem was the likelihood of the wind shifting, thus sending the clouds of gas back to the side that had released it. Using gas in artillery shells and small bombs effectively eliminated that problem.

Marshall continued, "We've had a number of requests from our own side to use gas against dug-in Japanese positions. A solidly built Jap bunker can withstand a flamethrower, but not gas, which will permeate through whatever flame-retarding barriers they have constructed. On my own initiative, I have sent more than five thousand gas artillery shells and chemical bombs to Okinawa. They are in place and can be transported for use on Kyushu at any time."

Truman started to glare at Marshall, but realized that the man had once again planned far ahead. "If the Japs use those shells, even if the number is limited, can our boys protect themselves? Do they have gas masks?"

Marshall laughed harshly. "While all of our boys were issued masks at some time in the past, I doubt that one GI in ten still has them. They are normally the first thing the soldiers throw away as excess weight to carry. It would take a while to resupply, and I'm afraid the danger still wouldn't be taken all that seriously. Also, the gases and chemicals now in everyone's arsenals are far more lethal than the ones used in the last war. In some cases, the merest touch of poison on bare skin can kill, which means gas masks would be useless. We would have to dress our men in rubber suits to protect them, and that is simply not feasible."

"We don't need more casualties," Truman said softly. "Particularly not from gas."

The American forces on Kyushu were going into a final defensive mode prior to the attack on Honshu. Casualties to date were well over the two hundred thousand mark and were still climbing, and civilian protests were mounting. Truman had canceled his daily walks. He couldn't bear all the heckling and shouts from the hundreds of people who surrounded the White House.

"Sir," Marshall said, "the real danger may come not from gas but from germ warfare. As I said, they've used it in China and tried to use it on Saipan. They are capable of sending infected suicide soldiers into our lines to spread anthrax, plague, botulism, and cholera. The Chinese believe the Japanese spread diseases by dropping crude bombs with infected fleas and other items like infected feathers on their cities. Based on our radio intercepts, that is an entirely likely scenario."

"Hideous," whispered Truman.

"It gets worse," Marshall said. "We now believe they will try to hit the West Coast of the United States with germ warfare. They have the capability, and in their current state of desperation, we believe they will make the attempt."

Truman was incredulous. "How? Their navy's sunk and their planes can't reach this far. Do they intend to send germs by balloon like they did the firebombs that were supposed to burn our forests down?"

"No, sir, but not quite all their warships have been sunk. We believe they could use at least one of their remaining large submarines for that purpose. These carry small floatplanes, which could be launched just off California, Oregon, or Washington, and the germs could be dropped from very small bombs or sprayed on a city much like a crop duster sprays a crop. We have no idea how much damage it could cause. Our medical facilities are much better than those in China, where many thousands may have died from germ attacks. Maybe only a few will die, maybe none."

"Panic," Truman said angrily. "If it happens, there'll be a panic and everyone in California will head east in terror-stricken waves. It's insane. It would unleash torrents of hatred that would take an eternity to cool down. Anami's people are fools!"

Truman turned and glared at Grew and Byrnes. "Here's what I want you two gentlemen to do. You will use your neutral-country contacts to tell that son of a bitch Anami that any use of gas or germ warfare will be repaid a hundredfold with gas attacks of our own. Tell him we will use every nuclear bomb we now have and can build against anything that moves in Japan, civilian or military, and that includes Tokyo and Osaka. We will, if necessary, pull our boys from Kyushu and then make sure that everything that lives in Japan is killed."

Truman took a deep breath to control his anger. "You will have them tell Anami that we also have the ability to use chemicals that will destroy their rice crops, and that will ensure that anyone who survives the initial bombs and gas attacks starves to death."

Grew was shocked at Truman's torrent of anger. One point puzzled him. "We have the ability to destroy their food crops?"

Marshall answered. "Not yet, but they don't have to know it. Experiments with plant-killing chemicals are progressing, and it may be a year before they are ready, but it will happen. Very soon we will be able to defoliate Japan. We have been performing a number of experiments at Camp Detrick, Maryland, and the only remaining concern is not wanting to kill civilians along with the crops."

"The hell with the civilians," Truman snapped. "If the Japs use gas or germs, then all restraints are off and everything in Japan is a target."

"The Japs will get the word," Byrnes said grimly.

"Good." Truman relaxed visibly as his fury dissipated. "And the navy will redouble its efforts to stop any germ-bearing sub. Now, General Marshall, I understand there is a bit of good news."

"Yes, sir, we have confirmed that the Jap sub that sank the *Indianapolis* and the *Queen Elizabeth* has finally been hunted down and destroyed. The sub was the I-58, and her captain was among a handful of survivors who are now our prisoners."

"Hang the bastard," Byrnes snarled.

Truman managed a grin. "No, Jimmy, the American way is a trial first and then a hanging."

Marshall did not think it was amusing. "His defense will be that he was doing his duty. Both the *Indianapolis* and the *Queen Elizabeth* were legitimate military targets, and he will argue that he was doing nothing other than what our own subs did to Jap ships. I'm afraid we may be considering him a monster only because he was so successful. He is also proving quite useful. Like most of the Japanese we've captured, they aren't the slightest bit reluctant about answering every question we put to them. It's ironic, but once they actually do fall into our hands, a lot of them tell us everything they know, almost without our asking. He may even be able to help us stop their plague sub."

Truman accepted the rebuff in silence. Marshall was right. Dammit, Marshall was always right. Hanging the captain of the I-58 was immaterial. He had to keep focused on the task at hand, the ending of the war. He did not want it complicated by some fool launching a gas or germ attack on the United States.

CHAPTER 66

KYUSHU,
THE NORTH SHORE

In the distance, the deep, dark clouds merged with the flat sea, giving the impression of a continuous oneness that was almost frightening in its totality. If he didn't know better, Dennis Chambers thought he could easily confuse the view of sky and sea with that of a definition of eternity.

Bringing himself back to reality, he shifted his weight so that the small rock jabbing his buttock wasn't quite so aggravating. Then he pointed the flashlight out into the void and repeated the signal: one long flash and two short ones. It was the Morse code symbol for the letter *D*. *D*, he'd decided, stood for "dark," for the night, or "dumb," for him sitting here and waiting. That it also could've stood for "dead" he ignored.

There would be no response from the sea. The signal was only meant to be seen, not responded to. It would be too easy for someone else onshore to pick up a signal from the sea. Of course, there was always the possibility that a Jap patrol craft would pick up his flashes and make their own inquiries, but that was a chance that Dennis had to take.

Dennis froze. There was the hint of movement on the water. Dark shapes moved closer. They were so quiet and so well hidden that he hadn't detected them until they were almost on top of him. He watched in fascination as the three rafts were beached and their occupants spilled out onto the rocky shore a few yards in front of him. Still silent, they lay prone and formed a skirmish line a few feet from the water's edge. Dennis signaled again, and one shape moved toward him. The man was dressed in black, had dark guck smeared across his face, and carried an automatic grease gun. It was an American, and the sight of the well-armed and deadly-looking newcomer sent chills down Dennis's spine.

"You Joe?" the man hissed.

"I'm Chambers." Nomura was discreetly in hiding, about a hundred yards behind Dennis.

The man leveled his gun at him. "I expected Joe."

"They told you there were two of us, didn't they?"

The man paused and stared at Dennis, fearing a trap. Then he relaxed slightly. Chambers obviously wasn't a Jap, and Chambers was the name of Joe's companion. "What's the capital of North Dakota?"

This was incredible, Dennis thought. A geography test. "Buddy, I have absolutely no fucking idea."

The man lowered his weapon and grinned. "I don't either. Maybe they don't have one. I'm Ensign Billy Swain and this is my team. Now, where the hell is Joe?"

"About a hundred yards behind me and watching us. What do you know about him?"

"Nothing. I was told it was best that I don't."

Nomura had thought it would be that way and Dennis responded, "Joe is Joe Nomura, a Japanese-American OSS agent who's now wearing the uniform of a Jap officer. He also has only one arm, which he lost fighting Nazis in Italy. He thought it would be prudent if I met you first and explained that fact so you wouldn't shoot him on sight and ask questions later."

"Makes sense." Swain passed the word that they would see a Jap and they were not to open fire. Dennis then gave the signal for Joe to emerge. "Jesus H. Christ," Swain exclaimed when he saw Nomura. "Damned good thing you didn't meet us. We'd have shot you and run like hell back to the sub. Now, let's get inland and get our gear hidden."

"Not so fast," Nomura said. "Is it clear who is in charge of this operation?"

Swain thought of making a smart-ass remark, but even in the gloom he saw the hard look in Nomura's eyes. "You are, sir."

"Good. The sub is still waiting for the rafts to return, isn't it?"

"Yes. While eight of my men remain here, the others take the rafts back where they can be taken back on board the sub and stowed. That way there's no chance that they'll wash onshore and be discovered."

A small touch, but a smart one, Joe thought. He gestured to Dennis. "He goes back with the rafts."

Swain blinked. "That wasn't in the plan."

"Plans change, Ensign."

"Indeed they do, sir. May I ask why?"

"Two reasons. First, Dennis is an undernourished and not very healthy airman, while all of you guys are trained killers who've been eating well and have all your strength. When this mission starts, I think Mr. Chambers would be a hindrance rather than a help. We've talked it over and he realizes that.

"There's a second reason," Joe continued. "There are some extremely important things about this operation that the top command has to know about, and they can't be trusted to radio. The message must be delivered in person. When your men return to the sub, the captain will be made to understand that he must rendezvous with a seaplane to get Captain Chambers to Okinawa as soon as possible."

"Understood," said Swain. The rafts were empty and ready to pull out with two paddlers each.

Dennis and Joe shook hands. Then Dennis got into one of the rafts and settled on his haunches. He sucked in his breath as he felt the craft bob in the water. It had just been freed from the shore of Japan. When he was shot down and imprisoned, even after escaping, he never really thought he'd leave the Land of the Rising Sun alive.

Dennis had argued with Joe about his leaving. At first he'd felt he was betraying the man who'd saved his life, but the logic of the decision quickly became obvious. Along with being an OSS agent, Joe was an infantry combat veteran and would be operating with skilled specialists, and Dennis would only be in the way. Besides, the need to deliver the message was real. It was imperative that Hirohito be handled correctly for the mission to succeed.

Dennis had exulted when he'd first seen fellow Americans, armed and ready, emerging from the sea. Now, as the land receded behind him, he felt a new wave of emotions that overwhelmed him. In a few minutes he would be safe on board an American ship. In a couple of days at most he would be on a military base. Maybe they would let him contact Barb and let her know he was okay.

The water in front of them seemed to boil slightly as the submarine rose from periscope depth. Seconds later, the raft bumped gently alongside her hull. As hands reached to pull Dennis to the safety of the deck and helped him down the conning tower, he hoped the wetness on his face would be seen as ocean spray and not the tears it really was.

CHAPTER 67

KYUSHU,
NORTH OF MIYAKONOJO

Major Ruger and Paul Morrell stood to attention as Brigadier General Monck entered the battalion's command tent. "At ease, fellas, relax," Monck said. An easy grin split his face.

As a platoon leader, Paul had only met Monck on a couple of occasions and hadn't even talked to the man since becoming company commander.

He did know Monck's reputation as a firm but fair commander who didn't care much for the formalities of rank, particularly in these circumstances.

Major Ruger caught Paul's discomfort. "The lieutenant really doesn't think he did anything special. After all, he was primarily interested in saving his worthless ass and not winning a medal."

Monck laughed. "Well, his ass isn't all that worthless." The general reached into a fatigue-jacket pocket and pulled out a small package. "Here. The powers that be have determined that your coolheadedness under fire deserves a Bronze Star. Congratulations, Lieutenant."

"I really don't think I should have this, sir," Paul said as Monck placed the box in his hand.

Monck looked at him coolly, but with a flicker of amusement in his eyes. "I'm not surprised you said that. A lot of people do when they see a medal. But the truth is, you do deserve it, and certainly more so than some of the politicians who get honors for being on the same continent as a battle."

"But why, sir? I just did my job."

"That's right, son. All you did was your job. But you didn't have to do your job, did you? You could have laid on the ground until somebody else did his own job and killed the sniper. Or you could have hid until it got dark and then you could have skulked away and let somebody else figure out how to get rid of the bastard, if he hadn't already fled the coop so he could do it again. By that time who knows how much damage even a half-starved little kid could have done. No, you did exactly what you were supposed to do, which is solve the problem, and that, young Lieutenant Morrell, is precisely why you are getting this medal. You did your job and you did it well."

Paul nodded and took the box. He put it in his own pocket. It would be examined later. "Then thank you, sir."

Monck shook Paul's hand. Paul was astonished at the strength of the grip. "Lieutenant, this may not seem like much now, but it means a lot to your men to know that people like me have confidence in people like you. A few years from now, maybe a lot of years from now, you'll take it out and show it to your kids. You'll be proud of it and they'll be proud of you."

Paul finally grinned. "First I gotta get home before I can have any kids to show it to, General."

Monck laughed while, in the background, Ruger rolled his eyes in mock horror. Monck's expression changed as he unfolded a map and spread it on the table. He was no longer laughing.

"Gentlemen, along with giving Mr. Morrell his medal, I am visiting all my battalion commanders to make sure they understand precisely what is going on."

Paul asked if he should leave and Monck said no. "This'll save the major a trip if you hear it from me. What has been rumored is now going to occur. Effective immediately, the U.S. Army and Marines on Kyushu are to cease offensive operations and dig in. General Bradley and Admiral Nimitz feel that we have accomplished our purpose, and that we now own enough Jap real estate to use as a base for the next phase, the invasion of Honshu.

"As a result, you are to entrench and prepare to hold the ground we have. The only actions you will take will be patrols to make sure the Japs haven't organized an army just over the next ridge. What I think will happen is that the Japs, once they realize we've gone to ground, will attack the first time the weather gives them an opportunity. Bradley thinks that will be their last great attempt to drive us out of here."

Instinctively, all three men looked out through the tent's opening. It was cloudy and there was a light drizzle. It was not quite bad enough to ground air support or hamper artillery, but the January weather was far from ideal.

"Bradley feels that the Japs will attack just like the Germans did in the Bulge a year ago December," Monck added. "I agree. They will try to hug us real close so our planes and guns, even those that do get off, will be unable to bomb or fire because the Japs are too close to us."

The other men nodded silent agreement. What was referred to as hugging had been standard operating procedure for the Japs on the defensive ever since the Americans had landed. That they would try it while on the offensive was something new and unpleasant to ponder.

"Will they have enough to hit us with?" Ruger asked. "If that sniper's condition is any indication, the Japs are in pretty bad shape."

"Their army is in terrible shape," Monck admitted, "but the bastards are still fighting. They may be sick, cold, and starving, but there's still an awful lot of them left. This is their home and they're gonna make us pay for it until someone like Hirohito tells them to stop. And one other thing. I don't just want trenches, I want forts. If they break through, I don't want our rear areas vulnerable to being overrun. Everyone is going to have a circle to defend, and that includes the lard-ass rear-echelon troops you all love so much."

Ruger understood. "So we dig trenches and set up observation posts outside them. Good. The boys will be thrilled to not have any more hills to climb. What about things like barbed wire and mines? Will we get enough of that to keep them at bay?"

"Probably not," Monck said sadly. "It's one of the many things no one thought we'd need in the quantity we'd like to have. You'll get enough wire for a couple of strands, but nothing like the thickets of wire that were used in World War I. As to mines, I don't even know if we have any."

A couple of strands of wire would be nothing more than an annoyance. Without wire and mines, any successful defense would depend on having at least some warning, as well as being able to focus overwhelming firepower on an oncoming enemy that wasn't afraid to die.

"Anything else we should know?" Ruger asked.

"Just one more thing. How are your men set for gas masks?"

CHAPTER 68

.

KYUSHU, CAMP 7

Col. Tadashi Sakei whirled as Joe Nomura entered his office, causing papers to fly from his desk onto the floor. "Captain Nomura," he snapped angrily, "just where the hell have you been the last couple of days? You should be here with me and your emperor! Don't you know that? Where is your sense of duty?"

Despite the difference in ranks and the fact that Sakei was an Imperial Guards officer, Joe did not let the other man bully him. After all, he wore the uniform of a *kempei* officer and, in theory at least, was answerable to no one, not even a guards colonel.

"I had other duties to attend to," he answered stiffly.

If Sakei was upset by the borderline insolence, he didn't show it. Instead, Joe felt he probably expected it and had simply been letting off steam. Sakei shoved a batch of papers at Joe. "Here, what do you make of these?"

Joe glanced at them. They were copies of the most recent transmissions that had been sent from his station in the hills. This time, the radio was different as was the code. The transmissions, he saw with satisfaction, had not yet been decoded, and the sheets were nothing more than pages of gibberish. He pretended to study them and then handed them back.

"The spy has changed codes. I knew that. We've been expecting it for some time."

"Is it significant, Captain? What do your superiors say?"

"I have been out of touch with my superiors," Joe answered with ironic truthfulness. He would never think of contacting anyone higher up in the *kempei* command structure. "American bombing has disrupted communications even worse than before, and we will not get much assistance from them for the foreseeable future."

Joe returned the papers. "My own opinion of the change, however, is that one of three things has happened. First, that the codes were changed simply because it was time to do so as they have been in continuous use for some time. Second, that the spy, doubtless an American as we've agreed, has been replaced. Perhaps he was replaced because he was killed? Third, it is possible that another spy hàs landed. Other spies have landed elsewhere, so why not here?"

"Good reasoning," Sakei mumbled, and Joe saw how the anxieties were wearing on him even more than in the past. Sakei looked on the verge of collapse. "The original American code was inferior in its architecture and easily broken. Our codes are not changed because they are unbreakable."

Privately, Joe wondered about that statement. It was typical Japanese arrogance to presume something's superiority simply because it was of Japanese origin.

"But what do you make of the planes and the dummy parachutists?" Sakei asked. "We have identified an American airborne division in Kyushu. Could they be planning a massive assault?"

The last couple of nights had been filled with the roar of hundreds of low-flying transports that flew over Kyushu and, in some cases, dropped dummy paratroops. It was all part of a massive distraction that covered the low-level drop of a platoon of airborne rangers that even now was reconnoitering Camp 7. As soon as possible, they and Ensign Swain's frogmen would move against it and pull Hirohito out of his cage.

"I think," Joe answered, "that the Americans are trying to distract and confuse us. By reacting and moving our troops to counter their phantom assaults, we expose our soldiers to further attacks from the air and at little cost to the Americans."

Sakei nodded. "Even so, I am tempted to move the emperor to a place of greater safety."

Joe was horrified. If that occurred, they would have to make an attempt to take him along a road and then fight their way back to an extraction point. All their plans were dependent on Hirohito's staying at Camp 7. If he was moved out of their reach, they would have to abort the attempt, and that would be tragic.

"Sir, with respect, I believe that it would be a mistake. To move the emperor now would subject the Imperial presence to the same aerial threats that would befall any column of soldiers or a convoy of trucks. Hirohito's presence is unknown here and the camp continues to be safe from bombing. In my opinion, Colonel, at this time this is the safest possible place for the emperor."

Sakei rubbed his eyes with his fists. He was almost groggy from worry and loss of sleep. "You are right, Captain. You are always right. I am glad I have you to depend on and help me think. You are a credit to your uniform. The emperor will remain here, although I will notify nearby police and militia units to be on the alert."

Joe bowed and walked toward the emperor's quarters. Sakei continued to be deluded and that was good. The colonel was a butcher, a sadist, and, to a large extent, personally responsible for the continuation of the war. Screw Sakei, Joe thought. Then he wondered just what effect Sakei's alerting police and militia units would have on the plans to extract Hirohito. Hopefully, Hirohito's taking would be done quickly and there would be no time for reinforcements to arrive.

Nomura knocked on a tent pole and received the invitation to enter. As he bowed before Hirohito, it occurred to him that he both respected and liked the little, bespectacled man who wanted peace. This was the embodiment of Japan, not fools like Sakei.

"How is the good colonel?" Hirohito asked.

"At the point of collapse, sir."

Hirohito smiled. "Confusion to our enemies, then. What news, Captain?"

"Soon, very soon. Perhaps even tonight. I will remain here and make sure I am with you when it happens."

Hirohito smiled grimly. "Soon cannot be soon enough, Captain Nomura. Every moment we wait is filled with death for the innocent. We must stop this killing."

.

CHAPTER 69

KYUSHU, ROUND TOP

The name for the barren and war-scarred hill occurred to several in Paul's company who had any knowledge of the Civil War and the battle of Gettysburg. The hill they were fortifying was fairly small, strangely symmetrical, and an extremely important piece of earth to the men of the company because, as they told him, they were on it. Thus, it was christened Little Round Top, although, they quickly dropped the adjective *little* and simply referred to it as Round Top.

The war and their efforts had denuded the hill of trees and shrubs. Many of the shattered trees had been turned into logs, which reinforced the trenches and bunkers that now crisscrossed the hill and provided comfort and protection for the 134 men in the company.

"Good job, Paul," Major Ruger said as he finished his tour. "The numbers are a little depressing, though. Didn't we start this thing with more than two hundred men in the company?"

More than half the company had been killed or wounded since the invasion, along with a handful who, like Lieutenant Marcelli, had succumbed to physical and mental illnesses. Both Paul and Ruger remembered the lecture back on Okinawa during which that half-crazed sergeant had predicted they would take such heavy casualties. It had seemed so unlikely then, but it had occurred.

"Look at 'em," Ruger said. He pointed in the direction of a half dozen confused, clean, and depressingly healthy young soldiers. "Replacements, and they're so scared they can hardly stand there without pissing themselves."

"I'll spread them out so they won't be together and feed off each other's fears," Paul said.

Paul was fortunate to get any more help. Only those few bodies who had already been in one of Kyushu's several replacement depots were being sent to frontline units. All other possible replacements en route or not quite landed had been shunted off to the Philippines or Okinawa to take part in the invasion of Honshu. Paul didn't really know which group was the luckier. Honshu didn't sound like any more fun than Kyushu had been. At least he'd got six new soldiers if they didn't wind up hurting themselves before they got acclimated.

"I love what you've done with the tank," Ruger joked. Sergeant Orlando's beloved Sherman was in the center of the perimeter and at the very top of the hill, where it was surrounded by an earthen berm. It had taken a great deal of time and effort to maneuver and manhandle the metal beast up Round Top and was only possible after the remaining trees had been chopped down. While it gave Orlando a complete field of fire, it also exposed the tank, which was one of the reasons for the berm. Someone had mentioned that from a distance the tank on the hill looked like a nipple on a tit, or maybe a fly on a pile of shit. Orlando didn't think it was funny.

"I just wish he still had the big gun," Paul said. While it was in the rear for maintenance, a tube had been inserted in the 76mm's barrel. This changed it from a cannon to a giant-sized flamethrower that could belch fire for more than a hundred yards out. "I have doubts about the change."

Orlando had heard the comment. He waved and grinned. "Don't worry, Lieutenant, we haven't failed you yet."

"No, you haven't," Paul said, laughing. "I just wish you had gotten more wire when you were in the back."

Ruger winced at the comment. There just wasn't enough barbed wire to go around. Literally. The perimeter on Round Top was surrounded by a thin line of fencing that would have been more appropriate for preventing cattle from straying from a Montana ranch, instead of protecting a fortified hill. The little ring of wire would not be much of a deterrent.

"Want some artillery?" Ruger asked.

"Sure," Paul answered. "What's the catch?"

"Nothing, although maybe I feel guilty about the little bit of wire and the absolute lack of mines. General Monck gave me two 105-millimeter pack howitzers, and this looks like a real good spot for them. They can protect the flanks of the companies to your right and left, and they can hit the high ground in front of you."

"Mount Ugly?" Paul grinned.

Ruger looked at the scarred and denuded hill in front of them and decided that the name fit marvelously. Technically, it was in Japanese hands, but Paul's soldiers had scorched it and stripped it bare of vegetation so that the Japs could not use it for concealment and sneak up on Round Top.

Mt. Ugly was a little higher than Round Top, and that was a concern as the Japanese could hide behind it and be out of sight. However, if the Americans took Mt. Ugly, there would be another, higher hill behind it, and they would also be sticking out of the American lines and be even more vulnerable than before. There was no choice but to make the best of Round Top. The howitzers would help there as well. With their high trajectory, they would be able to lob shells just over the ridgeline of Mt. Ugly and maybe shake up anybody forming up for an attack.

Paul shivered as a blast of cold, wet air hit him in the face. One of the advantages of entrenching was that there were places on the hill that were actually dry and fairly warm. Of course the trenches themselves were dank and ankle-deep in water, which might lead to trench foot or frostbite, but the bunkers were fairly comfortable.

"Want to go inside?" Paul suggested. "We've got hot coffee and some doughnuts left over from breakfast."

Ruger readily agreed. The war was getting a lot more civilized. Why stay out in the rain if you don't have to? The weather, however, concerned him. It wasn't yet bad enough to put a halt to air support or artillery, but it was making things difficult. It wouldn't take all that much more to shift a lot of advantages to the Japanese, wherever they were hiding.

Again the wind swirled. It was raining harder now. Ruger touched Paul on the arm and pointed across the valley to the scarred bulk of Mt. Ugly. It was scarcely visible.

CHAPTER 70

LOS ANGELES,
CALIFORNIA

The ringing phone jarred Barb Chambers from a deep sleep. After a moment's confusion, she turned on the light and looked at her watch. It was just after midnight. Who on earth could be calling her at this ungodly hour? She hoped it wasn't a drunk wanting a ride home. Her number was close to that of a local bar, and she often got calls from wives wondering just when the hell their no-good husbands were coming home. It would not be the first time her sleep had been interrupted by such a call.

She walked to the kitchen and turned on that light, somehow managing to pick up the phone on the fourth ring. "Hullo," she mumbled, her tongue still thick and uncooperative.

"Barb?"

She tensed. The voice was faint but chillingly familiar. Too familiar. "Yes," she said hesitantly. She had stopped breathing and her heart had begun racing. She dared not hope, would not hope.

"It's me, Barb."

"Dennis?" Her mind reeled. This couldn't be happening. This was a dream and she would soon awaken and find the happiness surging through her had been snatched away and replaced by cruel reality. Dennis was missing. The Japs said he was a prisoner, but Truman said the Japs lied. She hadn't heard from him in almost a year, and it was more likely he was dead than alive.

"It's me, honey. In the flesh."

Barb Chambers sat down in one of the kitchen chairs. The wood was cool to her buttocks through the thin cotton nightgown. She could feel things, sense things; therefore, she was not dreaming. This was truly happening.

"Where are you?" she said, half talking and half sobbing and all the while praying he wouldn't go away. This could not be an illusion, could it? Was she hallucinating?

There was a pause, and when Dennis responded, she could tell he was crying as well. "I can't say. Not just yet at least. But I'm safe, Barb, I'm safe. I'm on an American base and everything's gonna be okay." With that his voice broke down.

"When will you be home?" She tucked her knees under her chin, hugged them, and began to rock back and forth.

"Soon. Maybe a couple of weeks, but they're gonna get me out of here as fast as they can." He did not add that he wasn't going any-place until the attempt to free Hirohito was completed, one way or another.

Dennis'd had his conferences first with Ridgway, and then with Bradley and Nimitz. They all said they understood fully. Hirohito would be treated with all the courtesy afforded a head of state and not treated as a prisoner. Now it was rumored that Truman was fly-ing to Okinawa and that Dennis would meet with him as well. What a hell of a story he would have to tell Barb when he was allowed to tell it. If he was allowed to tell it, he corrected.

"Barb, I can't talk for very long 'cause this is costing the govern-ment a helluva lot of money and maybe someone else wants to use the phone. I just want you to know that I love you so very much and that I thought about you all the time I was, ah, in trouble. The thought of coming home to you was something that helped keep me alive when it got rough."

"I was so worried, so scared." She wanted to ask how rough it had been, but she was afraid of the answer. It could wait. He was alive and said he was well and that was all that counted.

"So was I, hon, but it's okay now. But, hey, how about you? How are you holding up?"

"Just fine, Dennis. My sister is here and she's helping out a lot."

"With what?" he asked, puzzled.

Barbara laughed at his confusion. "When was the last time we made love, dear Dennis?"

He thought quickly. He'd had a brief leave just before shipping out to Guam. That, he calculated, had been a little more than a year ago. They'd made love like bunnies for those few days as if there would be no tomorrow. There almost wasn't, he thought ruefully.

"I remember it well."

"Well, so do I and so will you. For the rest of our lives we're going to remember it. Dennis, you have a son. I didn't tell you because I didn't know at first, and then you went missing and I couldn't. I wanted so much to tell you, but there was no way," she sobbed.

"Jesus," Dennis gasped. "I'm a daddy."

"He's Dennis Jr. and he's got all the tools and digits he's supposed to." In the background, Dennis Jr. had awakened and was being soothed by Barb's sister, who was looking on incredulously. He would need changing and then he would want to nurse.

"Jesus," Dennis repeated.

"Dennis, have you suddenly gotten religion?" she teased.

"I'm overwhelmed."

"So am I," she whispered. "Now get home and let's get started on the next one."

Thousands of miles away, OSS agent Johnson watched as Chambers shakily hung up the phone. Despite trying to give the man some privacy, he had overheard much and understood more. The call had obviously gone well from the glazed and goofy look on Chambers's face.

"Congratulations, pop," Johnson said, extending his hand. "First cigar you get ahold of is mine."

"Fair enough." Dennis grinned. "Now, what do I have to do to get something to eat around here?"

"Whatya want?" Johnson signaled to a clerk who would make a quick trip to the mess hall. They still didn't want Chambers running around in public in case he slipped and said something. Even though it was extraordinarily unlikely that anything said on Okinawa would fall into Jap hands, there was no sense taking any chances at all at this late stage of the game.

"How 'bout a hamburger and a milk shake? Chocolate."

Johnson rolled his eyes and guffawed. That would make three of each in the last hour. "Dennis, you are nothing but a damned eating machine."

CHAPTER 71

KYUSHU,
NORTH OF ROUND TOP

Sgt. Yuji Yokota's plan to avoid further military service had fallen apart only a couple of weeks after Ens. Keizo Ikeda's frail plane had taken off and disappeared into the darkness.

Yokota's original idea had been to head north and lie low in the hills until the war ended, as he thought it surely must. He had what he felt was enough food to last him, but a sudden rain squall had ruined a great deal of it, forcing him down from the hills and into the camps to avoid starvation.

A roadblock set up to catch deserters had nailed him almost immediately. There had been no use even trying to lie his way through it. For one thing, he was still too well fed to have been anything but a soldier, and then he'd made the absurd mistake of standing at attention when a *kempei* lieutenant had interrogated him.

The *kempei* officer had sneered and given him two choices. He could "volunteer" for a shock brigade forming to attack the Americans, or he could be hanged right then and there. With false pride in his voice, Yokota had assured the officer that he would be honored to fight for Japan, which had been his intent all along. After all, he insisted, he had been on his way to find a new unit after his old one had been destroyed. The lieutenant's barely stifled laugh told him he hadn't believed a word of that declaration.

In the end, his sins had been overlooked because experienced NCOs were rarer than hen's teeth at this stage of the war. Yokota was delighted that they even let him keep his stripes. Even though he

was primarily a mechanic, he was still a sergeant. With even that little bit of authority, he thought he might be able to bluff his way out
of trouble. At the very least, he was still alive.

He was dismayed when he saw the unit he was finally assigned to.
It was called a company, although it had only eighty men and to call
the soldiers men, or the men soldiers, was to stretch either point.
They were all extremely young and in their mid to late teens, inexperienced, ill equipped, and scarcely trained. They all had rifles and
bayonets, although some of the weapons dated back to the turn of
the century.

They averaged only twenty rounds apiece, which wasn't enough
for a skirmish, much less a war. When Yokota commented on that,
he was told that their purpose was one grand and final attack on the
Americans, and that courageously thrust bayonets would prove more
effective than bullets.

Was this all that was left, Sergeant Yokota wondered, an army of
young boys? If this was the case, then Japan was in horrible shape indeed. Many of the young recruits looked terrified as well as cold and
miserable. At least as military personnel they had access to Japan's
dwindling store of rations, so they didn't look as bad off as many
people he'd seen.

Their company commander was Lt. Fumimaro Uji, who was also
the company's only officer. As the only experienced NCO, Sergeant
Yokota was second-in-command. Tall, thin, and extremely near-
sighted, Lieutenant Uji had been a supply officer until the army realized it had a desperate need for officers of any kind and, with no
supplies to distribute, had found a way to utilize him.

Lieutenant Uji was unqualified to lead a field command and knew
it. As a result and within hours of his arrival, it fell to Sergeant
Yokota to get the company organized and on the move toward the
Americans. Uji professed to hate the Americans and to be willing to
die a glorious and bloody death fighting them. He made a speech to
that effect that further terrified the youthful recruits.

Their trek south was fraught with peril. Even with the weather
deteriorating, the American planes were omnipresent threats. They
hiked the trails at night in an extended single-file column that made
them difficult to be seen and hit. Even so, they often heard the

crump-crump of bombs falling in their area, and several times came upon the grisly remains of others who had been either careless or unlucky. Knowing that the trails were in use, the Americans had started lobbing napalm bombs at suspected troop concentrations. On a couple of occasions they had passed the charred and blasted remains of Japanese dead. Whether they were soldiers headed to battle or civilians who happened to be in the wrong place was not always something that could be ascertained by looking on the mangled dead.

Under the circumstances, Sergeant Yokota wasn't in the least surprised when several of the recruits simply disappeared into the night. Lieutenant Uji was beyond himself with rage and disappointment, but even he recognized the futility of going after the deserters. It did not escape Yokota's notice that *kempei* presence was inconsistent the closer they got to the actual fighting.

Then came the day he realized they'd arrived at their destination. Their sector was quiet, but the Americans were only a couple of miles away.

"The rains are getting harder," Lieutenant Uji exulted. "Under their cover we will soon launch ourselves against the enemy and rid Japan of their scourge."

Yokota agreed that the weather was truly fucking miserable. A couple of the men had developed hacking coughs and now vomited their rations. As to whether the Americans could be driven off, he had doubts. Even though many hundreds of other soldiers were well hidden in the area, he wondered what they could do against the American army's legendary firepower. What use was courage and a bayonet against a machine gun? He'd seen that scenario played out in China when the roles were reversed. There it had been the Chinese who'd had the courage but not the weapons, and they'd been slaughtered.

And how would his men react when the time came? To his surprise, Yokota had found himself growing attached to them and not wishing them harm. He was their grandfather and they came to him with all kinds of problems. One had asked him why they were fighting and when it would stop. It was evident from the way the others watched this one that he represented all of them. They were all smart and most were educated. In earlier days, Yokota would have slapped them for being weak or even beaten them senseless and sent them back to work, but not now. Too much had changed. These were children, not soldiers, and he grieved for them and what they would suffer. He told them the war would soon end.

Worse, he knew that he was only a couple of miles and a day or two away from his own destruction. This was not the way he'd planned it, and he racked his brain trying to figure a way out of the mess he'd gotten into. He would do everything he could to save his newfound children along with himself. Only problem was, he hadn't the foggiest idea how.

.

CHAPTER 72

KYUSHU, CAMP 7

Joe Nomura was half-asleep outside Hirohito's bedchamber when he heard the first shout of alarm. It was followed by a burst of gunfire and a scream that ended in a gurgle. It had begun. He checked the time. It was a couple of hours before dawn. Joe pulled his pistol from its holster and ran the few feet to Hirohito's quarters.

"Where're you going?" yelled Sakei as he charged in. "Traitors are attacking us. They want the emperor. We must stop them." He had his own pistol out and was casting about in sleep-induced confusion.

"I'm going to protect the emperor," Nomura answered, and pushed past him. Sakei didn't protest. Instead, he went on to battle what he thought were the Japanese forces trying to take or kill his emperor. Nomura hoped it would be several minutes longer before Sakei realized his mistake.

Hirohito was seated on the floor listening to the battle. Apprehension was on his face, but not fear. "It is time?"

Joe plopped down beside him. "Yes."

Further conversation was cut off by a fusillade of shots punctuated by further screams. "Your men got so very close before being detected, didn't they?"

The bad weather had worked in their favor and hidden the approach of the rangers and the frogmen. Refugees remained huddled in their miserable tents and shelters and ignored the thirty-odd men who'd moved with near perfect silence through the camp and toward the hospital. Those who saw them noted nothing unusual as the men had been draped in blankets. In the rain and dark they appeared to be another group of refugees, or additional troops for the mysterious compound.

More gunfire erupted, this time close. The top of the tent shuddered and a line of bullet holes appeared in it. It reminded Hirohito of the time when Sakei had first taken him prisoner in the bunker beneath the palace in Tokyo. It was hard for Hirohito to remember that it had been only half a year earlier. As if to complete the memory, Sakei burst in on them. He had a pistol in his hand and his face was contorted with rage.

"Americans!" His voice was a shriek. "Americans are attacking us." He turned to Nomura. "We must move the emperor immediately."

"No," Joe answered softly. He fired his pistol twice, hitting Sakei in the chest with both bullets.

Sakei dropped to his knees and let his pistol fall to the ground. "Not you," he muttered as realization dawned.

A moment's anger twisted Sakei's face before his eyes rolled up in his head and he slumped to the floor. An enlisted guard retreated in on them and Joe shot him in the back. Another entered and, seeing the bodies, ran away before Joe could kill him as well.

"Roy," a deep voice yelled.

"Trigger," Joe answered, completing the signal. After a moment's delay, Ens. Billy Swain entered the tent and looked in disbelief at the small man with glasses who sat with Nomura. He had known whom to expect, but it still came as a shock that the emperor of Japan sat on the floor a few feet in front of him.

"Un-fucking-believable," Swain whispered as Nomura and Hirohito stood up.

"What's he saying?" Hirohito asked.

"That he's glad to see you," Joe responded. "Now let's get out of here."

They ran outside where a perimeter had been set up. A ranger said that their commander had been killed. "We've got to get out of here right now," Swain said. There was no disagreement. "We've got about two miles to go."

Nomura had not been privy to this part of the operation. Again, what Joe didn't know, Joe couldn't tell. If the operation failed and he was captured, he could say nothing that would endanger his comrades. Thus, he was slightly surprised when they did not make a direct run to the ocean, which was less than ten miles from the camp. Swain had said two miles, so that meant something else was up.

First they retreated through the refugee camp. There was confusion and consternation everywhere as a result of the gunfire. People swirled and screamed as they tried to avoid the compact group of armed Americans pushing through them. No one appeared to notice the small, bespectacled civilian in their midst.

Finally, they made the safety of the brush and continued through it. Joe watched the effects of the night on Hirohito. While sometimes looking bewildered, he would see Joe looking at him and shake it off. He had made a fateful decision and would stand by it.

They came to a clearing. A handful of rangers emerged and a sergeant told Swain that the message had been sent. The cavalry was on the way.

"How many casualties?" Hirohito asked. Two dead and seven wounded, he was told. It amazed and saddened him that these young Americans had died or been hurt on his behalf.

"How long will this take?" Joe asked.

"Twenty minutes max," Swain replied.

This did not constitute good news to Joe, who recalled Sakei's comment about alerting local police and militia. "It better be soon. There were survivors among the guards and they'll have sent for help. Things are going to get very interesting if the planes don't arrive real fast."

Billy Swain grinned. "Planes? Joe, who the hell said anything about planes?"

CHAPTER 73

NORTH OF KYUSHU,
THE USS MIDWAY

Admirals Nimitz and Halsey were uncomfortable with the situation in which they found themselves. The rain had kept the kamikazes away, but that was the only good thing they could say about the operation that had grown from the proverbial shoestring and now utilized a large part of America's naval might.

They both thought it unlikely that the operation would succeed, with Halsey going so far as to say it hadn't a snowball's chance in hell. Nimitz had initially gone along with it because it seemed remotely possible and wouldn't cost much, thus making it worth a try. Now, as they waited in the night, their doubts ran wild.

They were on the bridge of the newest and largest carrier in the fleet, the recently commissioned USS *Midway*. The *Midway* was almost a thousand feet long, displaced over fifty-five thousand tons fully loaded, and carried 137 airplanes. Of particular importance, she was the only carrier in the U.S. fleet with an armored deck. In a lesson learned from the British, it was hoped that any kamikazes that did attack her would bounce off, which was why she had been rushed to completion and sent to Japan.

Ironically, Nimitz and Halsey knew the impressive *Midway* was already obsolete. Even though a comparative giant, her flight deck was too short to handle the new jet fighters that were being developed. So far, jets had not played a part in the invasion of Japan because of the lack of bases with runways long enough to handle them, and since the Japs had no planes to speak of, the slower prop models were more than sufficient to the current task.

As further protection, the *Midway* and her important cargo were surrounded by a host of cruisers and destroyers along with half a dozen other carriers. This was just as well since the *Midway*'s planes had been forbidden to fly. There were more important uses for the flight deck.

"Fool's errand," murmured Halsey. "Goddamned idiot trip."

Nimitz did not contradict him. What had seemed at least marginally possible a few hours earlier seemed like just so much nonsense. How could a handful of rangers and frogmen possibly take Hirohito off Japan?

"They're brave," Halsey conceded, "but the whole thing's just a folly. I only hope they don't all die."

"I agree," said Nimitz. Normally he would have been at his command post at Okinawa or on the *Wasatch*; however, the situation was so unique that he felt compelled to be on the *Midway* waiting for success or failure. That he was not the only important person on the carrier was also not lost on him. Should anything happen to the *Midway*, history might well change dramatically.

A junior officer interrupted Nimitz's thoughts. "Sir, we have a message from Roy. He says send Dale."

"My gawd," said Halsey. "Something's actually happening out there, isn't it?"

Nimitz nodded. The question was rhetorical. *Dale* was the signal to begin extracting the troops. He wondered if the American raiders had actually taken Hirohito or were just running for their lives. Irrelevently, he wondered who'd thought of using the names of Roy Rogers and Dale Evans for the operation.

CHAPTER 74

KYUSHU, NEAR CAMP 7

Nomura looked at the clearing that was now surrounded by lights that pierced the foggy sky. Swain had said help was coming and that was good. Bad news, however, was that a Jap patrol had found them, probably attracted by the lights. It had been driven off, but the sky was getting brighter, and Jap reinforcements were coming through the brush and homing in on the beacons.

"When, Mr. Swain?" Joe asked impatiently.

"Any second now."

As he said that, a ranger outpost began firing at approaching Japanese. The Japanese shot back, and mortar shells began to drop near the perimeter. In the background Joe heard a distant clattering sound that rapidly grew closer. He turned and watched as what appeared to be a giant insect dropped from the sky.

"What the hell is that?"

Swain grinned. "That my friend is a helicopter. *Chopper* for short." As he spoke, a mortar exploded, hurling Swain on top of Nomura. Joe pushed him off and saw that the back of Swain's head had been blown away. Joe's leg was bleeding and he was covered with Swain's gore. He had picked up shrapnel and maybe pieces of Billy Swain. He picked himself up and managed to stand and control the pain.

The first chopper landed, quickly followed by a second. Sounds told Joe that others were approaching. He made a quick decision. "Get the emperor out on the first one and send one of the Japanese speakers with him."

"What about you?" one of the rangers asked.

"That's my problem. Hirohito goes first and then the rest of us."

Hirohito and a wounded ranger headed for the first helicopter. The emperor hesitated momentarily as he realized that the frail-looking craft was expected to fly him out over the Pacific. He turned, waved at Joe, then boarded. Joe was glad to see that the wounded man was one of the Japanese speakers. Good. Someone was using his head and killing two birds with one stone.

Hirohito looked out through the window as the helicopter began its slow, noisy ascent. Joe wanted to scream for it to hurry, to make all the dead and wounded relevant.

Prudently, the pilot kept the chopper low and headed away from the approaching Japanese. The second helicopter lifted off and two more landed in their place. These were quickly filled with wounded and flew away. Wounded now had the highest priority. The dead would have to remain.

The sequence of drop-down and liftoff continued despite Japanese fire, which got closer and heavier. As the Americans departed, it meant fewer and fewer remained to man the defenses, and Joe realized that he had a difficult decision to make.

Suddenly, a helicopter was hit and exploded in a burst of flames. It crashed to the ground. No one left it. The approaching chopper pilots ignored the fire and carnage to land and remove more men.

"How many left?" Joe yelled after still another pair had lifted off. The men sounded off. Only five were left alive, counting himself.

Two more helicopters managed to land, avoiding the flaming ruins of the burning one. Two men filled one and it lifted off.

"Go," Joe ordered.

A ranger looked aghast. "What about you, sir?"

"No room at the inn, buddy. I'll be all right. Just get your asses out of here."

The remaining rangers didn't need more urging. They sprinted to the last helicopter and flung themselves into the cabin, and the chopper immediately took off.

Joe turned and saw Japs approaching less than a hundred yards away. The sun was beginning to rise and the whole area remained lit by the lights and the fire. "Hurry!" he screamed at the approaching Japanese. "Hurry! The Americans are getting away. Kill them!"

With that, he stood and shot at the helicopter, which was now safely out of range. He only stopped when the wave of advancing soldiers raced by him.

A militia officer trotted up to him, saw the *kempei* uniform, and saluted. "Are you all right, sir?"

"Yes, but some of them may have gotten away." Joe gestured vaguely in the direction of some hills to his left. "Send your men in that direction." The officer did as he was told and Joe was again alone.

Joe thought he had a few minutes before they started to think and wonder just what he had been doing inside the American perimeter. They wouldn't believe for long that he'd been captured and escaped, or that he'd bravely followed the American raiders.

He staggered. His leg hurt like a bitch. The wounds didn't seem serious, but walking was going to be painful and slow. But what choice did he have? At least one guard had seen him shoot another. Did that man still live? Had he informed his comrades about the *kempei* officer's strange behavior? Soon the place would be crawling with investigators.

After all, one didn't lose an emperor and then just write it off. No, real *kempei* would be here soon. The time for masquerading as a *kempei* officer was over.

Joe limped down the path. His cache of equipment, food, clothes, and the precious radio were miles away. He would either have to get to them or find some other civilian clothing and, once again, let himself be swallowed up and made invisible by the throngs of refugees. Joe could only hope that the Japanese wouldn't be looking too hard for a man with one arm.

CHAPTER 75

USS MIDWAY

An honor guard of marines stood on the deck of the carrier. Halsey had personally checked to make sure that the rifles they carried were unloaded. The last thing they needed was for someone to go crazy with revenge and shoot the emperor of Japan.

Halsey still couldn't believe this was happening, and he was reasonably sure that Nimitz didn't either. The approaching helicopter had first landed on one of the smaller escort carriers, where it was refueled and sent on to the *Midway*. It was a shame that helicopters had such short legs, but Halsey was certain that future ones would see the problem rectified.

Almost daintily, the helicopter carrying Hirohito poised above the flight deck and lowered itself to land gently. There was a momentary wait while the blades stopped whirling.

An improvised red carpet was laid from the helicopter to the carrier's superstructure. Then a naval officer in a clean dress uniform walked to the helicopter with as much dignity as he could manage. The hatch was opened and the carrier's band began to play the Japanese national anthem, which was followed by "The Star-Spangled Banner." Halsey thought that the latter was played with more verve and gusto than the former.

Hirohito leaned out of the chopper and stepped onto the deck. There was a collective gasp from the hundreds of crewmen who had gathered around the flight deck for the historic event, even though it had been unpublicized. The carrier was a small town that kept few secrets.

Hirohito stood for a moment. Then he smiled slightly and walked forward to meet President Harry Truman, who had emerged from the shadows of the superstructure and was walking toward him.

As the men approached each other, the throng of sailors commenced to applaud and then cheer as they realized the significance of what was occurring.

CHAPTER 76

TOKYO

Japanese naval captain Minoru Genda was almost universally conceded to be a brave and extraordinarily brilliant officer who had a tremendous future before him. In his younger days—he was still only forty-one—many had despaired that he would not live long enough for his brilliance to blossom. He had been part of an acrobatic-flying group and had later been nicknamed the Madman because of his intense feelings that naval air was the way of the future. His fervor in proclaiming that carriers had made battleships obsolete had won him few friends in a big-gun navy.

Genda had helped plan the attack on Pearl Harbor and had taken part in numerous other battles. Some felt that if he had not been sickly during the ill-fated Battle of Midway, it and the war would have turned out differently for Japan.

Most recently, Genda had been assigned to help coordinate Japan's air defenses, which meant he had little to do since Japan's air defenses were virtually nonexistent. Thus, he could often be found at Anami's subterranean headquarters, and his presence was even looked forward to by those who considered him a hero.

After a cursory search for weapons—none of any kind were permitted in Anami's presence—Genda was admitted to Anami's private office. As he entered, a clerk closed the door behind him. As Genda expected, he and Anami were alone. The errand Anami had sent him on required a high degree of secrecy.

But first, there was a personal concern. "Your arm. What happened?" Anami asked.

Genda grimaced. His left arm was in a large cast. "Sir, the trip to

Kyushu was even more dangerous than I expected. This is courtesy of an American plane my pilot and I almost couldn't evade. It looks worse than it is, however, and it will heal in a few weeks."

"I am glad for your safe return," Anami said with sincerity. He wished he had many more Gendas to depend on. "But tell me, is the situation as bad as we've been led to believe?"

"It is," Genda conceded sadly. "If anything, it is worse."

The day before, Anami had received frantic coded signals from Kyushu that Hirohito had been kidnapped by an American raiding party. Anami had prevailed on Genda to fly to Camp 7 on Kyushu and verify the disaster.

Genda awkwardly lit a cigarette with his good arm. "I was able to confirm that an American raider force knew precisely where Hirohito was, and after a brief fight, they took him away by helicopters, which they used to fly him out to their ships. Witnesses saw a man fitting Hirohito's description with them, and it may be that the emperor went willingly. A Japanese officer was also seen assisting the Americans, which indicates a conspiracy, at least at the lower level. We must assume that the emperor is in American hands and will cooperate with them. The Japanese officer in question has not been found."

And doubtless won't be, Genda didn't add. Whoever the Japanese officer was and anyone else in on the conspiracy were in hiding and not worth looking for. Hirohito's taking had stunned the Tokyo headquarters, but, so far, the news had not spread to the rest of Japan. It did, however, present a unique opportunity for those brave enough to take it.

Anami took the bad news with surprising calm. Then he smiled grimly. "No," Anami finally said. "Hirohito was murdered by the Americans. It is an unspeakable atrocity that we will blame on them."

"But, sir, Hirohito may make public announcements for the Americans, even calling for surrender. What then?"

Anami slammed his fist on his desk. "They will be denounced as lies and fabrications. We will inform the world that Hirohito is dead and that his son Akihito is the new emperor, and that I have been appointed regent. We shall simply ignore anything Hirohito does and says for the Americans. We will announce that, after murdering him, the Americans have hired an actor to pretend he is the emperor."

Amazing, Genda thought. How could Akihito be proclaimed emperor of anything when no one knew where he was? Anami's control of Japan was far from absolute. Genda forced a smile. "Excellent. But how will that enable us to win the war?"

Anami chuckled. "Why, Captain, we have already won the war. This attempt by the Americans to undermine the Empire shows how bankrupt they are. Our counterattacks will begin very shortly and they will bleed the Americans so badly that they will sue for a peace that leaves us strong."

"And if they don't?"

"Then we will fight on, Genda. We will fight on forever. We will never surrender and be destroyed as the Americans have planned for us."

"Good. Then I will return to my duties with greater zeal."

Genda stood and bowed. The cast on his arm threw him off-balance and he nearly stumbled. He grasped the edge of Anami's desk for support while grimacing in pain.

Anami rose quickly and steadied him. "Genda, are you all right? Perhaps you should see a doctor before going back to duty?"

"I'm all right," Genda insisted.

As he said that, the hand encased in the cast squeezed a rubber bottle, which emitted a puff of misty fluid that hit Anami square in the face. For a second, the general appeared puzzled. Then his eyes widened and he began to choke and spasm soundlessly. He sat down hard on his chair and slumped forward. Genda waited a moment. There was no need to check for a pulse. He only wanted to be sure that it was safe to proceed.

The mist was a nerve gas, a particularly virulent derivative of a German gas called sarin that General Ishii had managed to bring with him from Manchuria. It killed on contact with the skin by paralyzing the nerves. It also evaporated into the air and lost its potency almost immediately, which made it useless on the battlefield, yet marvelously lethal in this instance.

Finally, Genda was satisfied that enough time had passed and that it would be safe to handle the general without fear of contamination, particularly since the air vent in the underground office had been humming and pulling out stale air. "Help!" Genda hollered. "The general has collapsed. Help!"

The door opened and others rushed in. They pulled Anami off his chair and laid him on the floor. At least two checked for a pulse that wasn't there, then started pushing on his chest as if that would start his breathing again.

General Homma rushed in from his own office down the hall and took command, chasing out gawkers. Only a couple of men who continued to try to revive Anami remained. "What happened?" he asked Genda.

Genda spoke clearly. It was imperative that his version be told and heard first. "We were talking when he suddenly clutched his chest and pitched forward. He didn't make a sound. He just fell over and didn't move."

Homma nodded and responded firmly, "A doctor has been summoned, but for what purpose I don't know. It appears that General Anami has suffered a heart attack or a stroke." He looked at the faces assembled just outside the open office door. Many looked stunned, but some appeared strangely hopeful. "I am senior here," Homma went on, "therefore, I am assuming command. You will return to your duties and continue as before. Captain Genda, you will follow me and make a brief statement for the record."

Genda's statement to a clerk was a formality. Anami was dead of a massive heart attack probably brought on by the immense strain of his duties. In a few minutes Genda was aboveground after watching Homma begin to take over the reins of the Japanese government. Only the plotters knew that a coup had just occurred, and that Homma and Ozawa were part of it. As part of their plans, "emergencies" had sent both Admiral Toyoda and Field Marshal Sugiyama away from the headquarters.

Even though political assassination had been a macabre kind of Japanese tradition in the decades prior to the war, Genda deeply regretted that necessity had forced him to do it. Genda was a warrior, not a murderer. Anami had been a warrior too before he had succumbed to the madness that was keeping Japan in the war. Now

Genda would inform his friend and mentor Admiral Ozawa that his mission was completed.

Even now, General Homma was setting more wheels in motion. There were others to round up or dispose of before a new government could be formed under General Homma and Admiral Ozawa. A government, Genda hoped, that would bring an end to the war that was destroying Japan.

As he walked toward his hidden vehicle, he chuckled. Who on earth was also plotting the overthrow of the government? Despite his disclaimer, he felt that the kidnapping of Hirohito must have had high-level help for it to have succeeded so neatly. He earnestly hoped that the various sets of conspirators didn't get in each other's way.

.

CHAPTER 77

KAGOSHIMA BAY

*T*he weather on the flight deck of the *Midway* continued wet and miserable. Despite this, both men had dressed formally and intended to be photographed without overcoats. It was important that they be seen as dignified heads of state, and not as ordinary people scuttling about in the rain.

Equally important was the need for a background that would convince the Japanese people that the emperor was both respected by the United States as a head of state, and that he was still in Japan. A picture of him anywhere else might be interpreted as his having fled the land and would mean his disgrace and the failure of his historic mission.

At first there had been hope that something in the city of Kagoshima could be used as a background, but little was left that was more than three feet tall. Weeks of hard fighting, coupled with the flimsy construction of most Japanese buildings, had resulted in an appallingly unrecognizable collection of ruins.

Then Undersecretary of State Joseph Grew thought of using Mt. Kagoshima as a background. While hardly as well-known as the snowcapped extinct volcano Mt. Fuji, it was well enough known to those who lived in the area as it dominated both the bay and the city. At any rate, it would have to do. The emperor and the president could only hope that enough Japanese soldiers would recognize the background as being uniquely Japanese and then be impressed by the message.

The weather refused to cooperate, though. Rain and large flakes of soft snow obscured the view of the mountain from the carrier. A photograph near the side of the flight deck could be posed to show nothing of the carrier, which might indicate that Hirohito was a prisoner, and all of the mountain, which would indicate that he was free. If only, of course, they could see the damned mountain.

Truman paced back and forth in the small room off the superstructure where he and Admiral Nimitz waited. "We can't stay here forever. Why not just take some pictures and get on with it."

"If it comes to that, we will," Nimitz answered wearily. He desperately wanted to get the *Midway* and Truman out of the area. "But I agree with Mr. Grew and so does Hirohito. We need to get that mountain in the background if there's any way we can."

"But we can't wait too much longer," Truman insisted. Indications were that the Japanese counterattacks would begin at any time if they hadn't started already. Who really knew what was going on in the misty hills beyond the bay? If it was too late to stop all the bloodshed, then they could at least stop some of it.

"Still think we should shoot the little bastard," muttered Halsey. Truman stifled a grin. The belligerent little admiral's thoughts weren't all that far from his own. He still had a hard time accepting that there was nothing Hirohito could have done to prevent the current phase of the war from ever starting in the first place, much less stopping it without outside help. Truman wondered if the emperor hadn't gotten a sort of religious conversion when he'd realized the war was lost. Perhaps he was actually maneuvering to keep his throne and for a place in history as a great humanitarian.

But, Truman thought, who the hell cares? End the war and worry later about what should have been done.

The phone rang and Halsey answered. "There's a break in the weather," he said as he hung up. "If we act right now, we might get some good pictures."

Truman and the two admirals raced out onto the flight deck, while Hirohito and Grew came from another room. Grew was the only person on the carrier Hirohito knew, and he had firmly refused to let the diplomat out of his sight. The former ambassador spoke fluent Japanese, which made him doubly valuable.

Hirohito and Truman took up stations by the edge of the deck. It occurred to Truman that, with just one little shove, one small emperor would suddenly find himself in the middle of a deep bay. The thought made him grin.

Cameras were hurriedly set up. In the background, the bulk of Mt. Kagoshima had become visible.

"Now," the photographer said. A movie camera was set up alongside the still photographer. It had all been well rehearsed. The two leaders stood beside each other, close but not touching. They would not shake hands as such contact was repugnant to Japanese males. They smiled and appeared as equals while the cameras whirred and clicked. More pictures were taken of them bowing toward each other at a depth that signified utmost mutual respect. Most Americans had little idea that a Japanese bow was filled with meaning. Too deep a bow and one signified subservience to the other; too shallow and it indicated dominance over the other. The bow had to be just right to convey the proper message of equality.

Several more pictures were taken while the light and the view remained. Halsey looked about nervously. If he could see the mountain, the Jap pilots could see the *Midway*. Granted the skies were filled with scores of American fighters and radar indicated nothing hostile in the area, but he remembered what happened to the *Augusta* and MacArthur. Halsey didn't want to go down in history as the admiral who lost the president of the United States. If the little Jap standing beside Truman got shot up, well, that was okay, but not the president of the United States.

"That's it," Truman said. "We have enough pictures and I'm freezing my butt off."

Grew translated the comment to Hirohito, who grinned and nodded. Truman wondered just how literal the translation had been and whether the emperor was a little less of a stick-in-the-mud than he appeared.

The executive officer of the carrier ran out onto the flight deck to intercept the group of men. He looked at all the assembled rank and directed his statement to Truman.

"Sir, we're receiving a broadcast from Tokyo. It says that Anami has been overthrown and that Admiral Ozawa and General Homma are now in charge. They're also saying they want to talk peace."

■

CHAPTER 78

KYUSHU, ROUND TOP

A Jap attack on Round Top could come from three directions. It could come from over the hill known as Mt. Ugly, or around either side of it. Because of the poor visibility caused by the rotten weather, a series of two-man listening posts had been established at each of the three points, with a fourth outpost coordinating and commanding the three.

Sergeant Collins had been in the command-outpost foxhole for several hours and longed for his watch to end. Along with being wet, cold, hungry, and miserable, the situation was scary. The weather remained bad, it was night, and he couldn't see more than a hundred feet in front. The thought that Japs could be just out of his view was unnerving at best.

But that, of course, was why he and Private First Class Hanks, his radioman, were in the hole. It was far better that he and the others in the outposts be overrun by a horde of Japs than that the entire company suffer that fate. It had sounded faintly heroic when it had been discussed back on Round Top. Now it sounded foolish and downright stupid.

Small, wireless walkie-talkies connected the four outposts to each other. As the closest to Round Top, Collins also had the luxury of a field phone connecting him with the rest of the company. Phones were not considered good ideas for the three forward outposts because the wires could be cut or even stumbled upon by the Japs and used to trace back to an outpost itself.

Communications with the three posts were limited to clicks, not words. Collins's command post would send one click out, and a one-click response meant everything was okay. The command post would then send one back as confirmation that the signal had been received. In case of possible danger, the men in an outpost would click twice and withdraw from their exposed position. They didn't have to wait for a response. A series of three or more clicks meant that everybody should run like hell. The posts were to respond to the clicks from Collins every few minutes. It was hoped that the discreet and muffled sounds would not carry.

The system was far from perfect. Several false alarms had led to precipitous retreats back to Round Top. These had been followed by sheepish crawls back to their positions by the men who'd just run from them. Lieutenant Morrell hadn't chewed out anyone for his actions, but the continued unnecessary alerts caused stress and fatigue. Collins chewed his gum and wished for a cigarette. Why the hell wouldn't the Japs come and get it over with?

It had been several minutes since the last outpost check. "Hit 'em, Hanks," he whispered.

Hanks grunted, crouched over the walkie-talkie, and made a clicking noise with his mouth. A few seconds later he looked up. "One reports okay, Sarge." He returned to his task. Then there was a pause. "Nothing from two."

"Do three." Two was at the crest of Mt. Ugly, while the others were on the lower ground flanking it.

"Three's okay. Should I try two again?"

"Of course." Collins's mind raced. Was something wrong? A delay in responding had happened before, and he'd chewed ass for it. People were supposed to pay attention, not scare him half to death.

Hanks looked up from his crouch, concern on his face. "Still nothing."

They tried a third time and again no response. Outpost two was a little more than a quarter mile away and well within the range of the handheld radios. Were they malfunctioning? No, in that case either of the two men would have realized they hadn't heard from Collins in a while and used the backup set each group had. Kerns and Fellows were good guys and wouldn't just be sitting there with their thumbs up their asses.

Shit.

Collins's next alternative was to crawl out there and find them, which he dreaded. It was bad enough that he had to take the men out there when their shift started and return to get them when it ended. At least then he had their replacements with him and wasn't alone. Maybe he should get some help from Lieutenant Morrell? Under any circumstances, he would have to notify Morrell of the problem. The situation was the stuff of nightmares and his fears were as normal as the next guy's. Christ, if only he could see!

The wind swirled and he thought he picked up movement in the distance, maybe a couple of hundred yards away. It couldn't be Kerns and Fellows, it was too broad a sensation.

But it couldn't be the Japs because they always began their attacks with yells and all kinds of noise to inspire them.

His mind raced. It couldn't be the Japs, could it?

Then he realized the cold truth: *the Japs weren't yelling!*

"They're coming," Collins blurted to Hanks, who immediately began making clicking sounds as fast as he could. Kerns and Fellows hadn't answered because they were dead. Now he had to recall his other men and get the hell back to Round Top. There was no time for a phone call to warn Morrell and the others. The Japs might be right on top of him in seconds. He simply began firing into the air. With all need for secrecy gone, the approaching Japanese began to scream and howl like a chorus of devils.

CHAPTER 79

TOKYO

General Homma was frustrated. He was now the de facto premier of Japan and commander of all the empire's armed forces, yet he found himself unable to function effectively in either capacity. Once again his communications officer had sadly informed him that they were still unable to reach Sixteenth Area Army headquarters on Kyushu. Damn the Americans! If they wanted the war stopped, they had to let him restore some semblance of communications so that he could contact his commanders and tell them to cease firing.

He had just completed meeting with Admiral Ozawa, who had taken control of the Foreign Office, where he had ousted Tojo. Field Marshal Sugiyama had killed himself when confronted with arrest, while Admiral Toyoda had disappeared; thus, they had no serious rivals. Many peace-inclined diplomats had been arrested by the previous regime, while others were in hiding, but the remainder, such as Togo and Marquis Kido, were now frantically trying to make contact with the Americans. Ozawa was confident that the Potsdam Declaration could be utilized as a basis for ending the war on terms that would guarantee that the Japanese world would not disappear. It would be shameful, but better than dying uselessly.

Lt. Gen. Shiro Ishii knocked. He entered and bowed. Homma wanted to dislike Ishii for all the despicable things he had done with his chemicals and germs, but the little man with the thick mustache had performed an invaluable service by providing the means to eliminate Anami and would be compensated by being allowed to live. Ishii would disappear.

Homma drummed his fingers on his desk. "Have you stopped the gases?"

"Like you, I have been unable to raise General Yokoyama on Kyushu. I have been able to ascertain, however, that very little in the way of chemical shells or grenades actually made it across the straits to Kyushu, and absolutely none of the bombs. Most are still in vaults here on Honshu or were on boats sunk in the straits by American planes. I now doubt that more than a couple hundred chemical weapons are on Kyushu."

Homma did not consider this entirely good news. Even a little bit of gas used on the Americans might provoke a devastating reaction from them. It was imperative that they somehow reach General Yokoyama and cancel the final phase of Ketsu-go #6, the plans for the defense of Kyushu.

"What about the submarine?" Homma asked.

The submarine, one of the large R-class types, carried a floatplane in a waterproof deck-hangar. The sub had more than enough range to cross to North America. There its orders were to launch its plane, which would be loaded with a number of small ceramic bombs that carried plague-infested fleas kept alive in an oxygen mixture.

"It attempted to leave two days ago. It was sunk by American destroyers."

"Thank God," Homma said, and wondered why he wasn't distressed by the additional deaths.

America was civilized, clean, and possessed excellent medical facilities. After the initial terror, the plague would easily have been eliminated and would only have added to America's fury with Japan. The attempt to spread germs in America had been total madness.

A staff officer interrupted. His expression was one of deep relief. "General Homma, we have finally established contact with General Yokoyama."

Homma virtually ran to the radio set. The reception was weak and distorted by static, but he convinced General Yokoyama that he, not Anami or Sugiyama, was now in charge.

"General," Homma said, virtually yelling to be understood, "you must not use the gas shells you have received."

"I wasn't going to," Yokoyama answered. "Apart from the fact that such weapons are not an honorable means of waging war, there were too few of them to make a difference, and we have no real way of delivering them effectively. I had them put in a cave and the entrance sealed."

Wonderful, Homma thought, such good news. "Excellent. Now, it is imperative that all aspects of Ketsu-go be halted. Do you understand? You must not launch your attacks. Neither your army nor the remaining kamikazes must attack."

After prolonged silence, Homma thought he might have lost contact. Finally, General Yokoyama's voice came through faintly but distinctly.

"My dear General Homma. I deeply regret to inform you that the attacks are commencing as we speak and there is no way I can stop them. The soldiers are marching and the planes are now in the air. The arrow has been fired from the bow. It cannot be recalled."

•

CHAPTER 80

ROUND TOP

Collins and Hanks narrowly avoided being shot by their own men as they crawled into the trenches on Round Top. Moments later, two more men from his outposts clambered in, their faces a mixture of relief and terror. No more followed, and it was reluctantly concluded that the four missing men were most likely dead.

"What did anybody see?" Morrell asked. "How many Japs are there?" The men, Collins included, shook their heads.

"We really didn't see much at all," Collins said. "Just a lot of commotion and noise." Behind and below them, the infernal shrieks continued, further emphasizing that no more Americans would be returning from the outposts around Mt. Ugly. "Sorry, Lieutenant, but we weren't in any position to hang around and count noses."

"They're going around us," Morrell muttered. "Open fire into the valley."

Gunfire rang out and rippled down the hill in all directions. It was a joy and a relief to be able to shoot. There was plenty of ammunition, and Morrell had earlier decided there was no point in saving it. Indirect fire against an unseen enemy was nowhere near as effective as shooting a target that was visible, but it would cause some casualties and maybe disrupt the Japs' plans. Similar firing could be heard from other American positions.

"Why aren't they coming?" someone yelled, and Morrell had to wonder as well. According to Collins, they'd been just a little behind him as he'd run for safety.

A Jap mortar shell exploded in their perimeter, followed by others. While they lacked heavy artillery, the Japanese had a large number of the extremely portable 50mm mortars and shells and were using them to effect.

Paul yelled for the company's own 60mm mortars to return fire and ordered the howitzers to open up as well. As the mortars responded, the sergeant in charge of the two pack howitzers told him the Japs were too close for him to shoot at. Effectively, they were under the barrels of his guns.

"They're hugging us," Morrell growled, and Sergeant Mackensen agreed. "Even if the weather breaks, nobody can help us."

Morrell tried division artillery and was told they were busy with other attacks, which he could now hear in the distance, and that the Japs were too close to his position to risk shelling blindly into the gloom and mist.

A plane hummed low overhead. It missed the hill by only a few feet. "Kamikaze!" someone yelled. Seconds later, there was a flash and the sound of an explosion behind them. The kamikaze had missed Round Top but had hit the hill behind them.

"Sonofabitch, that was close!" snapped Collins.

"Get to your men," Morrell ordered. Collins was in charge of a score of men Paul had designated their reserve. They were to reinforce any area where the Japs broke through.

Otherwise, the defense of Round Top consisted of two platoons that faced the front and curved along the sides of the hill. There they met the third platoon, which faced rearward and had the greatest length of ground to cover. Putting most of his defenders toward the front had seemed like the best idea, but now with the Japs hugging the hill and circling behind it, Paul was no longer so certain.

A group of men ran through the rear of the defenses, and Morrell recognized some of them from Ruger's headquarters and heavy-weapons companies. Then he remembered that theirs was the hill behind Round Top, the one the kamikaze had hit.

"Where's the major?" he asked, and was told that no one knew. A Jap plane had landed smack on the command bunker, then the hill had been overrun. The Japs were solidly behind Round Top. At least a couple of dozen men had made it through to him and were welcome reinforcements. Poor Ruger, he thought, then quashed it. If the major was dead, Paul would mourn for him some other time.

"Another plane!" came the cry. This time it was even lower than the last.

"Get down!" Paul yelled as it appeared through the mist. This one was not going to miss Round Top. The explosion of the crash was deafening, and the shock wave passed over him like a hot, sharp wind. Gasoline flamed into a smoky pyre right where his front-facing second platoon met the rear-facing third. Men were down and the trench was destroyed. Now he understood why the Japs hadn't launched their attack. They had been waiting for the kamikazes to soften up the hilltop fort. In the absence of artillery, the Japs were using suicide pilots.

They had succeeded in breaching his defenses. Fully a third of his defensive positions were destroyed, and the main Jap attack hadn't even begun.

CHAPTER 81

KADENA, OKINAWA

Lt. Gen. Matthew Ridgway didn't like dealing with the press. While some of the reporters were pretty good joes, others were nothing but sharks who'd sell their mothers for a story. That is, he smiled inwardly, if they'd had mothers. There were exceptions among Ridgway's compatriots, of course. Patton, for instance, had swaggered and postured for the press, while the late MacArthur always seemed to be onstage and never at a loss for a quote.

The press was, however, safely muzzled in this war and, with few exceptions, understood the need for it and cooperated with the wartime censorship regulations. After all, who wanted to give out military secrets that would cause the deaths of American boys? For that reason, and because the journalists in Bradley's press pool were men of integrity, Ridgway felt fairly comfortable with the men gathered in his office. Long after the war they could write all the books they wanted and analyze to their hearts' content all the decisions others made. In the meantime, every word they wrote was subject to review and removal.

It was a fairly eclectic and highly qualified pool of talent. Wilfred Burchett represented the London *Daily Express,* Theodore White was employed by Time-Life, Hanson Baldwin was from *The New York Times,* and Webley Edwards was a radio correspondent from CBS.

"Gentlemen," Ridgway began, gesturing toward a large map of Kyushu that hung on the wall behind him, "let me give you a quick overview. The Japs have launched major attacks against our positions, primarily along our right flank. This is the area covered by the I Corps, which consists of the 25th, 41st, and 53rd Infantry Divisions.

At this time there are no serious attacks against either the marines on our left flank or XI Corps in the middle. It appears that the Japs have concentrated their thrusts against I Corps only, and we first thought their goal was a penetration down to Ariake Bay."

"Can they make it?" Burchett asked.

"Not a chance. They are about seventy miles from the bay and we'll stop them well before they get anywhere near it. We are in the process of moving two divisions from IX Corps, the 81st and 98th infantry, into blocking positions behind I Corps. IX Corps had rotated back into reserve and is close enough to help out. No, gentlemen, their goal is not Ariake Bay. The Japanese are just squandering lives."

"Ours included, I presume," Baldwin commented.

Ridgway winced. "Absolutely."

White raised his hand. "I know it's certainly simpler on a map than it is in reality, but can any of the other units, such as the marines, attack north and swing behind the Japs?"

Ridgway stifled a sigh. Spare me from armchair generals. "Not in enough time to help out. While the Japs have stripped many of their defenses to form for this attack, the soldiers left behind are well dug in and in strongly situated positions. They would hold out for some time, and even if overrun, the mountainous lay of the land would preclude any quick move around the Japanese rear. No, the battle will be fought with the forces currently in place and those I mentioned as moving up to reinforce them."

"And the weather was the primary reason they got the jump on us?" This was from Edwards, and it was evident from his voice that he was used to being behind a microphone as well as a typewriter.

"Yes, although we knew it was likely coming, there was little we could do to prevent them from moving and massing their forces under the cover of cloud and rain. We dug in as much as possible and we can only hope it was enough."

"Sort of like the Ardennes all over again, eh, General?" This from the Brit, Burchett.

"Except that we are much better prepared. It shows that possessing overwhelming power is not always enough to prevent a desperate enemy from trying one last throw of the dice. The Japs will doubtless achieve local penetrations and overrun some positions, but they will be stopped." Ridgway faced Baldwin. "Like you said, we will suffer many, many needless casualties. Except for the fighting in I Corps area, the war is over."

"Any comment on the kamikazes?" asked White.

Ridgway's expression turned even grimmer than before. "That the Japs would use kamikazes on frontline positions came as a complete shock. With our warships pulled back, we expected suicide attacks on fuel depots, storage dumps, and command centers, but not on frontline trenches and pillboxes. Gentlemen, they hurt us badly with that tactic. Our antiaircraft guns were almost all situated farther rear. Just like the picket destroyers caught hell off Okinawa, our boys in the foxholes and trenches are taking a beating, and there isn't a helluva lot we can do about it."

"But why doesn't the weather hamper them like it does us?" Baldwin queried. He had seen Iwo Jima and was familiar with hell.

"Because they don't care. Jap planes by the hundreds, maybe a couple of thousand, are skimming a few feet over the hills, and when they see something that looks like our lines, they line up and crash into it. Since they intend to die in the first place, they are willing to take risks that we wouldn't even consider. If they lose some of their pilots through accidental crashes into the wrong hillsides, they just don't seem to give a damn."

It was White's turn. "What about Hirohito? Where is he and what's he up to?"

"Hirohito is now in Kagoshima City trying to coordinate an end to the hostilities. He has recorded messages for the Japanese troops and people that are being broadcast as we speak. Additionally, hundreds of thousands of leaflets are being dropped on the combatants. Hopefully, it'll work.

"The remnants of Japan's armies in the Philippines under General Yamashita have given up as a result of Hirohito's actions, and the garrisons of Rabaul and Hong Kong have also surrendered. Even in Kyushu, General Yokoyama is trying to recall his troops. It's working. It'll take time, but it's working." Then Ridgway sagged. "I can only hope that it isn't too late for our boys in I Corps."

Edwards looked up from his notes. "When will Hirohito be going to Tokyo, and what about General Homma's position with us?"

"The emperor feels that his place is on Kyushu, and everyone agrees with him. General Homma and Admiral Ozawa have pretty well shut down the Japanese military on Honshu and elsewhere, so there's no need for the emperor's presence there to help things along. Hirohito has told Bradley that if it would help, he would march to the front lines and try to stop the Japanese attacks in person. It won't happen, of course, but we believe his sincerity and it does show that he is fully committed to the goal of ending the fighting."

White was concerned. "But what about Homma? Isn't he the man responsible for the Bataan Death March? If he is instrumental in ending the war, does that mean he won't be prosecuted?"

Ridgway shrugged. War crimes trials were none of his concern, at least not yet. "Maybe his actions show he isn't as guilty as we thought? On the other hand, you may also be right. Helping to end this crap might just win some people a lot of forgiveness."

Burchett seemed to shiver. "In the meantime, God help the men in the front lines who are having to endure this awful fighting."

The reporters looked at each other. "I think we're about done, aren't we?" White said, speaking for the group.

"Yes."

"Well then, General, how much of what you've said will we be able to print?"

Ridgway laughed grimly. "Not a damned word."

■

CHAPTER 82

ROUND TOP

Paul Morrell was consumed with fear and anger. Japs were less than a hundred yards away in the trenches along where the kamikaze had crashed. The Japs had swarmed up the hill and overrun what remained before he could shore up the defenses and replace the casualties. Worse, a misunderstanding had sent Sergeant Collins and the reserve force of twenty men in a counterattack that had seen them chewed up by the Japs. Only a handful of men had returned, and Collins wasn't one of them.

"What now, Lieutenant?" It was First Sergeant Mackensen, and Paul saw fear in his face as well. The sergeant was normally a rock, but now he was as scared as anyone. Death in the form of untold numbers of Japs was only a little ways away.

Ironically, the long night had ended and the weather had begun to clear up, which meant that he could see the Jap trenches more clearly. Sometimes he could see their helmets and bayonets as they moved around and got organized. Shooting between the two groups was constant, and Paul wondered which of the many dead bodies on the ground between the two lines was his friend Collins.

"Lieutenant," Mackensen insisted, "what the hell do we do now?"

Paul began to shake again. With enormous effort, he gathered himself. There were orders to give. "We go to Last Stand. Order everybody out of their trenches and into Last Stand."

It was desperation, but what other choice did he have? Last Stand was the sardonic name given by the troops to the earthen berm that ran around Orlando's tank. In front of the berm was a line of trenches. It was Paul's idea. Men could shoot from behind the berm and from the trenches, which would effectively double their fire-power. It would also make them more vulnerable to machine gun and mortar fire because they would be so closely packed, but it was a chance he had to take. Already Jap mortar rounds were falling, and a number of his wounded had been pulled back to the narrow ground between the tank and the berm.

On signal, men raced from their positions and into Last Stand. Paul was dismayed at how few they were. Mackensen sorted them out and made sure there were no gaps in the lines. The Japs must be doing much the same thing, Paul realized. They were gathering for one last push past the useless howitzers and into Last Stand. He wondered just what the hell the Japs would do with the hill when they took it. The Japs had suffered badly. The slopes of Round Top were littered with dead and the trench was full of them.

"Lieutenant." It was Orlando from the tank.

"What?"

"I just want you to know that our hitherto inexhaustible supply of ammo is pretty well shot, pardon my pun."

It didn't surprise Paul. Everyone's weapon had been firing constantly. A lot of their reserve stores had been destroyed by the plane, while others were out of reach because of the Jap advance.

"When we run out of bullets we go to bayonets. When we're all out of weapons," Paul answered with an almost maniacal laugh, "we'll piss on them."

That brought nervous laughter from a couple of the men who heard it. Funny, but there was no talk of surrender. The Japs would kill anyone who even tried, so what would be the point?

"Banzai!" came the shriek from the trench, and he saw a sword waving in the air. *"Banzai, banzai, banzai!"*

A sea of humanity lifted out of the trenches and up the slope of the hill. The men in Last Stand fired as rapidly as they could, with the two machine guns on the tank joining in. They launched mortar shells at their highest possible trajectory so they would come down just outside the berm. Japs fell by the dozen, by the score, but they still came on. Many fired at the Americans as they advanced and the air became filled with grenades. The noise was deafening as men shot at each other at close range, screamed, and died. Neither the berm nor the trenches provided full protection, and more of Paul's command fell.

Paul turned to Sergeant Orlando, whose head was sticking out of the driver's hatch. "Now," Paul managed to say with a calmness he didn't feel. "Use firefly, Sergeant."

The brief and incongruous sound of a warning siren caused the men behind the berm to duck. Then, a second's pause that lasted an eternity. At last, a tongue of flame peeked out of the tank's barrel and then surged outward in a sea of fire. Some of the advancing Japs were caught in it, while others saw it and stopped in sudden fear while their ranks continued to be riddled by bullets. The bravest men in the world are terrified by fire, and the Japanese were no exception. Those who could began to turn and run from burning death. It was no use. Death caught them in its flaming grip.

Orlando traversed the turret so that the flamethrower mounted in the barrel of the cannon created a circle of fire around Last Stand. The Japanese on the hill were turned into human torches that jumped and fell and screamed. Again and again, the tongues of flame licked the land outside the berm, sucking and scorching the life from it. Paul huddled with the others on the ground behind the berm and felt the flamethrower's hot breath as the barrel propelled its fire over them.

Finally, Orlando turned off his death machine. Blackened, burning Japs were everywhere, and the stench of burned meat was overpowering. Most of the Japanese were prone, but a few were frozen in sitting positions, and a handful still moved and twitched. Rifle fire from the berm ended their suffering. Paul noticed that it had grown astonishingly silent around Last Stand. No one was yelling "Banzai," and no one was shooting at them. Firefly, the flamethrower replacement for the tank's cannon, had worked. The firefly apparatus had sent the flames out much farther than a handheld flamethrower could, and with horrifyingly deadly effect.

The tank's engine roar broke the silence. Orlando plowed his tank through the berm and over the dead and dying. Almost leisurely, he drove along the circumference of the original defenses atop the hill. The flamethrower surged again as he scorched the slopes leading to

Round Top, enlarging the circle of death, while the tank's machine guns added to the carnage.

The tank stopped and the driver's hatch opened. "They're all gone, Lieutenant," said Orlando. "Only dead ones left."

Paul nodded and sagged to the ground, exhausted beyond feeling. The Japs were gone, at least for the moment. Would they return? No, he corrected himself. When would they return? The Japs always returned. They never stopped and they were always there. Japs would be a part of his life forever. Then he realized that it had stopped raining and that he could hear planes flying high in the air above him.

·

CHAPTER 83

NORTH OF MT. UGLY

Sgt. Yuji Yokota grieved for the men of his decimated command. He had grown fond of the innocent young boys who had trusted him, and now so many were gone, their youthful lives snuffed out for no reason. He could only hope that some were still alive and were simply running from the horrors they'd witnessed. If so, he wouldn't blame them. It was the most awful death imaginable. There was nothing to describe the fear of being burned alive. His own personal bravery had vanished, and he had run with the rest of them, away from the hill and their hellish tormentor.

Even so, Yokota and his men had been fortunate. They had arrived late at the assembly point and had gone up the hill in the third wave, not the first. This had enabled them to flee when the jets of fire had commenced streaking down the hill, turning so many into screaming torches. Many of his boy soldiers had not made it back safely, but, overall, they had fared better than those who'd preceded them. Those brave soldiers of Japan were dead.

Lieutenant Uji staggered over to where Yokota squatted on the ground. Uji had lost his glasses and had to squint to see Yokota.

"We must attack again, Sergeant."

Yokota was incredulous. "Why? There's only us left. Everyone else is dead."

The temerity of the question shocked Uji and he cocked his fist as if to strike Yokota for his insolence. Then he changed his mind and merely shook his head. "It is our duty and our destiny. We must attack again."

"Lieutenant, there are only about forty of us left out of the eighty that attacked the first time."

Uji stiffened. "We ran, Sergeant. We ran like frightened dogs and I was one of them. We shamed ourselves and Japan by our actions. We must gain redemption."

"Plane!" a soldier yelled. Discussion ceased as the frightened men scrambled to make themselves small and invisible. The weather was quickly clearing, and there was no place to hide from the terrors of the sky. Yokota doubted if they would now get anywhere near the hill before being bombed or strafed. He squinted upward and saw a B-17. Its bomb-bay doors were opened and he awaited a rain of death, but, instead of bombs, thousands of sheets of paper began to fall like large snowflakes.

"Leave them," Uji commanded as the leaflets settled about them. Reading American propaganda was forbidden. However, it was a useless command as everyone grabbed a sheet. If nothing else, American propaganda leaflets made halfway decent toilet paper.

Yokota stared at the paper in his hand. On it was a picture of Hirohito standing alongside a little white man who was identified as Truman, the president of the United States, and they stood together as equals with the bulk of Mt. Kagoshima in the background.

In disbelief, he read the text. And then he read it a second time. The war was over. An honorable peace had been made. The integrity of Japan and her culture would continue. The emperor commanded that everyone withdraw from the American positions and head north to safety.

Uji crumpled the copy he'd been reading and threw it on the ground. Tears streamed down his face. "We attack."

Yokota stood and glared at the lieutenant. "No! You read the emperor's orders. We are to withdraw."

Uji was on the edge of hysteria. "They are lies, all lies. Even if we cannot succeed, we must give up our lives for Japan."

This enraged Yokota. Did the fool want to kill all of the remaining lambs? He grabbed the lieutenant by the collar of his jacket and jammed the paper in his face. "Would you disobey your emperor?

Read where he forbids further suicides. To do what you now wish would bring shame to us, not glory."

Uji sagged and began to sob. After a moment, he managed to speak. "You are right, Sergeant. Even though it is hateful, we must obey the emperor. Take the men to the rear. I will follow."

Yokota looked about at the surviving boy soldiers, who watched him with hope, fear, and confusion mixed on their faces. "No, Lieutenant," he said gently, "you will not follow. You will lead us back to safety. Just like the emperor orders."

CHAPTER 84

ROUND TOP

Gencral Monck and Colonel Parker left their jeep at the base of the hill and began the climb to the top of the battle-scarred mound. Both men were shocked by what they saw. The ground itself had been scorched, and the Japanese dead still lay where they'd fallen. Burned and blackened bodies with their clothes burned off gestured to them with charred limbs thrust upward. Body parts, many unidentifiable, had to be avoided as they walked. Monck slipped and recoiled in revulsion as his hand came to rest on what might have been part of a skull.

As they reached the crest, they stepped over the trench. There were bodies in it, but others were strewn about as if they had been pulled from the trench.

"Someone was looking for our boys," Parker commented softly. "And making sure the Japs were really dead." American dead and wounded had just been evacuated from the killing ground.

"The smell is awful," Parker added in understatement. The smell was nauseating. "I don't think I'll ever be able to eat roast beef again."

Monck corrected him. "It smells like pork." He wanted to gag.

They passed the blackened skeleton of a crashed plane. Its tail was pointed incongruously to the sky. They had seen many like it in their inspection of the regimental area. Kamikazes had caused almost as many casualties as the Japanese banzai attacks.

An American walked around the hill taking pictures while a second took notes. "Correspondents," said Parker. "I just hope they get the story right for once. It deserves to be told."

Monck led the way through the breach in the earthen berm. Numerous pairs of eyes were on them, but there had been no attempt to challenge or call out to them. For all their rank, Monck and Parker might as well have been invisible. They looked at the living men, many of whom walked or stood like zombies. Finally, one disassociated himself from the group and walked over to them. Monck was hard put to recognize the exhausted and filthy man as Lt. Paul Morrell.

Monck stopped Morrell from saluting and put his arm around the younger man's shoulder. "I'm sorry, General," Paul said, his voice and body quivering.

Monck was confused. "Sorry? For what?"

Paul's voice was choked with emotion. "I lost half my men."

"No," Monck said with gentle firmness. "You saved half your men. You and your men are heroes. You stood off at least a battalion of Japs and you're still here to talk about it. Son, I'm the one who should apologize. I tried to get you more help, but there was nothing to give you."

But Monck wondered what he could have done that would have saved lives on Round Top. Fewer than seventy had survived unhurt. Monck's doubts would haunt him for the rest of his life, just as Morrell would have to live with his. The fury and intensity of the Japanese attacks had stunned them. Someone who wasn't there had picturesquely described the assaults as waves from a stormy sea crashing over rocks with the rocks finally prevailing. Only the rocks and the waves were flesh and blood, not granite and water.

Paul was not consoled. "I should have used the tank sooner."

Perhaps you should have, Monck thought. But that was hindsight. Paul had fought the battle and won it. He was the one who had to make the decisions and not anyone else. He had done what he had to and done it when and how he felt was right. Morrell didn't know it yet, but he truly was a hero.

"If you had used the tank sooner, it might have been knocked out and been useless. No, Paul, the berm shielded the tank until the right moment."

Paul appeared to accept the statement. "All right, I guess, sir. What's the latest on Major Ruger?" Word had reached him that Ruger had been found just barely alive and under a pile of bodies and rubble.

"He's alive, but very badly wounded. With a little luck, he'll make it, but he won't ever be the same again."

"What'd he lose?"

"His legs. Both above the knee. They were terribly crushed and couldn't be saved."

"He's lucky, sir. He won't have to go back to fighting."

"Nor will you, Paul." Monck turned to Parker and ordered, "Get these men off this hill."

"Yes, sir," Parker said. "The relief from the 77th is just a little ways behind us. They'll be up in about an hour."

"Now," Monck snapped. "I want these men off this hill now."

The Japs weren't coming back, and the survivors of Round Top needed to get as far away from the hill as possible. Monck wanted to get them back to a land of clean clothes, showers, and food. They needed to forget the nightmare landscape that was Round Top as soon as possible.

"Leave the tank," Monck ordered Morrell. It was probably too risky to drive the damn thing downhill anyhow. God only knew how they'd gotten it up there in the first place. "Leave everything. Just get down off this hill." Again Monck turned to Parker. "When they meet up with the column from the 77th, they can use their trucks to take them to the rear."

Paul managed a small smile. "Sounds good to me, sir. Then maybe we can begin to put this behind us."

As Paul walked away to gather his men, Monck wondered if anyone would be able to forget what had happened on Round Top and any of the thousands of other battlegrounds on Kyushu. He hoped they wouldn't.

CHAPTER 85

DETROIT

Debbie Winston sat in the chair in her bedroom. Her bare feet were tucked under the long flannel nightgown. It was the middle of the night and she couldn't sleep. Too much was happening in her life.

Days earlier, the final end of the war had been almost anticlimactic. There'd been no dancing in the streets and few parties had been thrown to celebrate it. Instead, there'd been a feeling of enormous relief coupled with worry that this peace would also somehow fall apart. After all, hadn't the Japs surrendered once before? This time, thank God, it looked as if it would stick.

Debbie's brother, Ron, might yet be drafted, but not until after he finished high school. No fighting was going on, which meant he would be safe, unless, of course, he got sent to Palestine, where a small war raged. Maybe, she thought wryly, a little military discipline would help the spoiled and sulky little snot grow up. God only knew he needed it.

She took a deep breath and again read the letter from Paul. He was safe and unharmed, although his choice of words and phrases said there were things he wasn't ready to talk about, or at least put down in a letter.

This was not all that surprising. She had read with horrified fascination of the final desperate battles on Kyushu. One article in *Life* magazine had mentioned a place called Round Top as an example of the savage intensity of the final conflict. Not until reading Paul's letter did she realize he had been at Round Top. The thought that he had been so close to death had further reinforced her strong feelings for him.

Her friend Ann, whose boyfriend had returned an amputee from the war, had reached over and held Debbie's hands. "All you can do is be there for him. Hold him, listen to him, and understand that he's seen and done things that no one should ever have to endure and that we cannot possibly imagine, no matter how much we read or hear about them."

Paul's letter had been hopeful that he'd be stateside fairly soon, and the newspapers had confirmed it. Those men who'd borne the brunt of the fighting on Kyushu would be coming home in a hurry. They would be replaced by a far smaller number of Americans who'd be taken from the units forming for the now canceled invasion of Honshu.

If she was going to be there to help him through his nightmares, they were going to have to get married fast so she'd be there during his nights. She grinned to herself. She hoped Paul would realize the good that would come from their being wed as quickly as they could arrange it.

Debbie looked out the window of her second-floor bedroom. Snow was on the ground and she wondered if it would still be there when Paul returned. She hoped it would. That would mean they'd be together soon.

CHAPTER 86

KYUSHU,
NEAR MIYAKONOJO

Mitsu Okimura walked over to the bunk where the young man who was now her good friend sat propped up and reading a book. When he saw her, he dropped the book on his lap and smiled.

Mitsu shyly returned the smile, but decided to be a nurse before succumbing to the pleasure of his company. She pulled back the covers and checked the wounds on his leg. The infections had almost all but disappeared, and the color of the surrounding skin was healthy. In a way, this dismayed her, as it meant he might be well enough to move on.

"Will I live?" Joe Nomura teased her. She was so serious, he thought, but so pretty.

"Very likely," she answered primly, but the twinkle in her eye betrayed her.

It was an easy thing to say now. Earlier, it had not been so definite. Nomura had shown up at the hospital almost delirious with fever and with a leg swollen to twice its normal size. Dr. Tanaka had considered amputation but decided against it because the young man had already lost an arm. Tanaka, with Mitsu assisting, had spent hours probing the infected flesh for the pieces of shrapnel that had caused the problem. Against all odds, they had succeeded through a combination of Tanaka's skill, and American sulfa and penicillin. There would be scars, but they would recede over time. When he was fully healed, Nomura wouldn't even limp.

Mitsu dropped the blanket back over his legs. "I have a question for you."

"Ask it."

"Several times I have had night duty and come by to see how you were. On a couple of occasions, you were thrashing in your sleep and speaking words I didn't quite understand."

Joe was touched that she would single him out for such care. Peace had brought a dramatic reduction in the number of patients, which meant she was free to indulge in him if she so wished. That she so wished was a pleasant thought.

The American field hospital he'd been trying to reach had closed up and moved for the same reason—no more customers. But now, what did he tell her? Well, he would begin with the truth, at least a little of it.

"It was probably English, Mitsu. I speak it very well."

Her eyes widened. "I thought so. I have learned a little of it here, and I thought I recognized some of the words. Have you been to America?"

He laughed. She said it as if it were some sort of holy place. "Yes. I spent some years in Hawaii."

"I would like to see America someday," she said solemnly. Mitsu eased him out of the bed and up to a standing position. He put his arm around her slight but strong shoulders, and she put hers around his waist. It was time to strengthen his legs so he could walk unaided. Already she suspected he didn't need to have his arm about her, but it was rather pleasant so she did not comment on it. So too she liked the feel of his body under her hands.

"Wouldn't you be afraid of all the Americans?" he asked.

"No," she said firmly. "At least not anymore." Proximity to the American hospital had shown her that the GIs were nothing but little boys who were as normal as Japanese men, just larger and louder.

"But what about the war, Mitsu? Weren't they your enemy?"

Mitsu was puzzled. Why had he said *your* enemy rather than *our*? "Once I hated the Americans. Now I realize that the whole war was an evil wrong that should never have happened. Now I realize too that the Japanese people were duped by warlords. No, Jochi, the Americans are not my enemy. They never were."

They stepped outside. It was chilly, but far from unpleasant. Besides, he could feel one of her small breasts against his side, and that was definitely keeping him warm. In the distance, he saw a car coming down the road.

"Mitsu, did you hear about American-born Japanese who helped the Americans invade Kyushu by spying on the Japanese and performing acts of sabotage?"

She nodded against his shoulder in such a way that he couldn't see her face. "And you're one of them, aren't you?"

Joe took a deep breath. At least that's over with, he thought. "Yes. Will you hate me for that?"

Mitsu looked up at him. Her dark eyes were clear with understanding. "You served your country. How could you be hated for doing that? Tell me, did anything you did truly help end the war?"

He laughed, surprising her. "Yes, Mitsu, it definitely did."

She smiled and squeezed him. "Then that was good and you are good." The car was drawing closer. Probably more American doctors looking for possible radiation-sickness victims, she thought. They couldn't quite believe there weren't any at the hospital.

"Jochi, when you leave, where will you go?"

"Back to Hawaii."

"I wish to go with you."

He was stunned and thrilled. She felt as deeply as he did. He hadn't been imagining it. They'd only known each other for a couple of weeks, but it felt like forever.

"What about your family?" Mitsu's mother and sister had been located in the north. There had been a brief reunion and a parting that had left Mitsu unsettled.

"They will soon move to Yokohama to be with cousins. I have no desire to be with them. They are rooted in self-pity and the past, while I wish to live in the future. Now, will you take me with you to Hawaii?"

"Of course." He pulled her closer to him. The car had stopped almost directly in front of them. "It won't be a problem. I think I'm owed some pretty big favors by some very important people."

The car doors opened. OSS agents Peters and Johnson stepped out. They grinned happily and waved when they saw Joe. Joe laughed. "What the hell took you guys so long?"

■

CHAPTER 87

WASHINGTON, D.C.

"Gonna miss you, Jim," President Harry Truman said as he reluctantly accepted his secretary of state's letter of resignation. "You did a helluva job under some rotten conditions."

Byrnes shrugged, but the compliment pleased him. He had hoped to give it another year or so at State, but the pressures of the job in the past several months had accelerated the overall deterioration of his health. All his ambitions were now behind him.

"Harry, if I want to live to enjoy my retirement, I'd better go now. At any rate, General Marshall will do an outstanding job as my replacement. Sometimes I get the feeling Marshall's been prepping for this all his life. He's the man to shepherd the new world as it develops."

After a few minutes of small talk, Byrnes departed, leaving Truman with his many thoughts. First and foremost, World War II was over and now the world was learning the true nature of nuclear warfare. Scientists from many nations were examining the ruins of Hiroshima, Nagasaki, Kokura, and the residue of the straits bomb. Radiation, so casually dismissed as a factor in earlier calculations, was being redefined as a deadly killer that never stopped killing.

Truman knew that a portion of the world's population would forever castigate him for using the terrible weapon, but he had done so with a clear conscience and the hope that the bomb would bring an early end to the war. That the war had not finally concluded until the early months of 1946 was sad, but not as awful as it could have been for either side had it dragged on even longer.

In the war's beginning, many predictions had called for fighting the Japanese until the latter part of the 1940s. "The Golden Gate in '48" had been the GIs' sarcastic lament. It meant that they themselves did not figure to get home until 1948. Truman considered himself responsible for doing much better than that.

The "peace with honor" had been less than the unconditional surrender of Japan that FDR had first declared was requisite. American military occupied less than a third of Kyushu and were negotiating with the Japanese government for long-term leases for naval, air, and army bases in the Kagoshima, Ariake, and Sasebo areas. After the boys came home, the total number of Americans at the several bases would likely be less than a hundred thousand and would be more concerned with Russia than Japan. That American troops would be coming home had offset any resentment that perhaps the Japs had gotten off too easily. Of course, newsreel films of the devastation in Japan reinforced that the Japs had been brutally beaten.

Joseph Grew was ensconced in Tokyo with several hundred civilian and military "advisers" who now worked with the new Japanese government. Homma and Ozawa had announced their intention to resign and retire from public life. Hirohito had renounced his claim to being a godhead, and democratic elections were being planned. The political face of Japan was being restructured.

Japan had withdrawn any claims to Formosa or Korea, although Okinawa would revert to Japanese control. Japanese garrisons, many starving and in wretched condition, had almost all departed from distant parts of the Empire and, like their brethren on the home islands, were being disarmed by their own government while American representatives watched. It was all astonishingly peaceful now.

War crimes were a touchy issue. Many of the major possible criminals were already dead. Anami, Sugiyama, and Tojo, to name a few, had either been killed or had committed suicide, while Ishii seemed to have disappeared. Even so, an international tribunal made up of representatives from Spain, Portugal, the Vatican, Switzerland, and Sweden would judge those the United States wished to prosecute.

Homma would not be prosecuted. There was substantial evidence that he might not have known the Bataan Death March was occurring. He had accepted moral responsibility for the atrocity insofar as he had been in command of the Japanese forces involved. In light of his subsequent actions in bringing the war to an end, he was given the benefit of a reasonable doubt.

Truman received the latest on casualties for Operation Olympic, the invasion of Kyushu. The total stood at just under 350,000, and almost a third of those were dead. It was a staggering addition to the total of 300,000 Americans killed in all the other battles of World War II.

Many of the wounded were physically and mentally maimed for life. The medical profession took justifiable pride in that so many of the wounded would live, whereas, in prior wars, they would have succumbed to their wounds. While they might be crippled, they would at least have a chance at some kind of life.

It further grieved Truman that almost half the Allied POWs in Japanese hands the previous summer had died of various causes. These included starvation, mistreatment, murder, and death from American bombs and shells directed at where the Japs had placed them.

All of this, Truman thought, to conquer an area of Kyushu that was only a little larger than the state of Delaware. The hills must have been painted with dead. He thought it incredible that only a few months before, he and his advisers had debated just how hard, or even if, the Japs would fight. Now they knew. The Japanese had fought like tigers for their homes and their way of life. How could he and his advisers have been so wrong?

If he wanted good news, all he had to do was check what was happening to the Soviet Union. With their economy in shambles, ostracized by the Western nations, and living on plunder stolen from Eastern Europe, the Russians were now having a difficult time. In China, the collapse of the Nationalists and the departure of the Japanese had left a power vacuum. When both the Soviets and the Chinese Communists had tried to seize control, their forces had collided. Now, Chinese Reds and Russian Reds were killing each other, and the Russians, at the end of a long and tenuous supply line, were definitely getting the worst of it.

The Russians had also been forced to withdraw from Korea, this time urged on by a Korean national named Syngman Rhee, whose irregular armies had made life miserable for the Soviets. The Soviets' inability to succeed in Asia was not lost on European nations, which were gaining confidence in their dealings with the far from omnipotent Russian bear.

Only in the Middle East were American troops in any danger. Palestine was in ferment, and the British had informed Truman that they were no longer interested in policing it. Now that the British had Hong Kong back, there was little motivation for them to hang on in the bloody and not so Holy Land that had already claimed a number of lives.

The Arabs hated the United States for helping out the Jews, but that could not be helped. France and Holland were on Truman's back to help them reclaim their colonies in Southeast Asia, but he'd be damned if he would aid either country to enslave other human beings.

"What a helluva complicated world we live in," he said to the wall. He checked his watch. It was time for a drink.

Many of the characters were people whose roles in "real" history were, of course, different from those shown. However, care was taken to make their behavior in the story consistent with what is known about them, their personalities, and their motives. To satisfy the curious, here is a summary of what actually happened to a number of those historical characters.

Truman, of course, was elected president in his own right in 1948 and subsequently fired Douglas MacArthur over his handling of the Korean War. MacArthur was replaced by Matthew Ridgway, who is generally given credit for stopping the Chinese. George C. Marshall became secretary of state and sponsored the Marshall Plan, which rebuilt Europe, while Omar Bradley became chairman of the Joint Chiefs of Staff.

Most of the other Americans retired shortly after the end of the war.

The Japanese were not always so lucky.

After the war, Hirohito renounced any claims to divine status and continued to reign as emperor until his death in 1989. He was then succeeded by Crown Prince Akihito.

Defense Minister Anami committed suicide on August 15, 1945, after realizing that the coup attempt had failed because of his lack of support.

Lieutenant General Homma was executed in 1946 after being found guilty of war crimes involving the Bataan Death March. His degree of guilt is still debated.

Field Marshal Sugiyama committed suicide immediately after Japan's surrender.

Admiral Ozawa was never charged with any war crimes. He retired and died in the 1960s. There is confusion about the exact year of his death.

Captain Minoru Genda rejoined the Japanese military after the war and became chief of staff of the Japanese Air Self-Defense Force. He died in 1989.

Comdr. Mochitsura Hashimoto testified in the court-martial of the captain of the *Indianapolis*. After that, he disappeared and may have entered a monastery.

Lieutenant General Ishii was never tried for any crimes. Ironically, he was called upon to speak as a lecturer on chemical and biological warfare at what is now Fort Detrick, Maryland. Like Hashimoto, his ultimate fate is not known.

ABOUT THE AUTHOR

ROBERT CONROY is a
semi-retired business and economic
history teacher living in
suburban Detroit.